# Praise for Forever Blackbirds

"*Forever Blackbirds* is told in dual timelines as our narrator, Marta Gottlieb grows from a teenager into her late life. Greenwood deftly writes this important story, pulling at every heartstring and challenging what you may think the immigrant experience is."
—Leslie Johansen Nack, author of *The Blue Butterfly*

"The beating heart at the center of *Forever Blackbirds* is Marta, who is 14 years old when she and her family flee a bloody assault on their beloved home in Odessa. Dian Greenwood's powerful immigrant saga takes us inside Marta's psyche as the story alternates between her hard-scrabble existence in North Dakota in the 1940's, and the traumatic arrival on Ellis Island thirty years earlier. Marta's firm faith is tested by life-altering disfigurement, personal tragedy, marital strife, WWII casualties, and inter-generational rifts. When the war ends and women's roles shift, we journey with Marta through her growing realization that all is not determined, that things can change, and that despite shattered dreams, hope and change are possible."
—Gemma Whelan, author of *Painting Through the Dark*

"A poignant tapestry of love, loss, and reinvention, *Forever Blackbirds* unravels the story of Marta, a woman facing the brutal realities of war in 1943 and a tumultuous past fleeing Bolsheviks in 1914 Russia. Ensnared in a loveless marriage, Marta confronts the upheavals of war and societal change against shattered dreams of a storybook America. When tragedy strikes, Marta's evolution unfurls. With each turn of the wheel, Marta must struggle to reclaim control over her life in a rapidly changing world. This novel is an absorbing read, told in unflinching detail."
—Maryka Biaggio, award-winning author of *Parlor Games, Eden Waits, The Point of Vanishing,* and *The Model Spy*

"With lyrical, stirring prose, Dian Greenwood explores the universality of the human experience in a story about family, faith and the ties that bind. *Forever Blackbirds* is a thoughtful tale about a matriarch who emigrated to America as a young teen—her choices, struggles, and tragedies—and the powerful role family history plays in molding her and the family she builds. Through well-drawn characters, the author captures how we become our unique selves, muddling through love and relationships, searching for a path forward, striving for a sense of belonging and a belief in something. Sometimes we are able to break free of our past, and sometimes we cling to it like a drowning man. The story is set in the first half of the twentieth century, a time when the slings and arrows of life were particularly deadly. And although it was a time when suffering and loss were the norm, Greenwood still makes the suffering personal. A sad, splendid book that rings true."

—Suzanne Parry, author of *Lost Souls of Leningrad*

# Forever Blackbirds

# FOREVER BLACKBIRDS

## DIAN GREENWOOD

*Travelers Moon Press*
*Portland, Oregon*

This is a work of fiction. Any resemblance these characters have to actual persons, living or dead, is entirely coincidental.

© 2024 Dian Greenwood

www.diangreenwood.com

Interior design: Laura Stanfill and Gigi Little
Cover photographs by Albrecht Fietz and Nika Akin, Pixabay
Egg painting by Stephen O'Donnell

All rights reserved. No part of this book may be reproduced or transmitted in any form or by any means, electronic or mechanical, including photocopying, recording or by any information storage and retrieval system, without written permission from the author, except for the inclusion of brief quotations in a review.

Printed in the United States

ISBN 979-8-9895103-1-3

1 2 3 4 5 6 7 8 9 10

to my family

and in memory of Magdalena

*The woman who has grown old*
*And knows desire must die,*
*Yet turns to love again,*
*Hears the crows' cry.*

*She is a stem long hardened,*
*A weed that no scythe mows.*
*The heart's laughter will be to her*
*The crying of the crows,*

*Who slide in the air with the same voice*
*Over what yields not, and what yields,*
*Alike in spring, and when there is only bitter*
*Winter-burning in the fields.*

*The Crows*
*Louise Bogan, 1923*

## Chapter One

### The Bibles

### *September 24, 1943*

THE KITCHEN WINDOW ALLOWED me to take in the garden, the pigeon pen, and the outhouse beside the alley where the incinerator blazed. Albert, my husband of nearly twenty-five years, stood above the fire in his beanie, his coat collar up around his neck, his hands warming at the fire.

Today was Ozzie's twenty-third birthday. My eldest, my pride. A man who lived without explanations, a man who cared about who he presented to the world. Even now I could see him standing here in the kitchen at the small sink against the far wall, lifting his red hair into a pompadour following a clean shave. That last patting down before he turned and smiled at me. "How do I look, Ma?" he'd say. Then out the door to meet a friend or some girl. That was before he enlisted in the marines, before the war began and now only *Herr Gott* knew where he was. Somewhere on the Pacific Ocean on a ship destined for Herr Gott knows where.

There would be no birthday cake and no schnitzel, his favorite dinner. Much as I tried, I couldn't picture the Pacific Ocean, probably a place where there was nothing as far as you could see. Like our wheat fields here, butted up against the horizon, only shades of gray distinguished day from night. The Atlantic Ocean—yes, I'd seen and smelled those waters with their constant rise and fall. Something one never forgets.

I lifted my hands from the soapy water; the now-clean baking pans lay facedown on a towel beside the sink. Dark clouds gathered against the horizon where a mere slant of sunlight highlighted the telephone poles, their lines crisscrossing the sky. The blackbirds, forever it seemed, perched on intersecting arms. Blackbirds, an unfortunate omen, Mother always said. One should be wary of blackbirds.

My gaze dropped from the blackbirds to where my husband continued to feed the fire. Albert Gottlieb was an immigrant like me. How a Catholic found his way into this tribe of Evangelicals would always be a mystery to me. Showing up at Uncle Herman's back door looking for work. Father, already dead, would have never taken him in. But Uncle Herman was a different kind of man from his brother. More Christian in some ways. At least that was my thought.

Albert was never a man to smile. As I watched him there in the alley, as I saw him standing over the incinerator, his eyes had that particular stare that sees but does not see. I thought it peculiar that he kept tearing pages from a book and feeding them to the flames, except for momentary pauses when he gazed into the fire and smiled in a way I'd never seen. His smile frightened me.

I still trusted him then. No reason not to until I began to understand that the man standing before the incinerator kept tearing out and feeding Corinthians and Joseph, Matthew and the Psalms, one page after another, to the flames. My Bibles. He was burning my Bibles.

In that moment some instinct begged me to check, to see if the Bible stack remained on the far end of the small newspaper stand next to the rocking chair. Far enough from Albert's standing cigarette ashtray that he didn't have to see them. Far enough that he couldn't complain. But even as I turned toward the parlor, I knew they were gone. The German Bibles and English Bibles, even a Russian Bible Mother brought in the bottom of the trunk across the Atlantic from Kassel. The new King James. All the notations I painstakingly wrote around favorite passages, dates recording the births and deaths of Father and Mother. My brother Leo. The Bibles were always a source of tension between me and Albert and could be blamed for every disagreement.

Numb and horrified, I felt my mouth open, ready to scream. But nothing came out. I wiped my hands on a towel and stepped toward the door as if to stop him. But, as I focused on the many-colored beanie I'd knitted atop his still-black hair, my throat closed with incredible disbelief. It was those momentary pauses when he warmed his hands at the fire and smiled—a smile that sickened, then steeled me—that told me that burning those books was his one great life achievement. Yet, even as I watched with horror, Father's voice whispered in my ear, *Never question your husband, Marta. A man has certain rights. He is not to be questioned.*

The heat of the oil drum rose in waves even from where I stood, now inside the mudroom. Disbelief and my own muteness settled their weight inside me. The horror of what I was watching, the heat and gray ash like the turned-to-paper taste in my mouth. When I took that one step toward the back door and threw it open, the cold and stinging wind pressed against my cheeks, blowing the long threads of my gray hair, and Father's voice whispered, *A man is not to be questioned.*

*How, Herr Gott, could I stop this blasphemy against me, against you? Was this thy will and not mine?*

Autumn's harsh edge whistled around my ears, reaching down and into the well of tears I held on to. But I could not move forward onto the brick path, and I could not speak. My arms at my side and my hands clenched while silent and sinister flames rose from the ashes. Though my heart pounded inside my throat, I felt paralyzed in place. Yet with every ounce of will left in me, I would not allow the heat behind my eyes to spill, would not give in to this final assault.

I was this man's wife, and I had been a good wife all these years. In that moment I realized that I had one remaining weapon against this man who had husbanded me at eighteen, four years after Ellis Island and the scarring along both my cheeks and forehead, four years during which I prepared myself to be a wife to anyone who would have me. Now, after all these years of birthing this bricklayer's four children; of washing his socks and long johns, his work shirts and overalls, and hanging them on the clothesline despite the thick icing of winter and the Great Depression's hardships and, now, another war; despite his railing against Jesus's teachings, I would do what any self-respecting wife would do when her soul's longing is trampled with cork boots and spit on afterward. I would leave his bed. Forever. Yes, if it meant sleeping in my daughters' former bedroom, I'd take this man-pleasure from Albert in the hope he'd remember this day the way I would. This day that marked no turning back. *Herr Gott, forgive me. I am done.* And I would hold fast in the same way my mother held fast when my father fell into the white snow with the gun still tight between his fingers, the remnants of his body, like his sins, forever a stain on winter's snow.

The flames curled higher and wider, the ash floating like broken butterfly wings. I saw only one choice in that moment. I buttoned my coat and walked back into the house, across the kitchen's worn linoleum and the living room's frayed rugs, toward the front door we rarely used. One foot in front of the other, my feet found their way through the door and down one step, then onto the brick path toward the picket fence, my hand pulling back the latch and opening the gate. I walked onto the main road of this small town called Myra with its single grocery store, two taverns, and five churches. Five hundred and eighty-nine souls, the houses plotted on quarter-acre lots and often built too close to each other. These German and Russian immigrants who knew nothing but hard work and family, our daily life what Herr Gott had given us. Our faith was the great gift bestowed on those who sought it.

I took an immediate left, not into town where the gossips could see me walking but out onto the open road, the gravel under my best Sunday shoes, on toward my brother Oscar's place where summer combines had left their empty tracks in the fields after the summer wheat had come and gone. Like my father, the man behind me would never be questioned, and the unforgivable would never be explained, let alone justified.

THE LONG WALK CLEARED my mind and left me strong. Resolved. My feet carried me back toward home faster than I would have imagined. Past Fritz's Texaco and Jake's tavern, past the First Bible Church where I could have turned in and reported this grievance to Pastor Kinski, prayed with him. Home as fast as I could to save the only other memento I'd carried as a girl from Russia, the one remaining keepsake from my family and the life I'd known. I needed to safeguard my legacy from this vengeful and angry husband I could no longer trust.

I threw my mittens onto the rocking chair, but there was no time to take off my hat and coat. As quickly as I could, I stood behind the stairs to the upstairs bedrooms and removed the picture of wolves that Albert hung over the opening of this hiding place. I now resented Albert's forbidding the Jesus picture that Mother brought to America in our trunk from Kassel more than I could have imagined, my pulse rushing and my breath in my throat. The only reason that Albert had probably never seized this precious keepsake before now was because I had told Ozzie, our grown son, about it for safekeeping in case this moment ever came.

With the same urgency with which I'd walked away from Albert and the incinerator, I lifted the wolf picture away from the hiding place beneath the stairs, my fingers trembling when the wire got hooked on the nail. Under the dim light from the floor lamp, I gazed into the dark opening. First, I lifted the Jesus picture I'd placed on top of Mother's worn crewel purse. I stopped and held my throat, emotion rising even as I stood there. Here was my history's heart. Though it had been thirty years, I could still see Grandpapa Grozinski's large and burly hand extending the small silk bag. His hand into my small hand the day of my fourteenth birthday.

In the beginning Albert colluded with me in protecting this treasure, our only real valuable. Working together, we'd created the opening under the stairs. I was young. We were in love. Ozzie only a toddler. Albert originally conceived the idea of the hidden safe. "Better than banks," he'd said. In the evening after he'd worked long hours at Myra Brickworks, he came home and shed his work clothes in the mudroom, removing his socks before shoving his feet into felt slippers. After supper when Ozzie was well put to bed, Albert cut and then trimmed the sheetrock until he created the opening. Between the beams, he fashioned a shelf for Mother's tapestry purse. Inside lay the purse and, innocently dull without light, the treasure.

I now lifted the purse from its hiding place, my fingers stumbling in their nervousness. After undoing the purse's clasp, I reached inside to remove the small silk bundle. I peeled back the folds of lavender silk. And there inside my cupped hands lay the jeweled cloisonné Easter egg Grandfather had given me. Even in the dim light from the window's raised shade, the glint and shine of this particular treasure brought tears to my eyes and, at the same time, made something inside me dance and flutter as though coming to life. Multiple diamonds and pearls outlined a ribbon design forged into the cloisonné egg, its sapphire-blue background painted red at the heart of the ribbons. In my hand, the silk felt so light by contrast to the hard and heavy egg, forcing me to pull carefully at the fabric so I wouldn't snag the silk against the jeweled prongs. This magnificent egg, likely worth more than the house we lived in, had only rarely been outside of its hiding place. On random occasions, like now, I sometimes needed to be reminded that there was a world beyond carrying water from the well and baking multiple loaves of bread to feed my hungry family. I would then remove the egg from hiding just to hold it in my hand. The weight of it so reassuring. The luxury of the egg always made my heart jump inside my chest. More than once, Albert suggested we take it to Bismarck and sell it, especially when the Great Depression went on too long, and again when the war began and the brickyard was suddenly repurposed to make tank tires. Then again a year ago, when Albert's cancer diagnosis came and we sold our house mortgage to my brother Oscar. Both times I said no, remembering the moment Grandpapa handed me the Easter egg. For me, hocking the egg would be no less than a blasphemy against the memory of my parents and the life I came from.

Now, under the dimming light from the window behind me, the diamonds winked in reflected light and the pearls gleamed. Though I would rather think otherwise, this precious gift was never meant to rescue Albert, and it was never meant as an inheritance for Irene and certainly not for Ada, my two daughters. Either one would hock it for a new fashion or a piece of jewelry more to their liking.

Holding the egg in my hand, my fingers trailed the rough ridges of the jewels. I could still see Grandpapa lighting his pipe and settling back in his chair, the sweet tobacco I always loved floating into the air where we'd gathered around the hearth. Grand Mama with her embroidery lifted from her lap. Grandpapa's huskies with their thick winter coats huddled against my legs while Elvira, their maid, placed the silver tea service on a small table before the fire; outside, the Russian winter howled at the windows. Father always sat across from Grandpapa, the two of them talking about wine and crops like the good friends they had become. Father the substitute son Grandpapa never had. How could I have known then that it was our last time?

Later, following dinner, strawberry cake was served on Grand Mama's porcelain English dessert plates. Our family was seated around the oak table with the newly installed gas mantels lighted overhead. Centered on the linen tablecloth, the candlelit cake for my fourteenth birthday glowed in the dimly lit room. *I'm almost a woman now*, I thought to myself, blowing out the candles.

Leo, my youngest brother and constant companion, was first to rise and present his gift—a book, I could tell by the wrapping. He walked around the table, his chin tipped down in shyness. He set his gift on the table beside my plate and hurried back to his seat before I could stand and hug him.

Inside the wrapping, I couldn't help but smile on seeing a geography book with color plates. So fitting for our world lessons with Mother, a relief after English and math. I lifted the book and turned it to show everyone. Each family member then came forward with their gift. A new tortoiseshell comb from Grand Mama. A silver hairbrush from Oscar that Mother must have picked out. A pearl-handled mirror from Mother and Father. Last was Grandpapa. When he rose from his chair, he was so stiff he had to lift himself by putting his large hands on the table. He came around the table toward me. I immediately stood out of eagerness and respect. Because of his travels as a wine merchant, I always anticipated his gifts above all others. "Close your eyes now," he said. He stood before me, the gift in front of his paunch. "No peeking."

I giggled even before I felt the gift in my hands. First, my fingers recognized Grandpapa's trademark silk sack. The weight was heavier than I might have thought, the shape not quite round, oval. Something I'd imagined, hoped for. Maybe the same gift he'd given Mother on her fourteenth birthday.

"Keep your eyes closed," he instructed.

"The candles are melting on the cake, Papa," Grand Mama said.

"Okay. Now it's time," he said, his voice husky with unexpected emotion.

Though it was veiled by the gauzy silk bag, the lavender color a surprise in itself, my fingers couldn't work fast enough to pull the ribbon bow and see what hid inside. I had so long admired Mother's egg with its diamonds and sapphires, its rubies, the stones encrusted in a linked diamond design that wrapped around the egg. Once, when we were alone, Mother told me it was her most precious gift.

My hand dug into the silk bag and lifted out the cloisonné egg. The weight in my hand was a surprise I hadn't expected. Unlike Mother's porcelain egg, this egg was painted in a deep blue and wine red, a design of ribbons tied into bows. Small diamonds were attached to the tails of the streaming ribbons with similar-sized diamonds embedded inside the ribbon design. Best of all, the egg opened on hinges at the center. Inside, gold leaf overlay the secret compartment.

My chin lifted toward Grandpapa. "Please bend down, Grandpapa, so I may kiss you on the cheek."

"I wouldn't miss that kiss for the world," he said. The fragrance of pipe tobacco rose from his coat and beard. His hand rested on my shoulder. The kiss he returned on each cheek would always be with me.

Now, the urgency of the moment and my trembling chin told me I needed a new hiding place. Albert burning my Bibles changed any notion that this precious gift was meant for our joint protection. If this inheritance went to anyone, it should go to my namesake and eldest granddaughter, Marta. Only Marta had cared enough to ask, "What was it like to be a girl in Russia, Oma? How awful that you were so sick on the ship. They made you work on Ellis Island? How did you get the terrible scar on your face? How old were you?" Marta would be the one to carry forward the world I came from.

The decision's relief was almost palpable along my arms and in my chest. *You guided me once more, Herr Gott.*

I placed the silk bag holding the precious egg inside my apron pocket. There was only one place safe enough to hide anything from Albert, a place he'd never dare go given his health. I pulled a Ball jar and lid out from under the sink. Holding my paper bag of uncooked navy beans, I laid a cushion of beans on the jar's inside bottom. I then eased the silk-encased egg into the center of the jar and dribbled beans around it. Once the jar was filled and the silk camouflaged, I screwed on the lid.

The same urgency that forced me out the door an hour ago now rushed through my body. A kind of tingling in my hands and a rushing in my chest. I lifted the kitchen trapdoor and fastened the hook to the kitchen's central beam. I held on to the linoleum floor as I descended the cellar stairs with their steep pitch, down into the earthen hole below. On the fourth step, I grabbed hold of the light string, something Albert rigged so I wouldn't fall—though he forever reminded me of the great expense. I continued to ease my way down the stairs, my free hand tight around the jar, my eyes scanning the shelves. What would Ivan, my youngest, be asked to bring upstairs for his father? I finally set the jar on a shelf in the shadows next to the sweet pickles which my family rarely ate, though they were my favorite.

My stomach dropped in relief. No one would look for that jar here, let alone find what was inside. Back up the stairs, I pulled the light string. Lowered the trapdoor. After pouring a cup of tea, I sat at the kitchen table and folded my hands with their long fingers in front of me. I prayed, *Thank you, Herr Gott. Help me keep my secret safe.*

# 1914

OUR WORKERS THREW OPEN the barn doors, the barn alive with flames shooting into the night. After daily threats, the Cossacks had finally come, their pistols firing death threats into the night. When I woke in darkness, Father's hand gently covered my mouth so I wouldn't scream and give our family away. My body stiff, I cowered behind Mother and Father, my brothers, all of us hidden in the upstairs bedroom. Voices continued to scream from the yard below, and the horses, shrieking and panicked, threatened to trample anyone in their path when they finally exploded from the burning barn.

Though Kassel was the place where we'd always belonged, we climbed into Father's best carriage behind his Arabians and rode away the following Sunday. Turning away from the house that day, we dressed as though going to a church service, our satchels hidden under our feet. Our trunk, the only giveaway, had been lashed to the back of the carriage. The previous night, Mother had sewn all of Father's gold coins into the hem of his long coat. Now that morning had come, Mother, Leo, and I turned one last time to memorize the front door of our now-closed house, its white door dear in a way it had never been before. The upstairs window of my bedroom. The elder trees lining the lane, their lush clusters of small white blossoms welcoming spring. All that we had known and lived was about to disappear.

It was easy to blame the government's new regulation about military conscription. Or a plan to relocate the German farmers to Siberia. Clearly, Father couldn't accept either plan. More than anything, he wanted to save Oscar and Leo the fate of military service. How many times had I heard Father say that the Germans emigrated to Russia at Czarina Catherine the Great's invitation, with the assurance that our sons would never be conscripted. "War is senseless," Father said. "That is why we came to Kassel in the first place."

As the sleigh's runners carved a new path through the snow, I concentrated on Grandpapa's hearth, his huskies hugging my legs. Elvira, placing the silver tea service on the small table before the fire. The fragrance of the strong, hot afternoon tea and pastries. Russia's winter howling at the windows while Grandpapa lit his pipe. Father, across from Grandpapa, his carefully trimmed mustache and beard so much of who he was. Those dark eyes that could pierce or warm at will.

# Chapter Two

## Stealing the Bible

### 1943

WHAT AM I GOING to do without a Bible, Herr Gott, tell me that!

The Texaco gas station was ahead of me. I could see Ozzie's new Buick through the glass windows of the garage door. Ivan, my eight-year-old youngest, was bent over the air hose with his bike, probably filling the tire. His skinny legs failed to fill his corduroys and his plaid shirttails hung outside his trousers. No coat. The afternoon was cold enough that snow would fall before evening came.

I turned away at the corner before Ivan raised his head and saw me. The ten miles to my brother Oscar's farm was entirely unrealistic with or without my Sunday shoes. I veered toward the First Bible Church just two blocks away. Not that I wanted to talk to Pastor Kinski right now. I could see him tent his fingers and nod his head. *Oh yes, Sister Marta, you have your cross to bear with that man.*

That's not what I needed. I wanted justice. Retribution, yes. *Forgive me, Herr Gott.* Forget mercy. I might never find forgiveness from the ache in my chest that wouldn't leave me. *Forgive my frozen heart, Herr Gott.* How could I ever excuse that man in his cement-covered overalls, the wad of tobacco jutting from his lower lip—though Dr. Schmidt said, "Give it up, Albert. Your mouth is already in trouble." Not that Albert would listen, not that he ever listened. Not to me and not to Dr. Schmidt. *Certainly not to you, Herr Gott.*

The church. My refuge since I was a girl in Russia. For years now, I'd cleaned the pastor's study, then washed and ironed his vestments when he finally gave them to me. Truth be told, I couldn't live without the Lord's word, and I didn't want to walk to the church every morning just to sit in a cold pew and read scripture with the possibility that Pastor would walk in on me without warning. I needed to be alone with the Lord so I could say what I thought without someone telling me I should pray for forgiveness, should ask for mercy, should understand souls that are possessed by unholy spirits. Instead, I wanted to be in my own kitchen with a Bible laid out on the oilcloth, the bookmark given to me at my communion, and a cup of tea; the house empty. Albert mostly gone to wherever Albert went now that he was too sick to work—probably Jake's Tavern—and Ivan in school. I needed quiet and the peace of the Lord.

My key fit into the church's side door lock. I turned it this way and that to catch the lock just right. Once inside, a familiar musty odor met me, though the church was still half warm from morning service. But dark. The lights and all electricity were routinely turned off at the fuse box. To save money, Pastor said. At least he was gone for the day; Sunday supper in Horton with his missus and her sister at the Cozy Cafe. I would just find my way down to the basement where Frank Schreck likely counted the Bibles at the end of each study session. I could just see his grubby hands lifting each book and inspecting the pages while looking down his long, oversized nose. He'd want to know why I needed to borrow one, with my bragging about all the Bibles I had at home. Certainly, I didn't want to commit a sin by stealing one.

Down the basement stairs, the whiff of mildew grew stronger. The steps and the dark and no lights even if I could turn them on. I hung on to the railing, though I knew it wouldn't support my weight if I was unlucky enough to fall. *Unlucky* was the word of the day. Albert at the incinerator. My shoes just about ruined. Now me, prowling around the church like a thief. At least the egg was safe.

The basement was cold already. I was pretty sure Frank kept the Bibles on the bookshelf where we once kept the children's Bibles. Before Ivan was born, I used to herd the children down here. The girls already squabbling, Ada pinching her big sister in retaliation for Irene's being so bossy. Ozzie walked ahead of them like he didn't know those two girls. Who could blame him?

My fingers felt along the wall for the light switch, momentarily forgetting the fuse was shut off. Only the faintest daylight from the basement window, gray and of little use, let me know where I was walking. Slowly, one foot in front of the other so I wouldn't stumble and fall, I inched my way toward the bookcase that I recalled resting against the far wall. My eyes fought to get used to the near dark. Once there, my toe stumbled against the case. I reached out and felt along the spines for use, then the books' pages to make sure the one I wanted wasn't dog-eared.

The Bible felt good in my hands, the weight a reassurance. I adjusted my handbag on my arm and turned to find the stairs. Overhead, the floorboards creaked with someone walking. Not a heavy tread. Those footsteps could be the pastor, skinny as he was. Or some kid. But how would they get into the church? I'd carefully locked the door behind me. I eased toward the stairs and wondered, *Should I duck into the kitchen in case it was someone who shouldn't be here, this whole wide-open room and no place to really hide? Or, Herr Gott forbid, someone who would think I was stealing a Bible?*

I pulled away from the stairs and hugged the wall. Waited for the footsteps to stop. Then, sure enough, they were at the top of the stairs and a flashlight's blooming circle lit the stairs. The heavy tread on each step said it was a man. Heavy tread and too fast for a woman, at least any woman I knew.

His feet on the last few stairs were only an arm's reach away. I nearly panicked. First, I needed to get rid of the Bible. Quiet as I could, I lay the holy book on the floor beside my feet in order to remove the incriminating evidence. Lucky for me, whoever he was, he turned away from where I hid and went into the kitchen. But surely he'd see me when he turned that torch back toward the stairs. I'd be caught. Bible in hand or not, me standing against the wall like a thief.

*Now what, Herr Gott?* Should I holler and say, "Who's there?" Explain that I'd left something upstairs and didn't know how to flip the switch on the fuse box? Except I wasn't upstairs, I was here in the basement, but doing what?

Now, whoever they were, they rattled drawers in the kitchen like they were looking for something. "Damn it." A man's voice. Cursing. He threw open cupboards. "That damned Agnes."

Ebert, Agnes's husband. I couldn't believe he'd just cursed his wife, the woman who would never leave me alone. The woman who always looked for some bit of gossip she could whisper at Sunday coffee. For sure, my daughters gave her plenty to talk about.

Now that I heard him curse, I had ammunition. I bent to pick up the Bible, my mind working fast, searching for the needed words to explain. I stepped away from the wall into the shadow from his flashlight. "Ebert Fleischman, is that you?"

The drawer rattling stopped. A circle of light filled the doorway where I stood in the full blast of his torch. A couple of quick steps toward me. "Who's there?" he shouted, as scared as I was just minutes ago.

I stepped forward, forgetting that in my hurry to leave the house I'd grabbed the wrong hat, one without a veil. The minute he saw my scarred face, he'd know who I was. "It's me, Marta Gottlieb." My words were louder than I intended. I didn't want to completely shock the poor man. There was nothing like tramping around in the dark and being surprised by someone whose face resembled one of the gargoyle creatures I'd seen in a picture of Notre Dame.

"Marta. You just about gave me a heart attack."

"Sorry. Just stopped by to pick up a Bible for Myrtle McGinnis. She's laid up with arthritis, you know."

"It's lucky you're here," he said, his head and shoulders now in the doorway, his eyes looking past me so he didn't have to see my face. "You wouldn't know where Agnes might have left her cake serving knife, would you?"

"Didn't know she brought it," I said, relieved that Ebert Fleischman was nothing like his wife. In fact, I felt sorry for the poor scrawny man having to put up with that viper's tongue all the time. If she gave the rest of us a hard time, she must really give that poor man what for. "What's it look like?"

"She said it has a white handle with little roses in the enamel. Insists she has to have it before someone steals it."

I walked into the kitchen, confident in his flashlight's glow. "Come over here to the drain rack," I said. "Maybe someone washed it and left it here."

Sure enough, there it stood in the silverware drainer. The porcelain was still white as white and the roses so sweetly scattered. The cutting portion appeared to be silver, real silver, though it could have been silver plate. The last time I saw real silverware was in Grand Mama's parlor for afternoon tea, when Elvira served tea with real silver tongs for sugar cubes. Something else I'd never seen before. When I asked, Grandpapa said he bought the tongs from a trader he knew in Kiev. "Think this must be what you're looking for," I said, turning toward Ebert and into the light.

"I'm in your debt, Marta Gottlieb," he said. "If you're ready, let's get out of here. This place gives me the creeps when no one's here."

"How did you get in?" I asked. "Thought there were only two keys, mine and Pastor's."

"You'll have to ask Agnes. I don't know how or where she gets half the things she has."

*Isn't that the truth*, I wanted to say. But, of course, I didn't.

I tucked the Bible under my handbag arm, freeing my other hand for the stair railing. "I'll follow you and the light," I said. "Didn't know it would get dark so early."

"That time of year," Ebert said. "Everything goes into hiding."

I struggled up the stairs behind him, but he waited at the top. "Want me to walk you home?" he asked.

"Thanks, but I think I'll be okay with the streetlamps."

"Can't thank you enough," Ebert said.

"Thank you," I said. "I needed the light from your torch more than I knew."

# 1914

THE *RYNDAM* HAD BEEN at sea for six days and Leo still hadn't been able to keep any food down. He'd given up sleeping on the top bunk with Father and Oscar and resorted to the floor in front of my bunk, a goose down quilt beneath him, though we all knew it would never keep out the cold. But he insisted on being near the slop bucket, though he was nothing but dry heaves now.

I'd hoped that once we boarded the ship and put the night crossings and bribery of security guards behind us, that final night in the hay of a French farmer's barn, a night that cost Father a whole gold coin, our difficulties would end. Father had insisted the farmer feed our hungry family as well. When we woke the last morning, straw in our hair, Father sought fresh horses for our beaten carriage. Another gold coin. Then Hamburg, our immediate destination, was supposed to be the relief we'd all waited for. But the town was squalid with poverty along the waterfront and whole families begging in the street with no hope of ever boarding a ship.

On board the ship, Mother ushered me and Leo each morning up on deck for fresh air, no matter how the wind blew or the waves crashed against the side of the ship. We crowded together in the rain with other passengers who waited their turn for the bowl of gruel we'd be offered for breakfast. Standing in line along the deck, we saved a place for Father and Oscar who seemed to take longer than Mother and me. Poor Leo was now a permanent shade of gray, like the sea around us.

Standing on deck, Mother predictably pointed down below toward steerage. "We could have just come up from there," she would say. She pointed out children whose eyes were sunk inside their skulls, whose clothes were never thick or warm enough against the North Atlantic wind. "We are so fortunate," she would remind me and Leo. "We are blessed, really." And with those words, the three of us huddled together back from the rail and prayed, our heads bent and our words warm between us.

# Chapter Three

## The Farm

## 1943

"Appreciate you going out of your way, Millie," I said. "No way I'd get to Oscar's farm without the kindness of friends."

Millie sat forward, her town hat with its paper daisies upright across her wide brow and the black ribbon trailing her back. Her shoulders were hunched over the steering wheel and her eyes remained focused ahead on the road. Millie was one of only two women in town who drove cars. The other driver was Pastor's wife, who always drove to Horton's abbey to visit her sister who worked there. Probably the reason Pastor took this parish years ago. Sad to say, I never had a sister and never quite mixed with Tante Ketcha's girls, though everyone treated me tender and careful after Father died the way he did. My neighbor Millie was the closest to a sister I'd ever have.

"Sorry to hear Oscar's doing so poorly," she said. "Always the best at everything and so handsome when we were girls, not that he ever looked sideways at me."

"My brother had a one-track mind. Fields and farm reports all he's ever cared about. That's never changed." I'd often thought he was competing with Father's ghost, trying to make right Father's misdeeds.

The tragedy of Albert burning my Bibles was the reason we were going to Oscar's. I'd had no sleep and nothing but nonstop tears when I cleaned up the garden for winter. I'd already moved into the girls' old bedroom, and, as I expected, Albert never said a thing. In fact, I hadn't spoken more than a word to him since that day when I somehow thought I could walk the ten miles to Oscar's farm on old Highway 20. How foolish was that? But the fact I'd come to sleeping in the girls' room made me realize I needed to talk to my brother. Oscar always had an answer that helped me and even comforted me. Arthritis and its consequent pain had humbled him over time. He was no longer the gruff, know-it-all young man he'd once been.

"What time you think you'll be coming back through?" I asked.

"Told Ivan I'd be back by the time he got home from school."

"Isn't Albert there in case you're late?"

"If he's not at the tavern."

Millie nodded in the rearview mirror. She had the same problem with her husband, Henry.

We rode along in silence, the fields lying flat except for corn stubble. Winter wheat was planted. There was nothing to do but put up storm windows and wait for the first snow. Wouldn't be long, a chill in the air and autumn nearly past its prime and the leaves piled up. No matter how much Ivan raked each day, the incinerator overflowed. As expected, Albert hadn't been near the backyard since he burned my Bibles.

"Cleared out the car's trunk in case Oscar gives you meat," Millie said.

She knew I'd feel obliged to give her chops or a roast if Oscar gifted us—meat was so scarce now during the war. Newspaper said the black market had grown so strong that crooks were bold enough to approach individual farmers. Not Oscar. He'd never give in to that kind of sin. At least I hoped he wouldn't.

"Eleven now," Millie said. "Should be back by three. Unless the hospital visits take too long. Harvey Schelling and Horst Krauts are recuperating after being shipped back from France."

"They'll be happy to see someone from home."

When I tried to get out of the car, it was impossible to juggle the prune kuchen and two jars of jam—one strawberry, the other peach—as well as my bigger-than-ever body. There was no one to come out of the house to help. If there were hired men who hadn't left for the season, they'd be off in the fields. Oscar hardly got out of his rocking chair anymore except to eat and find his bed. He said that going to the outhouse had become a chore. A pity he didn't stay in Uncle Herman's big house with the flush toilet. But Oscar said he needed to save on water. What he meant was that he didn't want to replace the septic tank now that pumping out the current one didn't help. Too cheap to put in a new one. "What for?" he'd asked. "I'm not going to live forever."

Millie turned off the car and came around to the other side. "Here, let me hold the kuchen and jam while you get yourself out."

Though Millie wasn't as big as me, her joints creaked too, from bending over the garden and carrying water from the well. My daughters didn't begin to appreciate how easy they had it with running water and a flush toilet, not to mention a refrigerator. Next thing you know, they wouldn't be able to live without those things.

It took me a minute to swing my stockinged legs out of the car, to gather my purse and rearrange the veil on my small hat. Hardly ever went out of the house without a hat except the past Sunday when I was so upset. Never knew when I'd meet someone for the first time who'd never seen my face. Once I lifted the veil, I could count on the gasp. Then that quick look away.

Finally standing, I pulled down my dress. Looking down at my Sunday shoes, I saw they were practically ruined from trying to walk here a few days ago. I don't know what I was thinking. Three miles out of town, that's all I managed. Upset as I was. I never even walked to the farm when I was a young wife, no matter how mad I got at Albert or the girls. Usually just went to the church. Pastor Kinski was a young man then, young like me and Albert. So many of us recently emigrated at that time.

"Why don't I walk you to the door?" Millie asked.

She was still holding the kuchen and both jars of jam.

"Thanks," I said. "But you don't need to come in." Oscar needed to know these things came from me, though there was no mistaking my kuchen for somebody else's. Besides, I didn't know what kind of shape he was in and I didn't want to embarrass him.

Though my arms were full, I knocked on the back door facing the gravel driveway. I didn't wait for a holler or hello but walked right into the mudroom, the smell of damp from the recent rain on the inside rug. The place probably hadn't been swept since I was here last time, and that was three months ago. Didn't any of those men know how to hold a broom and sweep a floor? I had to maneuver through a tumble of work boots and galoshes, hip boots and waders, even though there wasn't a river or even a creek nearby for that kind of fishing. Must be bad in the field where they kept the cows. Likely hoof rot and the vet probably here already. Just another way Herr Gott reminded us of who was in charge.

"*Guten tag*, it's me, Marta," I hollered toward the living room.

The war's mandated blackout shades were still drawn closed. A lamp lit the back of the rocker where a familiar hand gripped the arm of the chair. The fingers grabbed hold at the sound of my voice. They strained against the rocking chair's arm as a head appeared at the side, the once-red hair having gone from gray to nearly white. The hair was almost down to his shoulders, and the beard fell to the same length when he turned toward my voice. I could already see today's job.

"*Guten nabend* yourself," came the voice from a face I saw only in profile. "Hope you brought something to eat."

"Let me get some light in here." I turned toward the long, rough-hewn dinner table, but there was nowhere to set down the kuchen. Bills and fliers, several days' worth of newspapers and used dishes from heaven knows when lay piled on top. He needed a woman to come in once a week, and it couldn't be me. Heaven forbid I'd have to take him home with me, the downstairs parlor the only place I could put him since he'd never again climb a set of stairs.

I shoved aside what lay on the table's end and set down the kuchen, careful to make sure it was flat. Hurried toward the main window across from my brother.

"Not too much light now, Marta. Hurts my eyes," he said. His voice sounded weaker since I last saw him, and the stench in the room told me he was having a hard time getting to the outhouse. He was still sitting in the same chair as the last time I saw him, his stained overalls and plaid shirt the same.

No one to cook or can for him anymore. Just a bunch of men living like field hands, which they were, jammed into what was no more than a bunkhouse now. My brother had insisted on moving back into the original house, the one Uncle Herman and Tante Ketcha lived in when we first arrived from Russia, the house our family ended up living in afterward.

"Millie brought me," I said. "Wanted to come in but didn't know if you were decent."

"Got my clothes on, don't I?"

"You been sleeping in them? That chair?"

"Sometimes it's just easier."

"Maybe we should get your bed in here."

"I'm not that bad, Marta." His deep breath betrayed the telltale wheeze of his lungs. "What brings you here this time?"

"Need to talk to you about something and Millie was kind enough to drive me." I handed him a napkin from the side table by his chair. "Here, wipe your beard."

He pushed my hand away. "You can see I'm not improving with age."

"Let's get you up and into a decent chair here in the dining room where I can turn on the overhead lights and feed you some of the kuchen I brought."

"Now that's worth getting up out of this old rocking chair. But you'll have to help me," he said. "You haven't told me why I have the pleasure today. Something wrong with one of the kids?" Like the rest of us, he was probably afraid to ask about Ozzie, his namesake. The only one any of us ever worried about since my other three lived in Myra. Ozzie had left from Seattle four months ago, likely headed toward Japan.

"No, not the kids," I said. I pulled his cane from the side of the end table and put it in front of him. "Here, lean on this while I pull from the other side."

"Give me a minute, will you?"

Oscar bent over and pushed on the arms of the chair to inch his way forward. He scooched first one hip and leg, then the other toward the edge of the chair. Once there, he started to lift himself, only to have his weight pull him back down.

"Tell me when you're ready," I said, intending to grab him under the arm like I had before.

"Should probably go outside first."

"I can help get you there," I said.

I gazed down on the top of my brother's head, a bald spot where his double crown once used to be. He was the brother I'd leaned on, trusted like no one else after the truth came out about Father. Oscar took it hardest, Father's lie inked like the devil's tattoo on our family. Oscar probably figured that's why he got the son he had and a wife who died. He once told me that Father was to blame for the scarring on my face. Now look at him, an old man not even fifty, bent and twisted like the gnarled oak in the front yard. He probably blamed his rheumatoid arthritis on Father too.

He stretched his hand toward me. "Now," he said. In one motion, he hoisted himself out of the chair, me pulling on his arm and his other hand around his black cane.

Once he was standing, we both waited to be certain his legs would hold. "Should have you around more often," he said. He tilted his head and smiled at me like he wasn't smiling. "Let's go outside."

It took a while to get him down the path and into the cold outhouse and back. I helped him into a chair near the window and dining table where I'd spread newspaper on the floor around the chair. I pulled an apron from my cloth bag, the barber scissors and a wide-toothed comb from the sink by the mudroom door. Another apron around his neck and shoulders. "Ready?" I asked.

"What about the kuchen?"

"After we clean you up."

"You get tougher all the time," he said.

"Have to. A lot going on."

We talked about the war but avoided any mention of Ozzie. He asked me about the girls and grandkids, how Ivan was doing with his pigeons. He asked last about Albert.

"That's why I'm here," I said, the *snip, snip, snip* of the scissors now on his beard. "Should take you outside and hose you down."

"You wouldn't dare," he teased. "Or maybe you would." I could feel his laugh in the heave of his shoulders.

I gathered the apron, folding the hair inside so I could take it outside and shake it at the edge of the yard. No sense adding to the mess that was already here.

"What's Albert *not* done?" he asked.

"It's what he *did*," I said. "Now, don't get into an uproar until I finish. I know how mad you get, especially when it comes to Albert."

"I promise nothing."

Would serve Albert right to have Oscar pounce on him like the wildcat he used to be, never taking guff from anyone and never backing down from a fight. Not at all like Father or Leo. More like Uncle Herman. Maybe that comes from being the oldest.

"He burned all my Bibles, Oscar."

Just like that, matter-of-fact now that the tears had dried and the walk left me with blisters and my shoes in need of repair. If Pastor Kinski had been in his office that afternoon, he would have been as shocked as I was.

"Goddamn it, Marta, that man has been nothing but trouble since the first day he showed up at Uncle Herman's looking for work and he couldn't take his eyes off your . . ."

"Chest. You can say it, Oscar. Off my chest."

"Alright, alright." His cheeks flushed to the color of cherry pie and his lips burbled with saliva. "He was a bad apple, but you took him anyway. Should have known the way he balked at a church wedding. He was from Cherson. We should have never let him in the family in the first place."

"He was a Christian, Oscar, remember that."

"He was a damned Catholic," he said. "Mother tried to tell you, but you were determined."

"Who else was going to marry a woman whose face looked like mine, Oscar? Who else, I want to know."

Oscar never liked mention of my face and the consequences of that fall on the dock. On one hand, he was probably grateful to Albert, since the unspoken concern in our family was whether I would ever marry given the raised white scar along the side of my face and my misshapen lips. Oscar sat quiet for a minute or two. Stared out toward the Willys pickup he'd bought off Ray Gardner when Ray left for the war. The bumpers were already rusted, and from the looks of it, Oscar never bothered to roll up the windows. Herr Gott knows how many mice had been born and died in that car. "At least it runs," he always said. Needless to say, he had nothing in common with my meticulous son, Ozzie.

"I'll come in and talk to him," he said. "Now let's have a big piece of that kuchen. Make us some tea, Marta. Yes, make us some tea."

## 1914

IN THE BLUE LIGHT of early evening, the boards of the wooden gangplank creaked beneath my boots, mine and the tramp of all the other boots and sandals. This mass of bodies shoved each other in their effort to get onto the dock. All around me, immense feather beds were lashed with belts across the backs of men and older boys. Peasant women in babushkas gripped their babies against their chests and followed close behind the men, their children darting like loosed animals, threatening to dislodge the precious bundle I carried in my arms. Old men with heavy jowls seemed bent in half from the weight of suitcases. A small child slept against a shoulder while men as tall as Father, some rounder, didn't seem to care who they trampled. I had to remain watchful to avoid being knocked one way or another. The screech of their voices and the cacophony of their languages, a baby crying out in hunger, only amplified the confusion. We were all too close, and after many occasions of saying, "Excuse me," I simply gave up.

Hurrying toward Ellis Island's main hall and just ahead of me, a girl my age, fourteen or fifteen, cradled a large wicker basket, the clasp clearly broken and the basket unravelling inside her folded arms. Her long chestnut hair was tied at her neck with a leather thong that threatened to come undone. She appeared to be alone. Alone and unprotected. Unthinkable for a girl like me, who had always depended on my family to keep me safe, something I didn't have to think about before the Cossacks burned our barns.

"Marta, wait!" Leo, my younger brother, ran out of breath behind me. "I don't want to lose you." My stomach was knotted and hungry. I momentarily resented him for slowing me down. When I turned toward his voice, Father's bearskin *shapka* rose above and behind Leo, where Father had lagged behind to stay with Mother. One glance at Mother's rabbit-fur hat, no longer the snowy white it had been when we left Odessa, told the story. At last we would be on the dry land that had been only a dream, a fantasy. *The hope of America* had been Father's mantra when we boarded the first ship in Odessa, the night around us and the marauding Cossacks spread through the countryside like snarling wolves waiting to hunt us down and turn us over to authorities, who would surely send us to Siberia with other German farmers.

"Leo, hurry. Mother and Father will find us." My heart was beating in my throat. I was tired and scared in a way I'd never been before, my feet swollen and squeezed inside my boots. I wanted to find a place to lie down. At the very least, to sit.

Leo couldn't hear me above the din of so many passengers. Oscar had scooted ahead as soon as the ferry docked, his red hair beneath a brown cap the flag I counted on to tell me where we were going. Two years older, he seemed to thrive on the ripe whiff of the bodies spreading forward into the damp and foggy night. The smell, Herr Gott, the smell of so many unwashed bodies moving like a giant river at flood stage. I'd lived so long inside my clothes that they felt stiff and crunchy against my skin, repugnant despite my stuffy nose. I agonized for those who had lived in the filth reported in the ship's steerage. For all Father's complaints that we didn't get the first-class cabin Grandpapa Grozinski reserved for us, I was grateful for the bunks we'd had in our small second-class cabin.

Leo carried a carpetbag in each hand, and one kept bumping against my hip. Because it was Leo, his dark, curly hair grown long beneath his cap, I could forgive him. The seriousness in his forward-jutting chin and his wrinkled forehead made me smile for the first time. Still we had to be careful. So many people were crowded together, and the shouting, oh, how the shouting hurt my ears. That's when I saw the old man teetering along, a crutch in place of his right leg. He could so easily get run over, especially by the exuberant boys. Or, worse, he risked being pushed off the wharf and into the water.

We shuffled forward, a few among many, this crowd of noisy people whose bodies, like ours, sagged with the ordeal of travel. One step at a time, we inched forward through the confusion. I held my bundle tighter and closer to my chest, my one last treasure, a cloisonné Easter egg, hidden inside. I'd had to leave so much behind.

Ahead of us, gas lamps lit the stairs and entrance to the main hall, where immense doors had been flung open by the swarm of immigrants. Massive arches with bulbous, copper-covered towers crowned each corner of the main building, the onion domes rising into the blue light. For a moment, I wanted to see beyond my disappointment, to feel the excitement swell again inside my throat and sting my eyes on first seeing the Grand Lady standing solid on her own island. Her torch held high signaled the welcome we'd all waited for. But we hadn't counted on being detained and forced through inspections. All because Uncle Herman hadn't met the first ferry at Battery Park with the agreed-upon train tickets.

Three piercing blasts behind us indicated that the empty ferry was leaving the Ellis Island pier. I took Leo's warm hand in mine, a comfort as we both looked back in the direction from which we'd come that afternoon. Though darkness surrounded us and foghorns would complain throughout the night, Manhattan's lights sparkled behind us like a lighted ship. Then, above and higher in the night sky, the lit torch held high by the Grand Lady, my new patron saint, rose into the starless night. Like a buoy on a wide sea, she reflected the promise we could depend on. America, our America.

## Chapter Four

### Oscar & Albert

## *1943*

Upstairs in my daughters' room, I leaned over the side of the bed, unable to move for fear the bed would creak and I'd miss a single word spoken by the men in the living room below me. Though they thought I was asleep, the wrought iron heating grate centered in the floor allowed me to observe them sitting across from each other in the two rocking chairs placed close to the stove. Below me, I could see that the top of Albert's still-thick black hair, as always uncombed, was quite a contrast to my brother Oscar's newly trimmed gray beard. Their heavy mugs thudded from time to time on a side table as the two men drank the strong tea I'd brewed for them. During the long pauses in their conversation, the only sounds were the snap of the kindling and the clang of the iron grate at the top of the wood-burning stove after Albert stoked the fire. For a long time, they talked about crops and weather until Albert, unprompted, said, "I would have come to get her."

If I had in fact walked to Oscar's farm the day Albert burned my Bibles, he would have had to ask Hector, one of Jake's regulars, if he could use Hector's team and wagon. Almost no one had a car except Millie's Henry, the pastor, and our son Ozzie. Ozzie, somewhere in the Pacific Ocean, had stored his car at Fritz's Texaco around the corner on Main. Albert would need an excuse to ask for the team and wagon. An illness at home, more likely a broken bone. He could say that the church had run him out of his own house. The men at Jake's would shake their heads in agreement. Offer to help, likely sympathetic to Albert's predicament, one they probably had themselves.

Below in the parlor, my brother, who somehow got himself into that old Willys and drove to town, shook his head, his turning-to-white hair now cut and clean. He pointed his pale blue eyes directly at Albert. "Wherever she walked to, it was a good thing," he said. "Gave her time to cool down."

Blood rushed up my throat and into my cheeks until I heard it pound inside my ears. *Albert's never been anything but trouble from the first day he showed up at the house*, Oscar had said at the farm. Now here he was, siding with Albert. I would remember this.

Quiet as I could, I got out of bed and eased down onto my knees, not easy for a body so heavy it could hardly crouch to sitting without a plop. With the rag rug I'd woven too many winters ago under me, I perched on one hip like I once did as a child. My braid hung over my shoulder while my eyes followed the two men below.

"Her church is a comfort, like Jake's is yours," Oscar said. "You need to understand that."

How infuriating. The blood felt hot in my face. How could Oscar make that comparison? Treating my faith as though it was a hobby I took up in the same way I tatted and embroidered. If I'd been willing to give myself away, I'd have gotten up from where

I hid and maneuvered the narrow stairs in order to make clear to those men what they so wrongly thought.

"Her church takes her away from me," Albert said. "It's changed our family."

"These things happen," Oscar said. "As you well know, my own family suffered great and unexpected changes."

He was referring to Emily, his wife who died giving birth to their only son, a fine-boned and sickly boy who, into his twenties, spent his days tending the chickens and pigs and managing the garden. Oscar's disappointment echoed whenever he mentioned Nicholas's name, every time they drove their wagon into town, the boy on the buckboard hovering beside his father. The boy's small hands and narrow shoulders matched a certain faraway look in his eyes that gave further testament to the fact he wasn't right. That boy never said a word. Not once. For my brother, the boy died the moment he was born, the same moment Oscar lost Emily.

Beneath the heating grate, Albert shook his head, his hair falling across his lined forehead. He stared at the circular pattern in the living room rug and said nothing. He had to know that living with a son you're ashamed of is worse than losing your twin brother in the Great War like Albert had. Made me think of Father's body lying in bloody pieces on top of the snow.

"We must learn to live with these things. Make the best of them," Oscar said.

More than a man-to-man, Oscar sounded like a father speaking to a son. In that moment, I felt vindicated.

"I haven't been able to work," Albert said. His voice sounded feeble, defeated.

Oscar said nothing. In the silence that followed, I nearly stopped breathing. For too long, I'd complained that once the diagnosis of mouth cancer came and his words became so garbled you had to know how to listen, Albert gave up on work, on our family, on life. Unwilling to stop smoking cigarettes, he retreated to Jake's Tavern the same way other men left home to work. What he did there, what those men talked about, I didn't need or care to know.

I lifted myself from beside the heating grate and crawled under the bed's down comforter. I closed my ears and let myself drift deeper into the pillows. At last my brother, the family elder, was talking to Albert the best way, the right way. The burned Bibles were no longer Albert's secret.

# 1914

WINTER'S MOOD SAT INSIDE Father. That's what I was thinking while our family stood in line for the Ellis Island inspections. Somewhere inside the pile of coats stacked before us lay Father's heavy wool coat with the black satin lining. Buried, except for a corner of the shiny hem that revealed the unnatural shape and sag of the gold's weight. The coat was otherwise indistinguishable beneath other coats. None of us, not me or Father or my brothers or Mother could take our eyes off the coat's ordinary but weighted corner. Without Father's coat, we couldn't survive. Never mind finding and reclaiming our own coats with all the people scrambling to find theirs or to choose a better coat. Though foremost in my mind, my trembling shoulders and chattering teeth made it impossible to distinguish the cold from my fear that we were lost, really lost inside the cacophony of noise and smells, the whole world's differences surrounding us.

Father finally stood at the head of the line where we had been waiting in separate aisles, all lines leading toward the immigration officials. Before Father, a white-haired man with a military-looking hat and gray uniform reminded me of the soldiers who increasingly came into our village. They took what food and wine they wanted without paying and chose both unmarried and married women as their nightly companions.

Father's ruby ring caught the overhead light when he handed over our immigration cards. There was a brief exchange I couldn't hear, though I recognized some Russian words. Father turned back toward us, the cards still in his hand. "I'm so sorry," he said. "We must go through the full inspection."

Mother, her hair nearly undone from its usual tight knot, dropped her head and stared at the marble floor. Oscar's lips tightened and his face reddened to the color of his hair. "But Father," he said, "everything was planned by Grandpapa. You need to tell the inspector that. Where is the interpreter?"

Father, his eyes straight ahead, his voice faraway, avoided Oscar's glare. "This is what we are told to do."

My body stiffened in the same way it did the night we watched the fires destroy our barn and outbuildings in Kassel. "Does this mean the eye hook?" I asked.

"No need to be afraid, kitten," Father said. He steered me toward Mother, who stood back from the uniformed officer, her half-open mouth and too-wide eyes reflecting the shock I felt inside. Father avoided Mother's glance when he pointed toward the line for women and girls. "Over there, my darling Marta," he said to me. "This won't be as bad as it sounds."

Not as bad as it sounds. The eye hook was all I'd thought about on the docks in Bremen and on the ship, then the moment we were told that because Uncle Herman hadn't arrived with the train tickets, we had to go to Ellis Island where we might be detained until he came. Ellis Island meant inspections. Inspections meant the eye hook, that barbaric tool meant to lift the eyelid and peer at your eyeball to see if you were infected with some strange malady. The very thought of having the eye hook lift my eyelids aroused nightmares, fantasies of being rejected.

Shoved forward like cattle, my shoulders and arms were bumped by people who were there and then gone. The odor of so many unwashed bodies was acidic. Mother's gloved hand wound around mine, tightening until it hurt. We proceeded, my heart pounding so loudly I could hear it. My hand sweaty inside Mother's glove. Mother and I shuffled behind those in front of us, two abreast, while Father and Oscar and Leo lined up opposite us. For now, we stayed close in parallel lines. I never took my eyes off Oscar's cap or Father's gray wool scarf. Our separate lines moved forward, then stopped, only to advance again, inches at a time. Our slow walk was reminiscent of what might be called a vague and unimagined punishment. In front and behind us, women grumbled in languages I'd never heard. Before long, the drone of their foreign words became familiar, like the ocean lapping against the sides of the ship. Standing in the opposite line, Father wasn't the same man I'd always known, his head bowed and his shoulders bent, the revolution having taken its toll on his pride. His new silence contradicted his previous bragging about the welcome we'd receive and the land we would own. On occasion, he smiled toward us as though he needed to believe this was simply one more awkward step in our journey toward the dark, rich loam that, in repeated telling, was now sprinkled with gold.

In that moment I began to wonder if Uncle Herman would ever come to rescue us.

The waiting. The shuffling. The odor of boiled cabbage and onions filled the hall. Somewhere, food was being served. Though my stomach grumbled, we had to wait. Without warning, a female guard in a gray uniform stepped forward and grabbed Mother's and my fur coats. She carried them off to a designated place where all women's coats were piled together in a haphazard manner. Once again, I held tight to the wrapped bundle under my arm while the now-familiar chill of the harbor felt too close.

Though I tried, I couldn't avoid looking at the men and boys in their long underwear, their clothes thrown over their arms, and what I was coming to understand was a barely masked helplessness that shadowed their faces. Uniformed men jerked the men's chins from side to side and sometimes pulled at their beards in search of lice. A hot flush ignited my cheeks and neck on seeing Oscar and Leo remove their shirts and trousers. They stood in their underwear. Father too. I was humiliated for them and for myself. Mother's arm hugged my shoulder, and her hand gently eased my chin in a forward direction. I stared toward the ceiling and high windows out of embarrassment for all of us.

One after another, the line shoved all of us, women and children, toward the uniformed doctors. I watched the immigrants hold out their tongues. Most remained silent while bending their heads in front of inspectors who parted their hair in order to examine their scalps. Ahead of me, the uniformed woman who separated Mother's hair said, "Put the clip away. Too nice for this place."

Mother grabbed at her hair, her hand covering her ivory clip. "No," she shouted, "I won't hide something beautiful in such a dreadful place."

This was not the mother I had always known.

## Chapter Five

## Albert in Decline

## 1943

"Is that you, Ivan?" I shouted down the cellar stairs.

"Yeah, Ma," came Ivan's voice. "Pa asked me to get him fresh strawberry jam. Wants it on his bread when it comes out of the oven. Not the nearly gone stuff left in the cupboard."

Canned peaches and pears, beets and all the pickles—both sweet and dill—lined the knotty pine shelves Albert built years ago against the dirt walls in anticipation of winter. The color of those jars, especially the jams and jellies, on full shelves at the end of summer always left me feeling rich. And now I had my special jar hidden there as well. A jar that lifted my spirits every time I pulled open the trapdoor, every time I thought about the Easter egg in safekeeping.

Ivan's thick brown hair led the way up the cellar stairs before the glint of his glasses reflected back at me above his plaid shirt and faded corduroys. With his hand on the linoleum at the top of the stairs, he held the jar of strawberry jam high in his other hand. Precious cargo, yes, his young fingers encircled the Ball jar and the heel of his hand caressed the bottom, the jar more valuable than the jam inside.

Out of breath, he asked, "Is the bread in the oven yet?"

"Do you see it on the counter?" I asked. I poured water into the dishwashing tub from the morning water pails, the teakettle behind me whistling with hot water ready to wash the baking utensils. "Turn off the light," I said. "And close the cellar door. It's hard enough to keep the cold out."

Ivan set the jar down next to Little Marta—*mein schatzi*, I called my four-year-old namesake, granddaughter, and Ivan's niece. Her pencil sat poised over her open notebook, her pigtails pulled to the front of her dress. Ivan unlatched the cellar door from the central beam, lowering the trapdoor until only the linoleum's outline indicated the cut in the floor. "Pa says the bread should be done by now."

"Give me a minute, will you?" I said. "Maybe your pa should be doing the baking."

I wasn't usually cranky with Ivan. He was just a child, and he didn't deserve my harsh tone or anything other than the understanding of a Christian mother. This boy played constant messenger now that his father lay upstairs in bed, his mouth discolored and swollen, the cancer spreading down his throat and working out toward the end of his tongue. Dr. Schmidt said there was nothing to do but wait. A little whiskey helped, not that I wanted whiskey in my house, and I objected every time Ivan took the jug to Jake's Tavern to be refilled. Not on his life would Albert ever say thank you. Not for any reason.

"I'm sorry, Ivan," I said, pointing a finger at my head. "I have a headache."

"I only asked because Pa wants to know."

My sigh came from deep in my belly and all the way up through my windpipe. "Tell Pa he'll have the first slice."

"He'll like that," Ivan said. His shirttail flapped behind him—partly loose, partly tucked in his trousers—when he turned toward the stairs. That shirt said everything I loved about Ivan. Not too organized and a bit of a dreamer. Like my brother Leo, Ivan would be forever innocent, and surely Herr Gott would reward him one day for the attention he gave his father.

"Tell Pa I'll bring up his soup right after I take the bread out of the oven." I hesitated before adding, "I'll pull the soft part out of the crust so it's easier for him to swallow."

Little Marta looked up from her handwriting lesson. "When will you roll out the dough for the cinnamon rolls, Oma?" She knew the cinnamon rolls always went into the oven after the bread. But it was the endpiece off a fresh loaf slathered with butter that she really wanted.

The kitchen counter next to the sink was spread with baking pans covered with clean flour sacks, the bread and rolls and kuchen lifting the towels higher as the kitchen timer ticked away. There were still ten minutes before the first batch of loaves came out of the oven. Lifting the bucket of well water, I was careful not to spill on the linoleum, already wet from the rain on Little Marta's boots when she forgot to take them off in the mudroom. "Can I go down into the cellar?" she asked.

I nodded toward the closed cellar door, the linoleum with its straight three-sided cut. "You know what happens if the trapdoor falls and lands on your fingers?"

"Next time Uncle Ivan goes down?" she asked.

"We'll see," I said. I pulled the first of the golden-brown loaves from the oven, the heat a blast against my already-warm face. All of my grandchildren had heard the story about Irene, Little Marta's mother, playing a game with her younger sister Ada and using the cellar as a hiding place. The crooked scars across Irene's knuckles were proof of their carelessness when Ada slammed the cellar lid before Irene descended, her hand still holding on to the linoleum flooring when she took those first downward steps.

Applesauce. I'd forgotten applesauce, about the only fruit that Albert could eat anymore, besides the jam. "As soon as I get the bread in the oven, *schatzi*, you can go down with me," I said.

When I reopened the cellar door later and latched the hook against the support beam, Little Marta came behind me into the smell of damp earth under the shadow of the single lightbulb. The shiny Ball jars, side by side, held the dark red of cherries this year and the warm gold of applesauce. They reflected anything I couldn't grow that arrived in crates at Hubner's Market. On the floor, a wooden platform made from dismantled orange crates lifted gunny sacks of potatoes and turnips off the damp floor. The leftover beets I didn't can.

Each time I opened the trapdoor to the cellar, each time I climbed down the stairs to that fourth step and pulled the light string, each time I set my foot on the next descending stair, my eyes went to the bottom shelf in the far corner where the whiskey jar, once used for pickles, sat in shadow until the light caught its swollen belly. Each time after Ivan went down, I marched across the damp floor and lifted the jar from its place in order to mark the place where Ivan last lifted the jug and carefully poured the whiskey into the measuring cup, half a cup at a time, then set the cup on the stairs while he screwed on the lid. When he started back up the ladderlike stairs, he treated the half cup of whiskey like molten gold. Slowly, again, he carried the cup up a second set of narrow stairs into the bedroom, where it was hoped the whiskey would ease his father's pain and bring relief from the cancer devouring Albert's mouth and throat.

The whiskey was ongoing payment from Kurt Reichel after Albert built a brick wall around his backyard to keep out the Hammer kids. His medicine, Albert called the whiskey. Now, after weeks of increasing daily pain, the jar was nearly empty.

"Keep him comfortable," Dr. Schmidt said. Because of the doctor, I credited myself with not giving in to my resentment until the last Wednesday of any given month, when the government check arrived and Ivan obediently took the jar to Jake's for a refill. I made sure I got down to the cellar first to erase the secret mark I used to assess how sick Albert thought he was.

ALL COINS AND DOLLARS belonged to Albert. I dared not question it. The man was dying, and the silence between us had climbed a new rung, the resentments so steep I couldn't trust myself with even a word. If I was to manage the household with whatever meager dollars he fished out of the tin can he kept under his side of the bed, I'd have to keep my mouth shut. Bad enough I had to ask for fifty cents here and there when I was unable to trade vegetables or eggs, an occasional chicken. The disdain in Albert's dark eyes became apparent whenever he opened his palm and allowed the coins to drop. I'd learned not to ask. Instead, I usually sent Ivan in my place.

But the rent was due. *Thank you, Herr Gott*; while my brother owned the mortgage, he'd be expecting some kind of payment, as he should. Oscar had been generous to let us slide for three months. Much as I dreaded confronting Albert, I took off my apron and headed to the stairs in the living room, a mug of cooled Russian tea between my hands as a peace offering.

Entering the bedroom, I took in the medicinal smell of rubbing alcohol mixed with the odor of soured body fluids, including the honey bucket beneath the bed that needed emptying again. The more repulsive odors were masked by the camphor rub I gave Albert each evening when I checked on him one last time before I went to sleep in the girls' bedroom. He lay on the bed as stiff as if he was in his coffin, his bony fingers clamped together on his chest, his eyes closed. Now, because his mouth wasn't open, I knew he was awake.

"It's me," I said, "bringing you tea."

At first he made no move and his eyelids remained shut. I waited, certain that if I were Ivan with his ration of whiskey, he'd open his eyes immediately. His silence was and always had been my punishment, though now, since he'd burned my Bibles, I used my own silence and disdain against him. Waiting for death changed nothing.

"It's not dinnertime," he said, his words garbled and growing fainter each day. "And it's not bedtime, so you must have come for money."

His face never changed, his lips partly invisible outside of the bandages that came up from his neck and covered the left side of his face.

"My brother has been patient."

"Now he owns both our house and Ketcha's too," he said.

"If it wasn't for Oscar, we wouldn't be here, Albert."

Albert never changed expressions; his resentment was pasted across what I could see of his tight lips.

My responsibility, next to miraculous, was to make everything work. I'd never know or care to know what kind of beer and whiskey bill he'd accumulated at Jake's Tavern when he could still go there. It had to be a sizeable sum considering his too-often jolly moods when he returned home. Even with his early pension, there couldn't be much left in that tin can at the end of the month.

"And we have to pay Dr. Schmidt," I said.

"If we were still in Russia, we wouldn't be paying a doctor." He pushed out his words, one at a time. I leaned over him to hear, but not so close that I smelled his sour breath.

"We don't know what they have in Russia today. Remember? They're in the middle of the same war we're in."

"Have you heard from Ozzie?"

Ozzie. Ivan. His sons were the only family he claimed. He'd never known what to do with the women, our two daughters as well as me.

"Not in two weeks," I said. "You'd be the first person to know if he wrote. Ivan would be shouting the news from the rafters."

"Good. No news is good news." His eyes remained closed. Even while Elaina, Dr. Schmidt's nurse, changed the dressings yesterday, I had to look away when seeing the raw tissue, swollen and yellow with infection. It was hard to know where the cancer lay beneath the cratered wound. A yellow stain and the resulting sourness from inside the white bandage gave daily evidence of the ongoing decay.

The tea warmed my hands for what seemed a long time as I stood there. Like a good wife, I changed the linens weekly when Elaina helped by turning him in the bed. I did the best I could to bathe Albert when he allowed me to do so. I knew without his saying that he preferred I see his naked body to having to endure the glance of a stranger. *Herr Gott, ease this man's suffering and help him find his peace as quickly as you are willing,* I prayed silently to myself.

When I opened my eyes, he was staring at me, his eyes wider than I'd seen them in some time. "Think that God you pray to will help me, do you?"

"Can't hurt."

Now I was impatient. I had cleaning up downstairs and dumplings to prepare before the day got too far ahead of us. "It's about the rent."

"Tell Oscar that as soon as my social security comes, it's his." His eyes closed again. "You'll have to sell more eggs, that's all."

"We only have two chickens laying. The raccoon got the other hen."

"You'll manage. You always do."

This man hardly deserved the kindness I gave him—and, predictably, he never acknowledged those of us trying to ease his misery. *Herr Gott, forgive me for hating him the way I do,* I said to myself, my eyes open when he reached for a cigarette on the bedside table. The cigarette lighter. *Will we ever find forgiveness for each other before he dies?*

His distance in that bed was greater than any continental divide. What happened to the beginning sweetness when he brought me a piece of chocolate on Fridays after he got off work? A yellow rose on my birthday? That first time he came to the house in a shirt and tie to sit at the kitchen table with the family, with his hand under the tablecloth searching for mine. His eager, excited face above me when Ozzie gave his first birth cry. The way he touched my hand, his fingers trailing mine, when I sang a German lullaby while rocking the children. Now it didn't matter that the full mug would go with me back down the stairs into the kitchen. Our marriage had trailed off onto a side rail and become nothing more than an overgrown path leading to either his death or mine. As long as I could pull myself up and down the stairs, it was unlikely I'd be the first to go.

# 1914

THE LAST MORNING ON Ellis Island, Mother and I made our bed according to the regulation. For some reason, I gazed at her and realized how much her beauty had changed since we'd left Odessa. Within weeks, the youth I'd expected around her eyes, her lovely mouth and heart-shaped lips, had slackened as though unseen weight had pulled her face into a new shape. Seeing her across from me, our satchels packed and ready for the anticipated train ride, I couldn't help but think that this was the mother who'd always been so mindful of her appearance. Had these big changes happened to me as well?

From out of nowhere, I blurted, "Mother, do I look pretty?"

It seemed a reasonable question after all those weeks since leaving home and seeing her as she was now, my own dress hanging loose where it had felt snug during the midnight carriage ride to Odessa with all of us fearful of being stopped and questioned. Now, when I lifted my pearl-handled mirror toward my face, my own cheeks had grown flat and drab.

"Pretty?" she said. "Why do you ask? The entire family has forever remarked on your beauty. Remember what Grandpapa Grozinski said?"

"That I was as rare as a fine pearl."

"There." Mother picked up her satchel. "Your uncle Herman will be happy to see how you've grown these ten years since he last saw you in Kassel. Just think," she said, "in a few years, you will make someone a good wife."

"What if I don't want to marry?" I asked. "What if I want to stay with our family?" The very idea of marriage made me fidget. Yes, I wanted to have what Mother and Father had. Grandpapa and Grand Mama too. But I wanted something more. Something I couldn't name but only felt when I was alone in my room watching the birch tree outside my window or down on my knees in prayer.

"All girls marry," Mother said, "eventually."

"What if I'm not a good wife?" I asked. "I would love to have children like those I worked with here in the nursery, with their sweet waddling when they're learning to walk and their eagerness in listening to stories. But do I have to marry to have them? And what if I don't love my husband the way you love Father?"

Mother laughed, the sound foreign after all these weeks. "First, it's hard to have children without a husband."

I twisted my hair in agitation. In my mind I only saw the rough and worn young men in Kassel who came from the fields with their boasts and demands, their dirty boots. Not unlike my brother Oscar. I rubbed my hands down the sides of my skirts to smooth the wrinkles. If I was to marry, I wanted a guarantee that any husband who presented himself would be a just like Father. Not someone who worked in the fields. "Do I have to marry a farmer?"

"Is not your father a farmer?"

I pulled my shoulders back and raised my chin. "I would rather marry someone who lives in the city like you did in Odessa with Grandpapa."

Mother's mock surprise disappeared. "I recall saying something similar when Grandpapa first suggested marriage to your father." She arranged her shawl around her shoulders. "I scoffed at the notion of living in the country. How could I leave Odessa's opera and symphony, the ballet?" she said. "Had I known we would be starting over in a new country, I might have reconsidered." Her eyes found mine and she quickly added, "And I would have been sorry. Your father made up for our life on the farm." Her glance drifted toward the window. "I always had monthlong winter trips to Odessa in your father's four-horse sleigh. Even before you and Oscar and Leo were born, your father arranged for me to have time with my parents." She stepped into the aisle that led to the hallway door. "Just wait, we will find you a husband just like your father."

I wondered what such a husband would demand in terms of children and a household. Would he question my delight in sitting alone with my books and writing notebooks? My carefree walks in the fields and along the river? Just the thought of being the wife to someone who might make unpleasant demands terrified me.

"How do you know I will make a good wife?"

By now, Mother's impatience layered her words. "A good wife, Marta, is learned in the home where she grows up. I would hope you've learned what it means to be a good wife."

# Chapter Six

## Mrs. Kinski's Talk

## *1943*

From my seat near the room's rear door, I scanned the entry hallway for my daughters' arrival. Mrs. Kinski's talk on womanhood would be the first of its kind in Myra. The room was filled with every woman from the church except Millie, who had no grandchildren. Her only child, David, was unmarried when he was killed in France. Most women sat up front and close to Mrs. Kinski, everyone in a hat and gloves under the overhead lights, an air of formality in the large room since it was so rare for the missus to participate in the congregation, let alone address the members. She probably didn't want to overshadow her husband, our beloved pastor. Except for Ivan, only women filled the folding chairs, my least favorite and always too hard after fifteen minutes.

I was too big for the chair, but that was the least of my concerns. With five minutes until the talk began, the heat of perspiration spread under my arms, which was why I wore a black dress. My best black hat with the heavier veil I continually adjusted because of being so nervous. Those girls had best show up and not embarrass me. If nothing else, I'd counted on Mrs. Kinski to spark renewed faith in Irene and Ada. I'd hate to think they, at twenty-two and twenty-one respectively, were too old or past due for being saved. All I could do was pray that you'd enter their hearts, Lord. Remind them that Herr Gott needed to be their guide, not their husbands. Everyone here had known for years how my family suffered division with Albert's refusal to attend church. Our wedding day happened to be one of the few times he stepped over the church threshold and then only because Oscar had a man-to-man with him. Albert acted sweet in the beginning, but then he went so far as to forbid any pictures of Jesus in the house. That was after Ozzie joined the marines.

I placed my pocketbook on the chair beside me. Ivan stood jittery and excited near the door. I threw my sweater over two more chairs in our row for the girls. They were already late. "Ivan, you'd better ask Mrs. Kinski if she wants you to unfold more chairs."

"Are we going to have cookies?" he asked.

That dimple in his right cheek made his brown eyes look so innocent. The worn brown corduroys were topped with the plaid hand-me-down shirt I found in the church closet. I called him *Herr Gott's gift*, a boy born later in life, one I could count on the same way I counted on his older brother, Ozzie. The girls were another story. Their screaming matches growing up, chasing each other around the yard. I knew Ada could be mean, pinching Irene whenever she had a chance. Then she'd duck out of drying dishes after supper with an urgent need for a long visit to the outhouse. Her red hair, so like Ozzie's but more auburn, should have been a sign. Not that Ozzie had a mean streak. Quite the opposite.

"Now what, Ma?" Ivan asked.

"You can go and ask Mrs. Kinski for a cookie. Then come sit by me. We'll save these two seats for your sisters."

Mrs. Kinski positioned herself behind a podium at the front of the room. She wore new wire-rimmed glasses with her hair rolled up on the sides the way they were wearing it now. That chestnut brown had to be natural. Couldn't imagine the reverend letting her dye it. Still slender, she had much to admire in her print dress and nice hose, the seams straight in back. How did she get silk stockings during the war? A higher heel than I'd dare to wear. She was from Minneapolis, maybe a rich family. Not like the pastor. Nebraska-born and raised, plain folk like us. She was nice enough, just not the inviting kind.

My eyes remained on the door and down the dark hallway, but there was no sign of those two even though I told them there'd be childcare. Millie signed up for that duty. I specifically told Irene and Ada not to wear the beads Ozzie sent them. Don't know what he was thinking. Good Christians don't wear jewelry. I also said they should wear something respectable, their skirts at least mid-calf.

For sure, if Ada taught this class on womanhood, you could count on her imparting her expert wisdom on how you get away with meeting your boyfriend after dark at the water tower or train station. She'd share her list of excuses for how to get out of chores and where to buy your lipstick and nail paint. How to hide it so your mother never found it. I didn't think that Pastor Kinski's wife, who'd brought the class back from the Evangelical Convention in Minneapolis, would dwell on how to pluck your eyebrows or hide the movie magazines. Neither did I think Mrs. Kinski would make you an expert on how to wear a hidden belt to hitch up your skirt once you left the house and which boys were the best kissers.

"Ma, do I have to sit the whole time?" Ivan asked.

"It won't be for long. You brought your writing tablet and pencil. Maybe write a letter to your brother. He'd like that."

"When is he coming home?"

"Maybe a month, maybe six. I don't know."

"Six months is a long time."

"The best reason to write him a letter."

Millie never had daughters. She was lucky. Agnes was here with her Susan, a stuck-up girl. Apple didn't fall far from the tree. There was Mabel Goebel with her Arlene. Fifteen and already taller than her mother. Ada and Irene would probably be the oldest. As a favor to me, they'd agreed to come and at least listen. Even married, Ada was too much on the wild side. Must be Albert's family line. Catholics have a way of acting holy, then doing whatever they pleased.

"We're here, Ma." The hand on my shoulder made me jump, my head down looking for a handkerchief in my purse. I lifted my veil toward Ada's red sweater and a skirt that was too tight. Irene stood behind her sister, rolling her eyes like she usually did around her sister. *One bad apple, one good apple; the challenges you gave me, Herr Gott.*

Ada slid into the chair two seats away, forcing Irene to sit next to me. Ada's feet on the rung of the chair in front of her. I could tell she was chewing gum by the cracking sound. She was determined to be disrespectful even though she admired Mrs. Kinski's style.

I patted Irene's knee. "Appreciate you're a little old for this but figured it couldn't hurt."

"As long as she's not *preachy*," Irene said.

Heat in my face and a tighter hold on my handbag. The eternal fussing with my veil. "What's that supposed to mean?"

"You know, Ma. Sometimes Pastor Kinski goes on and on about the same thing. He can get pretty boring."

"He's doing Herr Gott's work," I said. "So is his missus."

Irene stared straight ahead. Her profile probably what mine would have been without the accident. The straight nose, high cheekbones, a broad forehead that showed off nicely with the new pageboy hairstyle. Her almond-colored hair down around her shoulders and a sweetness shining through her face. If I didn't know she was my daughter, I'd say, "Now there's a *nice* girl." Still,

I couldn't believe she married that railroad bum with the black wavy hair. He was a hard man to trust.

Ada leaned forward. "How long do you think this will last, Ma?"

"Long enough," I said.

Mrs. Kinski placed some papers on the podium. "Good afternoon, ladies," she said. "And you too, Ivan."

Everyone laughed. Ivan looked up from his tablet where he'd been drawing what looked like a bird. He glanced at me. What was so funny?

"Let us pray." She bowed her head and everyone did the same, though Ada looked straight ahead like she was above bowing her head.

"Herr Gott," Mrs. Kinski prayed.

I heard little of the prayer; my eyes were on Ada, who was busy scanning the windows, the room, and Mrs. Kinski. Ada thought she lived in a world different from everybody else since she married that Jewish fellow, Philip. Her marriage was my main reason for wanting her here today. Maybe Mrs. Kinski could turn the corner in Ada that I'd failed to turn. *Maybe, just maybe, you, Herr Gott, will work a miracle with that girl.*

"We're here to talk about what it means to be a good wife," Mrs. Kinski said. "And being a good wife means being a good Christian wife. Don't you agree?"

Heads up front nodded in agreement. Mrs. Kinski adjusted her glasses and scanned the room, all the chairs up front were filled and those at the back of the room sat empty except for me and my family. Irene remained attentive, but she wasn't going to commit, and Ada actually smiled like she already knew the secret to being a good wife.

"The first thing I want to talk about is being faithful to the church and the teachings of the Lord. I'm sure you'll agree that's important, especially in these times of war when the world is changing and so is our country. Especially the women. Though called to do men's work, they're beginning to look more and more like men."

Again, everyone nodded in agreement. Because we didn't take magazines or the newspaper, I wasn't sure what she was talking about. Women becoming like men? But who hadn't been touched by the war and the needs of the country and our soldiers? I had to agree with her about the way women were changing. They were losing their . . . womanness if there was such a thing. Maybe that's what she meant by becoming more like men.

"The second principle I want to talk about is obedience. Obedience first to Herr Gott and then to your husband."

Murmurs filled the large room, maybe as shocked as I was, maybe in agreement. My fingers twisted the handkerchief in my lap. This wasn't what I'd come to hear.

"Yes, your husband," Mrs. Kinski said. "What we were told in Minneapolis is that your husband is a direct emissary of Herr Gott. You must remember that. Even when you disagree with his decisions, even when he loses his temper, especially when you have a different opinion. Your husband represents Herr Gott on earth."

I could hardly sit still in the chair. I lifted my veil to see if I'd heard right. I'd followed Herr Gott all my life and I'd never heard anyone say anything like this before. Not Pastor Kinski, never an interim when Pastor was called away. Never as a girl growing up did I think of Father as a direct emissary of Herr Gott. I certainly didn't think of Albert that way. Never. He derided Herr Gott. And Irene's new husband, Mac? No. Not at all. Philip? He was a Jew. We could forgive him for that.

Not only were my armpits sweaty but my hands were as well. A flush heated my face. I glanced around the room to see how this statement had landed on other women. Agnes, of course, nodded affirmatively. Her husband Ebert was the richest farmer in the county. A nice man, if I said so myself. Agnes's daughter glanced at her mother before nodding her head. Mabel Goebel and her daughter keep looking at each other, maybe as confused as I was. Mabel's husband was the banker, but that didn't mean he was a saint. He wasn't above visiting Jake's Tavern himself. Heard he liked to drink at home too. Someone smelled stale whiskey on him in the bank one day. In fact, how did we know what went on in any woman's home? How could anyone say that every man of the house in Haines County was a direct emissary of Herr Gott?

Ada smiled so big her teeth showed. You'd think she was going to burst out laughing. Irene stared at me, the same question on her face: *Do you really believe this, Ma? Given what you went through with your pa and now with ours? Men who only want what they want? Is that what I got myself into with Mac?* All of that was on her face.

"Third: keep your children in the fold. I know I shouldn't need to say that, but there are families in our community where the growing and grown youngsters are too influenced by the world beyond our gates. Movies and movie magazines. Cigarettes and alcohol. Dancing. Men with no religion. These are the things to be warned against."

I hardly heard her. I couldn't let go of her previous statement. I was so distracted I wasn't paying attention when Ada opened her pocketbook and fingered what looked like a lipstick. I'd be doggoned if she didn't take off the cap and run her pinky finger along the edge of the lipstick and apply the wax to her lips.

If anyone looked toward the back of the room and saw Ada, I'd be the laughingstock. They'd be talking about this over coffee and tea on Sunday morning when Agnes passed the doughnuts. She'd be waiting for me to come out of the vestry so she could waylay me. *Thank you, Herr Gott, Irene had the good grace to just close her eyes.* At least she wasn't humiliating me the way her sister was.

I felt a tug on my arm. "Ma, what does that mean, 'Keep your children in the fold'?" Ivan whispered. "What's a fold?"

He had sugar on his chin and around his mouth. More than one cookie for sure. I reached over with my wet thumb to wipe it away, then took my handkerchief and wiped again. "A fold is like with sheep, Ivan. Keeping sheep together."

Impatience laced my words. I was punishing my innocent son over my frustration with Ada and Mrs. Kinski. I leaned down closer to his head, that cowlick up in the back as usual. Slightly lifting my veil, I said, "You know, how the shepherd uses his crook to keep the sheep in the fold? It's just what people call keeping their family together."

Ivan was thoughtful for a minute, his pencil relaxed while he looked toward the side window. "Does she mean Pa is Herr Gott and the shepherd too?" he asked, his words louder.

"No, no, I don't think that's what she means," I said close to his ear. "I don't know what she means."

"Does Ada know? She's writing something down on a small pad from her purse."

"I've no idea what Ada's writing down. Just ignore her, Ivan."

Ada glanced over at me, a grin on her face and the lip color obvious so everyone would know. On her lap, she was writing a grocery list, of all things. No respect. None.

"Fourth: keep yourself clean and righteous. Free from sin," Mrs. Kinski said. "I don't think I have to remind you of this last one."

"Does that mean take a bath?" Ivan whispered loudly.

This was all a mistake. Besides, this chair cut into my back and hips. Irene had gone to sleep, probably because she and her sister were up late making taffy or popcorn balls or heaven knows what mischief. Playing house, those two, since they moved in together after their husbands left town; the Meyer house on First Street was just big enough for them and their four kids. Philip had already been gone too long, the same as Irene's husband, Mac. Now Ada was sitting there like she had a direct line to Herr Gott, and she had already disproved everything that Mrs. Kinski learned from the Evangelical Conference. Poor Ivan was so confused that he didn't know what to think. Whether Pastor Kinski knew it or not, we were in for another sit-down. Albert was *not* my Lord. And he never would be.

# 1914

I WAS CERTAIN TO find my older brother Oscar outside on the Ellis Island grounds, either behind the main building or by the infirmary where he organized the younger boys who were less filled out—skinny like Leo but eager for Oscar's new contest. Those who gathered the most trash or strewn clothes on the grounds would be allowed to participate in a game of kick the can after supper. When I—his younger sister—appeared, he assigned one of his so-called captains to take charge. We strolled around the building until we found a quiet place in the sun, away from the groaning noise of arriving ferries with the predictable tramp of feet on wooden gangplanks.

"I'm worried about Father," I said. "He hasn't been the same since we arrived here."

Oscar gazed toward the Grand Lady. He said nothing for several minutes. "You have such a big heart, Marta. The way you worry."

"I can't help myself," I said, my hand on his arm, the husk of his jacket woolly beneath my fingers. "What will our lives be like if he doesn't get back to his old self?"

He continued to gaze into the distance. "I know Father is restless. He sometimes leaves the room at night to go walking. But this is all because of Uncle Herman," Oscar said. "Had he been here with the train tickets when we arrived, things would be different." Oscar then shook his head, his red hair grown over the collar of his shirt, his hat pulled down to shade his eyes. "I'm going to have to put you on one of my teams if you don't stop worrying."

His half-teasing grin invited my smile. Oscar—his cheeks pink from the chill and his freckles darker, more pronounced from working outside—was always full of optimism. "Patience, Marta, that's what we need right now," he said. "At some point we'll be able to leave the island. This will be something we remember, something we talk about." He swept his hand, taking in the island, the buildings, the people crowding the main landing. "This is just a stop on our journey," he said. "Not what we expected, but I'm glad we're no longer on that horrid ship."

"Awful for you too?"

"You've never had to sleep with two others on the outside edge of a tall bunk, afraid you're going to fall every night."

Just the thought of Oscar, someone always so self-assured, falling made me laugh.

Oscar removed his hat and fingered it, turning the hat in circles in his hands. He stared toward Manhattan. "You'll see, Marta. Soon we'll be over there." He lifted his arm and pointed toward the city that had become more myth than reality. "At least we don't have the Cossacks at our back."

The Cossacks. I looked away, recalling the workers running in all directions while the uniformed butchers wearing their *ushankas*, the bear-fur hats, sat on their horses shouting directions from their mounts while we watched the barn burn.

I again lay my hand on Oscar's arm, the long muscles of his forearm already so firm. "Herr Gott was with us."

Even as I said the words, they didn't account for a strange loneliness that lived inside me ever since we'd turned down the driveway and left our home behind. A loneliness that might never go away.

Oscar took both my hands in his, the skin of his palm and under his fingers like the tough hide of an animal that had survived many winters. He held my fingers inside his own. "We're in America, Marta. Think of it. America. We're safe."

I gazed toward the Grand Lady. I wanted the same feeling I had when I first saw her the day the ship docked and ferries carried passengers to Battery Park. Before our assignment to a second ferry, the one that brought us to Ellis Island one long week ago.

"Sometimes I wish we'd never come," I said. "It's been dreadful from the beginning, and now we're going to have to leave, to make yet another change."

Oscar laughed his big laugh. When I wouldn't look at him, he spoke quietly. "We must have faith, Marta. It's our faith that will carry us through."

"I wish I could believe the way you do, Oscar," I said. "I so wish I could believe."

## Chapter Seven

### The Outlier

## 1943

MY TEA MUG FELT cold to the touch, Pastor Kinski now ten minutes late. We only had thirty minutes before Ivan came home from school. The Big Ben ticked away on top of Ozzie's shelf over the small sink where he shaved and fussed with his hair. I stood to pour fresh tea. I was the one who'd asked for this meeting. Someone needed to guide my daughters and who they'd become. They were not the young women that Albert and I had raised. As well, the men they chose were not our choice either.

I remembered the first time I heard Mac's name. Albert and I were sitting at the kitchen table just like I was now. That day, before they had husbands, both daughters drank afternoon tea with me and Albert. Irene was explaining why she'd come home late from Schubert's Creamery where she'd scooped ice cream since high school ended the year before. "He's a nice man and a hard worker," Irene said, describing Mac. "I know you'll like him. Please don't judge him until after you meet him."

"What do you mean, *judge him*?" I asked.

There was silence at the table, the kind of quiet where no one wants to be the first to speak for fear of being pounced on.

Our town was wary of strangers, especially since the Great Depression, when railroad bums hid in the rail yards and the cornstalks at the edge of town, or came begging at the back door. Just because this man worked for the Northern Pacific wasn't a ticket to acceptance. Besides, fancy, sweet-talking words were just that: words. They meant nothing without proof, and in this town, proof took years of knowing someone and their kin. Never mind that Albert was a stranger when he arrived in town. At least he was German and he was a Christian, though Catholic, so he said.

"Invite him to church," I finally said, "then to Sunday dinner."

Ada picked at her flesh-colored nail polish, though she knew I disapproved.

Irene kept her eyes on the oilcloth table covering, tracing the patterned roses with her index finger.

"Why not skip church and just invite him to dinner?" Ada said.

Albert fit a new cigarette into his amber-colored cigarette holder and struck a match. He gave both girls that sober, searching look he had whenever he was suspicious. His brown eyes said he didn't like strangers any more than I did. The question on the tip of my tongue regarded this man's willingness to attend church. But I didn't want to get into an argument over that with Albert or the girls, and I didn't want to become distracted from the real issue: Irene bringing a stranger into our lives.

Irene sighed. I wasn't sure if she was annoyed with Ada's attempt to save her or if she was rehearsing for the day she would introduce this fellow. Like her father, her mind was made up.

"How do you know he comes from a good family?" I asked. "Because he told you?"

"Ma, his father is still working," Irene said.

During the silence that followed, no one looked at Albert, who had only worked on and off the last few years, the Great Depression having taken its toll on regular shifts. Then there was the war just before his cancer diagnosis. Albert left the house each day, grabbing his coat and hat and walking through the back gate and down the alley to Jake's Tavern.

"Maybe it's time we got some fresh blood in this family. In this town," Ada said.

"Fresh blood? What do you mean, fresh blood?" I asked.

"People who are different but not different," Ada said. She tossed her red hair over her shoulder and folded her hands against the oilcloth, her nail polish nearly gone except for chips on both thumbnails. "He's from North Dakota, so he can't be all bad. He's working. His family owns their own home, and his father has worked years for the railroad, through the Depression and now through the war. I suppose he's different because he isn't German or Russian and he doesn't farm. Does that make him bad?"

"You seem to know a lot about this young man, Miss Ada. Is it possible you're thinking about him for yourself?" I asked.

"Ma, don't be absurd. He belongs to Irene. She saw him first."

I put my hand on Albert's sleeve, hoping he would say something.

He stared toward the telephone lines so full of blackbirds that the line sagged in the middle. "Just because he and his father have jobs doesn't mean he's cut from good cloth."

Good, he finally said something.

"What church does he go to?" I asked.

"Let's not get started with that damned church business," Albert said. "Irene already said he's working for the Northern Pacific and his family lives in Mandan. Isn't that enough?"

I folded my hands in front of me and pressed my lips tightly together. Why did he always turn against me at the mention of church? Why couldn't he stand by me at least once?

Irene stood to retrieve the teakettle from the back of the stove.

"Ma, you're scaring Irene," Ada said. "Give her a chance to meet someone who isn't cut out of a cloth you wove." Her tone changed and dropped a level. "His family is Catholic, like yours was, Pa."

I put my hands on the edge of the table and pushed to my feet, my chair scraping the linoleum when it scooted behind me. "Catholic" was all I said. I turned toward the drainboard and ladled more water into the teakettle.

Behind me, no one said a word. Out of the corner of my eye, I saw Albert smash out his cigarette in the ashtray just before the cigarette holder clicked into place in one of the ashtray grooves. A chair scraped back, then another. Had I won or lost, I didn't know. Time would tell.

Pastor Kinski was now twenty minutes late when he came in through the mudroom, not bothering to knock. I was already frying a chicken and boiling spuds for mashed potatoes. I wiped my hands on my apron and moved the chicken to the side of the stove and away from the fire. "Just about gave up on you."

His preacher's collar stood out white behind his black shirt, but he forgot to comb his hair. Not unusual for him, though he could have been caught in the wind. "Long day, Marta. You're the fourth house call today. Hope I'm not too late for tea and kuchen."

"Never too late, Pastor," I said. "Just wipe your feet on the rug and come in. The kitchen's warm from cooking."

"I can smell that fried chicken. I hope Albert knows how lucky he is to have you cooking his meals."

I said nothing. Sometimes Pastor annoyed me when he talked about Albert. You'd think Albert was an active part of our church family. "Have a seat. The tea is on the back of the stove and I have one piece of prune kuchen I've been saving for you." His being late goaded me to put the fresh kuchen in the cupboard.

"Bless you, Marta. Makes all the other calls worthwhile."

He took the chair at the head of the table. My chair. Put his coat over the back of the chair rather than hanging it in the mudroom where it could drip rain onto the rag rug set there for that purpose. Sometimes I had to forgive Pastor for being so doggone human he made me mad. "Will have your tea in a minute."

"That's fine. You can tell me what's happening with your daughters. Where are they? I somehow thought they'd be here."

"Said the children had colds; couldn't come today."

He settled with his mug of tea; the kuchen was already eaten, including his scraping the plate with the fork's tines. "Tell me what's bothering you, or should I guess?"

I turned in his direction and gave him that look that says, *Here we go again.*

"Must be about their church attendance. Haven't heard that anything's happened to their husbands, although . . ." He trailed off his sentence. No one wanted to say *hurt* or *killed*. Between rationing and the blackout curtains, the war was always with us.

"I worry about them," I said. "Look at Irene. Alone with three babies. No plan if Mac doesn't survive the war. They've already taken the train to the West Coast so Mac could make so-called big money in Portland's Kaiser shipyards. What's to become of those children if their father is killed?"

"They have you and Albert. Your brother. Our church community. Some things we just can't worry about, Marta." Pastor slurped his tea, his fork hovering over the empty plate as though waiting for another piece of kuchen to magically appear.

He'd heard all the stories about Portland. Irene working nights downtown at the Meier & Frank department store. Trying to hang diapers in their basement apartment's washroom only to find the hallway blocked by a man intent on throwing knives at a cardboard box. Said she'd never hated a place so much, with the endless rain and living in fear each day until Mac returned. She had Marta and

Sissy then; Louisa not yet born. That was before Mac thought the war gave them a better option. "At least Irene will have something if I'm killed," Mac said one night after supper when he and Albert drank too much beer.

"You know why I worry, Pastor." I sat down adjacent to him, a mug of tea all that was in front of me. I'd already eaten two slices of kuchen before he came. "Mac's too handsome for his own good. The two of them, Mac and Irene, running off to Glendive and eloping. No job, no apartment, not enough money for a loaf of bread let alone the baloney to put between the slices."

"Yes, I know," Pastor said, his tea mug empty.

I stood and retrieved the still-hot teapot and poured the remnants of tea into Pastor's mug.

He raised his head and gave me a long, penetrating look. But he said nothing.

"I know what you're going to say, Pastor. I need to bring both of the girls back into the church," I said. "At least I got them to your missus's talk on womanhood."

"She told me your whole family was there, including Ivan." He smiled and sat back in his chair.

"It's this war, Pastor. The romance of war. Even Ivan's been caught by Ida Reichel sneaking into the movies with his friend Robert. Millie next door overheard him retelling Robert stories about soldiers who scraped along in muddy trenches, the Nazis always over the next bunker. I've already lived through Albert going off to the Great War before we married. The Spanish flu afterward. I don't need to be fretting about the family I have at home when I already have one in the Pacific."

"You don't need to worry, Marta," Pastor said. "You need to pray."

Those words were his final remedy for any and all problems. What he didn't realize was that when things don't work out, when tragedy comes, the burden always falls on the women. Yes, I'd pray harder. *I'd talked longer and louder to you, Herr Gott. Surely you will bring Mac back home to care for his family. Do you hear me, Herr Gott?*

After Pastor left I was still thinking about how we all pay for the crime of war. Like we paid for Father's crime. I paid with my face down on the dock. The same feeling now, painful and familiar, reminded me of the night Mother and Father went out to the barn to sort the satchels from Russia so we could move into Uncle Herman's old house the next day. I was upstairs above the heating grate where Leo and I sometimes hovered in the evening when the adults thought we were in bed. Uncle Herman and Tante Ketcha were talking down below. "I know, I know, Ketcha, I shouldn't have trusted him to carry the gold from Russia. Reinmar had warned me that Jacob lost the acreage betting Reinmar's property in a card game. I just can't believe my own brother would gamble away all our futures."

"What's done is done," Tante Ketcha said. "He can't be trusted with money ever again."

It was true that they never asked Father to take the team to town for supplies. When cash was exchanged, they gave it to Mother. No one discussed what Oscar later told me about the card games that went on late at Ellis Island. That Father went out every evening for a walk, he said, but he rarely returned before dawn. What was done was done. Now I realized the same was true for me with my own daughters. War was the gamble none of us could avoid.

## 1914

THE MINUTE I HEARD the gangplank go down at Battery Park and saw first Oscar, then Leo and Uncle Herman fight their way through the upper deck crowd and descend the stairs—this our second landing at Battery Park—I descended the stairs, then the gangplank. Ahead of me, Uncle Herman and my brothers waved from the dock. Forgetting that I was prone to clumsiness and eager to be with my brothers and Uncle Herman on American soil, I broke free from the crowd. I ran onto the wharf and toward my brothers, the precious bundle holding my Easter egg in front of me, Mother's shawl dangling around my legs and feet.

The shawl tangled in my legs, tripped my feet, and, without warning, sent me too fast and facedown onto the wharf. My only thought was for my egg bundle when it flew out of my hands. Hands couldn't catch me fast enough before my face scraped along the splintered and uneven, horse-trodden wharf. It seemed to happen in slow motion, yet was over in a moment. My face, having scraped against the rough wood, throbbed with immediate pain. When I reached toward a painful gash on my forehead, my hand came back bloody. The pain in my forehead and along my cheeks, nose, and chin made it impossible to move. When I tried to turn my head, a single white tooth lay innocently inside the blood now leaking around my face and onto the wood planks.

Leo's black wool cap lay in the new blood pooled beside my face. Confused, I couldn't figure out why my skittish, sensitive, and shy brother was shouting, "Don't step on Marta's bundle!" Why would anyone step on my bundle? After all, I was holding it. But I wasn't holding it. My arms were not my arms and the pain that stung my cheeks wasn't my pain. People crowded around me.

What did they want? Why was I facedown on the wharf when I was trying to reach Uncle Herman and Oscar?

Leo's gasp confirmed that something was terribly wrong. A circle of forms that were maybe family, maybe strangers converged before a momentary blackness blocked them out.

When I looked up again, Mother leaned over me, her cheeks shiny with tears. What happened? Why was she crying? "Herr Gott," she said, over and over. Her moaning filling me with dread. Was she hurt? "Get back, get back," she shouted, pushing at the gathering crowd. She leaned over me, then timidly reached to touch my face. She pulled back. I didn't understand. My body lay in one place, but my mind could only see the tears falling down her face.

Father, his face fuzzy and shaking, lifted me into his arms, saying over and over, "Marta, my beautiful and darling Marta. This is all my fault."

There were tears in Father's eyes when I again opened mine. He laid me down outside of the foot traffic on the wooden wharf. He continued to repeat, "This is all my fault."

Why did he keep saying that? And why was Mother shouting in English, "Find water, a doctor. Someone to help."

When pain finally took over my body, everything hurt, even the tears soaking into my face. Father stayed beside me. Then the blue-gray uniform of what must have been a policeman, his frowning face shaded by his hat, came close. Yes, he told Father, he saw the incident, his face leaning close to mine when I heard myself scream.

A bareheaded man with white hair bent down, his spectacles resembling two shining orbs. People behind him pressed forward. I heard the clicking of tongues, someone praying the Our Father. Another exclaimed, "What a shame." Leo stood over the old man, my bundle under his arm. The white-haired gentleman knelt beside me, where he began to rummage in his satchel. He pulled out white cloths. Down on his knees, he leaned over me, holding a cloth stained a caramel color to my nose. I sniffed the strong spirits our family used only for birthday celebrations. After breathing in the spirits, he began to dab at my face with the wetted cloth. On contact, the cloth stung what was already burning. I screamed, and Father grabbed one of my arms and Oscar grabbed the other. The stranger continued to dab at my cheeks and forehead, the cloth now soaked with whatever liquid he was using. "A stitch or two," he said in German.

"Ja, ja," Father said, desperation in his voice.

The old man lifted what looked like the kind of tweezers Father's men used to pull thistles from sheep. He continued to dab the spirits at my cheeks despite my screams. Father covered my eyes with his hand. The man then pressed an instrument against my cheek and withdrew what felt like a giant sliver. Though I continued to scream with everything I had, Father and Oscar held my arms until I finally gave up. The man applied the whiskey-soaked rag again, the odor now reminding me of what it was. The screams that came from inside me may as well have come from the blue sky. Until I heard nothing.

Later, Leo told me that I'd blessedly passed out. According to him, the doctor swabbed my other cheek before lifting the needle he'd used to repair one side of my face. His concentration was so great that his glasses threatened to slide off his nose. He lifted out two, then three more slivers of considerable length from my other cheek. The doctor supposedly threaded the needle again and, quickly, whipped two more stitches into my forehead.

I remember nothing until we were loaded into a cart headed for the Jersey City Railway Station. Uncle Herman repeatedly said, "When we get to Dakota, Tante Ketcha will make her good as new." Tante Ketcha, the woman I dreaded more than anyone, her cruel slap on my three-year-old cheek forever imprinted there. "She can do anything, including small miracles," Uncle Herman continued to boast.

My hand drifted as though through rapidly moving water toward my face where I lay in the back of the cart on comforters Mother had pulled from the trunk. While everyone's attention focused on the tall buildings and the noisy traffic, I lowered my hand to my face. Gently—so very gently and almost not touching the gauze for fear I would add more damage, more pain—I touched my fingertips to the gauze along my right cheek. Not to disturb what was there, but to know for certain that my fall wasn't a nightmare. The rough gauze beneath my fingertips, then I quickly lifted them as though I'd just touched a hot stove. It was true, all of it. The gauze, the stinging beneath the gauze. My heart's pounding made it hard to swallow, my sobs quieter now as despair set in.

## Chapter Eight

### Coffee Hour

## 1943

I FINISHED CLEARING THE altar and carefully folded the altar scarves and vestments, checking for any stains that might need to be taken home and bleached before the next service. I closed the drawers behind the vestry and adjusted my hat in the mirror, making sure to place the netting well below my chin. I didn't usually pay attention to fashion, except in this instance when it was a blessing to be able to cover my scarred face and lips, always with me no matter how hard I tried to ignore them. In my mind's eye, I continued to have the lovely young girl's face with which I'd left Russia all those years ago. The fantasy held if I avoided the mirror behind the vestry. Whenever I saw the white scar that bisected my cheek and ran like a spider's web into my nose, I was filled with horror and immediately turned away. The horizontal forehead scar was easier to hide with my hair or a hat.

I glanced around the vestry to make sure everything was in order. The vestments, including Pastor's robes and stoles, were where they ought to be. His prayer books. A reminder that I kept forgetting to tell him I'd taken a Bible from the church. Certainly, if it came up, I'd talk directly to Frank, which I also kept forgetting to do.

Before lifting my pocketbook from the single chair left for Pastor's convenience, I spied a key lying on the floor. I picked it up, thinking Pastor dropped it in his hurry to get to the basement for morning pastries. He might still be there.

Today, like always, I approached Agnes Fleischman's table with hesitation, knowing that Agnes liked everybody else's business better than her own, her stiff shoulders up around her ears and her own black hat draped both in front and back with netting. I'd watched Agnes and her crowd destroy more than one person, Robert Shreve the worst after he was accused of chasing Emily Strickland and taking off her panties. The boy was only nine at the time, a big oaf for his age, and not well-liked except by Ivan. He couldn't help that his parents lived in a shanty at the edge of the town dump. Their only sin as far as I knew was that they'd never walked into the First Bible Church sanctuary. Once Robert was accused, Agnes and her friends made sure that Robert never worked for a churchgoing family again. He became the target of catcalls and fistfights. He started to skip school. Sayings like *stay away from Robert or your father will tan your hide* circulated over gingham tablecloths and baby peas climbing spring trellises.

Ivan often invited Robert to spend time with him in the pigeon pen. Because our place was located behind the Texaco station and not far from the center of town, everyone saw the two boys walk our alley to and from school. I was certain the Rumfords next door heard the boys talking in the pigeon pen, especially Millie, who could hear them from inside her propped-open kitchen window and would let me know if anything was amiss.

Walking past Agnes and her set that morning, my purse accidently swung against Helen Schneider's chair. Voices stopped. The ladies, circled around the table with their white gloves in their laps and their tea and coffee cups already empty, gazed down at the white dust of powdered sugar on their empty plates. Though this was usually where I lingered to have the remains of cold tea and whatever was left of the Myra Bakery doughnuts, I lifted my chin and thought to hurry past. For some reason, I recalled an incident with Karen Comebacker rattling on about Ada's name in the Dickinson Herald heading up a wives' club for servicemen. Leave it to Agnes to twist it around until Ada became the next Robert Shreve.

"Marta, you are far too busy," Agnes said, her voice breaking the silence around the table. The other women glanced up at me.

"Has anyone seen Pastor Kinski?" I asked. "He dropped a key in the vestry."

"Pastor has gone out to make Sunday calls," Agnes said. "Why don't you sit down and join us?"

The heat under my arms warned me that it was only a matter of minutes before a ring of perspiration would darken the underside of my light blue sleeves. "Thank you," I said. "But I have a ham at home I need to bake."

"Surprised you're having ham," Agnes said. "Seeing you have a Jewess in the house."

If I knew my face was red, so did the ladies sitting around the table, either with their heads down following Agnes's comment or looking elsewhere. They'd likely already chewed up my daughters and spit them out. They'd simply been waiting to land on me. Yes, Ada married Philip, and Philip happened to be a Jew. How sad to think that our German heritage had suddenly absorbed us as part of Hitler's mob. Was I now surrounded by Nazi sympathizers, ever loyal to Germany, no matter what? I surprised myself by staring at Agnes as hard as I'd ever stared at anyone. While the smile remained on her face and the full wattle of her neck moved with her head when she lifted her teacup, her eyes never left mine.

Pastor Kinski advised silence when you were tempted to say too much. Remembering his words, I said nothing. Instead, I kept my eyes on hers and remained standing, my handbag pulled against my hip. I then nodded without looking at any of the others. Pulling back my shoulders the best I could, "I recall hearing something about people who live in glass houses," I said.

It was one thing to fight a battle you had a chance of winning, another when the odds were against you. Nevertheless, if my family was under scrutiny, I wasn't going to run from the likes of Agnes. My only sin was that I'd raised two modern young women without the benefit of a strong man like Ozzie who, at that moment, was entirely out of reach. If Ozzie was home, one word from him would silence an otherwise trivial and regrettable situation. Not that the idea of Ada gallivanting around without my knowing was trivial; my face now plunged into the red ink of embarrassment. I told myself that this was how you knew your true friends, when your enemies descended and no one came forward in your defense. In that moment, I missed Pastor Kinski, who had been the church's backbone since I was a young wife. Pastor Kinski made people remember who and what they served and why.

Agnes returned her attention to her empty teacup and the powdered sugar crumbs remaining on her plate. "People who live in glass houses indeed," she said under her breath but loud enough that I could hear.

I lowered my handbag until it dangled from my wrist and, without intending to, put my hands on my hips. "Because someone is different doesn't mean they're bad," I said. "Or hasn't Herr Gott persuaded you yet?"

Agnes brought her napkin to her lips, maybe to hide a smirk, maybe to cover her own embarrassment. She then looked over her napkin at Helen, who sat opposite her. Agnes closed her eyes. My comment was clearly beneath her.

"And while we're at it, Agnes Fleischman, where is your own draft-age son at this moment? Hiding behind flat feet?"

*If you're going to curse me and strike me down, Herr Gott, this is the moment.* While I'd complained to both Ada and Irene, even to Albert, about the unfairness of the military service taking our only adult son when his father lay ill, to strike Agnes's own shame wasn't my right. That was Herr Gott's territory.

For once, Agnes didn't have a comeback. She narrowed her eyes and trained them on me the way you'd sight a rifle. It was over as quickly as it began.

When I left them sitting there, probably embarrassed for Agnes and furious with me, I had no thought but for home and the safety of my own kitchen. Never mind that the path was icy in spots after a heavy October snow; the sidewalk gravelly beneath the rubbers that fit over my shoes. There was a churning in my stomach that even you, Herr Gott, couldn't take away.

Then there was Ada. Was she hiding something? When I passed from the sidewalk into the alley, mudholes everywhere, I recalled her hurried wedding to Philip and the fact that Ada had been growing fat like me. At the time it never dawned on me that she might be pregnant. I knew everyone counted the months—Eli born six months later, his father shipped overseas just weeks after they married.

On the walk home, past Fritz's Texaco, down the alley between my house and Millie's, toward the pigeon pen and winter-buried garden, every step seemed too many and the way was too long. There was that stuck place in my throat when there's no way to let the frustration and shame out of the body. I pulled back the gate from the alley and stepped onto the brick path. Past the cooing pigeons in their cages and up the steps into the mudroom on the back porch. But I was finally home. Home to the comfort of putting on my apron and pulling out the bread bowl to start a new batch of rolls.

## 1914

WE WERE A FAMILY who had never wanted for anything. We threw better scraps to our dogs than the stale bread and cheese we subsisted on during that train ride. "Excuse me," Father said, "I need to see the money changer while we're in Chicago."

Our stop in the Chicago train station would be the longest on our journey west. Long enough for everyone to walk around the station, to feel some space around them at last. Maybe nap on one of the long benches that weren't overtaken by immigrant cases and bundles like the Jersey City station had been.

Uncle Herman raised his eyebrows. "Would you like me to go with you?"

"Not necessary," Father said. "Sit and finish your meal."

When he rose, Father's eyeglasses had fogged. For a moment, his were the eyes of a stranger, someone I'd never met.

We finished our bread and everyone took a sip from the wineskin. Oscar and Leo wandered close to the newsstand where I heard Leo read the English headlines aloud to our big brother. Sooner than anticipated, Father rounded the corner to join them and then disappeared. When he returned, the doleful expression on his face spoke of worry.

Before anyone could ask, Father announced, "They couldn't exchange the gold coin for cash but they did accept my eyeglasses. We now have enough money for food."

"Jacob," Mother said, her mouth drooping in alarm or disappointment. I wasn't sure. "How will you see?"

Father's smile was weak. "I will."

"Come, Jacob," Uncle Herman said. "We have time to leave the station and scout the street markets for supplies before we leave Chicago."

"You think that's wise? To leave the women and boys?" Father asked.

"Someone has to go," Uncle Herman said. "Either you or Oscar, but I think it will do you more good."

"Leo and I will stay," Oscar said.

Uncle Herman looked at his pocket watch. "We have three hours before we board the Great Northern."

Mother put her hand on Father's arm. "Herman is right. You can return and tell me and Marta what you saw."

Father glanced at Mother's small hand on his arm. He stood silent for the better part of a minute. Then, shaking his head, he nodded toward Uncle Herman. "Yes, a full pipe will brighten the day."

In less than half an hour, Father and Uncle Herman returned. A serious frown wrinkled Uncle Herman's forehead when he handed Mother the brown paper package. Without another word, he excused himself for the washroom.

"With you and Herman, what happened?" Mother asked.

"Let's stand over there," Father said. He saw me jump at the notion of being left alone. "We'll keep an eye on you, kitten. We just need a moment to ourselves."

Mother followed Father about twenty paces away toward the newspaper stand. Once there, Mother turned her back to me.

With Mother's face turned away, I couldn't tell if this was a good or a bad talk. Their heads nodded back and forth. Many people, folks not as peculiar or varied as those at the Jersey City terminal, hurried through the station. All seemed to be rushing toward the tunnel openings or lingering near the newspaper stand where Mother stood close to hear Father.

Throughout their talk, Father kept his eyes on me, only breaking the connection when he lowered his head to say something more to Mother. After a time, he put his hands on her shaking shoulders. She was crying when he pulled her toward him. Like an invisible trigger, a warm rush of sadness and anger filled my throat and a flush of heat spread up my neck.

Louder than usual and over the top of Mother's bowed head, Father pointed to my brothers' return. "See, here they are," he said. "Safe and sound." He pulled his pocket watch from his vest pocket. "Less than a half hour before we board the train."

The smile on Father's face betrayed the drop in Mother's shoulders with their apparent shaking. She was crying harder now. My own eyes began to tear up, for her and for whatever Father had just said to her. With her back to all of us, Mother pulled a handkerchief from her sleeve and dabbed at her eyes before blowing her nose. My parents continued to stand like that for another minute.

Though I was sitting down, my one leg began to shake while the churning in my stomach wouldn't stop. When Uncle Herman appeared, his usual smile had been replaced by a sternness I hadn't seen since Father came to the main hall stairs on Ellis Island almost too late for the ferry. Mother, her face red from crying just moments ago, walked back toward me, her arms falling heavily at her sides and her shoulders drooping. "We must prepare to leave," she said, a new weariness in her lifeless voice. She took my arm, but her hand was limp. Oscar wheeled the large cart that carried our luggage and Leo joined him on the push bar, both of my brothers seemingly oblivious to what had just happened. Without a word, Uncle Herman led our small procession toward Tunnel 18, destined for Bismarck, the westernmost destination for this particular train. I kept my eyes down, people stopping to stare at my face. Someone reached out to touch my arm. I quickly pulled away, realizing only later that perhaps they meant to comfort me. Even the conductor, who helped me onto the train, stared too long at my bandaged head. My heart had swelled inside my chest until I thought it would burst with a deep sense of unexplained loss at witnessing Mother's tears.

# Chapter Nine

## Recurring Dream

## 1943

THE INSPECTION LINE. IT'S my turn. My hands are shaking and my body trembles until I can hardly stand. Terrified and helpless. My eyes dart from side to side, jaw hard and locked, but my chin shivers. I can see Mother out of the corner of my eye, her hands inside the muff, her eyes as scared as my heart beating its way out of my chest. Why can't she help me? Stop him? The doctor's hand presses against my face. He says nothing. Just comes at me with what looks like a meat hook. I can't glance away. I can't close my eyes, though I try. Tears fall even as the doctor lifts my eyelid with his fingers. He raises the iron hook and smiles in what I see as a leering way. The iron hook comes closer, toward my eye. The doctor's hand grips my chin. He's insistent, demanding. The look never leaves his face. The hook comes toward the center of my eye. Its harsh edge grabs hold of my eyelid's delicate skin. The harsh pull of the steel. The hook latches on. I'm in immediate pain. Piercing pain that stabs all the way to the back of my head. There's a churning in my stomach and heat inside my mouth. Will I vomit? Will I faint? My eyes dart from side to side, looking for escape. My jaw locks tighter. Where is Mother? Why doesn't she save me? A scream awakens me.

## Chapter Ten

### Philip's Death

### *1943*

NEARLY THANKSGIVING IN THE middle of this torturous war. Our ladies' sewing circle had finished knitting wool socks to send back to Russia when the telegram was delivered by Harold, who wears a Yankees baseball cap all seasons. He worked part-time at Hoffman's Drug, where all the telegrams came in to Myra. The message didn't come to my house; no reason it should. Albert had fallen worse now, unable to come to the kitchen for any reason, all his food taken up and down the stairs by me or Ivan, along with the chamber pot, carried up and down by me as well. The message went to First Street where it should have gone, to the kitchen door where Irene walked the laundry from the new wringer wash machine to the clothes rack in the corner and Ada set up the ironing board whenever she got around to it.

I'd have never known the story about Ada's reaction if Irene hadn't come flying into the house shortly after through the only entrance we ever used, the mudroom next to the kitchen door. I wasn't thinking about unexpected messages when I saw the new fur-collared coat that hugged her neck. A fur hat to match in the Russian style of a *shapka* snugged on top of her brownish-blond hair. "What is this? Someone made you rich?" I asked.

Irene pulled at the fingers of new calfskin gloves, one finger at a time. She ignored my comment. While she unbuttoned her coat, she picked off a couple of my gray hairs from the sofa upholstery before she carefully draped the coat over the back of the seldom-sat-on couch. That coat would never hang on a hook by the back door where the rest of us hung our coats. The hat came off next and rested on top of the coat. Besides the coat and hat and gloves, an unfamiliar purple sweater—cashmere from the looks of it—betrayed a recent shopping trip to Dickinson.

Irene pulled the kitchen stool closer to the counter where I was busy shaping dough into a loaf of bread. "It's happened," Irene said. Her voice was filled with surprising emotion, and she stumbled over her words. "You should sit down, Ma."

*Herr Gott. Not Ozzie.* My mouth open, the shock of my secret fear spilled out. "Not Mac," I said, coming out of momentary panic.

"No," she said. We sat facing each other, her mouth trembling in a way I'd never seen. "It's Philip," she said. "Shot down over Germany."

The immediate sting behind my eyes seemed small beside the drop inside my chest, an emptiness I'd dreaded ever since the Germans moved into Poland and the whole catastrophe began. "Herr Gott rest his soul" was all I could say, a catch in my breath and my hand on my chest. This could be the death of anyone close to our family whose name had slipped from my tongue, someone mentioned during prayer circle at the church, or one of those faceless souls who would wear the knitted socks we shipped in a box to Kassel last week. But this was my son-in-law. Father of my grandson Eli, husband of a careless and undeserving daughter.

We'd braced ourselves against this kind of news since the war began, both denying and dreading that it could happen to someone in our family, in the same way it had already happened to the Reichels and the Rumfords. This, the worst of all news, now further united us to other families in our small town, often eerily quiet despite the back- and side yards being wide but close enough that you could hear your neighbor's radio without turning on your own.

Irene dabbed at her eyes. "She's an odd one," she said. "Not a tear. And not a word to Eli."

I pushed around the hill of dough on my breadboard, then paused, needing to catch my breath. "Eli's only two. He can't possibly understand his father's death when he's never known his father."

Philip was hardly more than a memory to me. His flying ace photograph rested on top of the bookcase alongside Irene's army-uniformed husband, Mac. Philip, no more than a romantic fantasy, grinned from his handsome face above the white scarf draped around his neck. The photo was Eli's only hint that there'd been a father somewhere in his life.

I punched down the dough, aware that the abiding fear locked inside the bulk of my body was that the name on the letter might be my Ozzie's. Like those of the mothers of other boys in other places where they didn't belong, my heart couldn't survive seeing the name of my eldest son in a yellow telegram delivering the news no one wanted to see or hear. Especially with Albert dying upstairs in our bed.

"I think it's wrong that she hasn't found a way to say something to Eli," Irene said. "But then, you know Ada. She won't listen to you, and she certainly won't listen to me."

I rolled the dough against the floured board, having put in extra shortening in hopes the lard would soften the dough and make it easier for Albert to swallow. The doctor, stopping by this morning, said what a shame we hadn't put him in the living room downstairs. "Would have saved a lot of bother." Dr. Schmidt was likely talking about himself and the effort to get his immense body up and down the narrow staircase. As far as I could see, Dr. Schmidt wasn't that far ahead of me weight-wise, yet Ivan and I did the bulk of the lifting and carrying.

"He's just a little boy," I said. "What about the body?"

"Ada said there'll be another telegram. When to expect the remains." Irene hesitated. "Can't imagine there will be much to return."

Her sudden callousness about the death of her sister's husband, and especially while wearing new clothes, made me stop with my hands buried in the floury dough, my heart beating too fast, and the war suddenly in my kitchen. What was happening to my daughters? How was the war changing them? Where had their hearts flown to?

"Of course there will be remains," I said. "There are always remains. And there will be a church service if his people will allow it."

"How can you be so sure, Ma? I don't know these things; you don't know these things. We've never had to deal with this kind of death before."

What Irene said was true. It was one thing to fix a chicken casserole for the Reichel son's funeral and to sit through another gray and dark service, hearing Marie, the mother, sob into her handkerchief while Pastor Kinski praised Roger Reichel for his service. Quite another to imagine sitting with a bent head and weeping into my own tatted handkerchief during a non-Christian service, or reaching for Ada's hand and trying to console her.

"I'll never get over it," Irene said. "Ada just stared at the telegram for a long time. Then she folded it and slipped it into the breast pocket of her blouse. When I asked what the telegram was about, she said, 'It's about Philip. He's been killed,' the same way she might talk about the grocery boy missing part of the order or a late notice from the electric company. What she's thinking is anyone's guess."

"That doesn't sound like a daughter I raised."

"Maybe she was raised by wolves we never saw," Irene said.

"For shame, Irene. That's a blasphemy against Herr Gott, against me, and worse, against Ada."

Irene lowered her head. "Sorry, Ma."

I began to roll out the dough for kuchen. Maybe this one should go to the Kesslers. It was time for all of us to appreciate Herr Gott's ways.

"His family must have their own tradition for dealing with these things," Irene said. "Maybe Jews don't have funerals. How would I know."

"Of course they do. Everybody does. It's Herr Gott's way."

"Ma," Irene said, "his family is different."

"They have to have some kind of service. It's only right. After all, Ada is his wife!"

"Barely," Irene whispered. She hesitated before raising her chin toward me. "I suppose this means his allotment will end."

I stared at Irene. I didn't know this woman. My own daughter, so hard and mercenary. When did Herr Gott disappear from her life? I pulled back from the rolling pin where I'd leaned heavily in order to thin the dough's elastic surface. "For shame, Irene. This is your sister's dead husband. What if it was yours?"

Irene placed the stool back near the door where she found it. "Ma, I have three kids. They like to eat and so do I. The whole reason Mac signed up was he figured there'd be more for us if he was killed in the war than if he fell off the high steel in Portland's shipyards." Hands on her hips, she walked toward me. "Or have you forgotten what it's like to eat fried potatoes and ketchup for supper?"

Without looking at her, I flipped the dough and rolled it

again on the other side, no longer caring that the kuchen might become too thin or tough to enjoy. "Obviously, you haven't forgotten either."

IRENE LONG GONE—GROCERY SHOPPING, she said—and I couldn't stop thinking about Philip's photo, that white scarf and leather bomber jacket, his sandy hair tousled and those sapphire-blue eyes. My daughter's husband. The man she lay with, the man whose seed became Eli, the man who promised he would return no matter what, standing there on the platform with all of us waiting for the train that would take him to Bismarck, then on to Chicago, and, finally, New York: a reversal of the train trip I once took with Father and Mother. His mother in her black dress wept into her handkerchief while his father remained stoic in his broad-brimmed hat, his mouth never twitching. He stared straight ahead, never once glancing at our family standing beside him. Ada standing there with her newly swollen belly and a baby that Philip would never see. That was the only time I ever met his people. Philip and Ada's elopement may have been as much a source of shame for his parents as it was for me and Albert. But elopement was what young people did in wartime. Now, his plane shot down. Philip would always remain the boy who tipped over my daughter's life when he first came to Myra High and Ada told me, "He's mine."

I was just taking the dinner rolls out of the oven when I heard the swinging storm door and Ivan's heavy tread on the mudroom floor announcing that he was home from school. "Just in time," he said. "Endpiece out of the oven is mine."

He slung his strapped-together schoolbooks down on a kitchen chair and piled his coat on top, likely smelling the bread even before coming into the house. First glance at my face, red from the oven and crying, and he asked, "What's happened, Ma?" Then, as if he was sorry, he picked up his coat and started back toward the mudroom where he was supposed to hang it.

"It's okay, Ivan. Just have a seat."

He stopped midway back to the table, the coat bunched under his arm. For a moment he didn't move in either direction. Then he abruptly sat, the coat filling his lap, his brown eyes wide and staring at me.

I lifted the loaf with my pot holders and brought it to the table where the floured board rested. The bread knife already there. "You might want to get a table knife and a plate," I said. The shakiness in my voice matched the look I saw in Ivan's eyes. I sat heavy in my chair at the head of the table. Determined to push out the words as fast as I could and get it over before I embarrassed my young son with tears, "It's Philip," I began. Began and couldn't finish.

"Is he hurt, Ma?" Ivan asked. He dared not take the next step to ask how in the same way I couldn't say, *Not coming back*, couldn't say *dead*.

"Shot down over Germany," I said. The fact of it closed my throat; a sob deep inside my stomach clawed its way up to the back of my tongue. "Irene told me." Those words the explanation meant to end any questions. "Best let me tell Pa," I finished.

"Shot down," Ivan mused, as though that meant something to him. Newsreels he kept telling Albert about. It was the only time Albert reported anything Ivan had told him that I might want to know.

I cut into the hot loaf even though it hadn't had time to cool. My fingers jumped from the loaf's heat and the steam rising from that first cut. Hot as it was, I managed to get the heel onto Ivan's plate.

"So sorry to hear this, Ma," Ivan said, his head down but his voice shaky with emotion. "Does Little Marta know?"

"Probably. Can't hide much from her."

"Should I take the Radio Flyer and go get them?"

"No, they'll come when they're ready," I said. "Eli doesn't know."

"That's his pa," Ivan said.

"I know." I rose to get the teapot off the back of the stove, my steps so heavy it seemed I hardly moved. "Want a half cup of tea?"

"Sure," Ivan said, his voice perky. He'd never been offered tea before.

"Half a cup of milk with it," I said.

"Some sugar?" he asked tentatively.

"No more than two teaspoons."

"Okay, Ma. Two's enough."

Now a funeral. A family I didn't know. A daughter I could never trust to do the right thing. But first I needed to tell Albert. He'd never go to the service. He had to be persuaded to go to the train station when Philip left. For shame, he never so much as greeted Philip's father and mother.

I poured half a cup of tea into my smallest mug so it wasn't too heavy for Ivan. When I picked up the milk pitcher to fill the cup halfway, Ivan's small hand touched mine. His fingers tentative on the back of my hand. Like a small, crawly caterpillar feeling its way, his fingers were so soft that I could have easily brushed them aside. Could have easily ignored this sweet gesture, the tenderness of who he was, this boy of eight who had already seen too much of life's dark side.

My tears were right there, their slow roll down my cheek. Without looking at Ivan, I took my other hand and placed it over the top of his. But when I grabbed the teapot to hold it steady, I accidently brushed his hand away. His brown eyes remained wide behind his glasses, his small lips quivering at seeing my tears. In that moment I wanted to fold myself into the chair and lower my head to the table. To let go of what felt so heavy in my body. My soul. My regretful distrust of Ada and Philip, an ache for their now-fatherless son, for all of us, really. Death, so far away but always present.

I lowered the teapot onto the trivet, where I kept my eyes focused. "Thank you, Ivan," I said. "For being you."

I dared not say more for fear I'd forget I was his mother and say too much. Or I'd give in to all the hurt that crowded my chest and visited me in dreams where, no matter how much or how often I baked, there was never enough bread and kuchen to fill the open mouths around me; my dream son so small he couldn't sit at the table, his hands holding on to my apron and no way to stop his hunger.

Moving back to the stove, I set the teapot on the warmer and busied myself at the sink. "Aren't you going to come and sit down, Ma? Drink tea with me?"

I lifted my apron and wiped away the tears. Removed my glasses and held them up to the light through the window. A quick glance toward Millie's kitchen. I cleaned my glasses with the underside of my apron. "Of course," I said. "Just need to make sure the tea stays hot for your pa." Any excuse to linger a moment longer, to still the strangling in my throat.

"I'll wait for you, Ma," he said.

Millie's curtain was pulled back, our signal that she was home. I'd talk to her after I thought about when to tell Albert. I suddenly wished my father were here, my father who in his better self would know what to say. How to take Albert aside, first laying his hand on Albert's shoulder, suggesting beer or a glass of Schnapps.

But Albert never knew my father. Or my mother. His family consisted of a twin brother who arrived with him on Ellis Island, young men of draft age, which became their ticket into the new world. I would now have to enter the Kessler house alone, explaining awkwardly that Ada's father was too ill to come. The faceless others would shake their heads in understanding, but it wouldn't matter. I'd once again be alone when facing a difficult moment in the same way I'd been alone since Father and Mother died and Leo disappeared forever from my life.

# 1914

Night whizzed by the train windows, my mummied face staring back at me from the glass, the lamps reflected both in front and behind me. I couldn't sleep with the odor of my wounds growing like a halo around me. I kept imagining the dreadful scarring that was happening to my face. First I was hot, then cold. So restless, I likely kept those beside me awake as well.

Leaving Chicago, the railcar may as well have been sitting unattended and without passengers on a side rail for weeks. It was as freezing inside as it was outside. As on Ellis Island, I began to wonder if they turned the heat on and off at certain hours. Leo twisted around beside Mother, his shoulder jarring both of us awake. At one point I turned at a different angle until Mother held me away from her. Though it was night, she tried to examine my mummy-like face. Thankfully, I couldn't see the white gauze or bandaging. I was just relieved that the pain had mercifully subsided. Something as simple as the warmth of our crowded bodies and Father's coat to protect us from the devouring cold gave me comfort.

But Mother's gasp woke me. Set off alarm inside of me. She lifted her gloved hand to touch the edges of the bandage across my cheeks, then pulled back, cringing with wariness and, yes, horror.

"What's wrong, Mother?"

"Nothing, Marta."

"But you see something."

"Yes, it appears that infection lies under the bandages and has soaked through them."

Though her squeamishness wouldn't allow her to remove the bandages and clean the wound, the unspoken question between us was how could we wait; Tante Ketcha, the midwife of miraculous healing, was still two days away.

The chill had seeped into my toes, where the calfskin boots proved no barrier against the numbing cold. I'd always been someone who preferred life inside the house unless it was to attend church. Father would then wrap a fur skin around my legs and feet. There'd been no need for the fur-lined, heavy leather boots of the farm laborers, boots meant to keep their feet warm in the worst weather.

Mother touched my fingers. They, too, were numb with cold. She reached for them, folding them inside her own and tucking my hands under her coat and against her bosom, where they slowly began to warm.

"Are you okay, Mother?" Leo whispered.

"Yes, my darling," Mother said. She reached across my lap in order to touch his arm. He nuzzled his head into my shoulder while she awkwardly attempted to stroke his hair but found, instead, the cap he wore to hedge the cold. "Maybe they'll turn on the heat in the morning," she said.

Even as she said those words, I wondered if she was making up a story to soothe Leo. From what Uncle Herman said, they might never turn on the heat. I hoped that wasn't true. Though I was cold, my forehead felt hot. I prayed it wasn't fever. An infection would mean scarring. Disfigurement. Like the child in our village who was scalded as an infant. The father's remedy of melted butter missed the fat under the baby's chin. When the little girl grew up, she had an ugly scar on her neck. I didn't want that or any scar. I didn't want people staring at me. Ever.

## Chapter Eleven

### Philip's Funeral

## 1943

THERE WAS NO FLAG-DRAPED coffin in the Kessler parlor; there was no body. Two candlesticks but no candles on a small table in the center of the room. No flowers, even though I left an order at Gardner's in Dickinson. No flag, no flowers; all the pictures or mirrors, whatever hung on the walls, had been draped in black. What kind of funeral was this? How could it possibly respect Philip, who had died for his country?

No music. Especially, no music.

These were my first thoughts after the front door opened; after a small woman, nearly as small as my young son, greeted me and Ivan. Her face revealed time's erosion around her mouth, her eyes. Under white hair covered in a black veil, her shoulders appeared permanently stooped, as though carrying her arms weighed her down. Perhaps she was an aunt to Philip. She extended her hand, another surprise. "Welcome." Then, "You must be Eli's other grandmother."

When she took my hand, the bones of her fingers were fragile, like they'd break if you squeezed them too tight. A deadly cold came through her hands and into my wool gloves. While her grip seemed solid and confident, the lines and wrinkles creasing her face told me I'd never seen her before, not on the street and not at Hubner's Market or Kresge's five-and-dime. But that was true of the whole Kessler family.

"Thank you," I said. "I hope we're on time."

She tried too late to stop her startled jerk on seeing through my black veil and noticing my face. She glanced away. "Not late," she said.

Though my scars had softened over time, the misalignment of my lips and the Z shape across my right cheek hadn't changed. I could forgive her reaction; I should have been used to it by now. This was just another time when I was reminded of what happened to my innocence. Indeed, if there was a blessing, it was the weight that had gathered and stayed on my face all these years. *Thank you, Herr Gott.* A little too much fat plumps one's unsightly facial scars and dissolves their edges. My family and I had become accustomed to the whitening around the dark spiderwebbing on the right side of my face. Rarely did anyone stare too long or give me a second glance except, like today, when we met for the first time.

In and among the elderly folks seated in the parlor behind her, old men huddled while one read from the Torah. Pastor Kinski had explained as much as he could about what to expect that day. I could hear their wives or sisters or female cousins weeping loudly and out of sight in the kitchen. The room carried the low drone that dominated the corner of the living room. None of the men glanced up at my entrance. Completing the almost eerie silence, my grandchildren, specifically Eli and Sissy, ran and played, sneaking behind the few empty chairs or shouting from somewhere down the hallway. Their sounds spoke of life not yet fouled by death and its grief.

In a corner toward the back of the parlor, Irene sat on a draped chair with Louisa, her youngest, on her lap. She glanced at me and smiled when I entered the front door, perhaps relieved from the trancelike faces of the dour men. Ada was nowhere to be seen. Because the service—or gathering, whatever they were calling it—was being held in a private home (a forbidden thought to any good Christian family), I was definitely the stranger here, as were my daughters and their children.

Behind Irene's back, a mournful song began to swell inside the room. The men's voices came together in a kind of chant—Pastor Kinski explained the word *Kaddish*, a lament for the living and the dead. The voices left me confused and even more uncomfortable than I already felt. Besides being strange to my ears, the words were unrecognizable, Hebrew being a language that belonged to Philip's family and their kind. I just wanted them to stop and get on with the regular service. Quiet music, that would make the funeral right.

I was reminded of my statement to Agnes about people being different, that it wasn't a sin. In the midst of all this strangeness, the self-righteous edge of those words came back to me. Now I was the one who wanted what I was used to, not this strange and foreign-seeming ritual that went against everything I'd been taught and believed about how the dead should be honored.

*Thank you, Herr Gott, Albert didn't come.* He'd have plenty to say, having fought in the Great War like my father. Never mind that Albert was so weak Dr. Schmidt said we should expect his death within days, a month at the most, the cancer having taken over his body and left him nearly absent inside his shriveled skin. All the doctor could do was keep Albert peaceful with daily shots of morphine. At least Albert was spared this, all of it because of Ada and her ways. I hoped we didn't all burn in hell because of her.

No one offered, and there appeared to be nowhere to hang

my coat. Irene sat with a shawl draped around her shoulders. Ada could have told me what to wear, maybe a scarf to cover my head instead of my veiled hat. At least my head was covered. Where Irene had laid her coat, I had no idea. Certainly, I wasn't walking back along a dark hallway to find the bed that was the likely repository. Finally settled in a chair with my coat open, I became aware that my neck scarf had fallen loosely down my chest. At least I could use it to cover my shoulders if need be.

When I glanced around the living room, the sofa had been pushed against a far wall, its wine-colored velvet arms appearing even darker beneath the picture or mirror's draped black covering. The matching chairs, also placed along the wall, were almost hidden inside the room. When one or two women finally appeared, the collars of their black dresses had been torn in seeming concert with the black bands on the men's arms, a custom that Pastor Kinski explained was part of their grieving ritual. Of the near six hundred souls who lived in Myra, no one I knew had ever been inside this house on Kraut Street, certainly not anyone from the First Bible Church.

The parlor was dominated by the odor of dust that had lived too long in the heavy brocade drapes, the same burgundy color as the sofa's upholstery. All other furniture, if there was any, had been removed except for the dining chairs we sat on. I doubted we'd have been invited if the deceased soldier wasn't Ada's husband and Eli wasn't his only child. I hated to think what Agnes would say if she were here.

I kept my eyes focused on the lace panels hanging in between the heavy drapes where winter's meager light reflected the constant gray sky along with new snow, heavy on the slender branches of a single oak tree in the front yard. It was easy to conclude that niceties and normal talk were either disrespectful or contaminating, bad luck at the very least.

Why I didn't notice, I don't know, but no one wore shoes. No one except me and Irene and the children. They all sat or walked in stocking feet. I'd never seen anything like it. No shoes, no deceased body. How could this happen? A casket gave one focus, a place to point one's grief, a distraction from the others who gathered together, especially here in the Kessler home, where the need for a moment of relief was nearly overwhelming.

This house had obviously been closed too long and through too many winters. Now, the formality that hung inside was stifling. Despite the crackling of a woodstove at the room's far end, the heat was nearly suffocating after coming in from outside. On seeing me, Louisa stretched her arms and cried, "Oma, Oma." She scooted out of Irene's lap and struggled with young steps toward me, where she knew I would lift her into my arms.

Eli—two and close in age to Irene's middle daughter, Sissy—came out from the hallway and grabbed Sissy's hand. The two of them lowered their heads in sudden shyness and crowded close to Irene. A woman I barely recognized had taken a seat near Irene. She wiggled her fingers toward Eli. He slid past Irene and went to sit on the other woman's lap. Of course, this was his other grandmother.

Even with Louisa on my lap, an uncomfortable twinge invaded my chest at seeing Eli not on my lap but on a stranger's. I found myself squeezing Louisa hard, so hard that she pushed against my chest. "Down, Oma," she said. She reached her arms across the empty space toward her mother. I set down my granddaughter, who twisted free and walked back to her mother. My lap was suddenly too empty while, across from me, Eli rested his head against the other woman's black dress and found comfort in his thumb, finally quiet after racing in the hallway with Sissy.

I was just easing back against my chair, the ache remaining in my chest, when the flash of Ada's dress appeared in the kitchen's doorway. The only thing that surprised me more than the broad navy blue and yellow stripes of a clinging dress was a neckline that revealed more cleavage than a Christian woman should show. I'd have been no less surprised if she held a cigarette between her fingers. I knew both girls smoked, though they hid it from me. They also indulged in a glass of whiskey now and then without realizing it hung on their breath long afterward.

Ada glanced at me, then turned away. Never mind that this was the day we were eulogizing her barely known husband. She was likely counting heads to make sure she had a seat for herself. Irene shook her head as though to say, *It's Ada, what do you expect?*

Heat flooded my neck, and my cheeks must have been red, though I couldn't see them. I suddenly remembered that day Ada told me that Philip was hers. *A lady doesn't talk that way about a young man*, I'd said.

Ada had flipped her shoulder-length red hair and said, *This girl does.*

Always incorrigible, always forward by any family's standards, she didn't surprise me when she showed up in the family way just three months before Philip was due to go overseas. A secretive family, his—Jews having come from Rohrbach like Albert's people.

To her credit, Ada served a purpose by standing at the juncture between the kitchen and hallway. Someone needed to herd the children back into the living room and get them seated on the floor, at least out of the way, for the anticipated ceremony. Ivan had already disappeared down the dark hallway in search of Sissy. Across from me, Little Marta shared the narrow seat with her mother, her pigtails wound into a crown on her head, her eyes directed toward me. I returned her smile. At four, Little Marta was already asking questions about Russia that I refused to answer for Ivan. Too many painful memories in between. But grandchildren are different from our own children. I wished Little Marta could sit with me, but there was no room for her to share my seat. My body already overflowed the narrow bounds of the chair.

An upright piano stood against the back wall. Perhaps the ritual would be performed at the small table, and someone would play the piano. Surely, food would be served in the kitchen, since the dining room table was absent. There was enough room for a casket, but there was none and no real reminder of Philip. Truth be told, whether Ada wanted it or not, her bones would never rest alongside Philip's and his people.

It was hard to think against the Hebrew words and what sounded like singing. I remembered that Pastor Kinski explained that the Kaddish, a prayer for the dead, was simply different from a Christian prayer. The body was supposed to be buried within twenty-four hours. That was impossible for Philip; his remains even now were turning to dust on ground that none of us would ever walk.

From the entryway of the kitchen, a woman draped in black lace entered the living room. She sat quietly and alone. Ada remained in the doorway as though she'd been instructed to manage the children.

Fortunately, when the children were finally seated in the living room, they were quiet, seemingly awed by the otherworldliness of the men's voices. When the so-called chorus repeated itself again and again, I began to hum behind closed lips as though I, too, knew the song.

Ivan, standing beside my chair, lowered his arm onto my shoulder and let the flat of his hand rest on my back. I wondered if he felt my humming resonate inside his hand. This young boy, so like my brother Leo, always surprised me with his sensitivity.

The elderly woman, hidden behind her veil, continued to sit in silence. Other women gathered and seated themselves opposite me. They wrung their handkerchiefs and wept, their faces masklike except for tears that trailed the grooves in their ancient skin.

Ada came last, her hands held low but together in prayer, her head bowed. However, a faint smile hid behind her closed lips. She was doing her best to appear somber and appropriately sad. No tears though. It was just as Irene said. And her dress, for all its gaudy stripes, didn't hide a thickened waist and swollen belly, the kind of thing a woman notices and immediately thinks of as pregnancy. But how could she possibly be pregnant with her husband absent these past few years? Fat, she was probably growing fat like me. No surprise. She must be eating her way through her grief.

The Kessler kitchen table was spread with food I didn't know was possible in wartime. A platter of beef and turkey and lox sat in the middle of the table. There were fruit and nuts, pastries I'd never seen before. And while the food was meant for the grieving family, we were considered family and happily filled our plates with the feast that had been provided by this community.

After heaping my plate, I smiled at the woman who had welcomed me. The kindness in her face, maybe the softness around her wrinkled mouth, reminded me of what Mother might have looked like had she lived a full life. As if there wasn't enough sadness today, remembering Mother brought back the image of her once-full and flushed face before the darkening of her eyes that made her grief transparent. This woman looked at me from inside her lived-in lines with a peacefulness that transcended the occasion.

I returned to my original seat. For a brief time Ivan ate beside me before disappearing down the dark hallway to find the other children.

"How are you doing?" Irene asked. She'd assumed Ivan's chair when he disappeared, Louisa clinging to her free hand. Her eyebrows were raised, not so much a question as a statement about the peculiarities we were experiencing.

"Wonderful food," I said. Then, in a whisper, "I wonder if we should have brought something. Kuchen or soup. Canned peaches at the very least."

"How would we know? Ada never told us anything."

At the mention of Ada's name, we glanced toward the doorway into the kitchen, where she appeared to be watching the children as they raced up and down the hallway. Though we never said a word, both Irene and I knew she was avoiding us.

Except for Sissy and Eli's squeals as they ran around the adults' legs, then in and out of the hallway, my stomach could relax now that the chanting had ended. Folks ate and talked to each other in normal tones, not to us but to each other. The living room had assumed an easy hum. But Sissy couldn't sit still. She began to annoy me with her darting around the living room where we held our plates in our laps. I put out my hand and grabbed her. "Stop," I said. "You must stop."

The look on her face mirrored both surprise and a hurt that forced the corners of her little mouth to droop. "Oma just wants you to slow down," I said. She squirmed out of my reach and in the process jerked against the small table with the candlesticks. Out of my chair to save the table from tipping, I spilled my full plate onto the rug.

I quickly righted the table, my embarrassment heating my face. "Now look what you've done."

Behind me, a chorus of gasps rose from those who saw the food scattered on the rug. They likely wanted to persecute me. In that moment I yearned to rush from the house, even from the room in the same way that Sissy had. I'd made a mess of everything. Bending over, my veil hanging like a skirt around my face, I scooped the scattered potato salad and turkey, the pickled beets and hard-cooked eggs, the bagel slathered with cream cheese and lox onto my plate. The mess incriminated me and underscored the fact that I didn't belong here. It was all Ada's fault for not keeping Philip out of her panties. For not considering the rest of the family.

Mercifully, both Ada and Irene were immediately beside me. Ivan. When Ada saw the beets lying on the sand-colored rug, she picked them up and hurried away, returning with a couple of kitchen towels. Irene, sensing my distress, wiped at my hands with one of the towels while Ada picked up the globs of food in another towel and hurried back to the kitchen. The entire time we retrieved the mess, the room remained silent—accusingly silent, shamefully silent. Only later, over tea and kuchen in my own kitchen, could I see the daylong occasion with humor. The whole incident proved an ironic ending to what had been an extraordinarily difficult day. The Kesslers would not soon forget us.

# 1914

Despite the sickening odor from my bandages, Father and Mother each held one of my arms, pulling me close against them as we moved forward inside the crowd toward the waiting train preparing to leave St. Paul. The engine roared like I imagined a hundred lions on the kill. The rising steam from the giant wheels warmed my hands and what little skin remained exposed. There were too many people and I couldn't breathe, the rush toward the train requiring me to move my legs, now weak and dead from the weight of too much sitting.

I was paralyzed with fear. Worse, humiliation. The moment I came near anyone rushing toward the train, I was sure they would recognize the smell of wetting myself mixed with the stink of my bandages. If I could smell it, so could they.

Now, seated at last on our train: "Mother, may I have my egg bundle?"

The Easter egg was all that sustained my faith. Though Mother reassured me it hadn't broken after the fall, I needed to see for myself. Mother unwrapped the egg from inside her shawl. She held it up to my face just to prove it was intact. Even so, I couldn't see beyond its shape now that we were seated inside the dim light of the train. Not until my fingers traced the whorls and curves of the diamonds and pearls along the raised ribbons, a backdrop of blue the color of deep water, did I feel reassured. I continued to feel along the ribbon outline, touching the tiny hinge that held the secret compartment closed. At least the egg was intact, though my belief in Grandpapa's declaration that the egg would keep us safe no longer seemed true.

"No husband will ever want me the way I am, scarred and deformed," I whispered to Mother.

"Don't think that way, Marta. Tante Ketcha will work her magic once we reach Dakota."

Hot tears gathered behind my eyes. "I don't want people to look at me, not even you and Father. Especially Tante Ketcha."

"My girl, we'll make this right," Mother said.

I wanted to believe her, but I didn't. She'd only tell me that accidents are unplanned, something that happens. I was certain that if we'd stayed in Russia, this wouldn't have happened. Yet, even there, when Mother and Father thought I was asleep in front of the fire, Father talked about a young girl my age, tied to two horses at the army's command and torn in two when the horses were sent in opposite directions. "We cannot stay. First the barn. Now this," Father had said.

Inside the pulsing pain of the moment, death seemed preferable to a lifetime of people staring at me or turning too quickly away.

Though Uncle Herman had been kind, I had no doubt Tante Ketcha would blame me for what happened to my face. Just the sound of her name took me to the dark tunnel of who I was at five years old, our first visit to Uncle Herman's farm when she slapped me. I'd stood up from Tante Ketcha's cushioned rocking chair at the end of a too-long day, the reeking odor and telltale circle betraying where I'd then accidently wet myself. Tante Ketcha's gasp of horror and her sharp fingers into my arm were immediate. My hand held my stinging cheek even as she scolded, "Bad girl," over and over. "Don't ever sit in that chair again."

Though Father spoke to her, none of us wanted to visit their farm again. Only once, sometime later, we attended the community party before Uncle Herman and Tante Ketcha left for America with their family of daughters. Remembering her now made my stomach burn as I sweated inside my bandages, the cold train car its own punishment.

Mother reached over and lay her hand on my forehead, her hand so cool compared to the heat coming off me. "Marta has a fever," she said to Father. "I'm afraid the wound has become terribly infected."

Father looked down at his hands. "I don't know what to tell you, Katerina. There's nothing to do but wait until we get to Ketcha's."

The wound was bad enough, but the reek of my wounded face and soiled dress drained what little hope I had for any kind of safe meeting with Tante Ketcha. I lay back against the hard wooden seat. Father was right. There was nothing to do but wait, though my empty stomach burned with dread.

## Chapter Twelve

### Smoke

## *1944*

FEBRUARY, THOUGH COLD, SUGGESTED we were edging toward spring. Midafternoon, the chickens began to squawk as though a fox or a dog had come too near the chicken coop. I grabbed my wool sweater off its hook. The air was heavy and too still for this time of year. I stepped out of the mudroom and down onto the path layered with snow and the freeze that hid beneath it. The walkway should have been cleared and salted long before today. I'd have to get on Ivan about his chores. He spent too much time with Robert Shreve, a nice enough boy. He couldn't help it if his father had a crippled leg that kept him from work and his ma barely got by taking in ironing in a town where women did their own ironing.

I passed the garden, where there was only a promise of summer squash and melons. Lettuce a dream yet to come. Everything stayed hidden beneath layers of snow. On my way past the pigeon pen, I could tell the weather was turning; those patches of what looked like rain betrayed the hidden ice. Ivan wanted to go ice-skating. "As soon as your chores are done, boy," was my predictable response.

Ivan was nearly nine. That marked the last time Albert and I ever thought to be naked with each other. I still don't know how it happened. Must have been when Ozzie dropped out of high school to join the marines. My brother Oscar's only boy died then. Was it grief that made us pant and sweat, or was it seeing our eldest leave home? I remember a hot summer night and me crawling into bed, removing my nightgown under the sheet. Never thinking how just being next to skin excites a man. Albert's hand on my breast. That always did it. I was as good as gone. It must have happened more than once. Me thinking I was too old to get pregnant. But there it was. On my way to forty and pregnant again; Ivan the blessing we never saw coming. *Thank you, Herr Gott.*

By the time I walked out back to the chicken coop, the chickens had finally settled. I smelled smoke, though, and it didn't smell like the incinerator. More like Albert's tobacco after he rolled it and put it in his cigarette holder, that first puff. It was coming from somewhere in the backyard.

Forget the chickens. I circled back around the chicken coop and headed in the direction of the pigeon pen. No, the smell was coming from the outhouse. Better not be the Hinkley boys. Nothing but trouble, those teenagers. Their mother was alone and raising them the best she could now that their father had been killed in the war. That's what living young without a father did to you: it made you wild and undisciplined, erasing all your Christian values. Bad as Albert was, I had to say he'd been a good teacher to Ivan like he was to Ozzie. Until he got sick. Now, nothing but that faraway look in his eyes and the pall of sadness cloaking the bedroom where he lived all the time. I couldn't walk in there without feeling the ruin inside his shrinking body.

The closer I got to the outhouse, the louder the voices. Ivan's.

Robert's. About the last place I'd expect those boys to be. The smell of smoke stronger. I stopped at the edge of the outhouse and peered around the corner. Cigarette papers on the snow. A pouch of tobacco like Albert's. Both boys hunched over in their heavy winter coats against the back of the outhouse, sitting on a blanket they must have dragged from the shed. Smoking.

Ivan saw me first. He coughed when I stepped forward. Started to put his smoking arm behind his back, but he was too late. Robert, his Heinie haircut leaving him nearly bald, was staring at Ivan. Both of them sat cross-legged with the papers and tobacco lying between them.

"What are you boys doing back here?" Anyone could see the obvious, but I had to say it. "Cigarettes? For shame, Ivan." My heart was beating too fast and I felt weak in my knees. After all I'd been through with Albert, here was my youngest with his friend, smoking. Wouldn't Agnes love to see this.

"We didn't mean to, Ma," Ivan sputtered. "Just trying it out."

"There'll be no *trying it out* in this house." I stared at Ivan, Robert out of the corner of my eye. Robert quickly stubbed his cigarette in the snow and began to shred the paper, and the tobacco as well, with hands that looked practiced at getting rid of the evidence. Without looking at him, I said, "Time for you to go home, Robert. And . . ." I said. "Don't come back again."

"Ma," Ivan protested. "It wasn't his fault."

"Then whose fault was it?"

"I took the stuff from Pa. Don't make Robert go."

"I'm not dumb. It takes two . . ."

I turned toward Robert, my chin shaking with anger. "My husband's upstairs . . . dying . . . do you understand?"

Robert was on his feet, his head bowed, his arms hanging heavy from his shoulders. "Yes ma'am."

"I can't tell you how many times I've defended you . . . because you're Ivan's friend. I've wanted to be generous and kind toward you." I paused, trying to catch my breath. "I don't ever want to see or hear that this happened again. Do you understand?"

"Yes ma'am."

"Ma . . . " Ivan started to say. He stood at Robert's side, a full head shorter and half Robert's size.

"Herr Gott will punish both of you if you continue to . . . sin and disobey . . ."

"Yes," in unison.

I turned and walked back toward the house, my feet hurrying as though I was running away from someone or something. Heartache pushed up all the disappointment life had allotted me. Leaving Russia, my face, Father gambling away the gold, then me marrying someone who said church was for weaklings. Now my son Ozzie, somewhere on a ship, his wool socks likely wet and his feet never dry, the chances of him coming home less than slim if I counted all the boys in this town who never came back except in a box. Ozzie's sisters pulling at their tethers and the town growing smaller by the day. My last hope had been Ivan. *What has the world come to, Herr Gott?*

A few minutes later the screen door slammed and Ivan entered the kitchen, his head bowed. He walked toward the stove, where I was starting supper. His head still down and that shyness that comes with shame. "I'm awful sorry, Ma," he said. "So's Robert."

"You know he has a bad reputation; I've talked to you about that before. I hope it was his idea." I smoothed the front of my apron across my stomach. "Taking the smokes from your pa's bedside table makes you the primary culprit."

"I know, Ma." He shook his head like he had a fly in his hair, which he didn't. He came across the room to where I was standing at the sink. "I promise I won't ever try smoking again," he said. "Can't stand to have you mad at me. Robert neither."

"You're nearly nine years old, Ivan. What would your brother Ozzie say about these shenanigans? He'd say I should whip you, which I've never had to do."

"No whippings, Ma. Please don't tell Pa."

We both knew Albert would try to get out of his sickbed and ask for the strap or the paddle, if I could even find them. He came down so hard on Ozzie. Only had to do it once or twice and Ozzie knew the difference between right and wrong.

"Go on upstairs and see if Pa needs anything. Tell him I made vegetable soup with the carrots extra soft so he can eat them. Can mash everything up if he likes."

"Sure, Ma."

He still had a tentative look around his eyes. He took another step toward me, then another until he was standing in front of me.

I turned away from the sink and the pans I was washing. Wiped my hands on my apron. "What is it?"

"Can I hug you?"

A sting, hot and sudden, crept behind my eyes while I kept wiping my hands. "Learned your lesson?" I asked, though my throat felt partly closed.

He didn't answer. Rather, he took that final step. He grabbed my waist, his hands only partway around me because that's all the way they'd go. His head just under my bosom and sideways. I hugged him close as I could, his hands hanging on for dear life.

## 1914

Leo, eyes closed, rested against the seatback, his head bobbing when the train swayed. He woke with a start, his arm jostling me awake. Leaning toward me, he whispered, "I dreamed we were back in Odessa in Grand Mama's parlor," he said. "Drinking tea and eating those tiny biscuits with anise she used to make."

His hair had grown since we'd left Odessa and the curls fell across his forehead, nearly covering his eyes. When he stood, his trousers were two inches shorter, a reminder we would no longer have our housekeeper Louisa measuring and stitching the clothes we wore.

My head a mass of bandages and my eyes nothing but tiny holes, I peered at him from inside my fevered waking. "A lovely dream," I whispered to him. "While I dream of Cossacks with their guns firing into the night and the screech of our animals escaping the fire."

"Marta, you must forget that," Leo whispered to me. "Think of what it will be like when we go back and have our farm again."

"You forget, Leo," I said. "We no longer have a farm."

"But we'll get it back."

"Have you forgotten running in the dark across the guard points? That awful ship with all of us in such a small cabin, you and Father and Oscar sleeping on the top bunk. Nowhere to change or wash our clothes. Three long weeks with what they called food. Then Ellis Island. All would be for nothing if we only dream of Odessa."

Mother leaned over the two of us, her shoulder against mine where Father's coat had momentarily slipped from around our necks. "You two must go back to sleep," she said. "Daylight will be here soon enough."

When I closed my eyes, I remembered Leo distributing the cheese and bread to our family that afternoon. He had to climb in and around peasants who crouched on the floor. First, he approached Uncle Herman, the eldest and farthest away, the one we most needed to respect. With great effort, Leo climbed back to where Mother sat, providing the simple supper Leo next delivered to Father and Oscar. On his way, he misstepped and dropped one piece of cheese onto a bundle where a mother grabbed it and held it out to her young son. Leo stopped. Stared. His hand reached forward as though to retrieve the cheese, but the incident happened so quickly that his mouth remained open in astonishment. Leo was still shocked when he gave the intact portion to Father. In turn, Father took the extra slice of white cheese off his bread and gave it to Oscar.

"Sorry," Leo said.

Father touched Leo's arm with his free hand. "Everyone is hungry."

Since leaving home, we were always hungry.

## Chapter Thirteen

### Albert's Death

## *1944*

How do we know when the dying begins? With Albert, who used to lie beside me in our bed under my wedding quilt—the stars so white against the faded ginghams and calicos—it was easy. The cigarettes and work layoffs, drinking . . . in that order. This, the ending, after years of bending and lifting, the eye measuring the exact placement of one brick on top of another, the cement-mixing and cleanup, the check or cash or chickens traded at the end. To his credit, Albert worked as hard as any man until he couldn't. His choice to continue smoking and drinking were just that: his choice. Yes, Albert had grown too thin in the same way I'd grown too fat. We would both pay for our sins one way or the other. Remembering Mother: no mystery there if you count heartbreak a reason for dying. America was never her place, no matter how bravely she tried. With Father, it was both harder and easier to understand. He was never robust like Uncle Herman, who worked the fields alongside his sons-in-law. Neither was Father as fragile as one might imagine, just someone whose vanity we had to excuse. Daily, he trimmed his mustache. He bathed long and often, even in winter and without considering others. I once overheard Tante Ketcha and Uncle Herman refer to Father as a dandy. Outside of port and sherry, which he drank in moderation, he had no visible vices. He should have otherwise lived into his eighties, like his father before him.

Perhaps Father's death began on Ellis Island with the humiliating inspection. Certainly not on the cross-country trip, though the railcars were cold beyond belief. Perhaps death took hold of Father when we reached Myra, where he never again seemed to find his place. Over time, he began to drink too much home brew, and he sulked late into the night, hardly rising before noon and never again taking the fastidious care he had before. From then on, he avoided Oscar and Leo for some reason, never looking either in the eye. While he seemed comfortable enough with me and Mother, and though I sat beside him in a feeble effort to cheer him, he eventually pushed me away as he had Mother. He no longer joined Uncle Herman on the wagon to town. And he no longer participated in Sunday services or the Saturday-night gatherings at the grange hall to discuss crops or weather or legislation regarding government subsidies. He stopped living long before he held the gun to his head and left the best parts of himself splattered across the snow outside the new barn. That was perhaps his one last favor: a reluctance to mess up the barn and create more work for those he left behind.

BEFORE DR. SCHMIDT shuffled down the narrow stairs from the bedroom, I'd already cleared the soiled bedding. The bedside table still held the milk of magnesia and a large box of baking soda;

Albert's stomach rebelled to the very end. Beck's Funeral Home would be here after lunch, not that I felt like eating. In the end, Albert's body exploded with all the poison he'd held inside. The memory of that stink and mess would plague me until I died.

But I kept my promise and stayed beside him until the end, my hand around the skin and bones that defined his hand, the veins throbbing until they didn't. With his eyes bloodshot and faraway, his breath was no more than a frog's croak. Two weeks earlier, I'd folded his wire-rimmed glasses and placed them in their black case on top of the bedside tray. Poor man had known no pleasure for too long, unless he counted the last time at Jake's, stumbling home down the brick path after being gone barely an hour. One drink, he'd said. That was enough to make him stupid. To want his bed.

Those last minutes by his bed after no words between us for how long . . . months? A full year? Since the Bibles went into the incinerator. His fingers remained cold inside my hand, the skin and bones as thin and fragile as chicken feet, so purple and darkly discolored. I imagined his breath hadn't reached those fingers for a long time. My other hand over the top of his, my warm and fat fingers such a contrast, the last-minute effort to warm something that had been cold in him for a very long time.

"Albert, can you hear me?" I asked.

He started to open his eyelids, but they seemed too heavy. The nod he gave me was so slight it almost wasn't there. He tried to turn his head in my direction, like he wanted to hear what I had to say, though I didn't know what that was. I just knew I had to start.

"I hope you can hear me, Albert," I said. I stopped and watched for a sign, any sign. "I so hope you can."

A slight nod at last. His hand with a faint twitch.

"I'm sorry we got so far away from each other," I said. "You know, Albert, at one time I loved you with all my heart. Once . . ." I began and didn't finish.

The chicken-feet fingers pressed into mine.

The press of that particular hand, so foreign these past years, was unlike the caresses in those early years after the Great War, the eagerness with which I waited at the door for him to return from work. My best apron. I even pinched my cheeks, though I thought that was wrong. His slippers always waited in the mudroom, where I stood taking his trousers and hanging them on a hook for the next day, his wool shirt on another hook. I held his hand while he inched off his boots. Blushed when he smiled up at me. Those dark eyes, the black hair across his forehead. He seemed to see past my face when he took me back into the warm kitchen, before we went up the stairs, where I always left the bedcovers folded down in the early days. First, he washed his hands and face at the small sink where I waited for him with a towel in my hand. He would then turn me around and untie my apron, lay it over a chair. His hand around my hand, we would climb the stairs like two children playing a game. My giggle so new to me. His smile like a flag in greeting. The pleasure of seeing that eagerness on his face was all that mattered. Afterward, we would lie next to each other, waiting for our breath to find itself again. I thought it would go on like that forever. Would remain unmarked by life and time.

What more would we, could we, have said to each other? Albert said it all when he stood before the incinerator, ash floating in the air and landing on the dead piles of leaves ready to be burned. A grin I'd never forget. He said everything he wanted to say that day. Afterward, we were polite, but he couldn't look at me. For weeks even before he burned my Bibles, we lay in bed together, his arms stiff against his sides, his hands I don't know where. Taut, as though touching me would contaminate him and hurry his death. He already knew his days were ending when he stood behind the flames, marking his territory for the last time. I'm sure he never anticipated living with my silence and disdain for what remained of his life. This ending as hard as the dirt I hoed each spring.

He tried again to open his eyes, the muscles straining in their effort to lift the skin. But he couldn't.

"I did love you, Albert. Remember that when you leave." I looked at him again. *You must have been watching, Herr Gott.* Because, against my will, I stood and leaned down toward his ear. "Whether you want it or not, Albert, I'll pray for your soul."

Then, after all the months when we both waited, his was the quietest slipping away I could have imagined. I just sat there, looking out the window toward the poplar tree with its bare branches. Not even the blackbirds wanted to sit there in all that empty sky. Quietly, the way he'd first come around to our back door at Uncle Herman's farm, he slipped back into the oblivion from which he'd come. My sigh in that moment felt like the sigh of the world, a world that ended with Albert and his coffee can, his cigarette holder still inside the empty ashtray, his glasses case beside the baking soda box. Now he'd never have to see blizzards arrive with their sudden whiteouts, or remark when the irises raised their purple heads, or the peas climbed the trellises. Somehow, he'd find his way to a heaven of his choice. I certainly didn't want him in mine.

DR. SCHMIDT CLOSED his medical bag on the kitchen table. Wiped his glasses. Without asking if he could, he sat heavily in the chair closest to him, my chair, where he always seemed to sit. "God bless Albert," he said. "Wasn't a whole lot I could do for him."

"You did what you could, Dr. Schmidt. There wasn't much any of us could do except keep him comfortable."

"He was a hard man, Marta," Dr. Schmidt said. "A terrific worker, but a hard man." He hesitated for a moment. "I hope God finds him an easier job." He laughed. "I could say the same for myself."

"How about some tea and kuchen?" I asked.

His eyes brightened. "Maybe an extra big piece?"

"I'd be happy to send the whole kuchen with you."

"No, no. I'd rather sit here and enjoy it. Besides," he said, "my wife would make sure I had the smallest possible sliver."

While cutting him a third of the round, I said, "He was a sickly man these last years since the children grew up and Ozzie left home."

Dr. Schmidt stroked his mustache and gazed out the kitchen window toward the garden. "Ozzie might explain why he seemed sad. Very, very sad."

I said nothing. A smaller piece on my plate and hot water, enough for two generous cups, into the teapot. "He brought it on himself."

Whether he heard me or not, he said, "Doc Heinz in Dickinson would say he was depressed. But I don't know any immigrant who isn't depressed."

"Is that just another word for *sad*?"

"Probably." He dug his fork into the pastry and ate bite after bite until it disappeared, his fork still scraping against the crockery plate. He sat back in his chair, his eyes closed and his hands folded on his expansive belly. "You make the best prune kuchen I've ever eaten, Marta. I would get even fatter than I am if I ate this every day."

We sat in silence. Slurped our tea. "I'll miss you, Dr. Schmidt. You've become one of the family."

He drained the tea mug. Held on to the table in order to stand. Crumbs covered the front of his vest where they joined the toast crumbs from breakfast. "You're a good woman, Marta. He wasn't an easy man to care for."

"We do the best we can. Me, you, all of us, Herr Gott willing."

Dr. Schmidt left through the kitchen door, then the mudroom door like we all did.

At last it was over.

The last brightness I saw in Albert was the day Ozzie came home from boot camp on his first leave. His dress uniform with the brass buttons, the smart hat. Always a handsome man, Ozzie embodied the best of me and Albert. His kind heart always watched out for us. Generous to a fault, he set Ivan up with all those pigeons after Albert built the enormous cage. Granted, Ozzie's so-called way with the ladies wasn't something I wanted to know about. Yet his coming home was the last time I remember Albert smiling like he meant it, the last time Albert put his arm around me like he wanted to.

I poured the last dregs of morning tea into my cup and cut another slice of kuchen, my arms too heavy when I picked up my tea mug. Even the fork was almost too much to get to my mouth. *I have to admit, Herr Gott, I'm happy that you've finally taken Albert from me.* I was thoughtful for a moment. *I trust you will help Ivan through this. He'll miss his father more than any of us, the daily up and down the stairs a thousand times. Help me love the boy a little more to ease his pain.*

I knew it was wrong to say I was glad he was gone. With Albert, I never knew what tomorrow held. So unlike Ozzie, who had an even temper I could depend on. Ozzie, who always put those envelopes full of cash inside my daily-reading Bible, then a monthly allotment when he left for the war. He took his eager little brother for a ride to Dickinson in the new Buick. New overalls as his going-away present for Ivan. Always, his assurance in saying what I needed to hear. Ozzie and my brother Oscar on the family farm, even my daughters and grandchildren, my family surrounding me at all times, that's what mattered. The only thing left to do now was burn candles in the bedroom and open a window for a bit of air despite February's freezing cold.

Before I pulled fresh linens from the closet, I remembered the Jesus picture Albert always forbade me to hang anywhere it could be seen in the house. My heart pounded high in my chest when I hurried as fast as my body allowed to the secret opening under the stairs. He never knew I slipped the forbidden picture onto the shelf and over Mother's purse, where my Easter egg had hid inside its silk cocoon.

My fingers trembled when I lifted the wolf picture away from the wall and opened the latch. Darkness had protected the contents inside the secret hiding place, but my fingers knew where everything waited. My hands were still shaking when I lifted Jesus' eight-by-ten picture from the top of Mother's purse. I held the picture to the light and, once again beheld Your lovely face, *Herr Gott*. My throat thickened with tears of relief. I turned and placed the picture on the back of the sofa while closing the opening and fastening the latch. The wolf picture was secured once again over the secret opening.

My kitchen tools were under the sink. A hammer and a nail were all I needed. Up the stairs again, my breath huffing the air. On the wall at the foot of my bed where I could see You, Lord Jesus, every morning I woke, the last face before I went to sleep. That's where I hammered the nail and placed Your picture. *Yes, Herr Gott, You and I live in my bedroom now.*

## Chapter Fourteen

### Daughters to Dickinson

## *1944*

WHEN THE KITCHEN DOOR opened, I was in the middle of rolling out the sweet dough for cinnamon rolls. Ivan at school and a quiet afternoon to myself after what had seemed a long winter of grief and more grief. Albert's death had left me more than financially strapped, the kind of poor that only a miracle from Herr Gott could save me. But, cinnamon rolls I could do, no matter what the state of my pennies. Sweets were especially possible since Irene gifted me with her month's sugar rations saying Ada's were enough and, besides, they were both putting on too much weight.

"You must have smelled the cinnamon," I said. Irene walked into the kitchen behind me and pulled out a chair at the table now covered with empty pans filled with sweet rolls rising beneath the dish towels.

"If you mean I knew it was baking day, I did."

Seeing her housedress made me happy, the flour sack material from what must be a hundred-pound sack. Where they got that much flour, I didn't dare ask, not those two and whatever conniving they were up to.

"But, that's not why you came," I said sprinkling the dough generously with sugar, but not too generously. I needed to make the supply last the entire month.

Irene looked down at her hands and turned the thin wedding band in circles. Her long nails were filed to a point but at least they weren't covered with the nail varnish that Ada tried to hide from me. "I need to ask a favor," she said.

I could feel my forehead wrinkle with immediate suspicion. "Favor?"

"Ada hasn't been feeling right, and Dr. Schmidt says it's female trouble he's not good at. Suggested we take the bus to Dickinson and see Louise Gluck, the midwife. She seems to know more about these things than he does."

"Says who?"

"Dr. Schmidt."

"When did you see him?"

"A couple of days after Philip's funeral. Doctor gave her some sulphur in case it was an infection, but it hasn't gone away. I called him this morning and he said I should take her. Already made the appointment."

"So, you want me to watch the children."

"It's a lot to ask because we'll be gone all day. Maybe overnight if they put Ada in the hospital. Don't know why they would, but you know what I mean. Just in case."

I couldn't help the automatic cluck of my tongue to the roof of my mouth. A long history of not trusting these two. For all I knew, this was a planned shopping spree. Even so, minding the children would be a welcome treat for both me and Ivan. Marta could sleep with me and the girls could sleep in their mothers' old bedroom. Eli with Ivan.

"What day are you going?" I lowered the butcher knife to section off the rolls before placing them in the pan. My fingers surrounded each section to make sure the cinnamon and sugar, along with the few walnuts I used in this batch, stayed inside.

"Louise said she could see us Friday afternoon right after lunch. I already checked and we can catch a ten o'clock bus in the morning, take the six o'clock back. At least there's a bus in each direction that works."

"And, if you don't get back?"

"I'll have to use what's left of Mac's allotment to stay over."

I smoothed a long strand of hair away from my face with my arm, the sweat on my forehead enough to make it stay. "You know I don't like the idea of you two staying overnight. Too many things can happen to two women alone. There are bad men out there just looking for the likes of you."

When I turned toward Irene, she was quick to erase the smile on her face. "Don't take this lightly, Miss," I said, my face flushed from the stove's heat. "You two better not be up to any foolishness," I said. "And absolutely *no* picture shows, you hear me?"

"Most likely we'll be home before bedtime," Irene said smoothing her fingers as though looking at me would only make her smile again. After a minute of silence between us, I lowered the pans that were ready to go into the oven.

"I'll bring their pajamas just in case." She paused, "And a couple of diapers in case anyone has an accident."

She stood, ready to leave. "Bring you some lemon drops?" she asked. Before I could answer, she said, "Licorice for Ivan?"

"You can't ask me a favor and then get up and leave," I said. "At least have a cup of tea with me."

"Okay, but just a quick cup. I need to get back and fix supper for the kids. Right now, Little Marta is in charge if Ada's lying down."

The smell of the cinnamon rolls filled the kitchen even as I poured the tea into two mugs and delivered them to the table. My body sat heavy in the chair, wearier these days and I wasn't sure why. My hands curled around the warm mug. "One thing," I said, my eyes searching hers. "Not sure why Dr. Schmidt recommended Louise. You know she has a reputation for . . . " I didn't finish. Couldn't say the word.

"I know, Ma. Wouldn't be going if Dr. Schmidt hadn't recommended her."

We drank our tea, mostly silent except for a few words from Irene about the kids and the mischief they'd been up to with the neighbor kids. Funny how we didn't really have anything to talk about outside of family. Ozzie, Mac, the war. Pa's death. That was it. I was afraid to ask and hear what she thought of Mrs. Kinski's talk now months ago. I hadn't forgotten it and I was sure she hadn't either.

Finally, my tea was about gone when Irene pushed away from the table. "Just try to be back by eight o'clock. Even if it means the two of you have to stay here overnight," I said.

"Thanks, Ma." At the door she turned back into the kitchen. "I'll feel better when we find out what's going on with her."

After she left, I realized I could have asked more questions and maybe found out if my feeling was right about those two. Wished I trusted them and didn't always have to feel this way.

FRIDAY AFTERNOON MILLIE FINGERED the handle of her tea mug, her hair frizzy with a recent perm. "Don't know why you don't just let your hair grow out, Millie. You'd save a lot of money and bother. You could knot it up like I do mine."

When she laughed, Millie's teeth were gray and coated for

some reason, something I noticed lately. Probably didn't use baking soda to brush like we did in this house. "You know Fritz as well as I do. Says it reminds him of when I was a bride. . .the old days. Kinda sweet, really."

I placed a couple of cinnamon rolls on a plate between us. Another plate under each of our mugs to hold our partly eaten rolls.

"You said the children are here overnight?"

"They're napping now. Their mothers took the bus to Dickinson to see Louise Gluck. Irene said that Ada wasn't feeling right." I picked up my sweet roll and took that long-anticipated first bite. "You know anything about that woman, Millie?"

"Agnes says she's being watched. Seems she takes care of things for some of the women, if you know what I mean. Agnes also says that Pastor Kinski and several clergymen in Dickinson are keeping an eye on her."

"I just knew there was something I didn't like about that woman. Those two daughters of mine sneaking off like that, maybe for an overnight. The whole thing's not right. Makes my stomach grind when I think about how I fell for Irene's story."

"Now, Marta. Maybe Ada has a legitimate problem. Besides, Agnes thinks she knows everything, but even she makes mistakes."

"I hope that's what it is, a mistake." My tea was still too hot to drink but the smell made me want to pick it up anyhow even knowing it would burn the tip of my tongue. "Agnes won't be happy until she has me hogtied and crucified."

"Sorry I said anything." Millie lifted her cinnamon roll and took the smallest bite. I didn't know how she did it, small as she was, not dainty like Mama, but small in the best sense. Not wolfing it down like I wanted to do but wouldn't because I had company.

"Don't be sorry," I said. "Sometimes I need to know things I don't want to know so I don't have to find out from somebody else. You know who I mean."

"I do," she said. She turned toward the side of the table. "Look who's here. That sweet baby, Louisa. Come to Tante Millie, Louisa."

Millie leaned over with her arms outstretched and took Irene's youngest onto her lap. Without warning, Louisa, now twenty-six months, grabbed at Millie's roll with her little fingers and started stuffing the whole thing in her mouth, her hands already covered with sticky icing and her big smile looking up at Millie as though Millie had just handed it to her.

"No, Louisa," I scolded. "That's not yours. It's Tante Millie's."

Millie laughed which didn't help. When she saw my stern glance and I wrenched the child from her lap, Millie's face puckered into a frown of disappointment. "She's just a little thing, Marta. Your grandchildren are the only ones I have."

I already had the squiggling child at the sink and was wiping her face with a wet cloth. "No, no, Louisa. That wasn't your cinnamon roll."

The child's small mouth pouted just before she let out a scream. I held her hard against my chest and rocked her back and forth. "Now, now, there's no reason to cry. You'll get yours after you have your soup."

Louisa didn't give up, hollering as though she's just been spanked. Little Marta appeared in the parlor doorway looking forlorn while her baby sister wailed. I relented and walked Louisa over to Little Marta who waited to rescue her sister. "Take her to see the pigeons, Marta. We'll have our supper when she calms down."

Once the screen door closed, Millie started to stand. "I'm sorry, Marta. Didn't mean to cause a ruckus this afternoon. Afraid I did you wrong."

"No, no. Sit down and drink your tea. Think I'm just upset about those two daughters of mine traipsing off to Dickinson for no good reason they would tell me, and now I'm worried about that Louise woman's reputation." I gave Millie a long look. "Guess Herr Gott didn't mean for life to be easy, did He?"

Millie closed her eyes, the lashes so pale they disappeared. "Unfortunately, I think you're right, Marta."

When the back screen door opened again at eight-fifteen, the children were in their pajamas and we were all in the parlor where I'd stoked the fire in the stove. Ivan had them playing pick-up sticks, and the girls were squealing with their shrill little voices. Eli rested his head against my breast in the rocking chair where we both sat quietly rocking back and forth.

"We're back," Irene hollered.

The girls screamed their excitement and Eli lifted his head away from my chest where he'd been so content. When she found us in the parlor, Irene was alone. "Where's your sister?"

"I took her home," Irene said. "She was pretty tired."

"You're not going to take the children, are you?"

"No, I just wanted them to know we were back and that I brought treats."

All the children including Eli abandoned their games and my lap and rushed to see what Irene brought them. I stayed in the rocking chair, more suspicious than I was before, especially since Millie told me what she told me. I waited until Irene had distributed small white sacks with a few pieces of candy to each child as well as larger ones for me and Ivan.

"Wow, sis. This is terrific," Ivan said, his smile lifting his glasses off his nose.

"Where'd you learn that word *terrific*, Ivan?" I asked.

He shook his head, his uncut hair falling over his eyes. "I don't know. School probably."

"Hmm," was all I said. Alone in the rocking chair now, "Want to go into the kitchen and talk about Dickinson?" I asked.

She knew better than to object. There were certain unwritten rules in this house. First rule, respect your parents and all other elders. If they asked a question, you answered.

In the kitchen, I lay my hand against the side of the tea kettle to see if it was still warm. When satisfied, I checked the tea pot and added hot water. Didn't want it too strong or we'd be up all night.

Little Marta's voice traveled into the kitchen. "Is Dickinson where you went, Mama? Why couldn't we go? When will you take us?"

"Not today, girls. Another time."

"Me too?" Eli said taking his thumb out of his mouth.

"Yes," Irene said. "Someday, all of you."

They were jumping up and down, Ivan trying to get them back to the game or at least to sit and eat their sugary treats. They seemed to settle once Irene pulled out her customary chair in the kitchen. The smile she wore with the children in the parlor vanished and my heart suddenly pounded just looking at her face.

"Is she okay?" I asked.

"Yeah, she'll be okay," Irene said. "Lost some blood when Louise did a D & C to clean up something she didn't like. A couple of days in bed and she'll be fine."

"What does that mean, 'D & C'?" I asked.

"Some kind of procedure when the doctor doesn't like what's happening inside. Basically, to clean it out."

"Must be something fancy," I said. "Never heard of it."

"She'll be fine, Ma. Don't worry." She looked into her teacup like she could read the tea leaves though they'd all been strained out. "Something else you should know."

Her eyes remained focused on her teacup. "Agnes was on the bus coming back. Kept asking me why Ada looked so pale. I tried my best to say she'd been to the doctor, but when she asked who that was, I said Dr. Kellogg instead of Louise. Didn't want her making up stories the way she does and spreading them all over town."

"Lord have mercy," I said. "That woman can't leave anything alone."

"You're right there, Ma. That's why I'm telling you." Irene kept staring into her cup, her fortune there somewhere.

"Maybe a good reason to get the two of you into church this Sunday. Stop that old hen's tongue from wagging."

"Afraid that will do the opposite. She'll think we're there to redeem ourselves."

"Let her think what she wants. Herr Gott is on our side."

When Irene glanced up at me, her half-smile sat crooked on her face. "What makes you so sure, Ma?"

I started to say something when she interrupted me. "Wish I could be certain," she said. "Certain that this war will end and Mac and Ozzie will come home and we can pick up our lives again. That's what I hope anyhow. That's what will make the likes of Agnes Fleischman's tongue wagging nothing but a bad memory."

I looked at her for a long time, the unlined face and smaller nose, her pageboy hair style and beige sweater. Small pearl earrings I'd never seen before. Must have shopped first.

"Hope you're right about that," I said. "We just need to keep saying our prayers . . . *all of us* saying our prayers."

## Chapter Fifteen

### Waiting

## *1944*

OUTSIDE THE KITCHEN AND beyond my open bible, blackbirds descended on the remaining snow, their black feathers held tight against their bodies. They waited. For what? A clear patch of grass where they might find a grub or stray seed? For the rest of their flock to descend? They congregated on the crossed-arms of the telephone poles, close to the glass knobs meant to protect the knotted wires, glass knobs that glinted whenever we had sun. From their high perch, the blackbirds analyzed the world below. Their eyesight had to be extraordinary, the way they spotted an unseen morsel hidden on the road or buried in the snow. Their job so simple. To eat and sleep, to fly through the day and care for their offspring. *Isn't that what You expect us to do, Herr Gott?*

The blackbirds waited and I waited, Mother's words bedeviling me. "Death comes in threes," she always said whenever she heard someone had died. Not that she wouldn't honor the deceased, but I knew she always waited for the next death to follow. And, wait she would, growing quiet after talking to one of my cousins in the kitchen or, when we were young, delivering afternoon milk and cookies to me and Leo. I'd find her sitting near the living room, staring out the window at nothing in particular. Waiting, like the blackbirds waited now. Like I waited.

## 1914

I KEPT SWEATING INSIDE the bandages, inside the cold railcar. "No food, Mother. I'm not hungry."

Mother reached over and lay her hand on my forehead, her hand cool compared to the heat coming off me. "You screamed, Marta. Another nightmare?"

"It was the horses this time," I said.

Mother opened the bread sack on Father's lap and rummaged inside. She placed a piece of bread on my open hand before lifting Uncle Herman's wine skin, awkward as it was, and directing the spout toward the piece of bread. We were ravenous soon after we left St. Paul and, now, both the bread and wine were nearly gone. While I'd grown tired of the wine's acid aftertaste lingering in my mouth, the wine-soaked bread succeeded in easing the pain.

"I dreamed we were in a buggy accident," I said. "The horses fell on top of me."

Mother stroked my forehead and sighed, her eyes in mine. "It was just a dream, Marta. Like so many dreams."

The train shrieked to a stop, steam hissing above the wheels. The infernal whistle made me wince each time we entered another town. "Fargo," the conductor announced. Strangely, there was little activity outside the train window where new snow lay patchy, melting off the town roofs and fence posts. The path appeared slushy and full of mud where horses and wheels had gouged their tracks. A baggage wagon waited beside the brick station, and a few passengers huddled inside the station door. There was almost no one inside our railway car now. The few men ready to step onto the train carried bundles that appeared to be vegetables. Uncle Herman explained that they were travelling west to market in

Bismarck, the largest North Dakota city.

With few stops since Chicago, both Mother and I needed to get off the train. "Just to freshen up," Mother said.

Fargo gave us a full hour's stop. Though we were still most of a day away from Tante Ketcha's, Mother wanted to look her best. Not that Tante Ketcha would notice or appreciate the effort. Reprimanding myself for being judgmental, I considered the fact that Tante Ketcha had made this same journey and would, hopefully, appreciate the difficulties.

"Uncle Herman, would you please come with us?" Mother asked. "We must find a chemist or a doctor, someone to look at Marta's wounds."

Uncle Herman sat back in his seat and stared at Mother. "We're only a day away, Katerina. Surely we can wait that long."

Mother rose until she stood over Uncle Herman, her hands clutching her small purse. "We can't wait," she said. "The infection will only deepen and. . ." She searched for words, choosing carefully. "I don't want to take that risk. A chemist, we surely can find. We have enough time if we hurry now."

Though I wondered why she didn't ask Father, I suspected it had something to do with Uncle Herman knowing these towns. Father, like the rest of us, had never been here before.

"Jacob, I would like you to take Leo and help Marta to the washroom while we're away. Oscar can hold our seats."

No one was used to Mother taking charge, let alone issuing orders. I was secretly pleased, both that she was willing to do something and that she told the men how they could help. She adjusted her hat and waited for Uncle Herman to pull himself up and out of his seat. Oscar stood at Mother's elbow. "Why don't I go with Father and leave Leo here."

"Would you be willing to go into the washroom and help Marta if she called for help?"

Oscar's cheeks reddened. I'd never seen him back down so fast.

"Father, must I?" Leo asked.

"We don't even know if she'll need you. Think instead of how much it will help Marta."

Leo lowered his head until only his hat and curls were visible. "I guess so, Father."

"You can get off the train when we return, Oscar. It won't take long, I'm sure of it. Especially if we all go now," Mother said.

Father and Leo escorted me through the softened snow and mud toward two women waiting for the washroom. The women turned and stared at me when they saw my father and brother hold me between them. The cold air and the slushy ruts added to my empty feeling and my throbbing face. I wanted to go home. To forget America. To not be the disfigured girl no one would want to marry.

While washing my hands, I grabbed onto the sink and gazed into the tin mirror. For a girl constantly praised for her beautiful eyes and the face of a princess, I gasped on seeing my mummy's head with two eye holes, nose and mouth slits, the bandages a pale pink on my cheeks and forehead, with yellow pus at the center of the pink. The stink of it trailed me like a barn gone too long without mucking out. How could I live with this face, the ruin of all my hopes for a family of my own? Whoever was in the mirror—behind the sagging and discolored bandages, the disheveled dress—was nothing but ugly. When the women stared at me in passing, I had to look away for fear I'd be ill from the shame of what had happened to me.

I knocked at the door to signal Leo that I was ready. But when the knob turned and the door opened, it wasn't Leo waiting but Oscar, his forehead wrinkled into a frown. "I was worried about you," he said. "I traded places with Leo."

Tears crowded my eyes, their sting unbidden. Oscar's kindness only added to my humiliation. I didn't trust myself to speak. Instead, I reached my hand toward him, grabbing hold of his arm and feeling his strength through his jacket. He swung the door wider, wrapping his other arm around my shoulders and anchoring me into his side. Together, we walked away from the restroom door and staring faces, back toward the train car and our seats.

Mother returned with Uncle Herman immediately after I sat down. She held a small vial in her hand and a sack was tucked under her arm with what looked like cotton bunting. She didn't wait to sit down but, instead, she stood over me. "Lean your head back, Marta," she said. "This may sting some." She began to dab at my bandages with a piece of cotton. The foul-smelling solution made me want to turn away, but Mother persisted. She generously dabbed two or three times at each place where I'd seen the pink and yellow spots in the washroom. I grabbed hold of the seat, bracing myself, my knuckles straining against the wood. She kept wetting the bandage. To my surprise, once the solution reached my skin, there was no added pain outside of what was already there. Mother explained that the chemist said that the sodium hypochlorite, even dabbed on the bandages, would neutralize the infection. Whether the solution eased the infection or not, I was proud of Mother for refusing to allow the men to persuade her to wait one more day.

## Chapter Sixteen

## After Dickinson

## *1944*

On Tuesday when I did my shopping, I was picking through the meat in Hubner's market, deciding between ham hocks and a couple of ham slices, when Karin Comebacker, her gray hair pulled back in a tight knot, stopped me near the milk case. "Has Ada been ill?"

Caught off guard, I could only imagine the startled look on my face. "Not that I know of."

"I was at the Dickinson nursing home visiting Mildred Shrift, and I saw Ada's name on the registry."

The downturn of her eyes failed to hide the smile at the edge of her mouth. Who knows how many others Karin had told before she ran into me? Given there were about 587 people in Myra, I could not—would not—be the first to know.

I didn't watch Elmer, the grocer, add up my groceries like I usually did. I filled my cloth bag, forgetting to put the cans in the bottom and, instead, threw in the groceries as he rang them up. Rather than going directly home, I carried my bag to my daughters' house on First Street.

Irene was still in her white chenille bathrobe when she opened the back porch door. Behind her, the children sat at the kitchen table eating oatmeal, the smell of cinnamon filling the kitchen. "Ma, what brings you here so early?" Irene asked. She quickly closed her robe with her free hand.

"Oma, Oma," the children shrieked in unison. They started to leave their chairs at the table, only to have Irene say, "Sit until you finish your breakfast."

"It's okay, children, Oma will sit with you."

I set my groceries down on the mudroom floor before wiping my shoes on the mat. "Are you going to invite me in?"

"Of course," Irene said. "Let me get you a chair."

Glancing around, I saw no sign of Ada. "Is your sister asleep?"

"No, just taking a bath."

My coat still on, I unbuttoned it and undid the scarf at my throat. I had no intention of staying here long. I nudged someone's teddy bear and Eli's Tinkertoys out of the way, scattered as they were on the linoleum under the table and beneath the children's feet. Irene poured me a cup of tea in one of the earthen mugs I gave Mother long ago. She set the cream and a sugar bowl in front of me.

My hands circled the tea mug, feeling the heat come through the crockery. I wondered what Mother would have done had I deceived her the way my own daughters deceived me. Maybe the contagion came from Father.

Little Marta stepped toward where I sat. "Would you like a piece of toast, Oma?"

"No, *schatzi*, I've had my breakfast, thank you."

Except for the children chattering, the kitchen, while warm and steamy, remained quiet. What secret had Little Marta been told to keep?

Irene cleared her throat and rose to refill my tea mug. "Looks like you've already finished your shopping."

"How has Ada been doing since Dickinson?" I asked.

"Fine. Just fine." She tried to laugh.

I sipped my tea. "Ran into Karin Comebacker at the market. She just came back from Dickinson Nursing Home and swears she saw Ada's name on the registry."

Color flooded Irene's face. "She must be seeing things," Irene said before she turned away. "Everyone knows Karin's a terrible gossip. That's probably the only reason she goes to the hospital. Likely digging up dirt so she has a reason to bother Pastor Kinski."

"There's nothing more wrong with Ada?" I asked.

"You can ask her yourself when she comes out from her bath. In fact, I'll go get her right now."

"Good," I said. "I don't want Karin gossiping about my family, especially to the pastor."

Irene gathered her robe around her chest and legs before she disappeared down the short hallway. The two youngest girls squabbled over the piece of toast Little Marta offered me. Eli cried as though he'd been left out, rubbing his eyes and sobbing until I went around the table and picked him up, holding him on my lap when I sat back down.

"She'll be right out," Irene said.

She busied herself at the stove, refilling the teakettle from the indoor faucet, something I didn't have at my house, where I still pumped water from the well as I'd done all my married life. Irene wiped the children's faces and lifted them down from the table, her back turned to me.

"Good morning," Ada said. Her mint-green robe set off her auburn hair, curly and wet from her bath. She wore a touch of lipstick. However, behind her wide smile, a new paleness spread across her face and made her green eyes even darker. Unlike her usual sparkly self, even emerging from nine hours of sleep and a refreshing bath, she appeared to have had the punch knocked out of her.

"Karin Comebacker saw your name last week on the patient registry at Dickinson Nursing."

"You know that old bat, Ma," Ada said. "Always stirring up trouble and now seeing things on top of it."

"Just wanted to make sure it wasn't true," I said. "Wouldn't want folks in town to know you were sick before I did."

Ada laughed. "You don't need to worry about that," she said. "Can't get away with a darned thing in this town." Ada stepped to the stove, a tea mug in hand. Her hand shook, and she was wobbly on her feet, grabbing on to the counter before pouring her tea. She reminded me of Tante Ketcha's story about a woman who was aborted by her cousin with a knitting needle. I was eighteen then, preparing to marry Albert. I remember sitting near the woodstove in her kitchen, the warmth of the stove against my back. From time to time, Tante Ketcha still applied poultices along my scars to ease the scar lines. I remembered wondering why she was telling me that story. Why was I remembering it now?

I put Eli down, and he scrambled back to his chair, where Irene had placed a half piece of cinnamon toast on his plate. I was standing when I rebuttoned my coat and tied my scarf around my neck before stepping onto the porch rug to retrieve my shoes. "I want to remind both of you," I said, "whatever mischief you're up to reflects on our whole family. Don't make me sorry you came back from Portland. If Ozzie was home, we wouldn't be having this conversation and you very well know that. Just remember, your reputation is my reputation."

"Ma, you're overreacting," Irene said. "Think about the source of this so-called rumor."

My heart was beating in my throat when I picked up my cloth bag. I turned my glare on Ada. "I don't think you completely understand how an untended infection, if that's what you had, can affect the rest of your life. Leave you scarred forever." I descended the one step into the mudroom. "You keep playing with fire, Miss Ada, and one of these days you'll go too far. There are always consequences. Remember that."

## 1914

BISMARCK. THE LAST STOP before Dickinson, where Tante Ketcha would meet us. While the wind howled around the train car's windows, Oscar and Leo escorted Mother to the washroom one last time before our arrival. I stayed on the train to rest, my wound eased since Mother applied the medicine all those hours ago. My head lay against the window, my eyes closed, my stomach dancing with dread in anticipation of meeting Tante Ketcha. Half-awake and half-asleep, I heard Father when he sat down beside Uncle Herman.

"I think we should talk now," Uncle Herman said, the same urgency and command in his voice that had become increasingly apparent since we left Ellis Island.

I kept my eyes closed. For all they knew, I was asleep.

"I've been thinking," Uncle Herman said in an unusually quiet voice, "about what we discussed outside the train car last night." When Father didn't respond, Uncle Herman said, "I trust you've given thought to the house plan?"

Father said nothing at first. "What is it you want?"

Uncle Herman's voice became louder, enthusiastic. "A house like the one you had in Kassel. Three bedrooms. A large kitchen for Ketcha. I will buy her a new stove in Bismarck. Oh, and indoor plumbing. That will please her." He sighed. "She always envied your house."

Father remained silent. Finally, he said, "Tell me about your current house."

"There's not much to tell," he said. "One great room for eating and living. Two small bedrooms for everyone. Outdoor toilets."

"That is the house you're asking me and my family to move into?"

"Yes," Uncle Herman said. "It's the only way I'll convince

Ketcha to welcome you considering the circumstances."

What circumstances? Prior to America, the house to be built was to be our new house. Father said so. He brought the gold to buy supplies and pay for necessary help. That was his promise to Grandpapa Grozinski, Mother's father. The only question had been the winter weather and if they could get the walls raised before the heavy snows came. The thought of living in Tante Ketcha's small house through the winter made me shiver.

"You're good at engineering," Uncle Herman said. "The houses you designed for the Rosins and the Ketzels are proof of that."

In that moment I realized this was a conversation no one else was supposed to hear. What did they discuss last night out in the cold between the train cars? Was Uncle Herman reprimanding or punishing Father for some reason?

"You know that Ketcha won't be happy about the turn of events," Uncle said. "She'll want me to send you back to Russia or make you work in the fields."

My heart was so loud I was sure they heard the pounding.

"In order to sweeten the sour, I'll tell her you'll design a new house that will better accommodate our growing family," Uncle rushed on. "In exchange, you and your family will take our house."

I wondered if Father's heart was pounding like mine. How could he bear what Uncle suggested? How could he break Mother's heart this way? Why did he continue to remain silent?

"While I need farm equipment, I can borrow or make do until you and Oscar are working with me and we've saved more money from next summer's crop. In the meantime we'll use the money I saved to raise the new house. It will be Ketcha's house."

What had Father done to create this turn in our family's plan? How would he explain this to Mother? To all of us? Now I was sorry I'd overheard the conversation and wished I'd gone with Mother.

Father remained silent for some time. "That sounds fair, Herman." But his tone was low, full of resignation.

"Good," Uncle Herman said. "Then we're settled."

## Chapter Seventeen

### Ada's Job

## *1945*

AFTER PHILIP'S FUNERAL, ALBERT'S burial close behind, the crocuses continued to withhold their purple and white heads the day Ada walked into the kitchen without knocking. She wore Irene's new coat with the fur collar, a coat seemingly shared by both daughters.

"Good thing you have the teakettle on," Ada said. "I could use a cup this morning."

"You look pretty fancy. Where are you going so early?"

"Out," she said. She flung her purse onto the table. Once she removed her gloves, she threw them on top of her black clutch. Her coat came off as quickly, though she carefully placed it across the back of a chair. Like her sister, Ada wasn't about to hang it on one of the nails in the mudroom.

Dressed in hose, heels, and a skirt, she was on her way to someplace special. I grabbed a mug from the cupboard and placed it in front of her. "You seem to be in a hurry."

Always headstrong and impulsive, she'd sneaked out of the house at night to meet Philip just before she shamed me and Albert with their hurried marriage. I'd never been surprised with Ada. Not today, not yesterday when that gossip Mitzi Gruenwald let it slip at the ladies' tea that Ada had been seen in Horton walking with Heinrich Bueller, a married man. This latest report was no less humiliating than when Karin Comebacker told me that Ada showed up in the Dickinson Nursing Home registry recently, about the same time they went to see Louise Gluck. I hadn't been able to walk down the street since without worrying that folks whispered about her behind my back. There was no God-fearing or God-believing in any of my children except maybe Ivan.

Before I could pour the tea, Ada said, "I got a job."

The top of her red hair shined unnaturally bright in the sun coming through the window behind her. Maybe that stuff they called henna.

"What do you mean, *job*? You're a mother. Of course you have a job."

"No, Ma. Not like that."

I sat down at the table, my body heavier than ever, the tea mug in my hand just something to hang on to. "What kind of job?"

"Waitressing," she said. "I'll get a paycheck, but even more important, I'll have tips."

"Where in Myra do you intend to work?"

"Forget Myra. I'm going to work in Horton. The Cozy Café."

For a moment, I was numb with surprise. "How are you going to do that? And what about Eli? Who's going to take care of your son?"

Ada tilted her head, her green eyes bold when she turned toward me. "Irene's happy to take care of Eli."

I sipped my tea. "Horton's nearly fifteen miles away. How do you plan to get back and forth?"

"I'll ride each day with Heinrich Bueller when he goes to the Horton First National," she said. "Arranged to give him a dollar a week for gas. Same as I'll give Irene for watching Eli."

This was the same girl who was first to run off to the shipyards in Oregon when her then-boyfriend Philip talked about the Kaiser shipbuilding plant. Eloped, the same as Irene. When Philip joined the air force, Albert put his foot down and said no daughter of his was going to live in a strange city among strange men. Made her come home. But there was no Albert now and Ozzie wasn't around to see that she stayed home. "You didn't waste any time, did you? I'm sure you had it all planned."

"I did," Ada said. "Day shift. Tips will pay for gas, Irene, and even our food."

"But Heinrich Bueller is a married man. There's already talk about the two of you around town." Even as I said the words, I knew there was no argument good enough for Ada. "What did I tell you about the importance of your reputation?" My fingers traced the worn design on the oilcloth, the old thickness blocking my throat.

She ignored my comment. "Ma, I've got to get back on my feet," she said. "Isn't it better to go to Horton than loll around Myra where there's no work?"

"What do you mean *get back on your feet*? You *are* on your feet."

She said nothing, just gave me a look, almost a smirk. She was done explaining.

"Is this an excuse to pay for the fancy clothes you and your sister parade around in?"

Ada's only answer was a smile. She'd never say a word. I might as well save my breath.

I lowered my head. What could I say? I had no idea how I was going to pay my brother rent since Ozzie's allotment hadn't arrived on time. I grabbed my tea mug with both hands, feeling the warmth of the mug as I lifted it to my mouth. "Your reputation... what about that?" I asked.

"Reputation be darned, Ma," Ada said. Her red curls trailed the shoulders of her too-tight green sweater. "I've been called a lot of names since I was a kid, starting with *squirt*. I always had to walk in Irene's shadow." She stopped to take a breath. "Someday I'm going to find a man who will take me out of this godforsaken country in the same way Mac will probably take Irene away. But it won't be a mere fifteen miles. It will be so far away that the small minds in this town will never sniff a hint of where I've gone or what I'm up to. That's right, Ma. The names I've been called could fill someone's little black book. But do I care? No. I don't give a damn."

"*Oh mein Gott.*" I grabbed hold of the kitchen table, the oilcloth slick beneath my fingers, and I started to rise.

"No, Ma," Ada continued. "You don't get out of this that easy. I want you to sit down and hear me out."

With her eyes on mine, a fierceness I wasn't used to, I lowered my heavy body into the chair. Mother would have never allowed me to talk to her the way this girl talked to me. I glanced away, wanting to hide my burning eyes, to wish away what was happening here.

"All our lives we've done what you asked. We attended church, went to Bible study and Saturday school even when Pa railed against it. We attended church dances with boys you chose. We stayed in Myra and worked at home, helping you and Pa with the garden and the house and raising Ivan. We did what we were told, and we showed nothing but respect to both you and Pa."

Ada leaned across the table, her hands folded in front of her, her eyes narrow and earnest. "But you went too far when you decided to pick our husbands," she said. "Yes, that's right. You wanted us to marry one of the Fredrich boys or Hal Schneider. Someone from inside the church, someone who had never stepped outside of Myra or, at least, had never been farther than Dickinson.

Someone who would live according to your plan."

Right then, ironing the vestry cloths or Ivan's shirts, even hauling water from the well or carrying canned peaches down to the cellar would have been a pleasure. I wanted anything but to hear Ada's rant. My hands gave me focus as I twisted my wedding band, worn thin after all the years and far too small for my fat finger. I could feel perspiration under my arms.

"Look at what we did. Ozzie joined the marines and went off to see the world. He found someone in California, someone he probably won't bring home until after he's married her."

"What do you mean he found someone in California?" Heat rose in my cheeks and my neck was suddenly too hot. "How do you know . . . and why didn't I know that?"

"Maybe he was afraid to tell you."

"Why would he be afraid?"

"Ma, think about it. He was probably afraid you wouldn't approve. Which is my point exactly. Look at Irene. She was lucky enough to find a man who came to this town through his job, and someday he'll be smart enough to take her away. I did the best I could by marrying someone who *was* from town, but he didn't fit into your righteous mold either. Now he's dead, and I'm left with his child. But *still* you want me tied to a place where women have nothing better to do than the drudgery of housework and gossip over the fence or in the church basement so they can feel justified with their tiny lives by taking everyone else into account."

Without warning, Ada pushed her chair back along the linoleum. She stood, holding on to the chair's back with both hands. "I'm done," she said. "Simple as that. At twenty-one, I'm going to live my own life. If I'm lucky enough to find a man who will take me away from here, I'll feel blessed."

If Ada had slapped me and stormed out of the house, she couldn't have had more effect. "I assume you're finished," I said, calm, like I was in control. In truth, my heart was racing and I could feel the blood, hot and red, flooding my face and arms.

Ada remained steady, unrelenting. "Finished, done. What does it matter?"

"You listen to me, missy. You may be a widowed woman and you may need extra dollars, but being alone in a car with a married man and being seen on the street in a nearby town, whether you're walking with him or hanging on his arm, isn't something a decent woman does."

"I didn't expect you to understand," she said. "You're old-fashioned, Ma. Women are working all over the place. Just because it doesn't fit your notion of who and what a woman should be doesn't mean it's not happening or that it's wrong. Wake up, Ma, this is America, 1944, war is real, and my husband is dead. So is yours. How do you think we're going to survive? Someone has to work and bring in real dollars."

My eyes remained on my hands. A sudden sigh escaped and unexpected heat rose behind my eyes. She was right. The war had changed everything. What was important in a woman's life, in my life and in Mother's only a few years ago was no longer important. The new heroes spread their faces across the newspaper and magazine covers I saw at Hubner's Grocery. This Rosie the Riveter was some kind of hero. My mother would have hidden her face in shame at the sight of the picture.

My fingers twined tightly through the loop of my tea mug. My heart was beating too fast, and while my mouth shaped the words I wanted to say, all I could manage was "This isn't right. You know that. It's not the way you were raised." After a moment's hesitation, I continued, "Maybe you should go as far away as you say you want to go and leave Eli with us until you're settled down and married again."

Ada sat down. She reached across the table. Rested her hands on the back of my hands, her touch lighter than I expected, her fingertips tracing my veins. Her voice dropped. "Ma, nothing's right about war. You've said so yourself." She hesitated. "Things are never going to be the way they were. You can count on it."

I gazed down at Ada's hands, the fingers short, the ends blunted with nails more square than oval. Worker's hands, like Albert's. His hands were made for threshing machines and pitchforks, scythes and harrows. The bricklaying he mastered to support our family. He could sort beans without looking. Guide a tractor while eating his sandwich. His hands lived on in Ada, now in Eli and Louisa. Only Little Marta had inherited my hands, the long fingers and shapely nails meant to play the pianoforte, to serve a formal tea.

I raised my chin to meet Ada's green eyes. "Decent women don't leave their homes," I said. But my words sounded weak and useless.

"That's the way it was for you, for your mother. For generations of women behind you. But the world is different, and it's been different ever since Pa joined the army for the Great War. Nothing is certain."

When I turned away from my youngest daughter, her red hair was a blur. There was too much truth in what she said. Truth I didn't want to face. We were both widows now. There was no man to do the simplest things. Storm windows that never went up. A clog in the kitchen sink. A hinge broken on the screen door. I'd never discussed finances with my daughters, so how could they know that Ozzie was the one who had picked up what Albert and I couldn't manage? If he married, that would change. Then what would we do? My brother Oscar watched out for us, showing up from time to time with a fifty-pound sack of flour, a bushel of apples, a quarter side of lamb. But I couldn't ask him to do more. Besides, he was so crippled that he hardly left his rocking chair. And there was no way to honestly talk about these things without Ada feeling justified in going to a job in Horton with Heinrich Bueller as her ride. Gone were the times when a woman remained silent until a neighbor woman, someone she trusted, like Millie, listened over a cup of tea. In truth, worry kept me awake at night and wouldn't leave me even when I kept my hands busy making bread and soup, crocheting and tatting. Helping Ivan with his homework. These were too much like the days when Father tried to turn the Dakota soil and we still lived in Tante Ketcha and Uncle Herman's house, where my brother still lived.

"I just hope this isn't some crazy idea. Because the next thing I'll hear is that you're moving to Dickinson."

When Ada smiled, her lips parted over small, white teeth. "I have no money to move to Dickinson, Ma."

"A job would solve that, wouldn't it?"

"Maybe, maybe not. It's not my plan. Heinrich Bueller isn't my plan. He's boring, Ma. Those spectacles and his bald head." She closed her eyes. "He's not a man I could ever want."

For the first time, I noticed the darkening of Ada's lashes, always so pale and nearly invisible. Like a further and silent slap against my face, her lashes were confirmation that I'd lost the fight that loomed between us. We sat silent for several minutes until I rose to move the teakettle to the back of the stove where the wood coals lay in hot embers. I lifted the stove's cast-iron lid and stoked the coals in order to start the borscht. Moments later, Ada's chair scraped against the linoleum.

Moving behind me, her heels clicked on the linoleum flooring. She lay her hand on my shoulder, her fingers squeezing my arm. "Let me try the job first, Ma," she said. "Before you go judging me and making me wrong."

I sat a long time at the kitchen table, my finger looped through my tea mug, the tea grown cold before Ada left. Ada getting a job. Ozzie meeting a girl in California. Everything I'd known and trusted was disappearing, and my daughters' lives and opinions were so far removed from what Mother taught me. The loneliness in that moment was unlike any I'd known before. My family was leaving me behind. I didn't know who I was anymore.

# 1914

WITH THE SUN OF a new day shining onto the side of my bandaged face, I remembered, even as I asked, what Mother last told us: our few mementos—her precious egg, the samovar and tea jar, our down comforters—were all packed safely inside the trunk. "They'll always take us home." She told me that in the carriage as we turned the last time to look back at our whitewashed house disappearing behind us. Her words were meant to reassure us. She must have believed that my Easter egg and her own would somehow carry our family forward. If the precious eggs were ever lost in the same way our home was lost, that simply proved we were like the nomads I'd studied in my history lessons. Wandering and lost, without a place to belong.

PULLING INTO THE DICKINSON train station, my throat swelled with relief and terror. Sometime during the night, cold as the train car was, I perspired through my dress and into the coat Mother kept tucking around me while the fever broke. For the first time since the accident, my head stopped throbbing and my forehead ceased to be hot with fever. Throughout the long night, Mother kept dabbing at my forehead with the medicine-filled bunting. Finally, the medicinal odor ceased to alienate those around me.

Now, a buckboard with two people and a couple of dogs sat back from the railroad tracks. When we stepped down from the train, a large woman in a long dress with a man's coat tightly buttoned hurried toward the train. The hat she wore matched Uncle Herman's. Except for the dress, she could have been another man. Beside her, a fellow in a wide-brimmed hat and what appeared to be leather trousers with thigh-high boots hurried with her. Two horses waited patiently in front of a wagon Father's men would have used to haul grain or corn, sometimes hay.

With Uncle Herman's hand in the middle of her back, Tante Ketcha nodded in greeting toward Mother, but there was no smile on Tante's face. "Welcome," she said, though there was no warmth in her words. The difference between the two women was never more apparent.

Seemingly forgotten, the young man introduced himself as Yuri, one of Uncle Herman's sons-in-law. He, with a wide smile the entire time, grasped Father's hand out of respect before taking Leo and Oscar's hands in firm handshakes. He stopped in front of me and immediately turned his head as though he had just trespassed, his eyes averting my mummified face. Beside him, Tante Ketcha strode toward me. "You are safe now, my girl," she said.

## Chapter Eighteen

### Ozzie

## 1945

I STOOD AT THE screen door facing the garden where the purple heads of crocuses finally stuck their heads above the late spring mud, a premature sign winter had given up its hold. Two men opened the alley gate and stepped onto the brick path. They were in military uniform; ribbons and medals hung on their chests. Their hats, trousers, and shiny shoes told me they were marines. The younger, shorter man used a crutch under his right arm.

My heart stopped. My mouth went dry and my stomach rose into my throat. This had to be a mistake. Instinctively, I reached to turn around and lock the door behind me.

Not until they were in full view by the pigeon pen did I see that the one man's pant leg was pinned back at the knee. The taller of the two carried a large manila envelope under his right arm.

They seemed a somber pair; their eyes focused on the wet brick path, perhaps to protect their shoes. They didn't look up until they were maybe ten steps away.

What did Millie tell me about the day they came to tell her about her son, David? Was the envelope part of the message? My hands wrung the sides of my apron and my heart couldn't let go of its frenzy. Maybe I should call Irene before I talked to them. Millie. Someone. Whatever they had to say, I didn't want to be alone to hear it.

They quickly removed their hats. The rush in my chest, the tightening in my throat, made me reach behind my back to untie my apron in response to the formality of their posture. But when my hands touched the knot behind my waist, my fingers didn't work right and I had to stop trying to untie the bow. I opened the screen door, although it was the last thing I wanted to do.

"Ma'am," the taller of the men said.

My hand found my throat and my eyes burned even before the men lifted their shoulders back and away from their chests. The man holding the envelope juggled his hat in his free hand. He seemed confused about what belonged where.

All I could think was to be polite; this had to be hard for them too. But the thickening in my throat created a strain in my voice and my words squeaked out. "Good morning."

"Ma'am," the legless soldier said. He held his hat flat and respectfully in front of him. His dark eyes said he was sorry to be at my back door.

The taller one brought his legs together as though about to salute. He appeared to be older. He cleared his throat. "We are here as representatives of the United States Government and the United States Marine Corps to inform you of the death of your son Oscar Albert Gottlieb on Eniwetok Atoll in the Marshall Islands on February 22, 1944."

He said this so fast I only heard *son* and *Oscar* but not that strange place they named. The rest was nonsense and unnecessary. *Son* meant something. *Son* had a face and a history attached to it. *Son* had my heart beating out of control.

I stared at both men, trying to understand what they'd just told me. A faraway feeling took flight. The far-from-here flew up onto the electric wire where the blackbirds waited and looked down on me and the men, the pigeon cage and the ragged garden, the brick path full of puddles from a late snowmelt, and Millie across the alley, pulling back her curtain.

We stood at the back door, me on the top step of the stoop, my eyes level with the eyes of the taller man. No one said another word. That made it worse. I wanted to scream, *Go away. Get out of here*, even while the one-legged man held on to his hat with shaking hands. Both men focused behind me, refusing to meet my eyes now filling with tears. Perhaps they momentarily forgot that they were messengers and, instead, were standing in front of their own mothers. All I could say was *oh mein Gott*. A deep breath while I still could. "How?"

I kept my eyes on the swell of the taller man's Adam's apple. The knot of it strained inside his throat when he swallowed and tightened near his ear from a jaw gone rigid. Anything to keep my eyes from spilling.

"In service to his country," the other finally said.

No one said anything for several seconds. "Where are you from?" I asked.

Again there was silence. Then the one-legged man said, "Bismarck, ma'am."

"Oh," I said, looking past them toward the water pump, and beyond the water pump toward the outhouse. "Did you know my Ozzie?"

"No ma'am," they said in unison.

"You've come a long way. Would you like tea?"

"Thank you, no, ma'am," the taller man said; there was a scar along his right chin line that I saw for the first time.

"Thank you for coming," I said.

I reached out and took the envelope, the weight of it numb in my hand. I no longer saw them or their uniforms, and I no longer saw the water pump or the pigeon pen or the outhouse or the gate by which they left. I saw only the disheveled garden with cornstalks fallen in disarray and the tomato vines spindly and dead. I turned, the envelope now under my arm like it had just been held under the tall man's arm. I walked up the one step, through the mudroom and onto the kitchen linoleum. Gathering my apron in both hands, I waited in the kitchen's silence, absently counting the ticks of the clock. Waited for the trapdoor to open, for the tears that would bury me alive.

"To hell with this death and dying, Herr Gott," I yelled at the ceiling in my steamy kitchen. "How can you do this to me?"

I screamed like I hadn't screamed since I was fourteen and fell facedown on the Battery Park dock. Screamed and sobbed at the same time because, of all my children, I loved my sons best. Now my eldest, my first, was gone. Gone in the way his father was gone. Philip was gone. Millie's David was gone. And I couldn't be there for my son the way I'd been there for Albert. I couldn't hold his hand and say a prayer; I couldn't reassure him that you, Herr Gott, would forgive whatever sins he held on to.

My brother Oscar was one of the first to reach me on the wharf, the first to lay his hand on my back, to whisper, "Marta, our little Marta," the panic in his voice ringing out at me as I lay there, the pain searing my face like small carving knives, a pain I had never known before and I would never know again in the same way. His hand on my back, his voice above me crying out, "Father, Father, we need help." The near-tears in his voice, the agony of his helplessness, the utterance as close to tears as he would allow. All of that before the darkness came and along with it the bliss of knowing nothing until the odor and the sting of whiskey brought me back to the nightmare I had mercifully escaped. Now the same desperation, the same agony and despair that would forever be notched inside a corner of my mind. The finality as dreadful as the pain of who had been lost, the one who would never return no matter how hard I prayed, no matter what miracle presented itself, no matter how you, Herr Gott, comforted me. My love had flown away like one of the blackbirds on the telephone line. And with it the faith that I would ever find it again.

## *1914*

Though I was separated from the table where the reunited family sat at their meal, the smell of food nearly overwhelmed me. I was far hungrier than I imagined. Tante Ketcha, sensing my hunger, said, "I will bring you a little something to eat. After I clean your wound."

Clean the wound. My heart pounded until I heard it hammering in my ears. I wanted no one to touch me. No one to put a hand or cloth near my face and likely hurt me more than I already hurt. I wanted to hang on to what numbness I had while I was finally feeling warm again. Even the thought of removing the bandages set me adrift, as though on a raft floating on the ocean under a grayer than gray sky without landmarks in any direction.

None of the voices on the other side of the stove seemed real. Not the laughter and high-pitched words or the bass voices of the men. Only the silence on this side, only the stool close to the warm stove, my raft bobbing on endless water and the promise of rescue unimaginable.

"This should help," Tante Ketcha said. With her oversized hands, she placed a small bowl of soup next to me, the steam alive with the smell of onions and garlic; the cut-up carrots and beets and a piece or two of ham floating toward the surface. My hands circled the bowl as though I've never held a bowl before. The warmth coming into my fingers.

"I'll make sure the others are served," she said.

We'd had no hot food since leaving Ellis Island. Nothing but bread and cheese, some apple, the wine my constant medication. Now even the smell of wine made me nauseous. I ate slowly: the spoon against the bandage near my lips, the warm and fragrant liquid, though hot, trailed my tongue on its way to my stomach.

"Not too much," Tante Ketcha said. "We don't want you to get sick."

*Was I not already sick?* I said nothing.

Tante Ketcha stood in front of me, garlic on her breath, her eyes searching the wrap of the bandages. "You'll feel better. I promise."

She was smaller than I remembered as a young girl. Not much taller than me, though I was sitting on a stool; her eyes with their heavy lids were a dark brown and intense, as though they could see beneath the skin's surface. She studied my face, turning my head and examining the wrap until she could see all sides of the bandage. "I'm looking for the end," she said. She lifted her head toward the stove. "Herman, bring me a lantern."

There was muttering as a bench scraped against the floor despite the laughter and clanking of spoons against crockery bowls. The mudroom door we'd come through opened, allowing the forgotten cold to come inside. When Uncle Herman appeared, his face was white above the lantern, his mustache and eyebrows a starker white. He looked for a place to set the lantern, finally pulling another stool close and setting the lantern near Tante Ketcha's elbow.

I swallowed the impulse toward tears, the effort thick and knotted in my throat. This wasn't the time to give in to tears. I concentrated on listening while Natalia, Tante Ketcha's eldest daughter, scooped the bean and vegetable soup with bits of ham and sauerkraut from a large kettle, the hiss of gray broth spilling onto the stove. The excited voices of my newly introduced cousins questioning Oscar and Leo about the journey even while they slurped their soup. Someone asked for more bread or butter; another spoke with what sounded like a mouth full of food. It took little imagination to see Mother sitting among these near-strangers as someone stranded on an island overflowing with creatures she'd never seen before, both amazed and aghast at the habits of a more primitive tribe. Yet their voices, along with the whistle of steam rising from the teakettle and the stove's warmth, consoled me.

While the others ate their dinner, the odor from my wound hung near where Tante Ketcha and I separated ourselves from the others. I could only imagine how much worse it would have been without Mother's ministrations on the train.

When Tante Ketcha rested her hands on my shoulders, I was both surprised and unsettled by the lightness of her touch. This tenderness so unexpected from the woman who ridiculed and slapped my hands as a child, a woman who had been the object of my fear from the moment Father said we were coming to America.

She leaned close to my ear. "We have to clean your wounds," she said. "The poultices will make you feel better. Then you'll be able to rest."

Though I remained hungry and tired, her gentle, almost whispered, words brought reassurance. Tante Ketcha produced a small piece of cheese she fed me through the mouth opening in my bandages. Once again I thought of the springtime baby birds I'd watched from my Kassel bedroom, the mother birds using their own beaks to feed their offspring.

"You need to be very brave, Marta" she said. "And you need to trust me."

That was the moment I looked past her overly large nose and the black hair on her upper lip, her thick and gray hair pulled back so severely she could easily be mistaken for a man. The person I saw before me wasn't just the most hardworking woman I'd ever meet, but a healer inside the guise of an ordinary peasant. Her dark eyes before me, I was hopeful for the first time since seeing the Grand Lady when we landed in America.

"I'm going to slowly remove these bandages. It may hurt because they're stuck," she said. "But I'll apply a warm, wet cloth to ease them away. If you're very brave, I have a stick of candied ginger for you at the end of your supper."

At first I nodded in agreement, not because I immediately trusted Tante Ketcha but because I had no choice. The cheese stuck in my throat along with the tears, and my heart beat faster while my hands lay sweaty atop my soiled travel dress.

The thought that the bandages might hurt made me swallow hard against the ongoing impulse toward tears. My wounds already hurt. How could removing the bandages be worse? It was nearly a week since I fell and no one had looked at the wounds, though Mother had tended them from the outside. I braced myself on the stool and my hands held tight to the wood. I was both relieved and scared while her fingers fumbled with the tucked and knotted bandage, still searching for the end.

I tried to relax as much as I could, allowing the warmth to comfort me and focusing on the other side of the stove, where Oscar's excited voice questioned Yuri about the community and who lived there that we might know. When he asked, "Who are the girls?" I smiled.

Tante Ketcha's fingers came into view as she unwound the bandage, crossing over my forehead, then to the back of my head and, finally, over my chin. While I knew she was doing what was necessary, I didn't want her or anyone to see what lay hidden beneath the gauze strips.

The first twinge came when she tugged at the bandage close to the deep cut on my forehead. I recalled how Father exclaimed in horror on seeing that original gash on the dock. Now, even when she applied the warm water and witch hazel–soaked cloth, intense pain stung my eyes and made them water despite my best effort not to cry. The wound's evolving smell made my stomach lurch. For once, I was happy my tummy was mostly empty, that Tante Ketcha had taken the bowl away. Even the promise of sweet ginger didn't stop the pain or the smell or my fear of permanent scarring.

Tante Ketcha stopped. "I know this hurts," she said. "Breathe deeply."

She soaked her cloth in more warm water and held the wet cloth longer against the wound. "Do you think you can hold this rag against your forehead?" she asked.

"Yes, Tante."

She clicked her tongue, and I wondered if that indicated the severity of the wound. She stepped back farther and pondered my forehead. "Just for a minute. This should do it." She placed the rag in my hand, its warmth a comfort against my fingers, and she directed my hand toward my forehead, where the warm wetness soaked into the bandage.

Except for the sudden stench, the water-soaked rag eased the pain while water trailed my hand and the inside of my dress sleeve. Tante Ketcha then took scissors to cut at the foot-long bandage she'd just removed. Taking the rag from my hand, she resoaked it in the water. "You'll sleep alone tonight," she said, as though talking to herself. "Beside my bed."

My throat thickened. I wanted to say, *No. I want to sleep near Mother and Father*. But I said nothing.

As though she sensed my apprehension, she said, "It will be safer for your wounds than sleeping with Katie and Blinka."

Her daughters' names sounded foreign to me. Though Leo had tried to prepare me, I recalled no one except Natalia, who was instructed to play with me when her parents visited our home that one time. When they left following afternoon tea, I missed a particular chair in my dollhouse, a chair Father had whittled for me from a piece of hickory we found together in the yard. I always suspected Natalia had taken it.

"Now, again," Tante Ketcha said. She pressed the rag against my forehead and lifted my hand to hold it in place.

This time I felt the bandage loosen, and an increased sting radiated from the wound. "Good," Tante Ketcha said. She removed my hand and tugged ever so gently at the bandage. "It's coming undone."

She teased the bandage away before following it around the back of my head by holding the bandage between her fingers. When her hand came into view in front of my face, she cut away at the rag and dropped it into a bin near her feet.

Exposed to the air, the wound stung and the pain overtook my forehead. I groaned and began to jerk my head away. "Shh, shh," Tante Ketcha said. Her hand grabbed my shoulder and her fingers dug into my arm to steady me. I wasn't sure if she was reassuring or scolding me.

"Marta, are you okay?" Mother called from behind the stove.

"She'll be fine once we get the bandages removed," Tante Ketcha said.

I watched her face when she said that, her jaw suddenly tight and her dark eyes narrow at this intrusion from the other side of the stove. I heard a shuffle, perhaps as Mother prepared to rise. Then Uncle Herman's strong voice. "Ketcha is skilled at this. It's bound to hurt some."

The shuffling ended and the table became silent.

"We'll allow the air to get to it," Tante Ketcha whispered to me. Her fingers unwound more of the bandage. I dreaded the dressing's downward turn when she neared my nose, then my cheeks where the splinters entered and were extracted at the pier. I again remembered the original pain.

Tante Ketcha remained steady, her face unchanged while she gently unwound the bandage, the wound becoming increasingly exposed. She cut and then dropped more of the soiled bandage into a bucket at her feet. She again handed me a warm, wet cloth, this time requesting that I hold it against my face before she attempted to ease the bandages away. At times the throbbing threatened to overwhelm me. At one point, when she eased the crusted bandage from my upper cheeks, I thought I would faint. She grabbed my shoulders again and clicked her tongue. "Tsk, tsk," she said. Her words settled me.

Only once did she comment, and that's when the bandages were completely removed and the stench escaped into our corner of the room. "My poor girl," she said. "You are so brave."

Those words, never forgotten, meant I was doomed. It was one thing to live with the bandaged wounds and escape the pain any way I could. It was another to have the wounds exposed and imagine my damaged face in the reactions of those who would never wish this wound on themselves. Those who loved me, despite the wound and subsequent scars, would need to be those who could see beyond my face.

My entire face was now bared to the steamy kitchen. If we hadn't been hidden, I'd have been forced to endure the reaction of every family member gathered around the kitchen table. In that moment, I was grateful to Tante Ketcha for being wise enough to hide me behind the stovepipe. For her willingness to midwife removing the bandages, for facing the wounds without flinching and scaring me worse than I already was.

I forgave the incidents from my girlhood.

Tante Ketcha, her hand hiding the mirror behind her back, asked, "Do you want to see your face now?"

I hesitated, gazing into her eyes to read whether my hesitation was warranted. A half smile on her face encouraged me to nod halfheartedly. She handed me the mirror.

Though hesitant, I held the mirror in my unsteady hand, and I saw the angry edged gashes on my forehead and cheeks, a long slice along my nose. Her gentle ministrations with the warm witch hazel and water had cleared away whatever infection had gathered there. What remained exposed was raw and red with inflammation. Stitched wounds zig-zagged my forehead and along my cheeks and nose. I saw the awful destruction of my once-lovely face.

"The poultices will heal and better close the wounds," she said. Gently, reassuringly.

I could only think to nod, tears falling from my eyes and blurring the image in the mirror. Polite daughter that I was, I said, "Thank you, Tante Ketcha. They hurt."

"I know they do, dear girl," she said. "Be patient with me while I apply the poultices." Unexpectedly, she took my hand and held it inside her own, the skin rough but warm, her touch reassuring while she gazed into my eyes just long enough to tell me that I was safe now.

## Chapter Nineteen

### The Women

## 1945

EXCEPT FOR IVAN, WE were now a family of women. Women and children. Only Mac remained, wherever he was in France. My brother wasn't much help. Worse now with rheumatoid arthritis and diabetes, Oscar no longer left the comfort of his rocking chair in front of the woodstove or the newspapers he scoured for news of the war.

How would I tell Ozzie's sisters that their older brother had been killed? Ivan? Ozzie, the man my young son looked up to. Ozzie, the one who allowed Ivan to sit in his new Buick and pretend he was driving, the man who permitted Ivan to wash and wax the blue finish to a reflective shine, the man who always fished a dime from his pocket and said, "Go get a Nehi, but don't tell Ma." Ivan idolized his older brother. I couldn't blame him. His often-sickly father wasn't someone a young boy could admire. Now Ivan was left with an aging mother and two sisters who were distracted by their own children. The one remaining husband, Mac, would never be a model for any boy, especially my son.

The details of Ozzie's death didn't matter. What mattered was that I would never know the men my son called friends. There would be no funny or sad stories about where they'd been and, never, about what they'd seen. My son was dead. And while I could say that Herr Gott had called him home, I would never understand this death any more than I understood war, the very thing my family thought they escaped when we left Russia.

"I do not deserve this from you, Herr Gott," I shouted at the naked ceiling, at the faded oilcloth on the table, the teakettle whistling on the back of the wood-burning stove.

"It's not fair," Irene sobbed into the phone's receiver.

"Maybe you should come over," I said. "We can talk better here."

The telephone party line left us too vulnerable to neighbors and gossip, especially in a town where there was nowhere to hide. Just saying what I had to Irene would be big news over supper tables that evening or dominate conversation following dinner when the families sat around the stove and drank evening tea.

"You're probably right," Irene said. "After the girls get up from their naps." Her tone dropped. "Ada and Eli will probably come with me."

"Bring them. I'm making *gruene borscht* and fresh bread. We can all eat together."

After we hung up, I counted to fifty, about the time it would take Alma Wright, the local operator, to inform the entire church that they should pray for me and my family, though she only knew it was bad news, not who it was. Ozzie or Mac were the only ones it could be.

I hollered up the stairs. "Ivan, your sisters are coming for supper. You need to set the table for eight."

Overhead, the rug muffled the stomping of his shoes but not the clamor on the wooden stairs when he came down.

"Don't forget the salt and pepper. The milk glasses."

Ivan had probably listened over the heating grate and heard me on the telephone. His eyes were red from crying and his face splotchy. He practically threw the plates onto the table, their clatter unnerving. Right then, I didn't trust myself to talk to him. Instead, I glanced to what I called Ozzie's mirror above the small sink where the door opened into the mudroom. I had to look away, emotion threatening to erupt whether I wanted it or not.

"They're only coming for supper, so don't get your hopes up that the girls will stay," I said. I took off my glasses and wiped them on my apron. Between my tears and the steam from the boiling soup, the lenses were so clouded I could hardly see.

Ivan glanced over from where he placed the silverware at each place setting, adult plates for his sisters and small saucers for the younger ones and Louisa, who would sit on Irene's lap.

His hand touched my shoulder where I stood facing the garden. My own hand reached up to cover his until the softness of his skin, his touch, threatened the onset of tears again. I patted his hand and turned toward the small sink by the mudroom door. It didn't help to stare at Ozzie's vanity, where I could still see him shaving and washing his eyes with his eye cups each morning and evening before he splashed on bay rum, applied the gels or wax to his pompadour, curving it up into a wave. The sink, the medicine cabinet, the mirror. These were his places.

I shook my head, my handkerchief wrung to a wad inside my hand. Irene's question about what was fair remained locked inside my mind. Was it fair when Albert's body, with his ash-gray face, was laid inside the white satin of his pine casket? No, it wasn't fair, only expected. Philip, with or without his jaunty white neck scarf and bomber jacket when his life was ended by bullets or fire, his body never recovered. Was that fair? Now Ozzie, named in honor of my only remaining brother, his red hair beneath a cocked hat, those open-necked white shirts in other photos when he stood with his arms crossed and a grin on his face in front of his new Buick, Fritz's Texaco behind him. Was this fair? Ozzie only proved that unexpected deaths are their own bullet to the heart. Like me, my daughters had every right to turn away and beat their fists against the wall. To sob until sleep finally came. *Yes, even to scream at you, Herr Gott.*

IN TRUTH, OZZIE WAS the one I counted on. Throughout the ordeal of Philip's death, then Pa's, I told myself, *Ozzie will come home and everything will be alright.* He will take care of us, all of us; his full-cheeked smile and white teeth, his neatly waxed hair a welcome sight each time he entered a room. Ozzie was the one who kept his father's once-bright spark alive. Only he could charm the town gossips with a ready smile, then say to me, "Ma, let it go. It's not you." Ozzie created the wherewithal to buy the new sedan and take his father west to see the ocean, then to Billings where Albert's twin brother was buried. Now, along with his returning body, his California girlfriend—whom none of us had met—was coming to Myra. *Fiancée*, she said over the phone. Cherry is her name.

What kind of a name is Cherry?

I WENT UPSTAIRS AND lay down on the wedding quilt, my head on the pillow I'd stuffed with chicken feathers when we lost the geese to a marauding coyote. To simply rest my eyes, to take a moment to relieve my back from the weight on my feet brought a vague but welcome comfort. My wire-rimmed glasses lay settled on the bedside table. I reached down and pulled Albert's wool army blanket over my stocking-clad legs and folded my hands, placing them on my stomach. "Herr Gott," I whispered. *I know I should be strong. My daughters have lost their big brother, and my heart* ... I couldn't finish the sentence, tears sliding from the corners of my eyes and down my face. *I need your healing salve, your ...*

Tears choked me, the sadness strangling my breath and the sobs that came up from my belly shaking my body. I tried to muffle them inside the blanket held tight against my face. Only a thin thread of faith held me in place. Pastor Kinski and Jesus had become a mirage a million miles away. Yes, release would come through tears, but every time I remembered Ozzie's face across from me the morning before he drove to Dickinson that last time, they threatened to swamp me again. His half smile, the wave in his hair, the blue of his eyes so like my own.

When I asked him about his life in California, he said, "It's different. There are more places to go and see. More jobs."

I'm sure I bristled. "What about church?" I asked.

He lowered his head, the wave in his red hair curling toward the back of his head. When he lifted his head again, he cocked it to the side and gave me a half smile. I waited for him to wink at me. Suddenly, the curve of his smile left his face. "California's not like Myra, Ma," he said. "I haven't forgotten the church or what it means to you. I know you'll be disappointed, but church isn't my priority right now."

"Priority? What does priority mean?" I asked.

"Important, Ma," he said.

"But what about Herr Gott, your heart? Your soul?"

Oscar laughed, his white teeth catching the light from the window over the sink. "My heart's fine, Ma," he said. "As far as my soul is concerned, I know I'm safe as long as I have your prayers." He took my hands in his, the trace of his military training in the rough skin around his hands, his fingers. He pulled himself into a half-raised position. "You worry too much," he said. He leaned forward and kissed my forehead.

I was so startled by his laugh when I'd asked him about Herr Gott, about his heart and soul, that an old heat burned behind my eyes and crowded out anything more I might have said. I sat there, a roiling in my stomach for all I wanted to say but hadn't, couldn't.

He rose from the table and straightened his slacks, checking the crease to make sure it was straight. "I'm going to Dickinson today. How about I bring you back a treat?"

Before I knew what happened, his back faced me and he was out the door. My unexpected tears followed him when the screen door closed behind him; that churning in my stomach and chest were there in the same way they were now. And neither the bag of lemon drops he brought me nor the licorice for Ivan would ever make that particular heaviness go away. Two days later he was on his way to Seattle by train, his Buick parked at the Texaco where Ivan could look after the new car with its gleaming blue paint. A flight to a Pacific island with a name that was hard to say, one more exotic place I'd never heard of before. That conversation at the kitchen table was the last one we had. Even today, I had to choke down my confusion and disappointment when he said, "You worry too much."

*What will you do, Herr Gott, with my son's soul now?*

THE CHILDREN'S VOICES ROSE through the heating grate in the floor of my bedroom. Louisa's squeals followed by *no*, an obvious reprimand from Little Marta.

The sides of my face were wet. *How long must I live with this eternal ache, Herr Gott?*

I fell into a dream in which it was summer. I was stooping over my garden pulling carrots and turnips. When I looked up, Ozzie stood close, holding a dead white rabbit by the ears. Even in the dream, I wondered at the strangeness of him holding the rabbit. He smiled as though he was making a joke. But the rabbit, still alive, cried, "Help me, help me."

Irene's hand on my shoulder nudged me awake. "The children are worried about you," she said. "They need to see you."

I reached for my eyeglasses, uncertain whether this was really Irene or if she lived inside the dream. As I turned toward her, her navy-blue dress appeared black in what must have been the fading light, the sun having moved off the bedroom windows and on to the south side of the house. "Why are the children worried?" I asked.

"Maybe too much death in the family, Ma," Irene said.

Her voice was so soft I strained to hear it. "Too much what?" I asked.

"Death," she repeated. She stood closer, so close I felt her warm breath against my ear, my hair.

I shook my head to clear the dream. "Let me gather myself. I'll be right down."

When I sat up, I reached toward Irene's face until I felt it between my hands. The high cheekbones and narrow jaw so unlike my own. "Thank you," I said.

"No need to thank me, Ma," Irene said. Her eyes had darkened with half-moon circles below them, her cheeks too pale. "You know how Little Marta worries about you."

"I do."

"Then come and join us." She glanced out the window at the fading light. "We miss you."

Before our eyes met again, Irene turned toward the door, a sag in her shoulders I'd never seen before. Even as I heard her footfalls on the wooden stairs, even as I sat up and lifted my legs to find my shoes, I was consoled that at least one of my children understood something about sadness too deep to explain.

INSIDE THE WARM KITCHEN, I pulled Louisa close, her still-round cheeks and baby fat a comfort, like her wonderful baby-powder smell and soft, fine hair resting under my chin while her chubby body nestled into my chest. Slowly, and with great patience, I undid her shoes so she could play with the others in the parlor.

"So glad you're here," I said to Irene, who stirred the soup at the stove. "Ivan is having a hard time."

"Ma, *I'm* having a hard time." She hesitated. "It was one thing to lose Philip. Then Pa, who'd been sick for years. But Ozzie? I'll never get over this."

Irene placed coloring books on the parlor floor where the girls had scampered and the wood-burning stove cozied the room. Ivan sat in the rocking chair, watching them but not watching them, his eyes on the oak tree outside the window.

"Marta, keep an eye on your sisters," Irene said.

Little Marta gazed up at her mother. Obviously, she knew something was wrong, but no one had told her what it was. There was a quick glance between me and my granddaughter before her mother returned to the stove.

"How is Ada taking it?" I asked from my chair at the table, my hands folded on the oilcloth. I marveled at the strangeness of watching my daughter attend to supper.

"The same as Philip and Pa. This has nothing to do with her." There was another pause. "Ma, there's something terribly wrong with Ada."

Irene wasn't the only one who had that thought. Ada often left me wondering how I'd been blessed, most likely cursed, with the likes of that girl, an alien soul crept into the family. "Just let Ada be," I said. "Think about Ozzie the last time he was home. Do you remember Pa's face when Ozzie's letter talked about the Pacific Ocean and the flash of green light when the sun goes down?"

"That doesn't make up for him dying, Ma," Irene said. "And I don't believe in Jesus the way you do. Especially these last six months. If there's a God, he's definitely abandoned this family."

"I don't want to hear that kind of talk, Irene."

"I'm sorry, Ma." She sighed. "I just don't know what I'm going to tell Mac. They were best friends. Before they were both sent to places where neither one of them belonged, all they talked about was hitchhiking to South Dakota for jobs after the war."

What was this about South Dakota? Did I always have to hear things secondhand? But I said nothing. As far as I was concerned, Mac was still a drifter, someone who came into town like other gandy dancer repairmen working for the Northern Pacific Railroad.

He just happened to land on our doorstep. "Don't tell him," I said.

I was surprised when Irene didn't scold me.

Everyone sat at the long kitchen table where, not long ago, my own brood of four once sat. My grandchildren's rosy cheeks in the warm kitchen matched the smell of their wet coats lined up on hooks beside the back door. Before long, the sound of soup being slurped filled the kitchen. The children ate their supper while Ivan stood with me at the stove. The distribution of fresh bread, a time-honored ritual, gave Ivan a position of importance. He handed each child their bread, then returned to them after he'd distributed each one a slice, helping them butter the bread if they hadn't already gobbled it down.

Even in a climate of death, the aliveness of sharing a meal overflowed with a particular warmth I first knew long ago in Russia.

Ada, who'd arrived after the others, said, "Good soup, Ma. Saved us cooking."

Irene nodded discretely toward Ada. There'd been no change in Ada's mood since news of yet another death in the family. Especially the brother who teased her but could turn around and grab her attention with the seriousness of a Dutch uncle.

"Ivan, take the children into the parlor and play a sitting game on the rug," I said. I gathered up the bowls and bread crusts. Eli, always a finicky eater, had left his soup untouched while he gorged on two thick slices of bread. With him being the only boy and now four years old, I'd have thought he'd prefer his uncle Ivan's company. But no, Eli would rather be with his girl cousins, normally scrambling into the living room with them, where a fire had been burning in the stove since morning. Today, he clung to his mother's skirt and began to cry. His fists wiped at his eyes, and his words became muffled in Ada's skirt. "I don't want to play a game," he said.

Ada pushed him away. "Don't be such a baby," she said. "Do as you're told."

I set down the dishes and wiped my hands on my apron.

"Come to Oma," I said, my fingers wiggling an invitation.

He bypassed his mother and reached toward me. Since Eli was too heavy to lift, I quickly found my chair before sitting down. I hugged him against my chest, where my warmth matched his. He began to suck his thumb, and for the moment he seemed comforted. Little Marta and Sissy and even Louisa followed their uncle Ivan into the living room. Though I would have preferred to talk without children present, Eli seemed innocent. The girls were often too eager to hang around the adult fringes and discover bits of information they imagined were secrets. They were no different than me, a much older child in Tante Ketcha's house who skulked eagerly over the upstairs living room heating grate. Like my brothers, Eli couldn't be bothered.

Eli's restless arms and legs finally settled. Irene started the kettle for the dishwater and Ada cleared the table. My first impulse was to speak in German. However, Ada, hands on her full hips, would chide me once again with "we live in America now, Ma."

"Her telegram said this Cherry person will be arriving by train Wednesday night," I said. "Which one of you will meet the ten o'clock train from Dickinson?"

"I'll go," Irene said.

"No, you stay with the kids and I'll go," Ada said.

Irene's dark look toward her younger sister was familiar. "What if Ivan came and stayed with the children so we could both go?" she asked.

Ada turned to me. "Where will she stay, Ma? Here with you?"

"There's your old room upstairs and the bed is made," I said. "You don't have room at your house."

"You're right," Irene said. "But how will we ever get Ivan home? Once he falls asleep, he's hard to wake up."

"Maybe I'll leave him home and watch the children myself. That way he can finish his lessons and go to bed before I come over," I said.

"Do you really believe he's going to go to bed and miss a big event, Ma?" Ada asked.

"He will if I tell him to."

Ada rolled her eyes. "Of course he will."

"Ada," Irene said. "Be respectful."

"Sorry, Ma," Ada said.

"It's settled then. I will watch the children. You might want to take the Radio Flyer. We don't know anything about this young woman except that she was Ozzie's betrothed."

"We'll be okay," Ada said. "With two of us, it can't be that bad."

LATER, AFTER BRUSHING AND rebraiding my hair—the long, gray strands captured in my nightly pigtail—I walked to Ozzie's medicine cabinet by the mudroom door. For a moment I seemed to be trespassing, yet I couldn't help myself. I lifted one of Ozzie's two eye cups and held it in my hand, feeling the concave bowl, the pedestal too cold. I could see him lift the clear glass to his eye and the abrupt shake of his head after he lowered the eye glass. Setting it down as gently as I could, I was reminded of the church altar where, with the same reverence, I handled the communion chalice and the wine cloths. Next, I picked up his hairbrush from the single shelf below the cabinet. Even in the kitchen's faint overhead light, the few hairs in the brush glinted, their redness so alive. I pulled a hair, then two, and rolled them between my thumb and pointer finger, feeling the texture, and what I wanted to believe was life that still lived inside those single hairs. My throat grew thick. In that moment I knew I would never be able to part with the contents of the medicine cabinet. Not the blue cylinder of talcum powder or his bay rum. Not anything that had been touched by him.

*Herr Gott, you can't mean for Ozzie to be dead. So far from home, from me. There has to be some mistake.* But some do-the-daily-work part of myself knew that it wasn't my place to question Herr Gott. Yet none of these thoughts eased the ache inside my chest, the voice that wanted to call out, *Let me die, Herr Gott. Let me die with him.*

## 1919

THE JULY DAY LEO and I went to the train station, I was seven months pregnant with Ozzie. The Spanish flu was finally ebbing. That was our hope, anyhow. First the war, then the flu. Uncle Herman and Tanta Ketcha were lost to the disease. My cousin Natalia as well. My heart was as heavy as my belly, my fear a stranglehold. Leo, my friend and confidant as well as my brother, was leaving Myra. I would never see him again. I knew that. Odessa was another life away and nothing but memories, the same as our stay at Ellis Island and, before that, the frightening midnight border and sea crossing we never thought we'd survive. Russia was changed now. Czar Nicholas II, weaker, more desperate and foolish at the same time, had been assassinated. The Soviets were in charge. Would Leo even find welcome now that Reinmar, Uncle Herman's eldest, was too old to plow? He had somehow weathered Russia's political storms, but his children had abandoned what was left of the farm in order to emigrate. My own young dreams had crashed after the incident at Battery Park. Mother and Father, long dead, would never be grandparents to my children or my children's children. Oscar remained preoccupied with acquiring land and had all but forgotten that Sunday was the Sabbath, meant for church and family and rest.

Leo's cap was pulled tight to capture his still-curly hair, though the walnut color had turned prematurely gray. Coughing into his handkerchief, he turned aside in order to check for blood or the yellow-green phlegm that prescribed his limitations on any particular day. "It's what I've always wanted," he said. "To go back."

He couldn't look at me, his eyes gazing over my head toward the ticket office. If he'd even tried, he'd have found my veil shielding eyes filled with tears. "The Great War is ended," he said.

"You have Albert now, a good life with children on the way, family close by, and the church you love." He hesitated. "It's all you ever wanted, even as a young girl, Marta."

My eyes followed the eastbound tracks. Everything he said was true, even his promise to return to Odessa. A scattered piece of newspaper danced along the tracks while overhead, blackbirds, the forever messengers of darker gods, perched high on the telegraph wires looking down on the two of us, maybe better at predicting our separate futures than we were.

"I wanted you here as my friend," I said. "To watch my children grow. To laugh and hold them on your lap." My voice dropped. "I wanted us to grow old together."

Leo laughed, though his skin was far too pale and dark shadows circled his eyes. Dr. Schneider feared the journey would be too much for his health, but Leo wouldn't hear it. He took my hands in his when he saw tears threatening to spill. He studied my fingers, the knuckles swollen and aching from pregnancy, the washboard. He reached across the divide between us and tipped my chin until our eyes met. "You've always been my best friend," he said. "That won't change."

I turned my head away, tears sliding down my cheeks. Though it was the joke he teased me with, the truth of his leaving had crept out of its hole and meant something this time it had never meant before. That love hurts. That love wounds. Love wasn't what you read in stories and heard in church services. Yes, Jesus's love heals. I did believe that. But the love between a brother and sister, two friends who had walked and run through the best and worst of their beginning and in-between, only added to the filled-in pages of too many life challenges. He might as well have asked me to lose an arm or leg. Standing beside him in the autumn wind, I couldn't say, *Yes, go with Herr Gott's blessing*. Maybe the blackbirds could, maybe that newspaper lifting in the wind and landing sideways on the tracks could, maybe the same wind sighing around the corners of the station could, but I could not.

"This isn't what I wanted for us."

"It's not what I wanted either, Marta," he said, the edge in his words building a wall. "Neither did I ask for the set of lungs I've been given."

The lungs. Yes, the lungs. A childhood of pleurisy and long stays in Odessa. Away from the farm, away from me. But I always believed Leo would return healthier and stronger than before. Each time I prayed we would sit again on the rag rug and play our stick game and checkers. Drink chocolate and eat the cookies Mother brought us, late afternoon, on the small silver tray that once belonged to Grand Mama. Now Leo seemed pale and thin, his hands nothing more than bones covered with tissue paper. Something new was happening in his lungs that the doctors couldn't or wouldn't name.

"Oscar is someone you can count on," he said. "Your husband as well."

I watched the newspaper lift in the wind. Heard the train whistle in the distance. Leo reached down to grab the handle of his satchel, the same satchel he arrived with just a few years before. He still seemed a boy at seventeen. Only his determination marked him as a man.

"Think of the war, Leo. How do you know anything is left of the farm, of Kassel? The war, the politics. How can you be sure they'll let you in the country?"

"I haven't even been to the New York sanitorium yet," he said. He smiled a helpless and giving-up smile, a smile that told me, *I have to do it my way, and I'll take my chances.*

I grabbed him around the neck and pushed as close to him as I could considering my expanded belly. I hugged him close, hoping that my hug would persuade him to stay, would lock him in Herr Gott's hold and convince him of the foolishness of leaving. The sanitorium was one thing, Odessa another. I squeezed him with everything I had; the smell of soap on his neck and something I'd not smelled before in his hair. A half day's growth of whiskers on his cheek.

When I tried to hug him tighter, he dropped his satchel. We both heard the sound of it hitting the ground, the tinkle of glass—possibly the jar of strawberry jam I'd given him. He gripped my fingers in his and loosened my hold. "Marta," he said in a voice I'd never heard before. "We're grown-up now. You have to trust me." He pulled my hands to the top of my belly, where he surrounded them with his own hands. Those four hands together on my belly was what I would remember. The back of his hat when he turned toward the conductor, the stepstool already in place and another passenger—an old farmer in patched overalls and muddy boots—in front of him. Leo's satchel with a wet spot at the side and that pensive look on his face, his hallmark, whether he was brooding or not. A quick turn on the stepstool; a blown kiss with his raised hand. The smokestack puffing steam as the wheels began their cranking motion. Blackbirds cawing at the backside of the train.

## Chapter Twenty

## Cherry Arrives

## 1945

*T*HY WILL, NOT MINE, Herr Gott, I prayed before I left my bed the next morning. After brushing my hair, I braided the length of it into a single queue that would become a circular crown until I brushed it again before bed. *Forgive me,* I pleaded over the soapy dishwater after Ivan, who was now quieter and more frequently retreated to the pigeon pen, left for school. *Everlasting Jesus, hear me,* as I pushed the broom in the mudroom and down the one step outside where the refuse landed its brown crumbs on what was left of the recent snow. *Heal my heart, Herr Gott,* when I walked through the house at bedtime to check the front door we rarely used and shoved the bolt into the back porch door like Albert used to do. *Bless me,* when I turned out the lights in the kitchen and parlor where that afternoon the ladies from my church gathered to pray with me, to drink tea and eat fresh bread with butter and strawberry jam. The pillows, now fluffed and arranged, had been returned to their place on the sofa. *I am a poor sinner, Herr Gott,* my breath blowing out the candle I used to find my way up the stairs to listen to Ivan's prayers. *Bless me, Lord,* when I removed my slippers and robe, before I pulled my braid forward in order to lie down between cold sheets. *Take this cup from me,* once I was in bed and finally let go, allowing the tears to escape into my pillow. And though I wanted to scream, *How could you, Herr Gott?* to wail, *This is your fault,* as I saw Mother do when Father, what remained of him, lay lifeless in the snow, I didn't say those words.

My curtain had been raised less than fifteen minutes when I heard Millie's timid knock on the mudroom door. She knew the outside screen door was unlocked during the day, that she only had to knock or say my name from the mudroom. Or just come in like the girls did.

I turned toward the opening door and her half smile greeted me, the first time I'd seen her since the soldiers were here the other day. She'd seen them too but had waited a day, having already experienced the tumult of sudden grief. Just seeing her standing there, timid as always, made my eyes burn with tears. Millie in her permanented hair, her tea mug in front of her, *DAVID* emblazoned into the glaze, the mug I always anticipated when she arrived at my door. I stepped away from the sink where I'd been washing breakfast dishes and trying to keep up with the day now that we were expecting out-of-town company. I wiped my hands before taking a step toward her.

We stood apart, awkward with what we knew was a river of feelings between us. We stood there, not quite knowing what to do.

"Thought maybe you could use some company today," she said.

"You saw them."

She drew back. Nodded. "I did." She set her cup down next to the sink. For just a moment, she didn't know what to do with her hands, her arms. Then her arms widened in a way they'd never done before, and she stepped toward me. Without a word, she put her arms around me, gently, holding me as though she didn't want to intrude in the same way she didn't say Ozzie's name or even ask who the men were. We'd known each other for so long that she didn't have to ask and I didn't have to say the words. In fact, they'd been to her house first. Not these men, but men like them. Her hands now splayed on my back, her small chest meeting mine, her hair beneath my chin. The smell of her recent perm lingered with its chemical odor. My friend, the sister I never had.

She pulled back. "Let's sit," she said. "I know you have tea in that pot."

Why I didn't fall into her arms and cry until I could cry no longer, I don't know. Why the tears didn't stream, I wasn't sure. Her hand on my arm, the touch so light, her eyes saying what words couldn't. We both knew she'd been where I was.

She sat in Irene's chair where she normally sat. Pulled her apron flat against her chest, her lap. Watched me pour the tea, her eyes alive in a quiet way. She already knew all there was to know.

"Thank you for waiting," I said.

When she nodded, her eyes never left mine. Her sorrow was still full of sharp edges and deep caverns. David had been her only child. I would shame myself to think that my sorrow could rival hers. That my grief was different.

I didn't need to tell her about the young soldiers. I didn't need to mention the envelope, and I certainly didn't need to tell her that the life went out of me. That my heart could never break as completely as it did then. I didn't need to say, *I don't know how I can go on without Ozzie.* She knew about the allotment, about his way with women, his generosity toward Ivan and his father. Toward me. She understood that Ozzie held a large measure of Herr Gott's radiance on any given day, though he was my greatest worry most nights. Ozzie had been my first prayer each morning and my last prayer at night.

"The girl is coming," I said. "His fiancée . . . named Cherry."

"I didn't know he was engaged."

"Neither did I until his sisters told me."

"I'm so sorry, Marta. Boys do that. Hang on to things until they think the time is right. David did that too. Not about girls but other things. So I wouldn't worry."

"But we always worry, don't we, Millie?"

"Always." She lifted her tea mug and sipped the still-hot liquid, her eyes never leaving mine. "What can I do to help?" she asked.

"Just be you," I said. "You know how I dread the whole thing."

"I do." She dropped her gaze and placed her mug on the oilcloth. "People mean well," she said. "But you can't know until you've been there."

I nodded. The tears I thought had finally dried threatened to erupt again.

"I could take the girl over to my place. We have room."

"No," I said. "She was the last person to see Ozzie alive."

Millie glanced toward the kitchen window and hesitated for a moment. "And now her dreams have ended too."

Her saying that made me realize I'd never thought about what this must be like for her. A young woman could start over again, but not without crossing the yawning river of sadness in front of us now. The grief for Ozzie would always be a stain.

"As usual, you are always so wise, Millie."

ONCE I'D SETTLED INTO my daughters' living room rocking chair, I drifted off to sleep. What woke me wasn't the sound of the door opening, heavy as it was. Neither was it the late-March storm or the sweeping wind whistling around the windowpanes. Rather, what broke my sleep's trance was Ada's loud laugh. Raucous and far too happy given the circumstances. When she turned the knob and opened the front door into the small vestibule, I was still vulnerable from sleep and the tenderness that lived inside a dream of being in Tante Ketcha's kitchen and her gentle attention when she eased away a poultice.

"Ma," Ada said, "who's watching the children?"

I immediately thought she'd been drinking beer or schnapps. And though she asked it as a joke, a flush of embarrassment filled my cheeks, my face. I quickly smoothed my dress and adjusted my glasses, hoping that, first of all, Oscar had warned this woman about my face. Second, that I hadn't been sitting with my mouth open or snoring like Albert did the minute his eyes closed. Only then did I realize I wasn't wearing a hat with its necessary netting to hide my face.

Behind Ada's red dress and heavy gray stockings, her boots shed at the door, stood a woman with extremely short hair, as dark as Albert's once was. There was nothing extraordinary or even pretty about this woman who wore eyeglasses. Dark eyes and a large nose, full lips. Her plainness was completely unexpected considering who Ozzie was, spit-polishing his shoes in the kitchen and spending a good fifteen minutes at the small vanity mirror over the side sink while he lifted his hair into a wave, then readjusted his shirt collar. This woman wore what women call *slacks*, not unlike what men wore. Uncommon in Myra and not at all what I expected from Ozzie's betrothed. Her shoes were the stylish penny loafers seen in the newest Sears, Roebuck and Company catalog. Yet nothing she wore, not her silk scarf and short coat or loafers, was adequate against the Canadian wind howling around the windows, the door. Given her outfit, I couldn't imagine what else she might have in the new-looking and oversized gray samsonite suitcase that Irene lugged into the living room. If they had to carry that suitcase all the way home in this wind after I suggested the Radio Flyer, I was glad I didn't volunteer to meet the train.

"Mrs. Gottlieb?" the woman said. She took a couple of steps toward me, where I still sat in the rocking chair. She extended her hand.

Whatever Ozzie had told her about my accident and my face, I credited her for not blanching or staring open-mouthed or turning away when her eyes met mine. She didn't seem to see the disfigurement, or she was looking past it. A response that angered me for some reason.

Except for Ada, new snow clung to their shoes and was now tracked into the living room, leaving wet spots on the hardwood floor. My daughters had no excuse for not leaving their boots by the threshold rug. Just plain laziness. Now two of them were guilty of tracking snow into the living room.

Her plainness was a contrast to the diamond on her left hand, a diamond that had to measure the size of a small hazelnut. I'd never seen stones that large, not even in the ruby and diamond brooch that once rested at the throat of Mother's dress before we left Russia. In the dim light of my daughters' living room, the diamond ring gleamed like a star. Surely Ada hadn't missed the ring either. Or Irene. In fact, the new fur-collared coat Irene wore appeared shabby and old in the presence of Ozzie's ring.

I grasped the arms of my chair to push myself forward, an ever-increasing weight having crept on since Albert died. My only solace rested in the baked goods I made each day, the soups meant to keep us alive. Now my movements proved awkward and clumsy. By putting my hands on the rocking chair and bracing myself, I stood at last, not unlike my brother Oscar. I reached toward the Cherry woman's hand, her cold fingers and hands as ordinary as my hands now lay flat against my warm, fat palm. This strange American custom of shaking hands compared to a Russian embrace. We dropped our hands after brief contact, Cherry pulling her arms to her side. I clasped both hands together in front of my too-large stomach. Though I was smiling, I couldn't help but cluck my tongue. "You are different from the way my Ozzie described you."

Cherry stepped back. "How did he describe me?" She blushed when she attempted to smile, then lowered her eyes. "Maybe I don't want to know. Ozzie was quite a storyteller."

"Indeed," I said.

Ada, not usually the responsible one, surprised me by saying, "Let me take your coat." She reached toward the stranger to lift the coat from her shoulders or at least help her out of the sleeves.

But Cherry—the name likely another California invention—shook her head. "I'll keep it on. I can't believe how cold it is."

Ada dropped her arms. "Of course, North Dakota isn't known for its dry, mild climate."

Irene rubbed her hands together. "Can I fix anyone a cup of tea?"

"Coffee, I would like coffee if you have it," the Cherry woman said.

"Won't coffee keep you up?" I asked.

When Cherry laughed, her lower front teeth appeared crooked in a way I didn't see at first. "It actually helps me sleep," she said. "I always drink coffee until bedtime."

All of the churchwomen, women who shared the same customs, who tended to be German or Russian like me, their homes like mine, never drank coffee after breakfast, if they drank it at all. We preferred tea, always had.

"Will instant do?" Irene asked. "I'm afraid we're down to the bottom of our coffee rations if you hope for coffee at breakfast."

I glanced at the dining room clock. It was already ten thirty. "Perhaps it's too late," I said. "I would think bedrest would be better than coffee after such a long trip."

"Not at all," Cherry said. "I'm something of a night owl. Besides, with the time change, it's still early evening." Her laugh was nervous. "Truth is, I haven't been able to sleep since Ozzie..."

Her eyes filled with sudden tears.

"The time change," Ada said quickly. "I almost forgot."

"It's really eight-thirty in California," Cherry said. She sighed, perhaps glad Ada rescued her from what might be more emotion than any of us wanted then.

Irene glanced at me, her eyebrows raised. "Ma, would you like me to walk you home? We can have Cherry bunk on the couch tonight," she said. Before I could respond, she continued, "I'll bring her things over to your house in the morning."

This unexpected change of plans, considering how hard I'd worked to get the girls' old room in order, irritated me. I hardly knew what to say. It wasn't even about the room. I was anxious to know something about my Ozzie within the quiet of my own home. To better know this strange and unknown woman he'd chosen as his fiancée. She was, after all, the last one of us to see him alive.

I said nothing, trying to adjust to the change in plan, though I felt resentful toward Irene. At the same time, I had no interest in staying up until midnight to accommodate a stranger. Besides, she should be grateful we'd gone to such lengths to include her in our family as well as the church gathering. If I lost this woman to my daughters and their modern ways, I might never have her alone to myself.

"Of course," I said. "I can't leave Ivan alone any longer, and the evening wind promises to blow more fiercely as the night goes on. One night on your sofa won't hurt."

"Thank you, Mrs. Gottlieb," Cherry said. She stepped forward. "I so appreciate all the trouble you and your family have gone to in order to make me feel welcome. As you can imagine, I'm pretty wound up from the train ride." She glanced from me to my two daughters, then around the living room of their small house. "I didn't expect it to be quite so cold. You must forgive me if hot coffee sounds good right now."

"Not to worry," I said. I took the woman's freezing hands in mine, the skin of a worker, the bones solid. "We'll have plenty of time to visit. Isn't that right, Irene? Ada?"

THE LATE SNOW WITH its huge flakes had come suddenly, falling all day and layering over the promise of spring. Snow was still falling when Irene insisted on walking with me the four blocks back home. She was silent during the walk until she grabbed hold of my outer screen door, which had never been replaced by the storm door at summer's end. Irene then grabbed hold of my coat lapels and brushed my cheek with a goodnight kiss. "We'll bring Cherry by as soon as we get the kids up and fed," she said. "I think I'll take Ivan's Radio Flyer. That girl brought enough in her suitcase to stay through the summer. That's one thing she has in common with Ozzie. Both of them are clotheshorses."

I clicked my tongue. "Coffee at night, now all that luggage, but no warm clothes. She's not what I expected," I said.

"She is a bit of a surprise," Irene said. "A disappointment even?"

"You could say that."

Inside the house, the chill indicated that the living room fire had died down. I removed my rubbers and shoes in the mudroom and stuck my feet into felt slippers. There might be just enough embers that a stick or two of kindling and a scoop of coal could get us through the night. At least the upstairs bedrooms would be warm. I kept my gloves on while I scooped the coal; the small shovel always threatened to blacken anything it touched. I glanced at the kitchen table where Ivan's homework lay ready for inspection. Good, obedient boy, he'd done it all. I hoped he'd been asleep a couple of hours. It was close to midnight and the short night would make it hard for both of us to get out of bed in the morning. Certainly, my daughters would be in no hurry.

I shuffled toward the narrow stairs and pulled myself up toward one of the three bedrooms. I couldn't help but smile. This fancy California girl had probably never used an outhouse. From what Ozzie said, everyone in California had indoor toilets, something you only found in the Dickinson courthouse and newer houses like the one Ada and Irene lived in. This woman Cherry wouldn't like that trudge down the icy path, only to sit on the cold wooden seat. Just the thought of her peeling off a page of the Sears, Roebuck and Company catalog made me smile. We might not be California, but we were still civilized.

## Chapter Twenty-One

### Before the Funeral

## 1945

THE NEXT MORNING, I woke to an even whiter world that somehow matched my sadness and felt deep as the spring snow. This was a world Ozzie would never see again. Even though the snow had settled and started to melt into tiny rivulets between the grooves of displaced gravel, I'd so hoped for a sign of spring. Some announcement of hope. The snow, pristine as it was, would soon be spattered by what few cars drove the rutted roads in Myra and, more predictably, the horse-drawn carts grinding through mud. What would this Cherry woman think? Ozzie said the sun shined twelve months a year in California. The way he talked, I'd expected to see that far country someday. Ozzie had already taken Albert there the last time he was home. When I asked Albert what he thought, he said, "Too many people and cars." That made sense.

After all, that's where the ships and airplanes were being built for the war. His final verdict: "It's not home."

Ivan rubbed his eyes when he came into the kitchen. He scraped a chair across the linoleum and sat across from me where I sipped my tea. "Do I have to go to school today, Ma?"

"Of course you have to go to school."

"But I want to meet Ozzie's lady, Miss Hendrix. Didn't you say that's her name?"

"You'll have all day tomorrow and the next day after the funeral to get to know Miss Hendrix."

*Funeral* was a too-common word in our household. And now, with Albert gone and Ozzie as well, I didn't know how long I'd be able to stay in the house. Sick as he was, Albert hadn't worked for at least four years before he died. Still, he received a pension. Not so for widows. My own Ozzie had paid for repairing the roof and the back stoop. His allotment covered the rent to my brother. Though we needed it, I never asked for a new fence. The possibility of that conversation ended with Ozzie's death. I couldn't ask my brother for more than he'd already done. On top of which, he provided us with beef and pork, a quarter sheep now and then when Millie was able to take me there to get it. I didn't expect Oscar to make me and Ivan his new charity. Irene and Ada's house wasn't an option. It barely accommodated them. Irene slept with Marta in the basement while Ada and her boy Eli had the one upstairs bedroom; the two younger girls slept on either end of the sofa except when they had company, like last night. Then the rag rug on the living room floor became their bed.

I hadn't told my two daughters about my situation, not wanting to worry them. If worse came to worse, Ivan and I could always move back to Oscar's farm, though from the looks of the mess there, it would take some doing. I now understood why Irene asked about Philip's allotment ending. Mine from Ozzie would likely end as well.

"School will help pass the time," I said to Ivan. "Besides, you'll learn something, and maybe someday you'll be the one who takes your old mother to California. I could use a little warmth in my bones right now."

THE FUNERAL WAS SCHEDULED for Saturday, Pastor Kinski's idea. That way Ozzie's childhood friends who worked the farms could come. We had three days to get ready. The church ladies would prepare the food, and knowing them, it would be bountiful. Ivan would be out of school and able to help. Right then I needed to start the kuchen dough as soon as Ivan left for school. Prune kuchen would make a nice treat with coffee when Ada and Irene finally brought the Cherry woman to my house. Besides, kneading dough gave my hands something to do, my mind a purpose, especially since my eyes were redder than they'd ever been.

First the dough, then the filling. Cottage cheese since I didn't have cream cheese, a richer flavor anyhow. I'd make one prune and one peach kuchen, two kuchen by eleven o'clock. Enough sugar to sweeten the filling, though I'd have to draw on rations I'd squirreled away. I'd never understood how those girls could make so much candy. Knowing my daughters, they'd have just finished breakfast when they'd come strolling in for tea and pastry. They'll be happy to find me baking and the kitchen smelling of yeast, the windows steamed.

Not long ago, Ozzie would have been standing across from me in the kitchen. That far corner in front of the small washbasin, the shelf below the medicine cabinet holding his eye cups and shaving brush; a soap dish, the comb, and lanolin bottle right where he left them. His hairbrush. From where I stood at the table, I could see the glint of red strands rising above the hairbrush, where they caught the cold springtime sun as it came through the small window. I'd never known a man to take so long with his morning toilet, humming some song to himself, then every once in a while catching my eye and giving me a wink that probably made the girls fall in love with him. Certainly, every girl in his Myra high school class was dazzled by him, the younger girls as well.

On impulse, I walked over to the small sink. Like a trespasser, my fingers shook when I again picked up his hairbrush. The rounded handle seemed awkward in my hand. The boar's hair stiff and black, with Ozzie's red hairs caught in the bristles. My pointer finger and thumb were timid as they pulled yet another red hair from the brush. I held it toward the facing window and watched the red catch fire in light reflected off the new snow. I lifted the brush to smell the bristles and there, hidden inside the bristles, rose the smell of Ozzie's lanolin and the faintest odor of bay rum. For a moment I was caught between feeling I had the body of my son in my hands and a sudden surge that was working its way up from deep in my belly. If I stood there any longer, I'd surely lose the gathering well of tears. I suddenly needed to find a sack or box or bowl in which to put these precious things—the talcum powder and bay rum, his eye cups and hairbrush. I wanted no one to touch them. They were mine. All that was left of Ozzie. I rummaged through the kitchen cabinets, bending down under the sink and behind the curtained pantry until I found a never-used mixing bowl. As carefully as I could, I scooped his eye cups, his brush and shaving soap, his lanolin and comb, everything that had touched his hands or his body in any way into the bowl. With more energy than I'd have imagined, the swell in my chest pushed me upstairs faster than I'd have thought possible. Once in my bedroom, I lowered myself to my knees, the flour barely wiped from my fingers. Bending down, I scooted the glass bowl under my bed. No one except the children would find them now. I'd forbid them to go into my room. These things were mine. Now and always, he was my Ozzie.

# Chapter Twenty-Two

## The Houseguest

## 1945

THE DOUGH HAD BEEN rising for an hour when I removed the flour-sack towel and punched down the elastic mound, the smell of yeast filling the kitchen. One more rising and I could roll out the dough, being careful to leave a raised edge so the filling wouldn't run and spill out. A kettle of cabbage rolls simmered at the back of the woodstove in case they wanted to stay for lunch. Fresh-baked dinner rolls. My grandchildren, unfortunately, never ate at a regular time, so I was prepared for whenever they came to visit. Had I been too lenient with my daughters? Didn't I demand enough in terms of help around the house? It was easier to do the work myself than depend on them with their bickering, pinching each other's arms or grabbing at one another's hair. Their one-year age difference only made matters worse, on top of which, Ada always managed to need the outhouse when it was her turn to wash dishes.

Ozzie. What would I do without him? It wasn't just the rent money. Or remembering him at the kitchen sink, or his laughter ringing from the back door those times he came unseen into the kitchen and startled me. Laughter that still lived inside these walls. Here at the kitchen table, his warm hand would lay on my arm. The weekly phone calls, like clockwork at noon on Saturdays when I waited next door by the phone at Millie's before Ozzie paid for me to have my own phone. "Not to worry, Ma. I'll take care of it," he'd said to any request I made of him. A consolation through Albert's awful last days and, I'm ashamed to say, the relief when Albert died.

My heart broke to think Ozzie's body had just arrived at Beck's Funeral Home in Dickinson. His death the last thing I expected. Standing at the sink washing dishes, I could still feel his small, warm body against my breasts as I cooed him to sleep all those years ago, standing where I now stood. The same window. Pulling back the flannel blanket just to see those tiny fingers with their sharp fingernails grab at the fabric, his fine red hair covered with a small cap to keep him warm inside the house. Nearly invisible eyelashes hiding his blue eyes. The comfort of holding him close and, yes, a joy that still filled my arms when I looked out at the snow piled around the pigeon cage, the outhouse, the alley.

I almost hated this girl, Cherry. Hated her because she was the last one to hold my son. Because she came from somewhere I've never been. Because she wasn't my Ozzie. And, though Herr Gott would punish me for thinking these things, I hated her for coming to our town.

I lifted my apron to my eyes, afraid I'd already rubbed them raw. I didn't want the girls to see me this way. Not the grandchildren, especially Little Marta, who was so sensitive. And not this Cherry person either. *Cherry*—not a Christian name. Was she named for a fruit or a tree? Would I call a girl *almond*? Or *peaches*? It wasn't right. Not the name. Not the girl. How plain she was with her eyeglasses and short, short hair. Her suntanned skin. I couldn't imagine who her people might be. You had to wonder what kind of person drank coffee late at night. Was that the way they did things in California? For sure, Ozzie didn't find this girl in church.

My back faced the door when the shrill voices of children cried out, "Oma, Oma," and the screen door slammed behind them. I'd barely turned around when Louisa grabbed at my legs, my apron, and for a moment I thought I might fall against the hot stove. "Children, let me sit down so I can hug you."

The three women trailed behind, Ada in slacks, though she knew I disapproved, and Irene in the plain wool coat. Out of the corner of my eye, I spotted Irene's new coat with the fox collar buttoned tight around this Cherry person's neck, unprepared as she was for the cold, the snowdrifts, and slush. In fact, one of the first thing Cherry said last night was, "I never dreamed of coming to North Dakota until I met Ozzie. I couldn't imagine anyone living here. Maybe Eskimos." She laughed, but her laugh was awkward and self-conscious. Sudden embarrassment had filled her cheeks.

"Sit down, everyone," I said. "I have hot water for Postum and tea. The kuchen just came out of the oven."

Irene sidled next to me. "Ma, Postum's not real coffee."

I stared at her. "It's what your Pa and I always drank."

Irene slipped me a small jar of coffee grounds. "Here. Use this."

Out of a cloth grocery sack, Irene lifted her percolator and placed it on the kitchen counter.

"But how?" I asked.

"I'll show you," she whispered. "Just take the kuchen to the table and ask Ada to get milk for the children. I'll fix the coffee."

My face felt hot. "This woman is a guest in my house; she'll drink what we drink." Only after I said the words did I realize I'd spoken too loudly.

"Ma," Irene said. She stepped closer to me, her head down. "She's not one of us. She doesn't understand that you don't like to spend your ration coupons on coffee."

"But why does she need to understand?"

"She's our guest, and she was Ozzie's intended," Irene said. "We can do it in memory of him."

I had hoped to get through the day without crying in front of my daughters and especially in front of a stranger. I looked past Irene's shoulder at the children reaching across the table for their slice of kuchen just as Ada intercepted Louisa's arm from spilling her milk. In another three days, the funeral and company would be over and this Cherry person would be on a train back to California. The insurance policy Ozzie took out before he left would go with me to Mr. Kreutzer at the bank. Not something Irene and Ada needed to know or worry themselves about. I'd already counted on the fact that Miss Cherry Hendrix didn't know she was co-beneficiary. Mr. Kreutzer and I would straighten that out.

I stepped away from the stove and left Irene alone to fix the coffee. "How do you like the kuchen, Cherry?"

"Quite delicious," she said. Her mouth was partially full when she nodded at me, her glasses glinting where they caught the light from the kitchen window. "I'd get fat if I ate like this all the time."

At the mention of fat, I backed away and folded my hands across my stomach. Of course I was fat. But I didn't need a stranger to remind me.

Ada and Irene always teased me about my girth. That, and sometimes they called me Marta the Martyr, mostly when they thought I couldn't hear. But I'd gained weight over the years, especially after Ivan was born. Except for my mother, Katerina, all the women, especially those like Tante Ketcha, carried extra weight. *Against the cold*, we always said. Albert never complained, skinny as he was and even thinner as he grew increasingly ill. Said I kept him warm at night. Even Dr. Schmidt said that being fat was a sign of good health. Yet all my children, with the exception of Ada, who put on weight after Philip died, were thin as birch trees in winter. So why was I embarrassed?

"A little more weight might be good for you," I said to Cherry. "Insulate you against the cold. That's what Albert always said."

Cherry's eyebrows arched above her black-rimmed glasses and she smiled halfheartedly. "Ozzie told me you might say that."

The room became silent, and even the children stopped talking. Just the mention of Ozzie's name, especially as a joke on me, knifed through my chest until I had to turn my face to the stove.

I grabbed Irene's arm. "I need to lie down," I said. "Please help the children to some cabbage rolls."

"Ma," she whispered. "She was just making a joke. Trying to fit in."

"There are no jokes where Ozzie's concerned," I said. Untying my apron, I looked down at my gray slippers, the felt now absorbing the tears as they fell. In that moment all the accumulated sadness, starting with Philip's death, swelled inside my chest. I left the kitchen before I started to wail like Mother did the day she found Father in the snow outside the barn, his blood splattered against the white drifts and the barn's new pine walls. A wailing that went on for days.

Saturday, the day of the funeral, I woke in early darkness to the howl of another March blizzard. Outside the bedroom window there was no light. I could barely see the snow except as it swirled around the darkened light pole, the flakes a blur midair. Inside the cold bedroom, my breath carried the vapor of my body's warmth while my feet stabbed toward the rag rug in search of my slippers. The house was far too cold. The coals I had so carefully banked last night must have gone out. Now I faced the awful prospect of relighting the fire.

The round face of the bedside clock said five o'clock, my usual rising time when the children were still home and needed to get ready for school. The honey bucket, likely full, meant a dreaded trip to the outhouse. I gathered Albert's wool robe around me, realizing that Cherry must be freezing in Irene and Ada's old bedroom.

At the top of the stairs, I stood outside the girls' bedroom door with a heavy quilt folded across my arm. When I peeked inside, Cherry's sound breathing told me she was asleep. Did I dare spread the blanket over her? Maybe she'd continue to sleep until I had the house warmed. From inside the partly open door, I heard a whispered hello.

I jumped back. "Thought you might like an extra blanket," I said, my voice uncertain and hoarse from the night's sleep.

"Come in," Cherry said.

"I didn't mean to bother you."

"I can't sleep anymore."

"Too cold?"

Since there was no response, I moved forward into the dark room. "Here," I said. "I was on my way downstairs to light the fire."

I spread the blanket across the faint outline of her body. "This will help you stay warm until I get the fire lit and the teakettle on."

"Thank you," Cherry said, her whisper full of sleep.

"It takes an hour," I said. "At least the kitchen will be warm. Come down when you're ready."

I backed away and started to leave the door cracked open. "I left you a warm robe at the foot of the bed."

My feet felt weighted when I descended the narrow stairs. I snapped on the light beside the rocking chair to discover the woodbox was empty. No kindling and no coal to start the fire. Not a shred of newspaper or even a catalog page or two to help. Must have used it all or forgot last night. While I always banked the fire before bed, the living room was now as cold as the upstairs bedrooms. Surely something would be stored in the woodbox near the back door.

This was not the start I wanted on the day of Ozzie's funeral. *Maybe you, Herr Gott, are punishing me for too many prayers begging relief from sorrow.* "You'd best not feel too sorry for yourself," I said aloud. "Worse things could happen."

But what could be worse?

The light from the living room floor lamp extended its circle into the dark kitchen, darker now that a blizzard enveloped the house. Ivan must have brought in wood for the kitchen stove after supper, because the stack of short-cut logs and scrap wood cut up for kindling gave me hope. I plodded into the kitchen, my body growing heavier as I imagined the day: a half-lit church, the organ music, everyone waiting with their backs to me when I walked down the aisle. I'd already practiced keeping my eyes on Pastor Kinski when Albert died.

No one should live with this much death. I'd said as much to Millie.

I lit the newspaper for the woodstove, the kindling piled on top, then the larger wood pieces. Having filled the teakettle before bed last night, it was a matter of waiting for the heat to rise from invisible flames inside the cast-iron stove. Hopefully there would be no other surprises today, outside of the cold air playing around my ankles when I bent to retrieve more wood.

The window revealed a first glimmer of gray light lifting into the sky against the white cover of snow. Mornings like this, I recalled the night our barn burned in Russia; flames rising outside Father and Mother's upstairs bedroom window. The shouts of horsemen carrying torches that awakened Father, then Mother. By the time Father pulled back the heavy drape, the barn was already gone. The flames leaping so high that the wild and frantic shriek of animals kept rising from the yard where they'd been set loose, then lost in the blackness surrounding the barn.

The blizzard had already blanketed the path to the outhouse. Best to make the tea and put on rubber boots before going out. There would be no quiet moments again until the house darkened and everyone went to bed.

Before I even heard Cherry's sandals on the stairs, I'd brushed and braided my hair at Ozzie's small kitchen sink. I'd already carried a small basin of hot water from the stove to wash up. It was impossible to stand in front of the mirror, winding my long braid atop my head, without sensing him there with the lingering smell of his bay rum.

I then put on Albert's heavy parka and my galoshes. Carried two empty pails from the mudroom to the water pump. But after all that effort, I'd forgotten to put on gloves. Without thinking, I grabbed the handle on the pump, again forgetting everything I knew about dangerous winter freezes. My heart was beating too fast when I lifted the handle as high as it would go. For the moment, I was relieved that the pump wasn't frozen. I quickly filled one bucket, then the other. But when I went to take my hand off the pump handle, I felt the tearing at my skin. My hand was now frozen to the handle. *Herr Gott, what have I done?* Out in the freezing cold, my nightgown flapping around my legs, and no one to help me. Ivan upstairs and still asleep. But what could he do? I didn't have a scoop to pour ice-cold water on my hand. There was nothing to do but stand there and pray that my blood would warm my fingers before too long so I could release the handle. Foolish, foolish woman.

Once inside, I stood beside the stove and quickly pulled my housedress over my head, finally warming after my forgetfulness. Next, I set up the coffee, trying to remember what Irene had told me. "If nothing else, fill the pot with hot water and throw the coffee on top. Just make sure you don't let it boil too long. It's not tea, Ma."

While the coffee brewed at the back of the stove, I skimmed the cream off a quart of milk and placed it in my best white crockery pitcher, the one normally used for syrup. I set a place for my guest with a tatted napkin and the last of Mother's bone china teacups.

"Good morning," Cherry said. Her long silk robe reached to the floor, its full sleeves reminding me of pictures of Japanese kimonos. That flimsy material couldn't possibly be warm enough.

"You didn't like the other robe?" I asked.

"Thank you, but I'll be fine in this." She lifted the shoulders of her robe to adjust them. "It's warmer than it looks."

Cherry's red-painted toenails appeared naked outside the open slippers that held her feet in place.

"Would you like some warm slippers?"

She nodded shyly. "Yes, please."

"Let me get your coffee first."

I'd been mentally preparing for this moment. Irene insisted that I keep it simple. "Put out the bowl of sugar, Ma," she'd said. "The cream pitcher, a cup, and a spoon." She spoke to me as though I'd never known nice things.

Cherry pulled out her chair, the sound grating as it dragged across the linoleum. "Sorry," she said, glancing up at me.

I poured the coffee into the paper-thin cup and arranged the spoon on the saucer. Albert and I, the whole family, had drunk our tea from heavy mugs for so long that the lighter weight in my hand felt unsteady. I circled the table, afraid of stumbling before I placed the cup, only two-thirds full as Irene instructed, in front of a woman who hadn't bothered to comb her hair, whose night-gown—a frilly thing with lace peeking out of the robe's opening—wasn't enough to keep anyone warm. The temperature read eleven below zero outside the kitchen window. I reminded myself that this was Ozzie's fiancée. I'd probably never see her again.

"Thank you." Cherry glanced at me when I set the cup and saucer in front of her. "Ozzie always described you as thoughtful."

Just hearing Ozzie's name, especially from someone who'd replaced me in Ozzie's heart, threatened the flood I'd been hanging on to, my heartbeat racing and the heat in my face giving me away.

"My son was a generous man."

My tone said more than my words. I wanted to remind this woman that the flesh-and-blood man Cherry knew came from me, from this body that moved away from the table now. *Ozzie's sisters and his younger brother were here long before you,* I wanted to say. *Who do you think you are, coming here and expecting sympathy from me? We are not fancy California people. We may sound a little backward, the old German creeping into our words, but we were once his whole life. And don't forget that he will lie forever in his grave beside his father and next to the place that is reserved for me. We came into the world together and we will leave the same way.*

I gazed at the top of the young woman's head where her hair parted at the crown. Why was I so angry with her? What had she done to me other than love my son? What would Pastor Kinski say about the way I was treating her?

Cherry's eyes remained on her coffee, where fine specks of coffee grounds floated on the surface. She had yet to pour the cream, and her spoon remained poised on the saucer. She just sat there, staring at the coffee cup.

Irene had said, "An egg, Ma. It will settle the grounds to the bottom." The egg. I forgot the egg.

I reached into the cupboard and retrieved the kuchen I hid yesterday from the children. Removing the dish towel from the top of the pastry, I set the rounded sweet on the table. With my butcher knife, I cut the kuchen into eight somewhat even slices, leaving one slice half again as big for me. "Would you like some kuchen?" I asked.

"No, thank you. Coffee's fine."

Unsure what to do, I sat down. "Here," I said, pushing the plate holding the kuchen across the table.

Her head remained bent while tears fell into her lap. Inside her flimsy robe and nightgown, her hair uncombed and her glasses steaming, she wept while her coffee grew cold. This was the same woman who had shared caresses and closeness with my Ozzie.

"Now, now," I said, pursing my lips and leaning closer toward her. "I will make you some fine eggs from my own chickens. You will feel better once you eat."

The room remained silent except for the clock ticking on Ozzie's shelf. Then, slowly, with my clean handkerchief pulled from my sleeve, I allowed my hand to creep across the kitchen table made for ten, the worn oilcloth faded from too many washings, the rose design nearly lost in the cream-colored background. There was probably no way to comfort this woman. Just the same, I held the handkerchief and pressed it toward her hand. When she took it from me, her fingers felt ice-cold.

"I'm so sorry," she said. "I shouldn't have come."

"Of course you should have come. You were Ozzie's beloved."

I couldn't say the words *you are family*. Instead, I scooted my chair closer to the table. "We need to be together."

My swallowed tears began to push up inside my chest. Against my will, my fat fingers held the long, much softer hands of the younger woman. Hands that Ozzie held, hands that held him.

Two years ago, Ozzie sat where Cherry sat now, his hair combed and shaped into his usual pompadour. He was too old and worldly-wise for me to ask why he needed to leave, even for a day, two, maybe a week. His shirt lay open at the throat and a small tuft of red hair rose toward his Adam's apple. His marine ring circled his finger, the one hand resting on top of the other hand, the fine orange hair curling along his fingers. He gave me a crooked smile. He knew I wanted to ask where and why he was leaving, but I wouldn't. "Ma," he said. "You worry too much."

"May Herr Gott always protect you, my son," I said.

Ozzie's face lost the smile he flashed so easily. "Like I said, you worry too much."

My mind's eye held Ozzie in his Marine Corps uniform, the whole family dazzled by the insignia on his sleeve and how handsome he looked. No one, least of all his father, questioned him when Ozzie said he needed to drive to Dickinson on a Saturday afternoon and wouldn't be home until Monday. When I tried to talk to Albert, his only response was, "He's a grown man. Leave him be." Twenty-five months later, even Jesus couldn't save him.

I rose from the table and reached for Irene's percolator. When I walked around the table to pour more coffee into her cup, the cup was already full.

Cherry turned her tear-filled eyes toward me and removed her glasses. She wiped them on the hem of her silk robe. Her weak smile faced me. "Eggs might be good."

I nodded. Half smiled. My eyes in hers for, really, the first time. The brown centers so layered with tears. Her own half smile, trying to be brave. Like I was trying to be brave.

Turning, I took her untouched coffee back to the woodstove, where it would remain on the warming shelf. As I pulled my frying pan down from the hook over my head, I couldn't stop thinking that her lips were the lips my Ozzie kissed, her folded shoulders the ones he held; hers was the hair he smoothed. This strange and oddly misplaced girl was the last link I had to my now-dead son.

## Chapter Twenty-Three

### Ozzie's Funeral

### *1945*

EXCEPT FOR SINGLE CANDLES in each window, the church remained dark, the light outside unable to penetrate the tar paper covering the stained glass. This morning on the radio, Sheriff Nelson in Dickinson once again announced total blackout restrictions. A big door sign saying the same thing greeted me when I entered the church. No lights and now no flowers for the vases. The March blizzard had taken care of that. Instead, the Ladies Guild had placed baskets of pine boughs on the altar and more candles than I'd ever seen at a service. That had to be Mabel Metzger's doing, her own son Raymond, Ozzie's classmate, never returned from Normandy. In truth, every day the town was weighed down by winter, by war, and by death.

I insisted we go early, anything to avoid the pats on my arms and shoulders; the words of condolence if I lingered too long near the entryway. I didn't want to explain the strange young woman who accompanied us until after the service. Arriving early made it easier to slip into one of the front pews with my family on either side of me and the rest of the congregation invisible behind us.

My one black dress with its white lace collar had seen too much wear this past year. When I stepped into the Dickinson JCPenney to choose the dress a few years ago, a dress bought for Albert's and my twenty-fifth wedding anniversary, I had no idea it would become my funeral dress.

Irene sat on my left with Little Marta between us. Ada on my right, their respective children beside them. At my direction, Ivan sat between Irene's two youngest. Otherwise, they would pinch each other or make faces during the service. Cherry sat on the aisle beside Louisa. She was, after all, Ozzie's intended. Even if he'd lived and breathed beside her, this church's curiosity about her would overshadow any reason for being here. Ozzie was, after all, a benefactor to many who sat silently waiting for Pastor Kinski to appear and adjust his rumpled robes before he started the service.

Outside, the wind howled around the sills and pushed against the stained glass, a reminder that winter hadn't passed. Likely, Pastor turned on the heat this morning, but the pews took more than two hours of a coal furnace to heat the too-cold wood. Drafts crept along the floor, and as the church doors opened and closed, more freezing air invaded what little warmth we held.

When the organ music began with "The Old Rugged Cross," everyone stood. Today, in front of another pine casket, I faced a single bouquet—must have been three feet across—of white roses from Oscar. Must be Gardner's in Dickinson, roses flown from California at great expense, no doubt. My brother said he was too crippled to attend the service. A disappointment since he was my son's mentor and namesake.

Pastor Kinski entered, his eyes momentarily settling on me before he sat behind the lectern. Just seeing him reminded me that we were all young once, all of us emigrated from somewhere else. Tears clouded my eyes and my throat closed off. I was being tossed inside a cyclone of sadness. When I pulled my handkerchief out of my sleeve, Irene reached for my hand. Without knowing, she squeezed too tight with her long, thin fingers, intertwining our hands until my wedding ring dug into my fingers. A hand rested on my shoulder, a squeeze I recognized as Millie's. She must be right behind me. Both of us with our tea mugs at my kitchen table early yesterday before the girls brought the Cherry woman to my house. Today, there would be food enough to take care of us for an entire week. I turned in the pew and Henry, Millie's husband and Albert's best friend, sat beside her. He stared straight ahead, his cheeks red, the capillaries broken across his large German nose. This was probably the last place he wanted to be. Albert's funeral was bad enough.

I pulled my coat closer. The pews behind me filled with people whispering and adjusting their coats before taking their seats. The weighted smell of wet wool and the clomp of heavy boots against the wooden floors accompanied the organ music. Whether in the field or church, those boots were the only shoes most men owned. The women, likewise, had one pair of shoes. Albert was one of the few to own wing-tipped Sunday shoes, thanks to Ozzie. I was saving them for Ivan.

The funeral program with Ozzie's picture in full uniform rustled in the many hands. These were my people, and, like me, every one of them in my generation was an immigrant. An immigrant with all the same fears and longing I'd had. They, too, had squeezed through the lines and barricades of Ellis Island. They'd stuck out their tongues before their eyelids were pulled up and back, perhaps wondering if they would be the family member for whom the white-coated authorities shook their heads no before marking their backs with an X in white chalk. Yes, fear was the one thing we could count on; our futures uncertain, like the wind here blowing a strange but familiar warning, and the ground too hard to bury the dead. We'd traveled to a life of ham hock soup and morning gruel, the wheat our greatest wealth.

The church lifted up *Abba lieber Vater*, our beloved father. There were the whispered greetings to one another, the shushing of a child. For the moment, I was comforted. Though Ozzie had seen the world differently and spoke of moving to warmer climates— of Ivan attending college in cities I'd never heard of, miles away from the wind shrieking outside the windows—these people, the people in this small church, were Little Russia to me.

Numb with sadness and worry, I dared not look around but kept my eyes straight ahead. I was again carried back to a dark and moonless night with only the trees' shadows lining the road to guide us. The driver's quiet *click-click* to the horses, Father's four best Arabians, meant to take us through the night to Odessa. I huddled against Mother, a bearskin robe encasing us from head to toe and Mother still in her Sunday dress with the high-necked collar, her pearls, and her diamond earrings Father brought from Kiev when he went to plead a farmer's case before the czar. All Mother's other valuables were bound and hidden around her breasts, Father's gold coins safe in the hem of his greatcoat. Never during that long night, when the wolves echoed their cries to one another in the forested distance and every branch on the road made me grip my Easter egg bundle tighter, did I imagine this would be my destiny. Death was the culprit then, and here it was again. That night, I feared a soldier's saber would find its way through my chest, where new breasts had barely sprouted beneath my camisole. My brother Oscar hunched beside Father on top with the driver while Leo cowered under the bear robe on the other side of Mother, our feet crowded with carpetbags and satchels, bedding we'd grabbed to keep us warm.

Millie coughed in the pew behind me, perhaps a signal to Henry, who had started to snore. They had their story. We all had a story about leaving the front doors of our homes behind and the first flutter in our stomachs at the good fortune of seeing the Grand Lady in New York's harbor before stepping onto New York's wharf in Battery Park for the first time. No one could foretell what came after.

"Rock of Ages" resonated throughout the church, the organ's bass notes rattling the windows. I didn't have to see her to know Maisy sat in front of the organ in her feathered hat and spectacles, playing songs her fingers knew by rote. Everyone stood when Pastor rose from his chair beside the pulpit, his vestments falling lopsided across his chest. I gripped my handkerchief. The church, the organ, and the ritual were all too familiar. Even Agnes, across the aisle in her fancy hat with the pheasant feather, dabbed at her eyes at least once.

I suddenly wanted these people gone. It didn't matter that they were friends and family, that they, too, were shocked by Ozzie's death and the now-pasty body inside the casket before us, or the fact that a stranger had come among us who knew Ozzie in ways no one else could. I held the handkerchief tight, the sweat from my fingers soaking into the tatted cotton until the handkerchief became a wet rag in my hand. I wanted to be alone with my son, not this skin-and-bone carcass painted too pink by Mr. Chalmers and his wife. The bow tie crooked and the casual jacket all we could find in his closet, his suits and good clothes shuffled off to some small apartment in California that none of us would ever see.

I wanted no organ music, no pastor, not Ozzie's grieving brother and sisters, no flowers or grandchildren, no whispers and coughing, no sniffles—Herr Gott, no sniffles. None of that. I should be able to have my son to myself, to throw my arms across the casket and cry as loudly as I wanted, to scream at Herr Gott if need be. To have that privilege, that right. In private. Not grief's public display. Not to be pawed over by well-meaning friends and neighbors who would take my rounded hands in their fat, worn fingers, as though my hands were supposed to comfort them. For once in my life, I should be allowed to shriek and tear out my hair, to throw myself onto the cold wooden floor. To pound my fists and shout this isn't fair, this isn't right. *He was mine, mine, and not even you, Herr Gott, have the right to take him away.*

Little Marta's hand reached inside my crooked arm and rested in the knoll of my elbow. Her hand inside my elbow, the squeeze of it against my side, those small fingers half curled around my heavy arm warmed the hard knot in my chest. I didn't have to catch her eye to know she understood as only a child understands that the surface of our lives is as deceptive as my straight-ahead eyes and stone face.

The casket, raised on a dais; Pastor Kinski's words. Little Marta's small hand inside my elbow, a hand that never seemed to disappear throughout the long afternoon and early evening. These were the things I'd remember. Not the whispered words of condolence and downcast eyes or sidelong glances. Not sandwiches and casseroles in the church basement. Not quick kisses on the cheek or the arms around my shoulders. I wanted to remember the children playing tag, not Pastor taking both my hands in his own too-soft hands and saying, "Herr Gott has Ozzie now." Nor Pastor Kinski's scripted reassurance at the cemetery, where the wind sleuthed beneath my coat and around my stocking-clad legs after Ozzie and Albert's friends lowered the pine casket into the ground beside his father's grave; Ozzie's grave hand dug with picks and shovels in the near-frozen earth by his friends and church volunteers.

## Chapter Twenty-Four

## The Insurance Policy

## *1945*

WE WEREN'T TWO WEEKS away from burying Ozzie, Cherry back in California a week ago. No sooner had she left when I went to the bank and talked to Mr. Kreutzer about the life insurance policy. Wearing my best black hat and veil, I sat on the edge of my chair while he adjusted his glasses. When reading the policy, he would *hmm* now and then. Finally, he folded his hands and gazed at me over the top of his wire-rims. "I'm sorry, Mrs. Gottlieb. In order for you to access the funds, you will need Miss Hendrix's signature. The policy is made out to both of you as equal beneficiaries."

When I stood to leave, I grabbed on to the arms of the chair to lift myself. With those few words from Mr. Kreutzer, the heft of my body felt closer in size to Oscar's prize bull. An old bull at that. One that required patience. Kindness. The haunches not carrying the bulk of the body as easily as they once had. Stiffness hung on and wouldn't let go, even when I stood at my full height. My veiled hat was all that rescued me from the disappointment and bellyache that seemed to invade my arms and legs. I lifted my head and nodded toward him. There was no need to disgrace myself with words.

Yes, I'd read that far in the policy. I kept hoping for something more, something else. Whether I liked it or not, Mr. Kreutzer confirmed what I'd read. I exited the bank, into the day; the sidewalk beneath my feet wasn't there, wasn't real. How could Ozzie do this to me? What was he thinking? That he wouldn't die? That it was "just in case"? *Look at where I am now,* I wanted to say to him. *Your father's dead. There is no widow's pension. No monthly allotment from you. Only a few dollars in a widow's benefit from Social Security. It isn't fair, Ozzie. It can't be what you intended!*

My eyes on my feet, careful where I walked, past Hubner's Market and Kresge's, fury working its way up from my stomach. Hadn't I lost enough? Our Kassel home. My face, once young and unmarked. Father taking us to the edge of poverty. Now all of this dying, life's road before me growing narrower every day. If it wasn't for Oscar's ongoing kindness—reducing rent for me and Ivan by half—I'd have no recourse but to move back to the farm. Back to a place that reeked of old age and death. Even the people in Myra remarked over coffee after church and at Hubner's Market and meeting each other on the street that our young people were leaving the farms. They wanted to live in town or somewhere shiny like California.

What persuaded Ozzie to think that Miss Hendrix and I were on equal footing? How could he be so blind, so uncaring? His own mother. And what had Miss Hendrix done to deserve any of that money? She had a livelihood. Her whole life was ready to blossom before her. Yes, she'd lost her fiancée. But there would be others. She was still young, while new prospects lay behind me like the end of summer's harvest. Sure, Miss Hendrix was nice enough.

But whether she knew it or not, she was just one among many of the girls Ozzie went after. And now the embarrassment of having to approach her to sign the papers. How humiliating. How unfair.

Truth be told, I never read the policy through. I was so busy seeing what I wanted to see. So busy keeping the policy a secret from the family that I fooled myself. *Herr Gott, if I ever needed you to intervene, I need you now.*

# Chapter Twenty-Five

## Heaven

## 1945

I SET THE TEAPOT down on a trivet after putting away leftovers. Irene at least had the good grace to pick up the plates and scrape them into the garbage pail for the chickens while Ada sat at the table without lifting a dish. The children played a game with Ivan in the parlor. I hadn't even had a chance to wipe the table properly when, without a knock or any warning, Pastor Kinski stuck his head into the kitchen from the mudroom step. "Hi ladies," he said. "I smelled the fresh bread all the way from the church. Thought surely you'd made prune kuchen, Marta."

Both my daughters' heads swiveled at once toward the door. Irene, a daughter who knew good manners, set down the kitchen rag and wiped her hands on a towel. She stepped toward Pastor and extended her hand. "Nice to see you, Pastor Kinski."

Ada remained seated and only half turned in her chair toward the door. "Ma must have called in reinforcements," she said. She then turned toward me, a smirk of defiance on her face. "You must be getting desperate, Ma."

"Don't be rude, Ada," I said. "Stand and shake Pastor's hand."

She scooted back her chair in a way she knew I didn't like. Slowly and deliberately, she took a few well-thought-out steps toward the pastor. "Lovely to see you," she said, a twist of sarcasm in her voice.

When he extended his hand, he took both of hers in his. His gaze toward her held what appeared to be genuine care and respect. However, Ada's smile curled with the same sarcasm as her first quip. In that moment she was her father.

Pastor ignored both her smirk and her forced, seemingly friendly, gesture. He dropped her hands and proceeded toward the table. Without being asked, he sat in my chair and rested his hands on the oilcloth covering. He nodded toward me where I stood at the stove, teakettle in hand. "I've come to personally invite you back into the church," he said, nodding toward each of my daughters. "Your family has seen too much death, and I suspect your faith has been sorely tested."

All in one breath, he said that.

Both daughters glanced toward where I stood at the stove, their eyes persecuting me in unison. It was true that I spoke to Pastor about my concern, but I'd hoped he'd at least give me warning before he came to talk to them. His arrival today, so soon after Ozzie's funeral, felt like an invasion.

Though I suspected he'd already written off my daughters and decided that being gentle and easing into the subject was useless, I wasn't expecting such a direct approach. Wasn't expecting I would now have to explain his visit, an already touchy situation. How would Pastor know that since Ozzie's funeral my family had come closer together, and our recent differences had gone underground for the moment, perhaps disappeared? At least, I hoped that was true.

"Nothing like putting your cards on the table," Ada said, her face scanning Pastor's. Without turning away, she asked, "Did my mother put you up to this, Pastor?"

"She didn't need to," he said. He pulled his chair around so he could face Ada. Irene remained standing at the sink. "Your church absence has put you on my calling list for quite a while, young lady. And if my own father hadn't passed this year..." He stopped for a moment, emotion having worked its way into his brown eyes. He took a deep breath, never allowing his gaze to leave Ada's. "I would have been here much sooner."

Ada's attention found me. "I suppose this has to do with my job in Horton?" she asked.

I turned away and reached into the cupboard for tea mugs, aware that Irene watched me. My hands shook when I lifted four mugs, barely managing my finger into the loop of the fourth. I stopped, having to think about how I was going to carry all of them at once. None of this was going the way I'd hoped. I dreaded what was coming next.

His tone softened. "I came because, like your mother, I care about you and what happens to you. Both of you." He let out a sigh. "I also care deeply about Ivan."

Whatever brashness existed in his tone before he mentioned his father, before emotion rose into his eyes, had disappeared. His voice now eased past the previous tension and a subtle warmth lit the kitchen, as though I'd just fed the cookstove another half dozen pieces of wood.

His voice dropped further. "This is a big moment for your mother and for our entire community."

He paused and no one spoke, the children's voices laughing and shrieking in the parlor just fifteen feet away. "Herr Gott wants us to come together, not to separate," he said. "These are hard times for so many families, including yours." He continued to direct his gaze at Ada. He folded his hands on the kitchen table. "Your husband is dead, Ada. Your father and now Ozzie. To break up a family, even with an out-of-town job, comes with a big price."

I half expected Ada to make a scoffing sound, or to snicker, or to twist her mouth into a shape our family had come to expect. Instead, she looked toward the window over the sink and let her eyes rest there. Her chin, taut; it was impossible to see her eyes while she gazed out the window. Irene circled the table and silently poured the tea. Pastor and I sat with our hands folded on the table. Everyone quiet for a change. I had no idea what either one of my daughters was thinking. But I knew that after he left, they would say what I didn't want to hear.

"Please pray with me," Pastor said.

I bowed my head, though I could see both my daughters in my peripheral view. Irene, still standing, folded her hands in front of her and let them drop below her waist. However, the window held Ada's attention. Her chin still tilted up; her eyes open. I was grateful she remained silent.

"Lord Jesus," Pastor began. "Heal this family and the resulting emptiness from their losses. Help them know your compassionate presence."

As Pastor went on, Ada sat back against her chair, her shoulders relaxed. Her eyes still focused on what looked like the pigeon pen. Her hands seemed to automatically find each other, and though one couldn't call it a prayer fold, her hands rested together in her lap, not too different from Irene.

Pastor stopped after a few minutes with "bless this household, Lord. The women and children who come together in your name. Amen."

When I glanced toward the living room, I saw Eli standing in the doorway with his hands folded, his head dropped. The minute he heard Pastor say amen, he took a step, then two, into the kitchen toward the table where we all sat.

"Sir," he said. His mother and Irene were surprised to see him, to hear his small voice address Pastor. "Sir, when is my papa coming home?"

An embarrassed silence filled the room. Pastor extended his hand to the small boy.

Eli moved quickly toward this man he'd only known from a distance. When Pastor reached down to take him into his lap, Eli lifted his arms in anticipation. Once settled on Pastor's lap, Eli looked toward his mother. "Mom doesn't know," he said. "Do you?"

Pastor glanced toward Ada, who remained focused out the window. "Do your cousins know when their papa will return?" Pastor asked.

Eli thought for a minute, his small hands holding on to the edge of the table. "No," Eli said. "Mama doesn't like me to ask."

"Could it be that she just doesn't know?"

"I suppose," Eli said. He leaned back and gazed up at Pastor. "Do you know?"

Pastor smiled. "I wish I did, Eli. I wish I did."

In that moment two things were clear. First, Ada hadn't told her son that the father he'd never met was dead. Second, at two that day, Eli didn't understand what was happening at the Kessler's when they held the service for his father. Now he was four, old enough to ask questions.

I waited and listened, stock-still where I sat. The tension that permeated the room just minutes ago returned.

Ada turned from the window and faced into the kitchen. "I'm sad to say that he's not coming home, Eli," she said. Her hands now on the table, her gaze softer than I'd ever seen. "Papa died in the war like your uncle Ozzie."

Irene's gasp forced everyone to turn in her direction. Her cheeks reddened and she swallowed. The children's voices in the parlor became suddenly quiet.

Why Ada chose that moment, I'd never know. A time so close to Ozzie's death.

"My papa's dead?" Eli asked, his eyes full of wonder at such extraordinary news.

"He's in heaven, Eli," Pastor quickly added. "With Uncle Ozzie and your grandfather."

"Where's heaven?" Eli asked.

Pastor glanced up at the ceiling. "With Herr Gott up in the clouds," he said.

Ada rose so quickly, her chair crashed to the floor. She rushed past Irene, past the table where Pastor and I sat, Eli on Pastor's lap, and upstairs into the bedroom. A door slammed.

Eli glanced first at Pastor and then toward the stairs in the living room. "Mama's upset," he said. "Maybe she didn't know."

He'd already forgotten that she was the one who spoke the words. "Maybe I should go see if she's okay," he said.

"No, child," I said, perhaps too quickly. "We'll let her have her sadness."

Eli's eyes pleaded with me for something, something he couldn't name and neither could I. The girls and Ivan crowded into the doorway of the kitchen, where the quiet swelled with unspoken expectations. "How about we make some cookies?" I said. "Chocolate chip and oatmeal together."

"Yes, Oma, yes," the girls agreed in a chorus. Behind them, Ivan headed for the mudroom, where he grabbed his winter coat. Without looking back at me, he said, "Need to feed the pigeons."

"Can I go, Uncle Ivan?" Eli shouted. He scooted off Pastor's lap and ran across the kitchen linoleum, nearly tripping on the throw rug. He got to the mudroom door where Ivan had already disappeared. He turned back toward me. "Oma, where's my coat?"

The boys were barely gone when the girls returned with their dolls to the rag rug in front of the parlor stove. The kitchen remained silent. Irene, at the sink, washed the dishes. Pastor and I held on to our tea mugs, a second piece of kuchen on Pastor's plate.

Footsteps on the stairs.

Before she entered the kitchen, Ada pulled closed the curtain that served as a door across the parlor entrance. She then stood in the middle of the kitchen linoleum facing Pastor. "You had no right to say what you did," she said. Hands on her hips, her head jutting forward in his direction and the fiery red of her hair now brushed back from her eyes. "No right at all."

"I don't understand," Pastor Kinski said. "You're the one who told Eli his father was dead. Not me."

For the first time, I heard the border of his temper, his wall of defense building invisible barriers—a warning to someone, anyone, who countered his authority. "What are you talking about?"

"That heaven nonsense, that's what," Ada said. "You, who pride yourself on being the church authority and a biblical scholar, clearly don't understand a thing about Judaism."

"And when did you become an authority on world religions?"

"When I married a Jew. That's when, Pastor."

"Do tell if you know so much."

"It's very simple," Ada said, stepping closer to Pastor, a sense of menace in the way she held her body so taut. "There is no such thing as *heaven* in the Jewish faith. And if you were the scholar you pretend to be, you would know that."

Ada spit out her words. Whatever lid she'd kept on her anger and grief had shot off into the invisible sky. "For you to put such ideas into my son's head is unforgiveable. You have no right."

Pastor sat back in his chair, his fork still midair. "I apologize if I've treaded where I shouldn't," he said. "I was only trying to . . ."

"Don't try," Ada said. "Not now or ever."

She turned and hurried toward the mudroom, where she grabbed my wool sweater, slamming the screen door behind her. Out of the corner of my eye, I caught the smile on Irene's face before she turned away and dropped her head, attending once again to the dishpan full of sudsy water.

Pastor set his fork down. He was silent for a minute before he pushed back his chair to stand. "Thank you, Marta, for the tea and kuchen. I'm sorry this didn't turn out quite the way I'd hoped." Without acknowledging Irene, he took his jacket from the back of the chair and knotted his scarf around his neck. "I'll see you on Sunday," he said, barely looking at me. "Think I'll leave by the front door."

Irene and I avoided looking at each other and remained quiet for several minutes. What had just happened in this kitchen was more than any of us could have imagined. I had the strange feeling it would reverberate for a long time to come.

## Chapter Twenty-Six

### Oscar for Advice

## 1945

SPRING CROCUSES ABOUNDED IN the most unlikely places, beside the brick walkway to the outhouse and along the gravel leading to the alley. Even in the garden where the carrots would once again send up their bushy tails.

"I'm going to Hubner's Market for soup bones, Ma. Want me to bring you anything?" Ada asked.

"I need ham hocks for the beans," I said. Impulsively, I grabbed Ada's shoulders in a hug, her bones curling beneath my fingers, her generous bosom meeting mine. Stupidly, awkwardly, I didn't know what to say. Her eyes in mine, the moment between us. "Thank you," I said.

Truth be told, I didn't know what else to say. We hadn't talked about or even acknowledged the incident with Pastor Kinski. Eli no longer asked about his papa. While the girls had to hear the entire argument, Little Marta—who would have been the one to bring it up, especially with me—hadn't said a word. Maybe they really hadn't heard the exchange and didn't know Eli's papa was dead.

"We're all going to be fine, Ma," Ada said. "You'll see." She twisted out of my grasp.

What she didn't say was *without Ozzie.*

My chest was too full to say more; the days empty in a way they'd never been before. Yet the sack of groceries Ada delivered every Monday, one of her two days off, proved to be a godsend. Fresh meat each week, Cheerios for Ivan when he'd grown tired of our standby oatmeal, the luxury of Tide, which I hated getting used to after years of shaving Fels-Naptha into the washer. Mrs. Wright's Bluing, another luxury. I'd never admit how much I looked forward to the white cloth bag Little Marta brought in the Radio Flyer with the younger ones tagging behind her. They always waited and watched me lift each item onto the kitchen table. Ivan, as excited, sat next to the younger children who crowded around me. Like a small chorus, they echoed *ooh* or *ah* at the bounty, sometimes from a list Ada asked me to put together, always with a surprise in the bottom.

Now that Ozzie's allotment had ended and my brother had reduced my rent, another miracle blossomed. When Mr. Kreutzer sent the insurance policy to Cherry, she very generously signed it over to me. I had thought for sure she would want her half, but no, she'd said, "You need it for you and Ivan." She clearly understood more than I gave her credit for. Now, if it wasn't for Ozzie's five-thousand-dollar life insurance from which I withdrew fifty dollars a month for groceries and utilities, I don't know what I would have done. Never mind I'd never told my daughters about the life insurance. Or about Cherry being co-beneficiary. For the time being, I managed, that's what I did.

Ada wasn't the daughter a mother wanted to depend on, especially when the church ladies didn't bother to hide their shielded mouths, their eyes pointed at me with a persecuting glare whenever I walked downstairs into the church basement for coffee and doughnuts after Sunday service. I no longer talked to Pastor Kinski about my daughters, though he continued to insist I bring them back to the church. I sensed blame in his gaze when he directed his dark eyes at me.

The screen door slammed shut behind Ada and I was once again alone. Alone with the memories of Ozzie and his stories those mornings after he'd gone away for a day or two. "Forgive me, Herr Gott," I said aloud. "For loving too much and not enough."

OSCAR'S FARM LANGUISHED IN the same state of disrepair as the last time I was here. More rust on the Willis and the yard full of last summer's weeds filled the gravel driveway. I pushed against the back door now smeared with mud from heaven knows where. Wiped my feet on the rag rug inside the mudroom door. Through the open door into the kitchen. "It's me, Marta," I shouted. "Where are you, Oscar?"

"Asleep, doggone it. Can't a man have a moment of peace and quiet?"

"I thought peace and quiet was all you ever had." I lowered the kuchen and loaf of bread onto his dining table; the stack of mail growing taller. He'd now flattened out and piled his newspapers against the wall alongside other newspaper piles reaching up about four feet high. Must have been his idea of maintaining order.

"You're about the last person I expected to see." Still no sign of my brother other than his voice in the living room, a hand on his rocking chair.

"Millie dropped me off for a couple of hours on her way to the Horton pharmacy and the care center. A friend of Henry's there. Some old war buddy I don't know. Lives somewhere up north."

The windows had frosted on the inside, and I was glad I wore my wool coat. Not a lick of heat and my brother still sitting in the same chair where I left him the last time I was here. "Came to thank you for Ozzie's flowers and to bring the rent check."

By now I was in the living room and standing in front of a body as ungainly as a sack of spuds, the lump of him twisted in the chair and his beard grown out something awful. "We have to do something with you," I said. "Get you to Horton to the doc, or Millie and I can bring Dr. Schmidt out here. You're looking pitiful, Oscar."

"I'm so glad you came to tell me that."

He barely looked at me, and when he did, he glanced away just as quickly toward the dark fireplace, his preferred place to stare—not at anything in particular but into a distance I couldn't see.

"You missed meeting Ozzie's intended," I said. "Nice enough girl, didn't stay but a few days after such a long trip."

"Was she pretty? I expected she was, knowing my namesake. He always liked the pretty ones. Not too practical that way."

"I'd never call her pretty," I said. Now I was staring into the dark fireplace too. "Nice enough."

"That doesn't sound like you, Marta."

"This whole thing with Ozzie has put me out of sorts. Can't stop thinking about Leo when he left. At least we knew where he was going. Never expected he'd come back. Not like Ozzie . . ." I couldn't finish my sentence.

"Leo was a whole other story," Oscar said. He sat straighter in his chair, his shoulders back as though he just remembered that's where they were supposed to be. "Too much of a dreamer, wanting what he couldn't have. Just didn't fit in here. Maybe too much like Father. Then the flu got Leo."

Outside the window facing the driveway, blackbirds sat on the telephone lines. Patient, ever watchful, looking for what they wanted. Ozzie and now my long-gone brother, Leo, disappeared as though into a drifting cloud. "We knew we'd never see him again."

"Everyone knew, including Leo. Determined to go back to

Odessa even with the Soviets in charge," Oscar said. "You can't go back. That's just the fact of it."

"I'll always remember him with that cap pulled tight over his still-curly hair. Always coughing into his handkerchief, thinking we didn't notice when he turned to check for blood or phlegm. All he could say was 'it's what I've always wanted. To go back.'"

"You were the last one to see him alive, Marta. Remember?"

"Alive," I said. Why mention that Oscar was the one who went east to retrieve the body? Not a job anyone would want to do. Then the question of burning the remains because of the flu. *No*, Oscar said, *put it in a box. I'll take care of it.* That's the story he told me.

I sat across from Oscar, my coat still on, my handbag on my lap. "He was already an old man before his time. You know what he said to me, Oscar?"

"Must have been memorable if you're still hanging on to it."

I shook my head at him. "He said, 'I'll always be as close as our memories of happier times.' I remember thinking, 'Why does love always hurt?' That was my question when I was just nineteen. It's still my question."

"I'm surprised, Marta. I'd have thought your faith in Herr Gott would have changed that." He pushed himself forward in the chair. "Here, help me get up before you get morbid on me."

I stood to help my brother out of his chair. "After the train left, that same piece of newspaper I'd noticed before still lay on the tracks. It was that piece of newspaper that left me feeling lonely. Strange I'd remember that."

"Well, you weren't responsible for his lungs or for him going away. Leo was doing what he wanted to do. Consequences be darned. Maybe that's the best we can do."

"Sad to say he wasn't the only one. Darned Spanish flu got Uncle Herman's family. Think Natalia's sisters lost heart after that. Just moved away. I lost track when the Christmas cards stopped coming."

"Can't help what other people do or what happens to them,"

Oscar said. "Now help me up like the good sister you are." He winked.

His wink made me stop for a minute. Not something I'd seen him do since Ellis Island. Always so serious. Maybe Oscar was getting his sense of humor back.

My arm went under Oscar's arm; his other hand grabbed the cane. "You want kuchen first or your haircut and beard trim?"

"I'm for eating first. Then I might even let you hose me down. Getting tired of my own stink."

We both laughed as I eased him toward the dining table and helped him to a chair, his left knee leaving him gimpy when he walked. I gave a swipe to that end of the table where even more papers and mail were piled in the middle. "Didn't mean to get sentimental," I said. "Mainly came to thank you for halving our rent. And . . ." My throat grew thick when I thought about the bouquet he'd sent. And it was especially strange remembering Leo. He didn't bring tears to my eyes the way Oscar's generosity did. Leo was right. Oscar would always be there for me.

"You're a widow woman now. Who knows, someday when Ivan takes off, maybe the two of us will take care of each other."

I couldn't help but laugh. "Who will be taking care of who?"

Oscar frowned. "That's not funny."

"Let me get the teakettle going so we can enjoy our kuchen."

"That's more like it." He smoothed the apron I'd tied around his neck. "I trust the flowers arrived at the church in time," he said.

"They were the only flowers there. A downright forest of flowers. Thank you, Oscar."

No sense in scolding him about not coming to the service, not when he could hardly get to the table.

"I'm glad you came," he said. "You're the family I count on."

Until he said that, I'd never thought about what it was like to be as alone as Oscar was. Two houses to himself, plus mine in town. Men he hired to work the crops. I doubt anyone stopped by anymore since he was so pitiful. No one to help in the house except when I came. Unlike me, he had no small, shrieking voices bursting through the door, no one to make him tea when he woke in the morning, not even grown children who argued and did as they pleased. A kind of alone I'd never imagined. Maybe one day I would move him into my parlor. Worse things had happened.

"Need to talk to you about Ada," I said.

"What's that girl done now that you'd never think of doing?"

"She took a job in Horton," I said. "If that isn't bad enough, she drives there every day with Heinrich Bueller."

"Smart girl. Always said that. Besides Ozzie, she's the one who will find a different life."

"You approve of that?" I pushed his second helping of kuchen across the table. Stood to refill our tea mugs. Even asking that question of Oscar, I should have known he'd side with Ada. He always admired the ones who stretched the limits of what was right, what we'd been taught.

"Don't suppose you read the newspapers, Marta," he said. "This war changes everything." He looked up from his plate, his mouth still partly full. Waited until he swallowed. "Wait and see. The world is never going to look the same. Especially for womenfolk." He gazed at me, steady and intense. "Mark my words." A grin. "Maybe you too."

I shook my head in disagreement. "Now you sound like Ada."

"What if she's right? Have you ever thought about that?"

"She already has a job with Eli."

"All mothers have a job with their children." He smiled. "I think she's downright enterprising. Good for her."

"Wish you hadn't said that."

He sipped his tea. He already looked livelier. "Mark my words, Marta. Nothing will ever be the same."

# Chapter Twenty-Seven

## Postwar Begins

## 1945

I WAS JUST FINISHING morning dishes when I heard the click of the back gate and the Radio Flyer's wheels scrape along the brick path from the alley and past the outhouse. I wasn't particularly surprised to see the children or the two empty egg cartons bouncing inside the wagon's bed. Millie raised her curtain and waved. I sometimes thought she loved my grandchildren as much as I did.

When Little Marta shouted, "Oma, Oma. Daddy's home," I was caught off guard.

The war was officially over. Not the grief of it, but the war. I suspected that the grief would travel down the decades and only end when many of us took our last breath. But the official end.

September 1945. Nearly four years since the war began. It took that long for the armistice to be signed. All of us sat around Ozzie's radio waiting for President Roosevelt's weekly program. Though I should have expected Mac would be home soon, his return surprised me. Maybe because it was Mac coming home and not my Ozzie. There was something unfair and disappointing about the fact of his return. I was slow to unlatch the mudroom door.

I wiped my hands on the flour-sack dish towel and laced it through the stove handle. I opened the screen for the children and received the empty egg cartons from Little Marta. "What's this about your pa?" I asked.

"Home, Oma. Middle of the night," Little Marta said. "Mama made me sleep upstairs on the rag rug."

"Yes, yes," I said impatiently. "But, how did he get home?"

"Mother said I had to."

"No, no, not that." I walked the egg cartons to the kitchen counter where the dish basin sat full of sudsy water soaking the baking utensils. When I turned, Marta's tears stopped me and I reached out with both arms. "I'm so sorry, my darling girl."

"Mama made me leave her bed." Marta pressed her face into my apron where the heat of her tears soaked into my dress.

"Oh, my dear, sweet *schatzi*," I said. I pulled her closer.

"I don't like him, Oma."

I held the girl close, rocking her where we stood. Eli, looking mystified, stood off to the side where he watched his cousin sob against my dress. "Now, now," I said. "It's going to be alright. You'll see."

"Marta's lucky, Oma," Eli said. "Her daddy came home. Pastor says my daddy's in heaven." He gazed up at me. "Where's heaven again, Oma?"

My back stiffened and my arms loosened around Marta. For shame, Eli had never once set eyes on his father. "Sit down, children," I said. "I have some nice cinnamon rolls and milk for you."

Little Marta accepted the handkerchief I pulled from inside my dress sleeve. She continued to sniffle at the kitchen table. Blew her nose and, for the moment, seemed comforted. Eli, looking more and more like his father each day—the blonde hair and dark eyes set inside the pale skin of both his parents—scraped his chair when he pulled it along the linoleum. He scooted close to the table, sitting with his elbows on the table, his chin in his hands waiting for me to bring the warm cinnamon rolls from the back of the cook stove.

"Oma, when the war ends, will all the fathers come home?" he asked.

"Yes, those who can come home," I said. I busied myself with separating the rolls and pouring the milk. I couldn't look at Eli without anger heating my stomach and my eyes wanting to weep for all that was lost.

"Daddy said we might move," Little Marta said. "Would we do that, Oma? Move away from you and Uncle Ivan? Aunt Ada and Eli?"

The sudden sting behind my eyes was unexpected. "Adults say a lot of things, child. I'm sure your father will need to find work and start over again. He's been gone for quite a while."

"I don't want to move," Little Marta said.

"Hush, now, *schatzi*," I said. "You don't need to worry about that today."

Eli's head bent over the table, his thick hair nearly covering his eyes. He ran his wooden car along the outlines of the oilcloth's faded pink roses. Children are innocent, so vulnerable to the whims and failures of the adults who raise them. Wasn't that true in my own house? Though Albert blamed his two years in the Great War before we married for his bad health, didn't he fail his family through his continued smoking and drinking at Jake's Tavern? Yes, he arrived in this country without a skill, and he did become a master brick layer. Something in my throat softened on realizing I was speaking of the dead. His hard work and determination made it possible to buy this house after Ozzie came along; it clothed our children. Put food on the table, even during the Great Depression when he often traded work for food. It was only after his health failed that we had to sell the house to my brother. All Mac had done, besides fathering his children, was rail repair and construction on war ships. He had no real skills and, worse, he lacked the determination Albert handed down to his sons. Even Ivan, who spent his spare time working with the pigeons, had succeeded in selling half a dozen birds to other families.

Take away Mac's white shirt and clean shave, that seductive way he cocked his head and smiled at you, and you still had a railroad bum. Worse, Mac was a drinker, he and Albert going off to Jake's Tavern and returning far too happy which always raised the bile at the back of my throat. Made me furious every time I thought back and realized those were the only times Albert actually laughed with his grandchildren. Stupid, drunken laughter. I couldn't blame Irene when she rolled her eyes at her husband and father before hurrying the children off to bed.

Irene could have found someone in town even though she was already nineteen with no proper beau when Mac came along. She brushed off the local boys and kept company with Frieda, her best friend from high school. Both girls talked of becoming nurses, but there was no money to send the girls to nurses' training in Bismarck. To Frieda's credit, she worked at the local rest home while Irene complained about the smell of sickness and refused to even fill out an application. Instead, she scooped ice cream at Schubert's Ice Creamery on Tuesdays and Thursdays when the Schubert's daughter took the full course on womanhood at our church. Now look at her. Three children in three years and a husband home from war with no job and even less ambition. Irene could be pregnant again inside a couple of months. What would they do then?

"Here's your milk. The rolls," I said. I set the plates and glasses down in front of the two children. Eli's chin grazed the top of the table where I've just wiped the oilcloth. "Do you need some cushions under you, Eli?"

"No, Oma," he said. Vanilla frosting covered half his face and the rest oozed between his fingers. "This is good," he said. "Really good."

Little Marta stared for a moment at the roll and the glass of milk. "I'm not hungry," she said.

"It will do you good," I said. "A little sugar heals all hurts."

She shook her head and closed her eyes.

I pushed the plate closer. "Come, come, child," I said. "Eat up."

I would eat another if I hadn't already had two for breakfast and, daily, squeezed the buttons on my dress to close them, ever aware of the growing gap between buttons. A sweater, unless buttoned to my neck, hardly covered my chest anymore when I walked downtown to the market.

I**T WASN'T UNTIL LATE** afternoon, an hour past tea and kuchen time, when the screen door pulled back and Irene shuffled into the mud room, wiping her rain-wet feet on the rag rug. I was standing at the kitchen sink cutting up beets for a pot of borscht.

"In here," I said. I wiped my hands on my apron and nodded toward the two sacks of groceries Irene lowered to the end of the table. "They look heavy. Would have thought Mac might have gone with you."

Irene slumped into one of the kitchen chairs. "Don't start," she said. "He's barely home. But, you already know because Marta told you."

"Marta and Eli," I said. "Eli wanted to know where heaven was. If that was a place he could go to see his father."

"Ma, I've told you, I'm not responsible for Ada or Pastor." She folded her hands on the tablecloth. "You got any fresh tea?"

"No, but some is already made." I indicated the pot at the back of the stove.

"I suspect it's left from breakfast, right?"

"You know I never throw anything away."

"Of course, and you have no ice." Irene's tone underscored the fact that I still operated with the old ice box, not a refrigerator with a freezer and real ice cubes like they had.

"You can chip some in the ice box," I said.

Irene set the tea kettle on the stove to boil. "No real notice except a telegram two hours before he arrived," Irene said. "Howard Kemper's boy brought it to the house."

I kept chopping the beets into small chunks, setting the greens aside. It was just me and Ivan for dinner.

"Discharged and free as a bird," Irene said. "Talks about looking for work."

"Why was he discharged so soon with the war barely over?"

"Army said two years in the trenches is enough for a married man with children," Irene said. "That's what he told me." She stared out the window toward the withered garden. "Lucky he didn't get killed."

"God forbid," I said. I set the vegetables to boil. "The children say you're thinking of moving away."

"Only if he can't find work around here," Irene said. She kept looking down at her hands. "Truth is, I wasn't expecting him so soon."

She and her sister enjoyed free reign with the allotment checks and being able to halve household expenses by living together. The fur collared coat and matching fur hat, the fine leather gloves. Without men, there were no meat expenses to bother with, my brother Oscar's generosity when butchering kept their freezer full. No liquor unless they drank it. Both Philip and Mac liked their beer and whiskey. Now, Irene would have to defer to a man again like she once deferred to her father.

"You know men, Irene; they have to have it their way."

"You're right, Ma." She picked at her cuticles. "Guess I got used to being independent."

"Understandable," I said. "Since your father died, God rest his soul, I buy what I please at Hubner's Market. If it fits into my budget, that is."

Irene said nothing. Budget was a word she and her sister didn't seem to understand.

"I hope he can find work here," I said.

"Look at Ada," Irene said. "Can't believe how well she's done."

Ivan was visible through the kitchen curtain, his shag of brown hair whenever he opened, then closed the pigeon cage, the latch catching after several tries. His lips moved as he muttered to himself or the birds, a new habit I'd recently noticed.

"Does Mac want to move?" I asked.

"South. Maybe the Black Hills."

I couldn't look at her. That was too much like giving in.

"Warm would be nice for a change," she said.

Though I hadn't intended to, I sat heavily in my chair, my elbows on the table. "Haven't I lost enough?" I blurted, my stomach suddenly roiling. "First, Philip. Then, Pa. Now Ozzie. And, you, Irene, how can you even think about leaving me and Ivan? It's not fair. Not right."

Irene's eyes widened and her mouth opened. "Ma, this is my husband we're talking about." She shook her head. "I wouldn't move to insult you. The man needs to work."

"You're the eldest now. It's your responsibility to care for our family, to watch over me and Ivan. Didn't my brother do that with our family? Where have I gone wrong that my two daughters have become so ... independent?"

For a long time, Irene said nothing. "Ma, Ada's not going anywhere."

"Ada only cares about Ada."

I pushed back from the table and walked to the stove, my body heavy with weariness. Maybe I was the naïve one, expecting that Mac would come home and settle in Myra, especially with Pa gone and now, his best friend, Ozzie, as well. Mac had no investment in watching Ivan grow up.

"Ma, you're upsetting yourself over nothing. It's just talk," Irene said. "We all need to calm down. The man's hardly home."

"We'll see," I said. I grabbed the bucket and headed toward the mud room and out to the water pump. There were dishes to be done.

A NIGHTLY HAUNTING OF bad dreams descended from who knows where. Over and over, the twisted smile on Albert's face, his calloused hands as he tore, then tossed one Bible page after another into the incinerator fire. His smile, always, his smile. That bruised lip, his smoke-yellowed teeth, and the multi-colored beanie pulled down over his forehead. His mouth leering as the ashen pages floated above the barrel and into the late autumn sky where they swirled above Albert's frosty breath.

Ivan's shadow filled the bedroom doorway. "Ma, I heard you shout."

"It's nothing, my boy. Come crawl into bed with your mother so you can get warm."

My nine-year-old Ivan slipped beneath the quilts, the warm sheets around him. "A bad dream, that's all."

"Ma, is it true Irene is leaving with Mac and the girls?"

I forgot that Ivan was a wiggler, not the cuddling kind. Still, I pulled Ivan closer, his spindly arms around my waist, my braid between us. I remained quiet, hoping my silence spoke for me. After all, it was a week since Mac returned home. If I reassured Ivan, I'd be lying. If I said nothing, I'd be lying. Finally, "It's true."

"South Dakota's so far away," Ivan said. The whine in his voice reflected the same ache I'd lived with since Irene and I talked at the kitchen table. Her reassurances had fallen like hollow echoes on my ears. Once the words were spoken by Little Marta, it was simply a matter of time.

I pulled Ivan close, but he pushed away, his hands against my shoulder. "I sure wish we had more family living here with us in our house," he said.

He was right. To have family around the table at mealtime, to cook for more than just the two of us would make our house feel like a real home again. If Ada and Eli came to live with us, she'd bring half her widow's pension. I could then breathe easier by saving the life insurance money. Yes, she'd take advantage of me for meals and childcare. I didn't care. I wouldn't have to let go of what little pride I had left.

"Ma, I can't sleep here," Ivan said. "Wake me in my bed when it's time."

I lay on my back, my head spinning. A new plan, that's what I needed. I'd talk to Ada in the morning, offer meals and minding Eli. Maybe she would be willing to pay ten dollars a week, no, every two weeks. Forget that. Keep things sweet. She'd bring more groceries. That would make the difference.

## Chapter Twenty-Eight

### Ada Moving

## *1945*

MY MIND WAS SET. Ada and Eli would live here with me and Ivan. When she returned from Hubner's with my navy beans, I'd talk to her. I had to. If she ever took Eli away, I don't know what I'd do. I went to the back screen door hoping to catch the tail of Ada's skirt. Instead, my eyes looked up to see the blackbirds in flight. Just moments ago they sat on the telephone lines. Then, just like that, they lifted off and flew high and away, tracing the sky with their flapping wings. Like the days themselves, they were here and they were gone. Only memories, like still photographs, remained. All those days I waited for the tomorrows. When tomorrow finally came, they disappeared in an instant like a blackbird on a telephone wire, returning to the unknown from which they came. Like Albert had. Like Ozzie. Their wings aching, they lifted up and away. Without my grandchildren, I'd be as alone as my brother was alone.

THE BEANS HAD ALREADY soaked and were in a rolling boil when Ada returned with the cloth bag I'd loaned her. She shoved the paper-wrapped package at me and turned, ready to leave. I pulled the tea kettle off the back of the stove and poured water into the waiting tea pot. "Aren't you going to sit for a minute? The kuchen just came out of the oven."

"No, Ma. I need to get home with the chicken for our own supper. Besides, you'll just want to argue with me."

"Is having you and Eli living here such a terrible idea?" I asked.

"Ma, you simply don't get it," Ada said. She smoothed the fingers of her left hand, her wedding ring long removed and the telltale line now blended into the color of her skin. "I'm not going to meet a new father for Eli in Myra, and maybe not in Horton either. I just don't want to date someone I've known since I was five."

I took a deep breath. "You've been widowed not quite two years. How can you even think about re-marrying? It's not right."

A smile crept into the corner of Ada's mouth enhancing the dimple that lay sleeping until a certain curl of her lip brought it out of hiding. "I want to remarry," she said. "But only if it's right. Why would I want to be an old maid at twenty-three? If I should live as long as you and Pa, I have another thirty, maybe even forty years. Besides, don't you want me to have other children so Eli isn't alone?"

I rose from the table. Half-way to the stove, I realized I'd forgotten the tea pot. I couldn't face Ada without betraying the scowl of my long-held anger. When I returned to the table, I lowered my head to avoid eye contact.

From the January, mid-winter day that Ada was born, things went wrong. The midwife's sleigh ended up stuck in the snow at Richter's Crossing. Albert was alone with me upstairs in our bedroom when the baby's head crowned and its blue body slid out of me. Waiting, Albert stood helpless at the foot of the bed where he'd spread clean flannel. The glint of our sharpest paring knife was raised beneath the overhead light. He held it in front of him, his blue flannel shirt behind red suspenders only enhanced the apprehension and, yes, helplessness on his face. "Now, what do I do?" he asked. Neither of us knew in that moment that the baby—born blue and tangled inside the umbilical cord, her frail body coming out withered like an old lady's—would end up being the feisty one.

At first she didn't thrive the way she needed to, and finally Dr. Schmidt said she had rickets, a lack of vitamin D. Yet an early death wasn't about to grace Ada's destiny. With her first cry, we knew that this child would never join those babies who collapsed like half-baked doughy bread, never to rise into the fullness of their bodies. When I first held the trembling newborn, I was angry that this child who had skirted death would demand extra attention. There were already two other children close in age.

The frustration of the past twenty-three years filled my chest when I leaned over the woodstove and poured hot water into the remnants of the once-strong tea. *Herr Gott, guide me. I don't trust myself,* I silently prayed.

I shifted my weight on the kitchen chair. "You should see Eli when he's with Ivan and the pigeons. He has half the birds eating out of his hand." To underscore my argument, I continued, "He's safe here. In fact, maybe you should just leave him with us and get a room in Horton, then come home on weekends."

Enough was enough. Driving with Heinrich, a married man, was something that needed to stop. Irene had already let it slip that Ada hadn't come home until after ten o'clock when her shift ended at seven the night before Mac returned. If that happened here in my home, how would I ever explain the late-night crunch of tires, even to Millie next door? If Ada failed to think of her son, she failed to think of her young, innocent brother as well.

If only Ozzie were here, he would take her into the parlor and close the curtain, his bass voice rising and falling behind the heavy curtain. More than Albert, Ozzie would know what to do, what to say. He'd been in the world and knew the consequences of a woman's lost reputation. The ruined chances for a child growing up in a hometown where he was forever scarred by his parent's mistakes.

"Ma, I don't have time for this," Ada said. "I already told you it's my turn to cook. I'm sorry. We can talk later."

"THE IMPORTANT THING, MARTA, is to keep going." Millie sat at the table, her finger looped through her mug; *DAVID* forever in the room if his coffee mug was there, with his name displayed in red against the white crockery.

"I know you're right, Millie. But it's been one thing after another with these daughters of mine. Ada's riding to her job in Horton with Heinrich Bueller, who you well know lives in Myra but can disappear into another world the minute he drives out of town. If it isn't already a scandal, it soon will be. I have no Albert, no Ozzie to talk to her, and my brother is useless. He's already sided with her. And she can't abide Pastor. She more or less told him so."

Millie stared into her mug, the tea leaves sunk to the bottom, her lower lip working against her teeth whenever she was deep in thought. "She'll just stray further away if you keep harping on her, Marta. You know as well as I do that she didn't get that red hair for nothing. Your only job is to love Eli. That's where the reward will come, not from your daughters. If I had even one of your grandchildren, I'd think I sprouted wings."

"What can I say?" I hesitated. "You're right, Millie. Appreciate what I have. Isn't that what Herr Gott tells me morning and night? Be grateful? But it just isn't in me." I looked into my tea mug. "A real shortcoming, and I don't know why."

Millie reached across the oilcloth, her skinny fingers toward my plump and fat hand, our hands together against the faded roses. "I'll pray for you," she said. "Isn't that what friends are for?" Her fingers laced through mine. Tears brightened her eyes.

Not two days later, I was so lost in thought I didn't hear Ada come into the kitchen until she pulled her chair away from the table. "Is tea ready?" she asked.

"Not yet." I turned back toward the kuchen I was lifting off the back of the stove. Reaching for a trivet, I placed the pan on the trivet so the oilcloth wouldn't scorch or pucker, careful to position the pastry close to my side of the table.

"Eli's outside with his uncle Ivan," I said.

"Good. I need to talk to you, and I don't want the boys around."

I sat down, my body heavy in the chair, heavy like the lump in my throat. I didn't know if I wanted to hear what she had to say.

"I found an apartment in Horton."

"An apartment?"

"You should be happy. I won't have to commute with that awful man anymore."

"Horton's so far away."

"Ma, it's not quite fifteen miles. Eli can go to school there and stay with Margaret Rossmoor while I work."

Ada slouched at the table, her elbows propped inside her mint-green sweater, highlighting her red hair. Something black smudged the skin under her eyes. The same way Albert looked after he sat up too late the night before at Jake's Tavern. Lord forbid that was yesterday's rouge still coloring her cheeks.

"But you can't," I said. "You'll be away from family." I sighed. "First Irene, then you."

I turned away, the sink a blur and the window full of springtime blackbirds, now melded into a black cloud. I got up from the table as though I'd forgotten something on the stove. But my hands gripped the sink to steady my knees suddenly gone weak. In that moment the bulk of me could have dissolved onto the floor and disappeared before I even knew it happened.

"It's not that far away, Ma," Ada said. "Besides, you know the way the old ladies' tongues wag in this town. It will be best, all the way around. We'll visit on Saturdays."

Saturdays. Of course she won't come on Sundays. Philip being Jewish had been a good excuse to skip church.

"You can move over here with me and Ivan. Take up your old room again."

"It's too late for that, Ma," Ada said. "I don't want to take advantage of you."

"But this is your second home. Eli would love to sleep upstairs in Ivan's room. Besides, Ivan already said we needed more family in the house."

"No, I don't think it's a good idea."

Moving away wouldn't keep the town from talking about Ada. Not just at church but in the grocery and probably among Albert's old cronies at Jake's Tavern. Even in a white uniform without the clingy dresses, her red hair pulled back in a heavy white net, I'd watched Ada strut at the grocery store in full knowledge that people were watching her full hips swing. She painted her nails red, now wore makeup, and her hair had taken on an unnatural shade of red. Though I clicked my tongue and shook my head, Ada was twenty-three now, her sister twenty-four. Without their brother Ozzie to chide Ada in his teasing way, I remained helpless. Forget Pastor Kinski. He'd failed me in this effort.

I looked past my daughter and out the kitchen window toward the garden and beyond to the outhouse at the far corner of the path. The blackbirds were just lighting on top of the pigeon pen, their black feathers held tight to their bodies. They were always hopeful for some odd shred of grain or leftover seed the pigeons missed. The blackbirds' lives seemed as simple as mine once had. To eat and sleep; to fly through the day. To care for their offspring.

Ada grabbed the fur-collared coat from a hanger by the door. She lifted her hair over the brown fox-fur collar and settled the ruff around her neck, throwing back her shoulders as though she had just won a long-awaited battle. Nothing would stand in her way.

Determined not to be tearful in her presence, I folded the flour-sack napkins. I breathed carefully. I didn't want so much as a sigh to escape. Ada should have no reason to think this conversation was over or that she'd won our long, ongoing battle.

I gazed at the empty tea mugs on the table, the crumbs on my plate where the last of the prune kuchen briefly sat. I should go down into the cellar and pick out potatoes for supper. Just imagining the open trapdoor to the cellar and the light flooding up from below reminded me of when Mother and I stood for the first time at the head of Tante Ketcha's cellar. An assembly line of jars lined the lip of the cellar's opening. Ketcha stood above the stairs handing one jar, then the next, down to her daughters, where they set them in an orderly fashion along the damp shelves. I was fifteen that first winter. I recalled the horror on Mother's face as she stood beside me, both of us staring into the black hole beneath the trapdoor, the shelves' mustiness rising from the narrow and steep stairs.

Mother never recovered. Not from the buggy pulling away from our Kassel home, or the endless night when we made our way to Odessa; not from the ship's long passage to Ellis Island, or my fall on the wharf at the Battery Park pier. Not from the crowded and cold train ride to North Dakota. Not the sight of Father's blood staining new snow on that December morning when Oscar and Uncle Herman found Father outside the barn. Mother's look of horror at the cellar door, then, later, seeing Father's blood. The memories were always there, always waiting for moments like this.

MY HANDS WERE DEEP inside the dishwashing suds, the S.O.S. scrubbing pad against the bottom of the pan. Outside the window, the pigeons cooed in their cage. It seemed that all I'd known these many years was death. First, Father's suicide after the discovery of what his lust for cards had cost us, followed by Mother's sudden spells that finally took her in the end. A few years later, Leo died on the eastbound train, another victim of the Spanish flu. He never did see Odessa again. Leo: my heart in Kassel, then again in Myra.

He was the only one who ever asked to touch my scar, who asked if it hurt, his fingertips feeling along the protruding and uneven ridges; so tender and gentle, as though he was handling fine silk. Long after my scar healed, the rough edges and unnatural red marks continued to make those who passed me look quickly away. Not Leo. He came closer, fascinated by how the scar tissue layered itself, then darkened to a rosy pink. He remained curious about what it felt like beneath the surface. After Leo died I went to bed for a week. I longed for his same fate despite my hardworking husband, Albert, and a child about to be born. Wanting to die and be buried alongside Leo was my greatest sin.

Until Ozzie.

It's the children I lived for, their small hands clutching a spoon or fork, smiling up at me with frosting spread on their faces. Spilling their milk. They weren't just my consolation—they were my future. To watch them grow was what I looked forward to, especially now that death haunted the back door and would eventually take me in the end.

# 1916

TANTE KETCHA WAS THE one who decided it was time I met other Myra boys and girls. Because of my scars, I'd refused to go to school when, in truth, the grades only went through eight, and Mother had already taught me and Leo well beyond that. But Tante took it upon herself to speak to the new pastor at the First Bible Church, a young Reverend Kinski who had just arrived in Myra along with his new wife. It was decided that I would teach Sunday school. Mother offered to go with me the first Sunday after Easter. The group was the younger children, five- and six-year-olds. They hadn't had a Sunday-school teacher since Mrs. Scholtz had died.

In front of the only mirror in the small house, one that Father hung over the small kitchen sink in Tante Ketcha's old house where we brushed our teeth, Mother arranged a hat with a short white veil that hung down in front to my chin. I wore my old velvet dress, taken in and lengthened once again this past year. For someone who rarely left the farm and had only gone into town once during the previous summer when Natalia needed help carrying supplies, I felt as scared as I did the first time I walked into Tante and Uncle Herman's house.

It was agreed that the new pastor would meet me in the church basement and introduce me to the children. When Tante opened the church's door at the top of the basement, her hand firm against my back, she all but pushed me down the stairs and into the dark hallway. I could hear her breathing behind me. My heart pounded in my ears while we waited for the door marked *Pastor* to open. Tante held my arm, her grip on my forearm tighter than she knew. I felt helpless to pull away.

"Ah, Miss Schroeder," Pastor said when he came out of his study, the open door revealing high windows lit by the gray light of a rainy spring day. At first his glasses glinted in the half-light, making it hard to see him. Outside of his glasses, his white collar above a dark suit coat became his most distinguishing feature. He extended his hand. "So glad you are willing to take this class," he said. "Here, let me show you the room."

He never questioned the veil on my hat, and he never seemed to see my face. He led us farther down the cold and unheated hallway, the half-light as dreary as a dungeon, the rooms not much better. He spoke over his shoulder as we continued to follow him. "The routine is simple. There is a Sunday-school book that teaches the children to pray and another picture book with stories about Jesus." He glanced over his shoulder. "This is as much babysitting during service as it is teaching," he said. His voice dropped into a slight laugh as though to say that this should not be a surprise.

Sixteen years old and only a couple of years away from Ellis Island, a strange déjà vu took me back to the island nursery. The white-coated nurse, guarded by her desk and her disapproving glance. Young children waddling toward the few toys, a top they weren't skilled enough to spin, some hand-carved blocks, and small balls of yarn. The smell of soiled diapers that hung suspended in the air. I remembered standing puzzled at first, a swelling in my throat just before I teared up. My hands dropped at my sides like a puppet waiting to be put right. That same feeling of being exposed, of possibly being ridiculed, coursed through my arms now.

"Would you like to take off your hat?" Pastor asked.

I pulled back, startled by his question and suddenly afraid that removing my hat was required. I reached for Tante Ketcha's arm. "I think she would rather leave it on, Pastor," she said.

"Very well." Pastor shrugged his shoulders. "You do look a little like a bride," he joked. "Don't be surprised if the children ask if you are one."

"No, Pastor," I said too fast, too loud.

"Here, this is the room. I'll leave you to it." He turned to Tante Ketcha. "Will you be staying?" he asked.

"Yes," Tante Ketcha said. "Until she gets started. Then I'll come upstairs to the service."

Fortunately, there were only five young children in the room, all sitting on the floor and playing with various toys they'd removed from the toy box, along with storybooks now scattered over the floor. Small chairs lined the wall. I could already see there was no chair my size. Once Pastor left, I stepped away from Tante Ketcha. "Okay, children," I said. "My name is Marta and I'm going to be your teacher today."

They all stared back at me. My strange hat. My aunt standing behind me. I selected a chair from the back of the wall and grabbed a couple of books from the case. With some finagling, they imitated me by dragging their chairs toward me, scraping them against the concrete floor. "Does anyone know the Lord's Prayer? No? Then that's what we'll learn today."

They crowded into a half circle. After we said the prayer a few times, those closest leaned against me in order to see the pictures in the book I'd selected. Telling the story in German, the children quieted down. Some few dared to come closer to see the pictures of geese, a red rooster. One held my shoulder, another touched my skirt. The feeling of their small hands brought unexpected comfort. I watched their eager faces, and in that moment I realized that these young children were no different than me; all of us looking for a place to belong.

I never knew when Tante Ketcha slipped away, never knew when the hour ended, until one of the parents came to retrieve her young girl, a girl whose dress came to her ankles—clearly a hand-me-down. No one asked about my veiled hat and no one said anything but "thank you, Miss Marta" when they left, tugging at the hand of a parent or gazing back over their shoulder. It would be three more Sundays before I left the hat at home.

# Chapter Twenty-Nine

## Pastor's Study

## 1945

The basement hallway was dark and a musty smell rose from the thin runner. The previous winter, so long and damp, had invaded the church walls that continued to sweat from snowmelt and cold that came from too many months when the building only knew heat for Sunday services. Always, the need to save money. The Great Depression not far behind us and the war effort all we could think about these last few years. Ahead of me, light leaked out from under the door at the far end of the hallway.

The borrowed Bible was held tight under my arm, and I finally intended to return the worn pages. Though unsure if Pastor said ten or ten thirty, I knocked quietly, not wanting to disturb him if he was praying. I'd been so muddled these days that I'd hesitated about coming, especially with his older brother ill and dying. My impulse to finally pick up the telephone seemed to be Herr Gott's way of guiding me. I'd all but lost my faith.

"Come in," said the muffled voice behind the heavy oak door.

"It's me," I said.

"Yes, Marta." Pastor Kinski stood from behind the desk facing the door, the daylit windows above his desk bringing nothing but gray light into the room. The only lamp sat on a corner of his desk. Otherwise, the room was the color of winter days when a blizzard has pounded at the windows and no one dared venture outside. A rainy day in summer could do the same thing.

I wasn't ready for his red suspenders over a plaid shirt. The same jeans that the farmers wore. I'd never seen Pastor outside of his robes and collar, or a black suit when he appeared for sandwiches and cookies following a wedding or funeral. The same suit when he came to call at the house. His white collar. Never suspenders, except that one time he surprised us in our kitchen. Never red like the farmers wore.

"What brings you here today, Marta?" He glanced at the Bible but said nothing.

"I don't know that I can live without my grandchildren, Pastor." My mouth went dry, and I squeezed my handkerchief as though it could save me. I lowered my gaze, the shame already on my face. "They're leaving Myra."

His eyes dropped to the desk in front of him. "Yes, Marta. I've heard as much." He placed his fingertips together. "This must be heavy on your heart. A great sorrow," he said. His eyes met mine.

"I don't know what I will do without them," I said. "Except for Ivan, my grandchildren are all I have."

Pastor leaned back in his chair and his eyes traveled to the ceiling, where they stayed. "This has been a hard two years for you. Your son-in-law Philip, then Albert. Ozzie, who I know you depended on."

I waited.

"You haven't been able to persuade your daughters to return

to church," he said. It was as much an indictment as a declaration of truth.

"I've had no luck."

"I can't imagine my calling again will help," he said.

"I know last time wasn't pleasant, with Ada in particular."

He rose from his desk. "Let us pray."

We lowered our heads, and Pastor rambled into a long prayer asking Herr Gott to guide me and press my daughters back into his fold. When he finally said amen, I realized I hadn't heard a word, my mind on Little Marta's face the day she came and told me her pa was home. Since entering his study, I'd never had a chance to take off my headscarf and was already having a hard time gathering my coat around me and managing my handbag and gloves, the Bible as well. I should have never come. We were back at the same place we always started. His urgency that I bring Irene and Ada back to church and their reluctance to come. The pastor saw no other solution than the one he proposed. I turned toward the door, ready to leave.

"I hope you know I've about given up on your daughters, Marta. I'm afraid they've been cursed by their father's attitude."

With the Bible still under my arm, I faced him with more energy than I thought I had. "They are *not* cursed, Pastor," I said. My fists clenched, my jaw so tight my teeth hurt. "They have strayed, but *never* will I consider them cursed."

Pastor turned to face the daylit windows. He stood with his back to me, his hands clasped behind his back. He was silent for what seemed like five minutes.

I stood behind him, wondering if I should leave. I'd never spoken to Pastor that way and I was immediately ashamed, the heat on my face and neck a dead giveaway. But how dare he accuse my daughters of being cursed. He might be a man of God, but with no children of his own, he couldn't begin to understand either the joy or heartache required to trudge a mother's path. Should I apologize? For what? For defending my daughters who stood accused? Absolutely not. My words were a mother's right and duty, though Herr Gott strike me down.

When he finally spoke, Pastor didn't turn but continued to stare out through the rain-streaked windows. His sigh defied explanation except for what it was, frustration. "I'll come and speak to your daughters again, Marta, though I confess I don't feel hopeful."

"Greatly appreciate it, Pastor. Thank you."

My words, automatic and rote, felt wooden in my mouth. With the Bible still under my arm, I took the doorknob in hand and pulled the scarf forward to shield my face from the rain. Closing the door behind me, my heart pounded frantically inside my chest. I was immediately grateful for the three blocks home and a chance to talk to you myself, Herr Gott. The Bible was mine to keep.

## Chapter Thirty

## Robert Comes to Dinner

## *1945*

The kitchen window contained a full line of blackbirds on the telephone line when I saw Ivan and Robert walk by the pigeon pen without stopping. Unusual in itself, the boys were whispering. When they turned toward the mudroom, I couldn't help but gasp when I saw Robert's face. Not only was his eye black but bruising covered his face, as though he'd been beaten by an entire gang of boys. Ivan preceded him when they stepped into the kitchen.

"What happened, Robert?" I asked, grabbing a wet towel as I walked toward the boys.

"Nothing, ma'am," he said.

"It's not nothing, dear boy," I said, wondering what I thought I was going to do with that towel. "Ivan, what's going on?"

Ivan turned to Robert. "You might as well tell her. She'll find out anyhow, especially if you stay here."

"Stay here? Find out? Come, boys, take off your coats and sit down. I'll get some kuchen and milk for the two of you."

They turned back into the mudroom and left their coats on the hooks along the wall and removed their boots—not because they were wet, but out of respect, it seemed. My heart beat too fast and my thoughts were a jumble as to what or who could have destroyed that poor boy's face. "Now sit down when you're ready. Maybe some tea with your milk? A little sugar?"

Ivan sat in his usual place, Robert beside him. Their backs were against the wall, where I could see them both. I marveled at what might have attacked Robert. "There's more kuchen if you want it," I said.

If I were Catholic, I would have crossed myself at this sight. But that would have been a heathen thing to do for an Evangelical. Instead, I ate my peach kuchen too quickly and was rising for a second cup of tea when I noticed tears on Robert's cheeks. Then Ivan's hand reached for his friend's shoulder. My own eyes burned just watching those two boys.

"Herr Gott says we have to tell the truth when we hope for healing," I said. I sat back down. The words sounded awkward coming from my mouth, considering Robert's face. I didn't know what else to say. His lip was cracked and bleeding, his nose as good as broken. Who could have done this to him?

"Ma," Ivan started to say, his eyes pleading in a way I'd never seen before. "Would it be okay if Robert stayed with us for a while? Maybe just for a night or two?"

"Of course," I was quick to say. "Should I call Dr. Schmidt to make a house call?" I was looking at Robert, but my question was directed toward Ivan.

"No ma'am," Robert said. His head remained bent toward his plate. Though he'd taken a bite or two of the kuchen, he was reluctant to raise his head and look at me.

Ivan shook his head. "No, Ma, don't call anyone. Robert will be okay in a day or two. Maybe he just won't go to school."

"Did this happen at school, or on the way there or home?" I asked. I realized that my questions came from the nervous fidgeting of my hands, the towel still in my lap and now my fingers twisting and untwisting it, moisture sinking into my apron and then my housedress. "Can I see your hand, Robert?"

"I'd rather not, ma'am."

He never looked up from his lap and he didn't respond to Ivan's hand on his arm. But the tears stopped coming, and eventually Ivan removed his hand and ate his kuchen in silence, slurping his milk and tea.

Not knowing what else to do, I picked up my plate and the empty mug and took them to the drainboard. The blackbirds were now mysteriously gone and the pigeons cooed in their cages, waiting for their supper. I pulled a large pot down from over the stove and set it on top of the stove. Stirred, then added more kindling to the fire. "Having leftover cabbage rolls for supper. Hope you like cabbage, Robert."

Behind me, he muttered, "Yes ma'am."

"When you boys have tended the pigeons, maybe you'll let me put some witch hazel on your face, Robert?"

"No ma'am. That would hurt."

"We need to do something so it doesn't get infected," I said. "Would you wash it yourself at the small sink over there if I gave you some Ivory soap?"

He glanced up at me for just a second, his still-short hair exposing his bruised forehead. "Yes ma'am, I'll try."

"Good," I said. "Then we'll be ready to sit down and eat."

"Thanks, Ma."

My eyes went to Ozzie's sink to make sure there was a fresh towel there. Not that a fresh towel would make any difference, not with these two boys and especially not now.

I WAS WAITING FOR Ivan when he came down to breakfast the next morning. He was alone, as I expected he would be. While I'd heard the boys whispering in bed when I went up last night, I must have fallen asleep before they did. I'd given Robert, such a big boy, a pair of Ozzie's old pajamas. The towel I handed him had barely been used and now hung on the rack in the mudroom where we kept our bath towels.

"Robert won't be going to school today," Ivan said. He scooted into his usual chair and put his elbows on the table, his chin in his hands even though he knew I didn't like that.

My eyes over the top of my glasses. I didn't need to say anything. We both knew I had a question he needed to answer.

"It's his dad, Ma," Ivan said. "Seems he drinks too much home brew. You know."

"No, I don't know, Ivan. But I can guess that what you're trying to tell me is that when Robert's dad drinks too much, he gets angry and strikes out at those around him. Is he the one who hurt Robert?"

Ivan shook his head, his hair floppy and over his eyes before he brushed it back. "Robert said he was going to run away," Ivan said. "That's why he's here." Ivan's eyes teared up. "I don't want him to leave."

"Of course you don't."

I spooned up his oatmeal, putting brown sugar on top as a treat, and milk; the raisins were already cooked into the oatmeal. Set it in front of Ivan along with a piece of toast. "Should we let his mom know he's here?"

"Don't know," Ivan said. "I don't want them coming here and causing trouble. His pa isn't like mine was."

I said nothing for a few minutes, busying myself at the sink. Then, picking up my tea, I sat down across from Ivan so I could see him better. "That was a nice thing to say about your pa."

"Well it's true. He never whooped me like other dads do. I tried not to give him any reason," Ivan said.

"Robert can stay for a night or two, but eventually he'll have to go home. Can't be adopting more than I have, even if the war just ended."

"Thanks, Ma. I'll ask him to call his ma and tell her where he is. Just so she knows. Mac's home now, so I don't think we need to be afraid."

Ivan had more faith in Mac than I did. "Think you should ask Robert to go to school, though. Either that or I'm going to call Dr. Schmidt."

"Don't do that, Ma. Will just make Robert mad." He stood up and took his bowl to the sink. "I'll tell him to get ready," he said. "Robert said that if Dr. Schmidt comes, they'll have to tell the sheriff. He doesn't want to get his pa in trouble. You know what I mean?"

"I've got some salve we can put on his face. Will start the healing. Tell him that."

"I will, Ma."

The dishwater was good and hot, the suds a relief. I'd always loved washing dishes. Dishes and ironing. Two pieces of toast on a plate left on the heating rack in case Robert changed his mind about eating. He'd hardly eaten a thing at dinner last night. Big boy like that shouldn't go without eating.

I thought to call Pastor. He would surely know a safe house where Robert could go. Appreciated that Ivan didn't want the sheriff involved. Besides, he'd have to come all the way from Dickinson, and that would create an even bigger fuss. That face, though—the black eye, red in the white of his eye. I wished I could call Dr. Schmidt without upsetting the boy.

When Robert came downstairs, he didn't look any better than the day before. He wouldn't look at me, even when I said, "Robert, some toast here for you."

"Thank you, ma'am," he said. "I'm kinda hungry."

"Want to sit down and eat it?"

"No, best not. We're already late."

"Run on, then," I said. "I'll expect you back for dinner, Robert."

Ivan pulled on Robert's arm. There was the beginning of a smile on Robert's face then. They grabbed their shoes from the mudroom floor and were gone before the sun hit the outhouse.

MUCH AS I DIDN'T want to, I set up the ironing board near the stove. Knew the morning would go faster if I kept busy. Grateful I had a prune kuchen in the cupboard that hadn't been cut. Wouldn't have time to bake before Dr. Schmidt got here.

Millie called Dr. Schmidt for me just so the operator wouldn't know. Now Millie knew Robert's situation too. The doctor agreed to come by midday. I needed to think over how to approach such a delicate situation. Another woman's son. A drunk father with a temper.

Like family, Dr. Schmidt hollered from the mudroom just before he stepped into the kitchen. I'd already set out the tea mugs and a couple of plates and forks. Kept the water hot on the back of the woodstove.

"Good to see you, Dr. Schmidt." I wiped my hands on my apron, unsure whether to shake hands with him or not. Would have liked to hug him but didn't know if that was right. "Have a seat and I'll have your tea right there. The prune kuchen as well."

"Marta, you're a woman after my own heart." He lowered himself into my usual chair. I'd never bothered to correct him.

Once we were seated, I sat there eating and trying to sort out whether I should mention Robert's name or not. Finally, I said, "I have a strange dilemma, Doctor." I explained about Ivan bringing a school friend home yesterday and the boy looking pretty beat up. That I'd wanted to call him, but the boy refused. Ivan said they were afraid the law would get involved. "I'm just not sure what to do, if I should do anything. Told the boy he could stay here a night or two, but I'm a little worried about what his pa will do."

Dr. Schmidt sat back in the chair and took off his glasses. "Wish I could see him," he said. "Sounds like his nose is broken from what you told me." He was thoughtful for a few minutes. "No need to report this to the sheriff. He can't do anything about it anyhow. Sounds like the family is in bad straits."

"That's what Ivan told me. He was only at their place once. Said he didn't care to go back again."

"Wish I could be more help." He thought again for a minute. "Don't suppose I could have another piece, do you, Marta?"

"I'm sorry, Doctor. I forgot my manners."

Before he put a fork into the pastry, he said, "Sometimes the fathers, when they haven't worked for a long time and they drink too much, go mad and don't really know what they're doing to themselves or their loved ones." Dr. Schmidt stopped, his fork to his mouth and a hum of satisfaction. He lifted his fingers to his lips and kissed them. "Marta, you are an absolute angel," he said. "You don't ever have to worry about calling me. I would come here for your kuchen any day . . . and your good company, of course."

"You're always welcome, Dr. Schmidt. You've done so much for us over the years. A slice of kuchen now and then is small payment, especially for all the times you never bothered to bill me."

Dr. Schmidt was thoughtful for a moment, his fork at rest on his plate. "There's a place in Nebraska run by some priests. Suppose he could go there. They call it Boys Town. Mostly for boys who get in trouble, but sounds like this one is in trouble not of his own making as far as we know."

"How do you get in touch, Doctor?"

"I'll see what I can find out when I get back to the office. Will ask Gertrude, my nurse, to call there. See what they require."

"Sure appreciate it, Dr. Schmidt. I'd hate to send him back home."

"Know what you mean."

Dr. Schmidt made two attempts to rise from his chair. He wasn't successful until the third try. When he stood, he wiped away the crumbs on his tie, his vest.

I listened for the back door to close, then covered what remained of the kuchen and tucked it back in the cupboard under its flour-sack covering. Standing at the sink, I watched the blackbirds taunt the pigeons. Madness. Was it madness that impelled Albert to smoke until the day he died, his tongue half gone and his throat so closed he could hardly swallow his nightly whiskey? Was it madness when Ada insisted on driving with Heinrich Bueller, knowing she was marked by sitting alone in a car with a married man? Was it madness when Irene ran off with Mac after six weeks of knowing him?

Best to finish the ironing and get on with the day. Grateful for Dr. Schmidt with his good heart. He was anything but madness.

# 1916

THE MORNING THEY FOUND Father outside the new barn, I refused to leave my bedroom. Through my single bedroom window, I watched Oscar and Uncle Herman wrap Father in a white cotton blanket Tante Ketcha took to them. The shroud was wrapped again in an old gray military blanket. A mummy in a homemade case. They then lay Father's torn body on the bed of the utility wagon. Drove off, the body alone and heavy on the slatted bed. Numb with disbelief, inside and out, I was as frozen as the snow. My arms, my legs, my eyes. If I had a heart, I had no idea where it had gone. I watched alone from my room as the horses pulled the wagon out of sight. All day, my tears dried before they began. I sat there watching Tante Ketcha swing buckets of well water against the barn and the snow, erasing the blood that splattered the new walls. Bucket after bucket until the walls were as fresh as they'd been before Father held the gun to his head, before his blood sprayed like buckshot across the new snow.

I was too scared to go to Mother's bedroom. She was likely hiding, the same as me. Or she was simply swallowed by a grief so deep it sucked all the remaining courage she'd depended on. Leo? I had no idea where he'd gone. Maybe the cellar. I wouldn't know. I hadn't left my room.

My chair faced the window when Uncle Herman and Oscar returned with the empty wagon bed. They were like strangers to each other. No words came from their tight lips, not a glance between them. Just their hunched shoulders. Uncle hung on to the reins and Oscar's hands clutched the buckboard seat, his eyes, if they could see, looked dead from where I sat.

All that time, I could hear Tante Ketcha in our kitchen. Not hers but ours. Heard her light the woodstove fire. Then the soup pot clanged on top of the iron cookstove. Water from a bucket filled the pot, probably half full, the way she always started soup. The meat cleaver down and down again on the cutting board. She must have hauled vegetables from her own cellar, because the bushel basket squeaked when she set it on the floor. I could see her scraping carrots and chopping off the ends of turnips. I might as well have been sitting on the kitchen stool and watching her, which I wasn't.

After the men put the horses away, they came into the house. Their boots shuffled against the new linoleum floor. "More wood," I heard Tante say. "Some bacon. And you might as well get the chores done even though it's early. That way we can all go to bed when the sun's down."

The clomp of boots back out the door into the mudroom, then gone. A knock on my door. Not a hard knock, the way Tante usually rapped at the door. I knew it was her. The men wouldn't dare come to my door for fear of disturbing emotions that might cloud the air they breathed. Gently, she knocked, not to disturb what was broken. "Marta," she whispered at the door crack. I heard her but continued to sit. To do nothing. Father was dead. After all we'd been through.

"Marta," a little louder. "I need your help. Come out please." *Please* from a woman who never said it. "Now," she added. More like her. When she didn't hear movement, her loud whisper filled the crack once again. "We can do this."

Her tone was firm and demanded a response. *We can do this*, words she leaned on when she didn't know what else to say, and the only path was forward. *We can do this*, when the calf came backward through the birth canal. When Uncle Herman's index finger disappeared behind the saw. When Father confessed the truth about the gold. I remember she sat there like she'd been shot just hearing those words from him. Then, with her big and strong arms, she pulled herself up from the table. She never looked once at Father, and she didn't look at Uncle Herman. Her eyes were on her feet when she pulled her body upright. *We can do this* was all she said.

## Chapter Thirty-One

## Marta and the Buick

### 1945

MILLIE LOOKED LIKE A child pretending to drive. We were in the Texaco garage and she'd settled behind the Buick's steering wheel, both hands on the wheel, her straw hat in place. "This is the biggest car I've ever seen, Marta."

"I wouldn't know," I said. As an afterthought, I added, "Is Heinrich Bueller's car this big?"

"Don't think so," Millie said. "He has a Ford, the same as us."

Millie pulled out the choke, carefully, oh so carefully, before turning the key in the ignition. She tried once, twice, a third time. Her frustrated sigh made obvious the fact that the car wouldn't start, the key making an awful grinding noise. Before I could open the car door to go into the Texaco station, Fritz came running into the garage, shouting, "Stop, stop, for Pete's sake."

Millie didn't see him, not until he waved his hands in front of the windshield. "You'll ruin the starter," he yelled. A powerful smell of gasoline filled the garage. I hurried toward the open garage door, shouting over my shoulder, "We'd better get out of here, Millie, before the car explodes." I could just see us going up in a ball of flame, the photograph blazed across the headlines in the *Bismarck Tribune* tomorrow morning.

"No, no, no," Fritz continued. "You've pulled the choke out too far and now the car is flooded. Give me a minute." He lifted the immense hood of the car and buried his head inside. "Ozzie disconnected the battery cables before he left." With the hood still in the air, he came back around to Millie. "You wait out front until I get it ready," he said. "I'll start it."

Poor Millie, just trying to do a good deed and already getting yelled at. We held our handbags on our arms and stood outside the garage door. Embarrassment stabbed me more sharply when I realized Ivan and Robert were watching the whole scene. When they exchanged a glance, I didn't like the impish smile on Ivan's face.

"Go home, boys," I said. "Tend the pigeons and keep an eye on the house." As an afterthought, I added, "No smoking, understand?"

Millie and I were nervous enough. She said she's never driven such a big car. "Maybe my Henry should be teaching you to drive, Marta. You know I'm only good on the open road. Why, I can't even back our car out of the garage."

I opened my pocketbook in search of my handkerchief. Kept my head down. Surely Fritz would get the car started before Millie chickened out.

"I've never taught anyone to drive, Marta," Millie said. She was now hunched over the steering wheel and we had just driven onto Highway 12. Her hands clutched the steering wheel of Ozzie's Buick. Even though I'd brought two pillows from the house to put under her, she still looked like a kid Ivan's age driving a grown-up car. "Maybe we should turn around and go back to town."

My eyes focused straight ahead. If Millie was nervous, I was terrified. My sweaty hand held on to my hanky, and I could hardly swallow. It was one thing to have the idea of driving, another to actually do it. Learn, anyhow. What if I wrecked this beautiful car the first time I tried to drive? What if I killed somebody? Even myself and Millie? Who would take care of Ivan? With the girls practically gone, I was all that Ivan had.

"I know a place where the road ends," Millie said. "Out past the water tower and away from town. That way we won't hurt anyone."

"Fine," I said. She was thinking like me. Wishing Ozzie hadn't bought such a big car. Even with two cushions, Millie still had a hard time seeing over the steering wheel.

"What year you say this Buick is?" Millie asked.

"I don't know, Millie. I never knew there was a year."

"Our Ford's a '39. This has to be a whole lot newer. Nice cloth seats and all this chrome. The car looks like no one ever sat in it before."

"Only Ozzie. Oh, and Albert when Ozzie took him to Butte and then west to see the ocean," I said. "I'm sure Ozzie told his dad he couldn't smoke in the car."

I could just see Albert bite down on his lip and stare straight ahead, never saying a word. It wasn't often that someone told him what to do. I doubt anyone except Ozzie could have gotten away with it, and that was only because Albert adored his son. Probably wished *he* had been Ozzie.

"You'd never know anyone rode in this car. Not a crumb on the seats. No mud on the pedals or even on the tires. Oh, there is one small burn mark."

"Probably Albert smoking in the car."

"Bet Ozzie had a fit."

"I never heard about it, but then I wouldn't. Ozzie knew how I felt about Albert smoking. It was the one thing he asked his dad not to do. Would have loved to have been a mouse in the car."

"All this time in Fritz's Texaco?"

"Only drove that one time to Butte and the ocean. Once in a while Ozzie took it to Dickinson."

"He liked the girls, didn't he?"

"Too much, if you ask me."

"Wish my David had liked them more. But getting married wasn't going to keep him out of the war. Look at Ada and Irene. They both have kids. Their men went to war anyhow."

"Mac volunteered," I said. My tone insinuated he was trying to get away from his responsibilities, his children. "Said Irene would be better off if he was . . . you know, killed."

"How could she be better off?"

"Money, I guess. Said she'd get money from the government like Eli does now from his pa dying."

Millie steered the car to a dead-end road. She pulled up the hand brake and put the car in neutral, double-checking that's where it was before she took her feet off the floor pedals. "Let's just sit for a minute. Leave it running. Actually, I'm afraid to turn it off."

"Fine with me," I said.

Sometimes I became nervous with silence, especially today, when we were doing something I'd never done before. Reminded me of the first time I was asked to make a beef stew for the whole family, Uncle Herman's included. Natalia volunteered to help. But I hadn't cooked anything since Russia, when Tante Louisa taught me how to cook that one dish that used sausage. I couldn't remember what they called it. Not sauerbraten, not beef brisket. Maybe I couldn't remember because I was so nervous—not only my hands sweating but the armpits of my dress felt soaked. In the end Natalia did most of the cooking. I was too nervous, threatening tears the whole afternoon.

"See that hawk on the fence?" Millie asked. "Henry says that means a storm's coming."

"How does he know that?"

"You know men. They know everything." Millie smiled and turned toward me. "At least they think they do."

Smiling lightened the mood. I sighed, then smiled myself. Millie and I were the only ones who could talk to each other this way.

"Maybe put your handbag in the back seat," Millie said. "For a first lesson, we'll trade places and you can just get used to the seat." She turned toward me. "Now, don't fuss. I can see you're getting riled up. All you're going to do is sit here where I am."

I took a deep breath. Turned toward my friend, her eyes smiling in an attempt to make this easier for me. "Guess I'm never going to learn from this side of the car, am I?"

"All you have to do is sit here and see how it feels."

It was never easy for me to maneuver my big body, and now, being nervous, it seemed even harder to get my legs and then my big self out the door. All Millie had to do was scoot across the seat. I couldn't believe how nervous I was, my heart already beating too fast.

"Careful with your feet when you get in," Millie said. "Don't touch the pedals at all. Not until I tell you."

I stuck my head inside the driver's side and stared down at the floor. Three pedals. "I thought there was only one pedal."

"No, there are three. The far right is gas, the far left is what's called a clutch. And the middle is the brake . . . the most important one."

"I get what the brake does. The gas makes you go. But what does a clutch do?" I craned my neck toward the floor, but it was too dark down there and I could hardly make out the three pedals.

"Maybe just feel with your hand down there to see where they are and what they feel like," Millie said.

"Will I get my hands dirty?"

"You will." Millie reached over the seat to get my handbag. "I'll let you get a handkerchief out of your handbag if that makes you feel better."

"Doesn't look dirty down there, but you never know where shoes have been."

"Right," Millie said. "Can never be too careful."

THE FIRST PERSON TO ride in Ozzie's Buick with me was, of course, Ivan. It had been three months of twice-weekly lessons while he was in school. We kept practicing where the road ended. Finally, I drove on the highway for ten miles, as far as Oscar's farm, although we didn't bother to stop. I still wasn't good at the clutch and brake thing, but Millie assured me that would come in time.

On a Thursday in summer, I invited Ivan to go with me to see his uncle Oscar. This would be the first time I drove there alone. After he settled himself on the seat, he said, "Don't wreck, Ma."

"Is that a kind thing to tell your dear ma when you're her first passenger?"

"You know what I mean."

His comment didn't lift my confidence, but I figured if we went slowly and I concentrated, we'd be fine. We chose a midweek day when I didn't think there would be much traffic on the highway.

Since learning to drive, I'd kept the Buick in front of the house, right outside the gate. Ivan had been sworn to secrecy as far as his sisters were concerned, especially not to tell Little Marta, who couldn't be trusted to keep a secret. "It's one thing that Robert knows, but your sisters don't need to know until I'm ready to tell them."

"Will Tante Millie keep the secret?"

"Yes, she understands that once it's out, the whole town will know. Bad enough we're parking the Buick out front. Just can't afford the two dollars a month your brother gave Fritz to keep the car in the garage."

Since we lived close enough to old Highway 79, I figured the only folks to see me drive were Millie and her Henry next door. Henry had been sworn to secrecy as well. The gossip at Jake's Tavern was likely where most of the town gossip started. And the church, of course.

From our front street, it was easy enough to pull onto the road and turn left at the end of the block and onto the highway without anyone knowing the difference. Anyhow, that's what I wanted to believe.

Wouldn't you know, that day, maybe because I had Ivan beside me, I pulled the choke out too far. Then I had trouble coordinating my feet on the pedals. I killed the engine once, twice, and almost a third time when the flooded engine finally took hold and we lurched forward.

"Take it easy, Ma," Ivan said. He grabbed hold of the armrest, his whole body leaning forward, his other hand against the dashboard.

"Ivan, be quiet," I said, my voice snapping in a way Ivan rarely heard.

Once we made the left turn at the four-way stop, I was on the road, shifting into third gear when we'd picked up just enough speed. We both sat back, listening to the hum of the engine. I stayed right at twenty-five miles an hour, afraid I'd kill the engine again if I slowed down too much. Then we'd really be in trouble. Texaco Fritz would have to come get us and the whole town would know. My armpits were already sweaty. Those ten miles to Oscar's farm would be the farthest I'd ever gone without Millie. Somehow, I decided to go there just to see that I could. No idea what I'd do if someone tried to pass us or we came behind a slow-moving cart or wagon. But I especially wanted to prove my new accomplishment to my young son before I dared test my daughters. With Mac back, it had become urgent that I learn to drive. Something told me that one of these days he'd be coming by to ask about Ozzie's car.

By the time I pulled off the road at Oscar's, we'd been in the car for an hour to get exactly ten miles from town. I could have blamed it on needing to follow a hay wagon I couldn't see around. Then I forgot where to turn off the highway to Oscar's place, the hay wagon blocking my view. Fortunately, I was driving slow enough that I recognized Oscar's mailbox with the extra-large red flag permanently raised and right on the highway. Easing into the gravel driveway, I was careful not to get too close to the house for fear I'd get mud on the tires.

I'd barely turned off the ignition when Ivan leaped out of the car. "I'll go and tell him we're here."

"You haven't seen your uncle for a while," I said. "Maybe we should go in together."

Ivan beat me to the front porch. "Wait until I tell Robert I'm the first one to ride with you," he said, so excited he pulled the screen door open in my face.

"Ivan, slow down," I said. But I had to smile. Seeing him so enthusiastic was worth all those lessons and all the worry and, now, the new gasoline expense. For sure, we wouldn't be driving too far too often. Already, I figured Ada could give me the dollar she gave to Heinrich Bueller. That would persuade her further that living with me and Ivan was the best solution, especially since she hadn't yet moved. Wasn't that half the reason I learned to drive? To end that scandal with Heinrich once and for all? In fact, I hadn't bothered to tell Pastor. Strange, because I'd never kept anything from him. But that last time in his study, something in my feelings changed. I didn't need to be shamed by my own pastor.

"Yoo-hoo, it's us," I called into the house. "Marta and Ivan. Remember, I called and said we were coming."

"Don't stand there letting in the flies. Come in," Oscar shouted back.

Ivan ran through the kitchen and into the living room, where he stood in front of his uncle. "Hi Uncle Oscar," he said. "Guess who drove us here."

"If Millie's out there, better keep her in the kitchen until your mother gets me cleaned up."

Ivan took a giant step back from his uncle and looked at me coming into the living room. "Millie didn't bring us," I said.

"Then who?"

"We came in Ozzie's Buick," Ivan said.

"I'll be damned," Oscar said. He leaned forward in his rocking chair and turned back toward where I stood a few steps away so Ivan could have his excitement. "You teach Ivan to drive? He's kind of short for that big car."

I lifted my veil and removed my hat. "Your sister drove us."

"What sister? You're the only one I have."

By now, Ivan was pointing at me and grinning in a way I hadn't seen for a long time. "Ma drove us, Uncle Oscar. Ma drove us all by herself. With me."

"I don't believe it." His eyes wide and his mouth hanging open. "I don't believe it, Marta." He sat back in his chair. "How?"

"How do you think? I learned to drive," I said. "Only way I could think to get Ada off the road with Heinrich Bueller."

He sank back against the chair, the same grizzled look and the same shirt he wore the last time I was here. "I'll be damned."

"Don't keep saying that, Oscar," I said. "Not what the good Lord wants to hear."

"Can't help myself," he said. "I'm shocked."

He stared at Ivan as if seeing him for the first time. "When did you go and get all growed up, boy?"

"Fourth grade now," Ivan said, a grin on his face. "Isn't it great about Ma, and she didn't even wreck."

"I sure hope not. Your brother would turn over in his grave."

"You think he'd be happy?" I asked.

"He'd be happy that car isn't sitting in Fritz's Texaco," Oscar said. "I'm surprised Mac hasn't hit you up for the car."

"The girls don't know yet. I swore Ivan to secrecy until I'm good and ready to tell them."

"They'll be shocked, I've no doubt. Their mother going and getting all modern on them."

"I hope they'll be shocked. They think they know everything," I said. "Now look at you. Let's get you cleaned up. I brought kuchen and homemade sauerkraut hoping you had some sausages left from butchering."

Oscar scooched toward the edge of his rocking chair. "Just let me get out of this chair," he said. "If you're staying for lunch, you'll have to help me get cleaned up." He grinned at Ivan. "Only time I clean up is when your ma comes. She won't feed me unless I do."

Ivan backed away to give his uncle room. But I could see Oscar struggling more than ever. "Here, let me give you a hand."

"You're getting kind of old for this, sister."

"But I'm not crippled up with arthritis either," I said. "Here, Ivan, you pull from the other side, but not too hard or he'll fall on both of us."

Ivan laughed. "Then who will come and take us home?" he asked.

"We'd have to call Tante Millie," I said.

"Not Pastor?" Oscar asked.

"Not Pastor," I said. "Not today."

# Chapter Thirty-Two

*July 12, 1945*
*Dear Miss Cherry Hendrix,*

    *I apologize for not writing to you sooner. After you left, spring finally came and I needed to get the seeds in the ground. I hope this letter finds you well and settled back in your apartment.*

    *It is now months since we buried our dear Ozzie, months of learning to live without his smiling face, his many kindnesses. A time during which the tears never stopped for me. Maybe not for you. As the months passed, I have greatly appreciated your courage in coming to our small town from so far away. The effort and expense that trip must have required. And though I haven't written before, it seemed only right as time passed to say thank you. Thank you for coming but also, even more, for loving my Ozzie. Also, for allowing my family to meet you and to know you even briefly.*

    *I also want to thank you for signing the insurance papers. That was very thoughtful and generous of you. I appreciate it more than I can say.*

    *Enclosed in this package is Ozzie's hairbrush. This may seem like an odd gift, but I have held on to it as one of the last mementos belonging to him. I don't know why I thought you would want it, but I'm sending it anyhow.*

*Again, thank you for coming. May Herr Gott bless and keep you.*
*Mrs. Marta Gottlieb*

I SEALED THE ENVELOPE and folded it over the cigar box Ivan secured from Jake's Tavern when he returned the half-full whiskey jar, thinking someone there might want it. Crumpling newspaper, I surrounded the hairbrush so it wouldn't rattle. If it hadn't been for Millie saying, "We can't keep hanging on, Marta," I might have never found the courage to pull out the hairbrush and all those other things I hid under the bed. Except for the eye cups and bay rum, I put everything in the trash while Ivan was in school so he wouldn't see them and be tempted to covet those things for himself. It was now stored above Ozzie's sink in the medicine cabinet. When Ivan needed his first razor, I'd give it to him. A gift from his big brother.

A paper bag cut open served as covering, twine to wrap around the box. A half hour later the package was addressed, my letter tucked inside. Because Miss Hendrix was a hairdresser, I thought she might appreciate this gift most of all.

I had to sit and have a cup of tea and a slice of kuchen when I'd finished. Then my galoshes on my feet and a trip to the post office. All before Ivan returned from school.

# Chapter Thirty-Three

## Ada's New Ride

## 1945

I WAS READY WHEN Ada walked past Millie and up the brick path, Eli pulling the Radio Flyer behind her. I quickly moved the teakettle onto the hot coals at the front of the cookstove and pulled two mugs from the overhead shelf. A cup of tea might ease any tension. Ada never liked a plan that wasn't of her own making.

"Ma, I don't have time for tea," Ada said, laying her summer sweater across the back of the chair. "Was hoping to leave Eli here for a bit. Millie said she could take him if you were too busy."

"Never too busy," I said. I refilled the teapot with fresh tea and set it on the trivet atop the kitchen table. "Please take a minute to sit. I have a surprise for you."

Ada raised her newly drawn eyebrows. Plucking them, I could

see. Another sign of the times.

"Just for a minute," I assured her. "I have good news."

"We could use some good news around this town," she said.

"Then please sit down and let me pour you one cup of tea. That's all," I said. My heart pounded in my throat the way it did when I got excited.

Even when she wasn't working, Ada had become the picture of fashion I saw in the *Life* magazines that Millie gave me after she was finished. We both knew such magazines were forbidden by Pastor, but we read them anyhow. A new white blouse on Ada with what they called a Peter Pan collar. Olive-green slacks. Loafers. You'd have thought she found the pot of gold at the end of the rainbow.

"Make it quick, Ma," she said. "Promised Althea I'd watch the creamery while she went to the dentist in Dickinson. Could be all afternoon." With the teacup raised to her lips, she asked, "What's the good news?"

"If you'll stand for a minute and go with me into the living room, I want to show you something."

"Is this a game, Ma? If so, I don't have time for it."

Though she was reluctant, she pushed back her chair and followed me into the living room. Despite the chill, I opened the front door. "There, look out front," I said.

"That's Ozzie's car," she said. Surprise registered in the lilt of her voice and a puzzled look covered her face. "How'd it get there?"

"I drove it there," I said.

Her mouth opened and her green eyes narrowed like she didn't believe a word I said or even what she saw parked near the fence. "When did that happen?" she asked. "You? Driving? How?"

My smile seemed to have a strange effect on her because all she could do was shake her head. "I don't believe it," she said. "You're always railing against modern women and who they've become. No, don't tell me. Millie? Your brother Oscar? The pastor?"

"I didn't ask a man," I said. "Our neighbor taught me how to drive." Before she could protest further, I continued, "You can ask Ivan. We drove yesterday to see your uncle."

"I'll be doggoned," she said. "I've never even thought about driving myself, even though that big Buick's been parked at Fritz's Texaco since before Ozzie left for the war." She gazed at me with new respect. "Good for you, Ma. I have to hand it to you."

"Let's go finish our tea and I'll tell you how it happened."

Returning to the kitchen, I folded my hands on the kitchen oilcloth. *Herr Gott, I need all the help You can give me now.* Ada continued to look at me with wonderment. "One of the reasons I learned to drive is, firstly, we had a car that was just sitting in a garage." I hesitated, my hands nervous when they held my tea mug. "But my greatest motive was you."

Her face was a question. "Why me?"

"So I could take you to Horton and pick you up myself."

"Ma, you know that's not necessary. Besides, we don't have gas coupons."

"I can get them and so can you," I said. I wanted to say what I had to say without mentioning Heinrich Bueller's name once. "I believe your ride has been worth two dollars a week lately. If you put that much gas in Ozzie's car, I'll be more than happy to drive you."

I wasn't expecting Ada to start laughing. And laugh she did, never taking her eyes off me, though I know I had a puzzled expression on my face. "Yes, Ma. Yes," she said. "I can't believe you went to all this trouble so I wouldn't drive with that awful man anymore."

The heat of embarrassment invaded my face and my neck. I should have known better than to try to pull the wool over Ada's eyes. She was too smart for me.

When she finally stopped laughing, she said, "I think you need to practice a bit more, or at least take me for a long ride before I get rid of the ride I have."

Though I didn't want to agree, I said, "Yes. That'll be fine."

"I have to hand it to you, Ma. I never thought you had it in you."

Was that a compliment or an insult? I wasn't sure. "One thing," I said. "I'd rather we kept this between us, you and me. Mac's just home, and I'd rather they don't know right now."

Ada grinned at me. This was the conspiracy we knew it was. "Agreed," she said. "Until you tell them yourself."

She became thoughtful. "Remember, Ma, this doesn't change me moving to Horton. Just so you know."

"Of course," I said, straight-faced and appropriately somber. What Ada didn't realize was that we were both the same kind of smart.

## Chapter Thirty-Four

*August 10, 1945*
*Dear Mrs. Gottlieb,*

*I hope this finds you well and enjoying summer. No doubt, it's much warmer than when I was there. Your garden must be beautiful.*

*Your letter and package arrived a week after you sent them. I was so touched by your kind sentiments and your thoughtfulness. I appreciate how difficult it must have been for you to part with such a powerful memento of Ozzie. Thank you for this kindness.*

*Since your letter, I have met a gentleman barber who works next to my salon. He is widowed and has a daughter who is eight. We have begun to see each other. Having a caring person like him in my life has helped ease the loss of Ozzie. We take his daughter to the park and swimming.*

*I wanted to tell you this because you were so kind to me. Because we both loved Ozzie so very much. Because, for the first time, I feel hopeful about my life again. I would be so happy to know you also feel hopeful. You are a wonderful woman, Mrs. Gottlieb. I count myself lucky that I was able to meet you and your family.*

*Best regards,*
*Cherry Hendrix*

## Chapter Thirty-Five

## Mac's Request

## *1945*

Seeing Mac at the back door wasn't a surprise, although it was the first time he'd appeared at my door since he came home from the war. I'd already anticipated he'd come as soon as he knew the Buick was out of Fritz's Texaco. How he knew it was parked in front of the house and not in the alley where the children would see it, I didn't know. It didn't matter. I was expecting him.

He walked up the brick path from the alley past the outhouse and pigeon pen and the abundant garden, now that we'd been blessed these last months with summer. Irene strolled beside him and all the children, including Eli, followed behind like ducks waddling behind their mother. Little Marta brought up the rear, pulling the Radio Flyer with Louisa riding inside, her three-year-old legs still taxed by the four-block walk.

I wiped my hands and greeted them at the mudroom door. "Welcome home, Mac," I said, reminding myself that he was the father of my grandchildren.

He was sheepish when he leaned down to kiss my cheek; the smell of Old Spice on his face and his black hair combed back and gleaming. "Hello, Mother Gottlieb," he said. Formal but affectionate-seeming.

"Come in, come in," I told Irene and the children. "I have the teakettle on and some fresh rolls if you'll have them." Now who was being formal?

The children scurried to their usual places, all of them with their hands folded on the oilcloth as though they'd suddenly acquired new manners. "Think I'll stand," Mac said. "Can't stay long."

"Sorry to hear that," I said. "Had hoped we'd have some time after . . . after all you've been through."

"Thanks, Mother Gottlieb." He hesitated, his hands on his hips and those dark eyes right into mine. "Irene probably told you I got a job in South Dakota. Fort Meade," he said.

I chose to stand as well, even while Irene sat at the table with the children, all of them looking up at us. "Why so far away?"

A half smile I didn't trust before he suddenly grinned. "Got a job at the hospital because I can type, if you can believe that. My mother made me learn." He laughed to himself, waiting for me to join him in the joke.

"What's important about typing?" I asked, a defensive tone undercutting my words. If I heard it, so did everyone else.

"It got me a job as a hospital ward clerk," he said. "And it qualified me for postwar housing for my family."

When I sat, the heaviness I always felt in my body doubled when my hips found the chair. "Could you have done that here?"

He was still standing, his white shirt open at the neck like Ozzie, though his chest was absent the thick tufts of hair that always filled Ozzie's upper chest. When I glanced at Irene, she was all eyes on him, the smile on her face the same as the first time she brought him home and Albert shook his hand. For all her brave talk when Mac was gone, she was clearly as crazy about this man now as when he left. I didn't have a chance.

"Would have to move to Bismarck, but it's just as cold there as it is here." He hesitated. "Nice town, Sturgis, where we're moving to." Then, as though he suddenly recalled why he was here, "Actually, I came to talk to you about Ozzie's Buick. Wondered if you'd sell it to me so we can take it to South Dakota."

Now it was my turn to wield a half smile. My full face, scars and all, right up at that man still standing like he was king of the mountain. "Wish I could help you, Mac."

I'd been preparing for this moment. Rehearsed it over tea with Millie. I knew he would come wanting that car, and, much as I loved my grandchildren, I'd already decided who should own that car. It wasn't him.

He stood there with the dumbest look on his face. Disbelieving, really. And Irene frowned at me, like *what are you saying, Ma*, though she never said a word.

"It's taken, Mac. I'm so sorry."

"Taken?" he asked.

He'd clearly forgotten his manners. "Yes," I said. "I'm driving the Buick."

His mouth opened in surprise, as did Irene's. Before they could say anything, Little Marta, joined by Sissy, shouted, "Can we go for a ride, Oma? Can we, can we go with you?"

When Mac recovered himself, tightness gripped his jaw. "That doesn't mean you can't sell it to me."

"I need it here, Mac. I'm so sorry. If I'm going to be alone, I need to be able to get to my brother's and the doctors in Dickinson if need be," I said. "I'm sure you can find another car in town that suits your budget."

I added the last point because, even if I agreed to sell him the car, I doubted very much that I'd have seen more than the first payment. Besides, Mac had his parents in Mandan to ask for money or a car. He didn't need a widow's only foreseeable asset. He'd find a way. Men like that always did.

The conversation and the visit ended as soon as it began, signaled when Irene rose from her chair. Maybe she needed to get her husband out of there before he became more forceful. "I'll be back later, Ma," she said. A promise, no doubt, to try to talk me out of my resolve. Mac tried to smile, following this sign from his wife. But his smile was forced; his teeth still clenched. Only when Irene started toward the mudroom did Mac's hands come off his hips. "Yes, we'll be back . . . Mother," he said. He didn't nod or look at me again, but rather followed his wife toward the mudroom door.

"Can we stay?" Little Marta begged her mother.

"They can stay and help me bake," I said, my eyes directed toward Irene and away from Mac and the children. "Will give you two time alone."

"I'll come back in a couple of hours," Irene said. To the children, "Don't fill up on sweets now, you hear?"

There was something hypocritical about her admonishment, considering she and Ada spent their evenings making popcorn balls and fudge, exhausting their double sugar rations between the two of them. But I'd have to learn to ignore my judgments. For all I knew, the family will have left town by the time the leafy tops of the carrots had come and gone.

## Chapter Thirty-Six

## Mac & Irene Leaving

## 1945

THE DAY MAC DROVE up the gravel drive, the new used Ford packed tight, three small heads bobbed in the back seat. I waited at the screen door. I was right that the carrots had come and gone by the time Mac and Irene would finally drive south to Fort Meade. Since none of the girls were yet in school, it wouldn't matter if they arrived in mid-September; they'd still have relatively warm weather to get settled. Irene said I should come on the bus once they were in their new home. I could stay for a week or two, or I could bring Ivan with me and stay for a month in summer. I doubted she'd consulted Mac about this plan. He'd barely said two words to me since the Buick incident, and he'd never again graced the mudroom stoop, except once for a welcome-home pot roast dinner. Even then he remained painfully silent throughout the meal.

Irene's offer for us to visit was likely a consolation prize for their determined departure and another tear in the family curtain. Like our family's move from Russia and my resulting facial scars, this was a deep wound that might never heal.

The children, excited, ran in and out of the screen door, checking upstairs in the bedclothes for a lost teddy bear or baby blanket, then under Ivan's bed for stray socks they might have missed on their overnights, any toothbrushes still sitting in a cup at the kitchen sink. To them, this was a great adventure. None of them had been outside of Myra except for a single train ride to Mandan to visit Mac's parents the month before.

I'd insisted that Ivan go to school. "We never know when Mac will get here," I said, having considered the pace at which Mac moved into action. Add three daughters and a disorganized wife, and they were bound to leave after lunch rather than midmorning as they claimed. In anticipation, I'd prepared ham, potato salad, fresh bread, and cinnamon rolls for the family to eat here and take with them. Predictably, Mac would be anxious to get his family on the road. Irene had likely packed bologna and cheese or peanut butter and jelly sandwiches. Still, a good meal wouldn't hurt them, and they'd only be delayed in leaving by half an hour.

Lying in bed the night before, I wondered again if I should reconsider giving Irene my Easter egg, still wrapped inside the silk and once again hidden in the wall safe. The diamond and pearl egg fit easily into the palm of my hand. Though I'd decided to save it for Little Marta, I remained conflicted and didn't know what to do. What if they lost it on the trip? What if they were tempted to hock it? I carried the egg in my apron pocket all morning, reaching inside to feel the sharp edges of the diamonds, my fingers trailing the raised pearls. My uncertainty held throughout the day, as did the egg inside my pocket.

No early or midday parting for this family. By the time they were anywhere ready to leave, the sky had darkened and Eli had fed the pigeons. I stood on the back stoop facing the alley where Mac loaded the last of the suitcases and blankets into the car's trunk. The moon had climbed through the oak tree and seemed to look down on us, the night air holding the day's heat. The smell of late-mown hay swept across the outlying fields. With that slight breeze came the particular freshness of things settled for the night now that the day had been abandoned by the sun.

Irene, a bandana around her hair and tied on top, wore slacks and what my daughters dismissed as sensible shoes, the saddle shoes and white socks meant to keep her feet warm, though the night wasn't that cool.

I hugged my arms where I stood, not that I wanted them to leave, and not that I wouldn't carry the day's heaviness long afterward. The tension about the Buick would likely always build a wall between me and Mac. So be it. The Buick was definitely a flashier car than the Ford he ended up buying. I could wait out his silence as I'd learned to do throughout my long marriage. Not that anyone noticed or cared how much a woman's life was spent waiting.

This departure reminded me of the first evening my family waited in the ship's hold. When we stood in front of the stacked bunks before the ship left the harbor, Father said he and the boys would take the top bunk and leave the lower one for me and Mother. We waited for the ship to leave, for the night to begin. On this evening, like then, there was the sense of leaving everything that was safe and known, everything we'd counted on to keep us secured in place. Hopefully the blue light at the end of day would prove a good time for them to leave. Maybe the growing darkness would mask what was being left behind.

With Mac's presence and this new resentment between us came an unspoken dictate for me to only mention practical things. Enough blankets and pillows? Do you have the necessary teddy bears? Socks on the children's feet? Have you been to the outhouse? Enough jars of water?

Irene hurried in and out of the house, avoiding my glance and rushing past me where I stood in the kitchen trying to decide whether it was better for me to stay out of the way or find a way to be helpful, awkward as that was. Though we ate the planned lunch and the rest of the ham was packed in waxed paper, dinnertime was at hand. A pot of vegetable soup simmered on the back of the stove, but no one made a move to suggest dinner or say they were hungry or it would be good to eat again now that it was so late.

It was nearly six o'clock when Ivan wandered into the kitchen. "Guess they're still getting ready," he said. He took a few short steps toward where I stood at the sink, and unexpectedly, he reached around my waist and hugged my back. "I'm kinda hungry, Ma."

"Why don't you set about six places at the table, just silverware and small plates. I'll tell Irene there's soup if anyone wants it."

He squeezed me again, maybe afraid to say anything the same way I was afraid, the tears we were hanging on to while not wanting to make everyone else sad.

"Don't forget to wash your hands," I said.

Outside, the girls had already taken their place in the back seat, their three heads only visible when I walked closer to the car. Stuffed animals crowded their laps. They'd draped blankets across their legs, though the day was still warm. Pillows rested on the floorboards under their stocking feet. While the girls were smiling and eager, there was a silent tension between their parents. Mac avoided any glance toward me, and Irene busied herself with a couple of half-filled cardboard boxes that Mac seemed to have a hard time fitting into the car's already-full trunk.

"Can't you just put that stuff in one box?" Mac asked, the edge of his words betraying his impatience.

"I don't want to mix the girls' stuff with our own," Irene said.

Mac, hands on his hips, his hair falling into his eyes, said, "For

God's sake, Irene, it won't make a damned bit of difference. Just cram the stuff into one box, for Pete's sake."

I backed away from the two of them and, at a safe distance, turned and walked back into the house, the egg still in my pocket, where it would stay. "You can take the other plates away," I said to Ivan. I went to the stove and dipped up two bowls of soup and carried them, one at a time, to the table. Pulled the rolls from the warming oven. Butter on the table. "It's just the two of us, son."

His eyes found mine and he nodded. This was the way it would be.

## Chapter Thirty-Seven

### Ada Moves

# 1945

THE LATE-SUMMER LIGHT BEGAN to fade and the children's laughter and squeals had slipped into the walls. Ivan was outside working in the pigeon pen. Ada busy cleaning up at home now that everyone had left. Said she was getting ready to move at the end of the month. Late as it was, I turned on the teakettle. In the cupboard, I spied the one piece of peach kuchen I'd saved for this moment. A sad ending to a major chapter in my life.

*What now, Herr Gott?* Ozzie dead and both girls as good as gone. Ivan only nine years old. Never in my life had I thought I might leave this town, my church, these wheat fields, winter coming on like it did with its wind and blizzards, then the crocuses announcing spring, the summer garden. Fall canning. All my loved ones lay buried in the First Bible Church's cemetery. Who would take care of their graves? Who would I have tea and kuchen with? What about Millie? Why was I even thinking that way?

The outside screen door squeaked open, followed by the squeal of Eli's voice. "Oma, Oma. I'm here."

"Indeed you are. Come give your oma a kiss."

"Do you have more?" he asked, seeing my empty plate.

"I'm sure I can find something. You're up awfully late, aren't you? Where's your mom?"

"She's by the alley talking to Tante Millie."

Eli scooted his chair closer to the table before sitting down, scraping it along the linoleum like he always did until the chair was in the same place he sat when the girls were here. "Milk?" I asked.

"Yes, Oma. And a *cimmamom* roll."

He made me laugh with his notion of what he wanted.

"Here's your mom," I said, glancing at the door from the mudroom.

Ada wore a bandana tied around her hair and tucked on top. "They left a mess," she said.

"Have a seat; I'll fix you a nice cup of tea."

Ada plopped into a chair close to Eli, who reached out and patted his mother's hand. "It's okay they're gone, Mama. Now you have me all to yourself."

Ada's smile was half-dismissive.

"How soon do you have to be out of the house?" I asked.

"This coming Friday, and I have to work on Thursday and Friday."

"You can bring your things over here. Ivan will be happy to help."

"I need a man for this job, Ma."

"I'm sure Pastor can find someone."

"I don't want to talk to Pastor. Not after last time."

"Suit yourself."

I busied myself at the stove and the sink. "It's hard to see them go. You two living together the last couple of years. I loved having you close by, and I think you actually had fun together."

Ada said nothing for a few minutes. She kept her eyes on her hands, smoothing the cuticles now that they'd started to bleed. "Think I could store some of my stuff in the shed until I find a place?"

"Sure, Ivan can move things around," I said. "What kind of stuff are you talking about?"

"The sofa and bed. Won't need it if I stay here awhile. That is, if you'll have me and Eli."

*Herr Gott be praised, just what I'd prayed for.* Casual as I could, I said, "You two can have your old room."

"Eli's restless. Kicks me all night."

I looked at Ada long and hard. The top button on her flowered blouse was undone. Would be a blessing to get that girl married off again. "He can sleep with me if it gets too bad. Or his uncle Ivan."

I pulled the cinnamon rolls out of the cupboard and sat down in my usual place. "Want some soup, something to hold you?"

She continued to smooth the square shape of her fingers, massaging their length, her eyes on her hands. "No, Ma. I want an apartment."

Hard as it was, I was learning that the more I kept my mouth shut, the more she'd say. I cut between the cinnamon rolls to separate them. Eli had already eaten and gone out back with Ivan, their voices trailing through the pigeon pen, where they'd latched themselves in with the pigeons. "Thought you were set up in Horton."

"Thought so too. But they don't want a single woman, especially one with a child. A boy child in particular. They say boys are too noisy." She lifted her cup. "I don't need that kind of prejudice."

When she looked up at me, there was an unexpected shine in her eyes. "Hate to say it, but she's hardly gone and I miss her already."

I said nothing. She spoke the words my heart was saying. A tug

I was trying to ignore. "Not a bother to have you here," I finally said. "Has helped to have the groceries." I didn't want her to think she was a burden. And I was secretly glad she was having a hard time. Now that I drove her back and forth to Horton, she had no excuse for having anything to do with Heinrich Bueller. I often wondered what his wife thought of the previous arrangement.

"Do you ever miss Pa?"

Out of the blue, just like that. "Sure, I miss Pa," I said. "But I especially miss the girls and your sister."

"Me too," she said. "We had it good until Mac came home."

I gazed out the window to the overhead wires from which the blackbirds had retreated for the night.

"Mac's okay," she said. "But you should see the mess in the bathroom. He may be handsome, but he's no charmer when it comes to cleaning up after himself."

I lifted the teakettle off the stove and filled the teapot. "Men are different, that's all."

"Not Philip. He was fastidious. Now there's a word."

"Are you talking about Daddy, Mama?"

Eli had appeared at the side of the table, his small hands hanging on to the table's edge, his blue eyes searching his mother's face.

"Yes, darlin', I am."

"He's never going to come home and take us away like Uncle Mac did, is he?"

"No, Eli. He's not," she said. Her usual impatience with her son disappeared in those few words, and a kind of acceptance filled the void where her resentment once lived.

"I felt like an intruder from the night Mac came back. Then they left that mess. I don't blame Irene. He was chomping at the bit with a new job waiting. Couldn't believe all the stuff they jammed into boxes and suitcases. She said she was sorry, but there wasn't much she could do. She has three kids and now an even bigger one."

I ran my fingers over the plate, cleaning up the last of the crumbs. "Shame they had to go so far away."

"Can't blame them for wanting to get out of here," she said. "Don't know why they didn't move to Dickinson and find work there. But no, Mac thinks it's warmer in South Dakota. I think he just wanted to get away from his family and ours. Too bad too. If they'd gone to Dickinson, we could have found a big enough house, one where Eli and I could live with them."

Getting away seemed to be all this generation thought about. Getting away from what? We were family. "You'd still be far away, even in Dickinson."

She laughed a wry and bitter laugh. "An hour's bus ride from here. Not nearly as far as South Dakota." She smiled for the first time since she came in the door. "Now look at you, Ma. You can even drive to Dickinson."

She poured more tea. "Yeah, I'd like some soup, Ma. Some toast if you have bread in the cupboard."

Though she was entirely capable of getting her own soup off the back of the stove and toasting her own toast in the fry pan, I was more than happy to comply, seeing she and Eli were still here. *Thank you, Jesus, for answering my prayers.*

"How much are they asking for apartments?"

"Six dollars a week, more or less. I wouldn't be paying for gas or buying extra groceries. I could eat at the restaurant. Eunice Shriver said she'd keep Eli for three dollars a week, including his meals. I'd still have a few dollars left over."

This girl had it all figured out. Three dollars a week I could use. Six dollars a week would pay the rent on this whole house. Does she ever think of anybody but herself? She seemed to forget that I was her mother. That I depended on her help. She'd never breathed a word about what she got from the government for Eli since his father died. "It's been a big help having the extra groceries, Ada. I appreciate it."

"No problem, Ma. You're saving me three dollars a week I'd be giving to Eunice, and I'd rather give you two dollars for gas than Heinrich. Besides, I'm sure you're a little strapped yourself."

Truth was, even with what was left of Ozzie's insurance policy, Ivan and I would be eating less chicken and more potatoes if she moved away. "Pa's pension didn't include widow's benefits. Your uncle Oscar cut the rent in half. If it wasn't for the two of you, I'd have to think seriously about moving back to the farm and cooking for your uncle and his workers."

The soup went to the side of her plate with the toast sliced diagonally the way she liked it. She ate too quickly, but I wasn't saying anything.

"Are you around home tomorrow?" I asked.

"No. Thought I'd take Eli with me to Hubner's Market and stop in at Kresge's."

Ada's bandana and blouse needed washing badly, but I didn't want to start doing her laundry too. She walked toward the sink with her dirty bowl and set it down. "Suspect this has been especially hard for you, Ma. Ozzie passing and all."

At the mention of his name, I had to focus toward the pigeon pen to stop the sting behind my eyes. Pastor would say I should count my blessings. I still had part of my family at home and I was still in my house. He reminded me that Ivan had years to go. But without my Ozzie and those little girls, half my heart was missing.

My arm warmed where Ada lay her hand against it. A warmth so unexpected and gentle. A rare gesture from this headstrong daughter. I didn't know what to do or say. I keep staring out the window, afraid to see what was inside her green eyes.

Outside, Eli shrieked at something the pigeons had done or a joke his uncle Ivan had told him. Over time, I was sure that the two of them would become more like brothers now that the girls were gone. The two of them holding us together. Ada removed her hand before she turned to leave the kitchen, stopping at the door to the mudroom. "Only Russian tea from the store, Ma?"

# Chapter Thirty-Eight

## Pastor & Pot Roast

## *1945*

"Pastor, you're early," I said. The screen door squeaked behind him where the hinge needed a squirt of oil. He set his Bible on the table and looked around the kitchen. "Smells like one of Marta's home-cooked meals."

"Pretty basic," I said. "Bet Mrs. Kinski does better than basic."

He laughed, the gold teeth at the back of his mouth shining in the overhead light. He sat once again at what was usually my place.

"Hope you're in the mood for pot roast, Pastor. Big treat in this household."

"Smelled it the minute I walked in the door. Missus says she's grateful I'm being well cared for while she visits her sister in Horton."

Strange that I never spotted Missus around town, only at Sunday services. She always left right afterward. The only other time she made herself known was the day she gave the talk I'd never forget. A husband as Herr Gott's direct representative indeed.

"Ada got called to take Irene's old two-hour shift at the creamery. Should be along in a half hour."

"Just as well," he said. "Gives you and me a chance to catch up." He moved the Bible to his right. "How's it been since Ada and Eli moved back home?"

I had to be careful how I answered him. Next would be *why hasn't Ada been in church yet?* But he didn't know Ada the way I did. Having to walk around on tiptoe for fear she'd walk out the door and leave me without Eli and the weekly bag of groceries, the three dollars a week she started paying me for taking care of Eli. Another two dollars for gas when I drove her to her Horton job and back. Pastor hadn't had to put up with Ada's moods, or her complaints about a woman not having her rightful place in the world. At the same time, she probably sized up every man who came into the cafe as a possible husband. No, he hadn't lived with half of what I'd lived with—church attendance being only one of Ada's failings.

"Lovely to watch Eli with Ivan and the pigeons," I said.

"It's good for Eli to have someone like Ivan to look up to, especially now that there's no man in the house. You should bring Eli to Sunday school, Marta."

"Can't bring him right now," I said. "The Kesslers take him Saturday until Sunday afternoon."

Pastor said nothing, fingering the handle of his tea mug and staring down at the crack in the mug's lip. "Hate to see that happening," he said. "Loss of a Christian soul, as I see it."

I picked up my pot holders and pushed myself out of the chair. "I do what I can here at home, Pastor."

We hadn't had pot roast in more weeks than I could remember. It was Ada's gift, though she reminded me, "Probably ruined our supper by inviting Pastor."

Without my pressuring her about church, we got along better. And now her general attitude had improved since I started driving her to work in Ozzie's Buick. Hoped she wasn't right about inviting Pastor. He'd undoubtedly ask her to come to church. *Herr Gott, forgive me for lying about Eli's other grandparents.* He only went there every other week.

"What's this I hear about your kuchen on the menu at the Cozy Café in Horton? Agnes said she'd been there for lunch. When she asked Ada about the kuchen listed along with apple pie, Ada was happy to tell her they were your kuchens, your pies."

"Their pie maker got too old," I said. "So Ada took a piece of kuchen to Mr. Cummins. He said it was better than the pies. Asked her if I'd bake for them. Mr. Cummins especially likes the prune."

"Enterprising family, this one," Pastor said. "Ivan with the pigeons and you with your kuchen. Just goes to show how much my prayers are working."

His prayers, my eye. More like my hard work. I fussed at the sink, which wasn't like me. Would be a mistake to tell him they pay me a dollar a pie and provide sugar to boot, even though sugar's still on the ration list.

"You're gonna be famous, Marta," he continued. "There's a certain ring to *Marta's kuchen*."

"That's what they call it. Was Ada's idea."

"Will probably be able to increase your tithe now," he said.

Of all the things he'd ever said to me, that took the cake. Took the cake and sliced it hot. I lifted the pan of biscuits, putting them into the oven ahead of time. Inviting him was a mistake. Every question he asked and every answer I gave ended up in a rat's nest of trouble. First, Ada and Eli, now my baking. *Probably able to increase your tithe.* As if I hadn't done Herr Gott's work all these years. Prayed with the sick, cared for the vestry and Pastor's vestments. Cleaned up after others who thought they'd cleaned up.

I wiped at my forehead until I realized it was my eyes that were leaking.

"Going to call the boys in to wash up," I said.

Rather than hollering out the back, I closed the door behind me and walked slowly toward the pigeon pen.

WE WERE WELL INTO dinner when the screen door squeaked and Ada appeared. Summer slacks and a white blouse, the top button undone again. Pastor had been talking to the boys about the pigeons. I was about to fill his plate a second time when Ada set down her purse and pulled back her chair.

"Hi Pastor," she said. "Ma told me you'd be joining us. How's the pot roast?"

Pastor wiped his mouth with his napkin. "Sorry I didn't get up to pull out your chair."

Still standing, Ada laughed. "No need. I'm perfectly capable of pulling out my own chair. How's your dinner, Eli?"

Eli shook his head until his long hair fell into his eyes. "Good, Mom," he said before he directed his fork to stab a potato.

Ada went to the stove with her plate and reached into the central pot. "Your wife's in Horton, Pastor?"

He waited until he swallowed. "Her sister has female troubles," he said. His face reddened as soon as he said the words. "You've probably seen her sister in the café. Works for the Benedictines doing housecleaning."

"She's a widow, as I recall," Ada said.

"Good memory."

"A shame she has to do housekeeping. That would be at the bottom of my list."

"We do what we have to do," Pastor said. "I understand both you and your mother have done quite well by Cummins."

"It's a job," Ada said. "Plus, it's given Ma quite a reputation."

"That's what I understand." He paused, looking down at his

twice-emptied plate. "Should take your recipe back to my wife, Marta. That's about the best pot roast I've ever eaten. Please don't tell Irma I said that."

"Ma's the best cook I know," Ada said. "Didn't seem to rub off on me."

"You're a lucky young woman," Pastor said. "Your mom's as good as a second mother to your son and . . ."

"And?" Ada asked.

Herr Gott, with that one word, this whole meal could turn upside down. Pastor had no idea what he'd just stepped into. Ada might not be easy, but then neither was he.

"You're lucky to have your mother to care for your son," Pastor said.

"If I didn't have Ma, I'd find another good woman who could do the same."

"But," I started to say, then stopped myself. My daughter had just implied that any woman would do to take care of her son. That there was nothing special about her own mother. At least she was paying me now, like she would someone else. Hoped she didn't mention me driving her back and forth to work. He'd likely pounce on the expense of that too. Never mind his own wife drove that road at least twice a week. I could always say I was delivering the kuchen and my pies. Which I was, indirectly.

"You started to say something, Marta?" Pastor asked.

I smoothed my apron across my stomach when I rose from the chair. Avoided the pastor's gaze.

Ada glanced up at me. "Eli's right at home here."

"My point exactly," Pastor said. "A child belongs in a home with loved ones, not someplace among strangers, no matter how well-meaning they may be."

"Everyone has a right to their opinion, Pastor," Ada said. "What's a woman going to do if she's somewhere without family?"

"A child should always be with family," he said. "That's the way Herr Gott meant it to be."

"Seems to me *always* is a big word," Ada said. "It doesn't fit every situation."

I could feel the wet circles beneath my arms. Ada was spoiling for a fight. "Anyone for more pot roast?" I asked. "Or can I clear your plates and get ready for fresh apple pie with ice cream?"

Pastor pointed his glare at Ada. "Pie is good," he said without veering from his target. "Herr Gott promotes certain values that leave no alternative to *always*, Ada. And it's best to abide by them. Family is one of the *always*."

"Family is changing, Pastor. Look what's happened because of the war. So many widows now alone with their children. I hate to tell you this, but the same rules don't apply."

"One should always be with family, like you are with your mother," he said.

"Only because I can't get anyone to rent me an apartment," she said, her voice up a notch and both boys staring at Ada.

"If you're finished, boys, you're excused," I said. "Go on outside. I'll call you in for the pie."

They scooted off their chairs without further encouragement.

"Maybe that's because you're meant to stay close to your mother until you are ready to marry again."

"What if I decide not to marry again?" Ada said.

"But you have to marry again," Pastor said. "And marrying someone inside the church would be best for both you and Eli."

Eli lingered at the mudroom door, though Ivan tugged on his arm. "C'mon, Eli. Let them figure it out."

"What would you do, Pastor, if you lost your wife?" Ada asked. She didn't wait for him to answer, her half-eaten plate in front of her. "You'd find another wife, that's what you'd do." She took a deep breath. "That's what men do, but it's not always what women do."

Ada set her fork down at the side of her plate. She said nothing for a long time, but that only seemed to magnify the icy silence. If I'd said anything close to what Pastor just said, we'd be in a yelling match with her accusing me of being old-fashioned and pig-headed and not living in today's world.

Ada pushed back her chair, her plate still half-full and the red flush of anger in her cheeks. "Now if you'll both excuse me," she said, rising from the table, "I have important things to attend to."

When she turned to leave, she didn't go upstairs as I expected her to, but rather grabbed the handle of her handbag off the nail by Ozzie's mirror. She turned and left through the kitchen door. The screen slammed shut and my heart dropped into my stomach. All I could think was *what next?*

*Thank you, Herr Gott, for keeping Pastor silent.* I couldn't look at him and I couldn't say a word. Without meaning to, I dropped a dish in the sink and it shattered into a hundred pieces. The breaking crockery was magnified by the boys' laughter in the pigeon cage and the pigeons cooing a chorus of their own making.

"Do you always let her go off in a huff like that?" Pastor asked.

My hands clenched the cold edge of the porcelain sink. My jaw was locked in place. "Pastor, she's a grown woman. She lives her life as she sees fit, whether I like it or not."

"A shame," he said. "Reflects back on you. That's the sad part."

My face red, I had to stay turned away. For the first time I felt sympathetic with Ada and why she had to leave the kitchen. "Boys, are you ready for your pie?" I hollered out the screen door.

Ada was right. The world was changing and so were women. That meant her. Look at me, driving Ozzie's car and selling my baked goods. Yes, it meant me too.

"I can see your challenge, Marta," he said.

I poured the tea water into the teapot and sliced up the pie. Retrieved the ice cream from the ice cream churn. I smiled when I placed the teapot on the table, then brought two slices of pie. Smiled as a peace offering because I didn't want to hear his serious tone or what more he had to say. Smiled because Ada was right. The world *was* changing. Smiled because for the first time ever,

I had money I'd earned that didn't belong in Albert's coffee can. That didn't belong to anyone but me. Smiled because I could smile.

"Don't call the boys in just yet," Pastor said. He lifted his fork and cut into the end of the pie. "It's imperative that you bring Ada back into the church. You know it's for her own good. For Eli's good. We can't have the child influenced by a family of Jews. It's imperative that we keep all our families together in the fold."

I interrupted. "Pastor, I've been meaning to return a Bible I borrowed from the church after Albert burned all of mine," I said. "I won't be needing it anymore."

"Oh, I didn't know it was you who took it," Pastor said. "Frank complained that one was missing."

"Sorry. I meant to tell both of you. I guess it just slipped my mind under the weight of what's happened this past winter. I have it wrapped in paper right here," I said. I lifted the package from the chair beside me.

"Thank you," Pastor said. "The end of a mystery." He smiled for the first time, then his face became dour again. "I've been meaning to talk to you about Ozzie's Buick," he said. "I've heard word that you've been driving it around town. You . . ." He sputtered for a minute. "I was frankly surprised. Even more surprised that you didn't give it to your son-in-law, who probably has far better need for it."

I smiled because I could. "Yes, Pastor, you're probably right about Mac," I said. "But how can his need be greater than mine? Can you explain that, Pastor?"

"Well, first off, he's a man who will need to go to work."

With the greatest effort I could manage, I said, "And I'm a woman with obligations who also has to work. Because I have the car, I can deliver my pies to Cummins myself." I lifted my hand in anticipation of his response. "Pastor, you yourself have complained about Ada driving back and forth to Horton with Heinrich Bueller." I smiled. "That's no longer necessary."

The pie was the right state of warm with the ice cream melting nicely, though the Pastor didn't seem to notice. I nodded appropriately at his further argument, but I kept my eyes on my plate. For some reason, I saw Mother, so incredibly broken after Father shot himself. She may as well have gone to bed and died. Then Albert's face when he handed me two quarters, a grim tightness to his lips, his eyes on our hands when he placed the coins in my palm.

Pastor continued to talk about the fold and what it meant to be Herr Gott's children, especially what it meant for a woman to know her place. I nodded at times, but I heard nothing. In my mind were the first three one-dollar bills inside a white envelope, my name on the outside. Three dollars Albert would have never handed me at the same time. Three dollars for three beautiful kuchen I made in my kitchen oven right here. Three dollars that were now fifteen dollars that I kept in my old music box in a bedroom that was now mine alone, with Jesus's picture on the wall and no Albert to complain. A pot roast that Ada earned by serving others, even though she resented doing that at home.

I offered Pastor a second piece of pie and wrapped another in waxed paper for him to take home. But my thoughts had flown away like one of the blackbirds that perched on the high wires, flown higher and farther than they'd ever flown before. Right out of Myra and into a bigger sky. Across the fields and plains and gullies, into less weighted air, into a faith different than I'd ever known. I was able to do something I'd never done before. I earned my own money. I drove Ozzie's car. Neither Father nor Pastor nor Albert could ever take those things away from me. I felt like I would surely burst, the same way I felt before I fell on the wharf. That I could fly even if I was scared, that I'd land when I was ready to land.

# NOTES

THOUGH *FOREVER BLACKBIRDS* IS based loosely on my maternal grandmother, it is crucial for the reader to understand that her life provided only a scaffolding on which I built a story through other people's stories, research, and my imagination until it became a work of fiction. The events in *Forever Blackbirds* never happened in real life. My grandmother did leave Kessel, Russia, and she did immigrate to the United States, settling with her family in central North Dakota. But the life events and the characters, including Marta, are creations of a fiction writer's mind. Though my sister Peggy still attests to our grandmother Magdalena's cinnamon rolls, and I will likely always taste the kuchen baked in her kitchen, it's the small details like the well, the outhouse, the garden, and pigeon pen that are lifted from memory. Again, all events in the novel are works of fiction. In her lifetime, my grandmother was a lifelong Christian, deeply devoted to her faith, her church, and her family. I simply attempted to capture the "spirit" of who she was in the small details of her daily life.

A bibliography of the research is available upon request.

## ALSO BY DIAN GREENWOOD

*Double Fire Burning* (Press 22, 1979)

*About the Carleton Sisters* (She Writes, 2023)

## ACKNOWLEDMENTS

My gratitude goes to my son, Brian Frary, who shares my interest in family genealogy and helped with the German language questions, who also encouraged me to write the book. Thanks to my sister, Peggy McMillen, always my first reader. To my Seattle family, especially Craig, Linnea, Grace and Madi. I'm grateful for your love and support. To Jan Faber and Vicki Baker, thanks for faithfully reading draft after draft. David Ciminello and Patsy Kullberg for our weekly critique group, thank you. The Henry Writers gave helpful feedback and first heard me read the last line of the book which remained the last line.

I owe a huge thanks to Gigi Little, both for the cover art and the inside layout of the book. Our long friendship and comradery are a staple in my writing life. Suzy Vitello, I couldn't finish a book without your developmental edits and encouragement. You are one of a kind. Elise Le Sage, you have faithfully carried out my marketing/publicity campaign one more time. Thank you. To Gina Walter, Judy Reeves, June Cressy and Nancy Lashbrook Townsley for your editing expertise, thank you. Mary Desch, thanks for your moral support. To those who endorsed the book early on—Leslie Johansen Nack, Maryka Billagio, Suzanne Parry, and Gemma Whelan, my heartfelt thanks. Thank you to the bookstores and book clubs that have graciously welcomed me.

Last, there aren't enough thanks for my long-time writing companions and friends, Judy Reeves in San Diego and Laura Stanfill in Portland, Oregon. They listen to the near-daily ins/outs and help me problem solve the many challenges in publishing a book. Thank you.

If I have forgotten anyone, my apology. The writing community, the friends and family and, also, the readers who support a writer and lift her up are many. Thanks to all who have touched my life in any way. I'm forever grateful.